DEATH SPEAKER

Published by Kalambakal Press

ISBN: 978-0-9853973-0-2
Library of Congress Control Number: 2014958255

Book design by Stacey Aaronson

Printed in the United States of America

DEATH SPEAKER

A Novel of Ancient Gaul

VICKEY KALL

K
kalambakal
press

To Katie

Note to Readers

Once upon a time, Celtic tribes populated most of Europe. The tribes had different names and customs; some were more warlike and powerful than others. Over the generations, they fought with each other and with outsiders—like the upstart Romans from the south.

In this story, the village of Samarnum is just a bit east of the present city of Amiens, France. The river that runs by Samarnum is the Somme. The story moves along the Loire (or Liger) River to the French province of Brittany, around the Morbihan Bay. To date, no one has located the Veneti capital city that I call Venetona, but without a doubt there was such a place. And there were such people.

Character List

Visitors and People of Samarnum

Emyn, the Death Speaker
    Isminos, her father, whom she calls A'er or Ater
    Nonicos, her oldest brother
    Esmios, her older brother
    Aumios, her son

Iomat, the village healer and midwife

Almer, a friend of Emyn's brother Esmios
    Hentios, his father and the village drunk
    Micco, his younger brother

Cesua, Emyn's best friend
    Sinia, her younger sister
    Sonios, their father who brews ale

Lausos, a local farmer and shepherd

Volio, the village headman
    Tulia, his niece

Bodocnos, a visiting druid
    Rialos, his student
    Coath or *Cothuacos,* a student, son of a Carnute chieftain
    Morodag, a student, son of the Bellovaci king, Motirix

Ferdiath, a visiting druid from Ireland

Nanto, a visiting druid

Omullos, a druid of Virmandum skilled at healing

Men and Women Near Gundori's Island

Gundori, the self-proclaimed king

Vinnia, a wealthy widow and niece of Gundori

Darsa, her cook

Gorio, a child slave

Haebro, keeper of an alehouse

Laurina, the widow of a fisherman

Oleda, her child

Lorsus, a merchant

Suttia, innkeeper and gossip

Residents and Visitors of Venetona

Vlidorix, the Veneti king

Nanto, the chief druid of the Veneti, now very old

Nerrus, an innkeeper

Satto, a warrior and friend of Rialos

Teuto, a merchant and shipowner

Iotros, a visiting warrior from Bellovaci lands

Historical Characters Mentioned or Present

Ariovistus, a king of the Suebi and other Germanic tribes who allied with some Celtic tribes, fought with others, and challenged Caesar.

Julius Caesar, the general and statesman who took control of the Roman republic and turned it into an empire. He spent years conducting wars against the Celtic tribes of Gaul and wrote about that in a book still studied today: *Conquest of Gaul.*

Marcus Crassus, the wealthiest man in Rome and a general who suppressed the slave revolt. He was a political ally of Caesar

Publius Crassus, his son who served under Caesar in Gaul

Diviciacos, a leader of the Aeduan tribe, favored by Caesar

Dumnorix, a leader of the Aeduan tribe and brother of Diviciacos

Orgetorix, king of the Helveti tribe and father-in-law to Dumnorix

Spartacus, a leader of Rome's largest slave revolt

The Eighth Day of Elembiu

Emyn never thought before she spoke. Maybe that was why the dead had such an easy time speaking through her.

What were the ghosts saying as she stirred? The words faded, but battles had raged in her sleep. Emyn remembered seas lit with flame; men shrieked as they ran out of the water. There she stood in the middle of it all, unable to look away as waves lapped at her feet.

She heard the dead chattering over the rustle of leaves and muttered, "No one listens to you."

The boy curled beside her, then shifted and rolled his head onto her arm. Emyn didn't move. She had seen too much death in her twenty-three years, but so had Gorio in a lesser span. She let him sleep and soon she dreamed again.

The skull temple burned around her. Roman soldiers trampled and smashed the bones until only a circle of broken skulls remained—a sacred circle that no one could cross.

Was time a line or a circle?

Emyn jerked awake, sure that a real voice had asked the question. Gorio slept on. She stared at the stars, the only side of the world left unchanged. They shone like the year's first snow dusting a field.

Questions raised in dreams had no answers, did they? How could time be a circle? The druids said it was, but they could argue the stars into daylight given the chance.

Time had no end and no beginning, the wise said.

That was silly; everything began somewhere. She'd been born. You philosophers, Emyn told a druid once, you are tricksters who play with words and tell lies that wouldn't fool a child. He tried explaining time to her, but she was stubborn and didn't want to understand.

"Our lives continue in a circle; they don't end."

"But when you make a circle you begin it," Emyn had insisted. "You start somewhere. Don't laugh . . . ."

She could almost hear his deep voice in the darkness. "Rebirth, over and over. We're in this world or the next. We are never nowhere."

The druids were wrong, Emyn decided. There were beginnings and endings, even to time. Her own people were gone and Rome had destroyed the last hope of the Veneti yesterday. Her death was near; she knew that as if she'd caught its scent on the breeze.

The holy places, the secret gods and stories known only to the people of Samarnum—all this existed only in her mind. No one would tell her story when she died; it seemed important to recall it now.

BOOK ONE

The Girl

 1

W here did she begin?

The ghosts were the only reason anyone noticed Emyn. Her story began with them.

When Emyn was six, she followed her brother Esmios and his friend Almer as they hiked to higher ground west of their village. Weeds but no grass grew there, and pits and rocks were scorched. She picked up a stick and dug a few exploratory pocks into the ground, exposing charred earth below.

The boys found charms here. They said they found bones once, but quickly covered them with dirt. All children knew better than to disturb the honored dead or any spirit that guarded their remains.

As Emyn crouched and scratched the loose dirt with her stick, Esmios whispered to his friend of a place beyond this one, a place with ruined and smashed huts where metal had been worked over fires and hammered into knives.

"This was a road." Esmios led Emyn and Almer down a slope and away from the dead earth. A long stone marker lay between clumps of dandelions, carved on one side with a horse. Flecks of white paint still clung to it. "That means that our people lived here," her brother said. "Viromandui. They put that up. Then enemies came and shoved it down."

"And they killed the people who lived here. Slit them open and burned them." Almer swung an imaginary sword at Emyn. "I bet there's more bones around. You're probably standing on some now. Are you scared?"

"No." Emyn meant it. Why should she be afraid of bones, when she hadn't stolen from them?

Disappointed, the boy pivoted from her, jabbing and grunting. Emyn looked up at her brother. "Don't take charms off the bones. Or they'll come after you—"

"I *know* that," Esmios scowled. "Everyone does. But I want to find out who attacked this place. Was it the Ambiani? It was a long time ago. Maybe there's an enemy we don't know about."

Almer menaced them again, this time with an invisible ax. "Maybe they're still around."

Esmios rolled his eyes. "Iomat probably knows."

Iomat was a tall woman who gathered plants and brewed potions for people when they were sick. That Esmios named her confused Emyn; their father was the person who answered their questions. "Did you ask A'er?"

"He doesn't know. Will you ask Iomat for us?"

Emyn blinked at him. "Why don't you just ask her?"

"You're the one who'll be staying with her."

"I'm not going to stay with her," Emyn protested.

"Yes, you are. A'er said so."

"When?"

"In three nights, he said."

"Liar!" She'd never lived anywhere but with her own Ater. Where would she sleep? Who would feed her and sing to her?

Esmios and his friend laughed and called her a baby, so she threw rocks at them and ran away.

She *wasn't* a baby. If she were big or a boy, they wouldn't mock her. They wouldn't dare.

Another path branched away from the old road and wound into shadows. Emyn followed it, watching the ground carefully so she wouldn't trip on roots or rocks. The boys' voices faded. They stopped laughing and began yelling her name, but she didn't answer. Because now she knew: people waited for her at the top of the hill.

How Emyn knew *that*, she could never say. As far as she remembered, that afternoon was the first time she stood among the oak trees of the sacred grove; the first time she'd seen the dead king and the white ladies. She felt she knew them and they certainly knew her, so maybe they had met in dreams. She sat and listened as they told her wonderful stories and showed her pretty things, magical things that she could never quite describe or make sense of later.

"We will stay with you," a silvery woman said. "We will sing you songs."

Emyn rubbed her eyes. "I want to go home now."

The ladies giggled and began to dance. Emyn dozed and when she woke, she was alone.

The sun had set and no moon was out as she stumbled back down the path in darkness. Little sparks of light danced before her, showing the way; the display seemed funny, but not impossible. She wondered if the new month had begun. That happened when the moon rose too late for her to see. Esmios said the month was unlucky.

Emyn heard her brothers and neighbors call her name and ran toward the sound. Someone scooped her up; by the light of a torch she recognized her oldest brother. "Tell my father!" Nonicos called out as he squeezed Emyn tight. Water filled his eyes. "He's at the river—"

His voice broke. "You brat," he muttered into her ear. She giggled at the hot air from his mouth and the tickles of the little hairs of his new, golden moustache. "You worried us all! Where have you been?"

Emyn stopped giggling. "Between the trees. I fell asleep."

"We've been calling and calling."

She hadn't heard. More people joined them; Emyn had never seen so many torches except on holidays. Everyone seemed anxious to give her a hug or a pat and then scold her. She and Nonicos were almost home before her Ater pushed through the group.

"She says she fell asleep in the trees," Nonicos told him.

"In the trees?" A'er's voice grew loud. "Little girl, you know how dangerous that is! There are wolves—did you think of that? You don't go off alone!"

"The ladies said I could."

"Prettiness." Her father buried his face in her hair. "Don't ever run off like that again."

Emyn's father pulled a cask of ale around to the front of his house, and all the men and women who'd been out looking for her —everyone she knew and some she didn't—drank heartily from bowls and cups. The moon smiled as it rose in the dotted sky. The fire pit outside was filled with branches and split logs and the flames danced up to touch the stars, sending out little red, glowing stars of their own. She and Esmios sat leaning against the house as it grew late.

Esmios, she noted with satisfaction, was subdued and pale. But he hadn't been lying. The ladies had told her that she was going to live with Iomat at the headman's house, and Iomat would show her how to make medicine and read the stars.

"I know the name," she said to Esmios. He'd been crying earlier and his eyes were red. "Sadonu, the place where we went. Men made swords there. They made swords for kings. I saw some of them."

Esmios wiped his eyes. "That's wicked, Emyn. You're telling lies and teasing me."

"I am not. You wanted to know—"

"You are too."

"Am not—"

"Can't you two sit together without fighting?" Ater pushed himself between them. He tried to glower, but the firelight danced in his eyes as he smiled. People would tell Emyn later that she had her father's eyes, large and quick to express emotion.

"Emyn's making up stories," Esmios said.

"I'm not. It's true. I saw the king's sword, and I saw where they made it."

"And where was that, prettiness?" her father asked.

"At the forge, but it's all broken now."

"Then how did you see it?" Esmios demanded.

"The ladies showed it to me when I was between the trees."

"You were dreaming, then, if you're not lying."

She opened her mouth to answer, but her father shushed her. "You should be dreaming, both of you. That's enough for one night. To sleep, now."

WITHIN THREE DAYS, Emyn traveled with her father to stand on planks over the river. They said prayers as A'er tossed two offerings into the water: a carved cup and a smooth rock with designs cut into it. One to bless her new life with the healer and one to thank the gods for letting her stay in this world a little longer. It was sad for a child to die too young to earn a place of honor in the next world.

Emyn lived with Iomat in the headman's large house after that. She followed Iomat on walks in sunlight and darkness, reciting after her the names of flowers that they passed. The woman showed her paths and hidden shrines that Esmios probably never dreamed of, swearing Emyn to secrecy. Iomat chopped up plants and Emyn washed down the wooden boards afterwards. Her hands were busy and her head full.

Her father's home was near, and no one made a fuss if she picked up her softest fur and walked back to A'er's when darkness fell. Maybe they half-expected it; she was still very young.

Before the moon got full again, all the grownups went off to shear sheep. Those not old enough to help were ordered out of the way. Esmios tried to follow their father to the sheds but was sent back, so he wandered by the headman's house. Emyn brought him inside and pointed out the boxes and pots that held Iomat's plants. The drying branches that hung from the rafters were mostly hers as well. Her brother grinned when she whispered that the headman snored.

"I wasn't lying about Sadonu," she told Esmios very seriously. "That's what it was called and you said you wanted to know. Robbers came down the river in ships. The robbers burned the houses and workshops seven generations ago."

Esmios rolled his eyes, but before he could say anything, Iomat's voice rang out from the other side of the half-open door. "Where did you hear that?"

"Now you're in trouble," hissed Esmios.

Emyn bunched up her skirt with her fist. "I'm not lying."

"I didn't say you were," said Iomat. "Where did you hear that?"

"The ladies told me. When I was between the trees."

"When she was *sleeping* between the trees," Esmios corrected. "When everyone was looking for her."

"Well, I want you to tell me about that. What trees, to start with?"

Emyn described the tall oaks that ringed the top of a hillock beyond the dead town where she'd run from her brother. Iomat asked Esmios if he knew the place, then took him to the door and sent him home. Before he left, Iomat warned the boy in a hushed voice to stay away from the hill with the tall trees on it.

"Is it a bad place?" Emyn asked when Iomat came back.

"For some. Not for you, apparently." Iomat leaned against a post. The distaff that held her wool was tucked in her belt as always.

"So." The woman began to spin thread. "Tell me about those ladies. What did they say?"

Iomat's face bounced between amusement and concern as Emyn talked and the spindle whirled. She told of the ladies and their sad sighs, and the embroidered edges of their gowns that sometimes hung in tatters. "They had shiny metal circles. The ladies held them in their hands, and I could see their faces, like water."

"Mirrors." Iomat gave the spindle a flick. "They made mirrors there as well as blades."

Emyn spoke of the king who commanded the town and the forge. She jerked in surprise when the king appeared beside her, but Iomat didn't seem alarmed. The king whispered the names of tribes who sent emissaries and reminded her of the ships that brought metal from the islands down the river to the forge.

"Tell her this, too," he ordered.

"Why don't you tell her?" Emyn could see right through him to the sunshine outside the door.

"You are my voice. You must do as I say. Tell her that soon this village will need help. I will provide that help so that all will know my power."

Emyn repeated the words to Iomat: when the village needed help, he would tell them what to do.

"Oh, indeed?" Iomat sounded skeptical. The king didn't argue or scold; he simply vanished.

Emyn wondered what else she should say. "They were very nice, but they didn't have any food."

"Of course not," said Iomat, leaning down to catch up her spindle and wind the new thread. "Dead people don't eat."

And that was when she began, really: the day she learned that she could speak to and for the dead. That gift would carry her far from home to speak before the wise and the foolish alike. After that day, Emyn heard the word *Gutumaros* whispered when she passed: Death Speaker.

2

Emyn missed her A'er, but people said that it was not fitting for a girl to grow up in a house full of men. Someone had to teach her the things a girl must know; Iomat needed to pass on her skills as well.

On their walks Iomat taught Emyn how the moon told roots to grow deep on certain days, how new leaves were favored at other times, and what words to say as she cut or dug up plants. At night, if they felt like staying up late, Iomat explained the stars.

Once that summer Iomat woke Emyn, wrapped a shawl around her, and led the half-awake girl down the road and through unfamiliar pastures to a house. There a suffering woman poured curses on her husband and all his ancestors while Emyn dozed until Iomat shook her roughly. "Stand up and learn!"

Emyn saw a baby born that morning. The creature emerged from an impossible location, becoming an infant out of blood and ugliness as Emyn watched, amazed. Days passed before she recalled that her own mother had died giving birth but it wasn't hard to believe that such an ordeal could kill.

* * *

As SUMMER PASSED and dampness crept back into the air, an old man came to the village and stayed with A'er. Emyn was summoned and introduced to her grandfather.

He studied her face in the afternoon light, peering at her from up and down and both sides before grunting, "You don't look much like your mother."

He nodded at A'er. "Pretty girl. Don't spoil her."

The old man had masses of hair the color of rain clouds on his head and face. His pale, runny eyes fixed on her for a moment. Then with a snort, he rose and walked out of the house.

What had she done? Nonicos, her oldest brother, touched her shoulder and said quietly, "Your grandfather came a long way to see your mother. He didn't know she was dead."

Emyn's mind tripped over "your grandfather." Hers, not Nonicos'. She'd always known that her brothers had a different mother. Now she realized they must have different grandfathers and maybe other cousins and aunts and uncles as well.

The next day her grandfather asked Iomat if Emyn could walk with him. He did the same thing the following day and whenever the weather was dry.

Her grandfather didn't talk much, so Emyn recited some of the stories she'd heard from A'er and from the ghosts—tales about brave men who died and were brought back to life by magic, or about loyal sons who were cheated out of their birthright and forced to live as outlaws without home or clan.

"He wasn't really alive," she mused after telling of a warrior who had been decapitated and whose head continued to entertain and sing to his companions for many years. "He never got to be a grandfather."

"Heroes live faster than farmers," the old man grunted. "You never heard that?"

"No. Why?"

"The blood runs hotter. It's a better life."

Emyn thought about that. Grandfather came from another tribe, the Nervii, and they were supposed to be very brave. "Do you know heroes?"

He snorted.

Maybe not everything people said was true. She'd heard that Nervians didn't drink ale, but Grandfather was more than happy to share a cup with A'er or the headman in the evening.

One day Emyn sang with the white ladies and another spirit who played a lyre and said he was a bard. Grandfather was surprised but not afraid. "You hear ghosts, do you?"

"Yes."

"My grandfather used to hear ghosts. They told him where to find game."

Emyn thought of how the headman's dogs whimpered and crawled away whenever she passed. No dogs came near her lately. Iomat said they feared the dead.

"Were dogs afraid of your grandfather?"

"Ha! Of all the things to ask . . . they were, they were. I remember."

Grandfather taught her Nervian songs after that, saying that the words to the white ladies' tunes were foolish. His songs were mostly about courage and never giving ground.

Once he told her about the time her mother had fallen and skinned her knees and how she'd walked all the way home without shedding a tear. He was very proud of her that day; she wasn't any older than Emyn. She asked if he missed his daughter.

"Her choice. She knew it would be a long time between visits."

* * *

A SPRING FED THE wood-lined well in the center of Samarnum, which was what people called the village when they needed to name it. The source of water was important; Samarnum would not be where it stood if the water gurgled up in a different spot. The well filled with rainwater daily so no one noticed its lowering at first.

One day, the water nearly disappeared.

Buckets and basins appeared outside every house to catch the rain. Folks gathered in small groups and walked through the fields, tracing barely-discernable paths of water on the muddy ground. The river was close but if the well went dry, Iomat told Emyn, they'd have to accept it and move.

"Where?"

"The ancestors will show us, one way or the other."

Emyn was still six. The ice and storms of winter kept her grandfather from returning home but he no longer called on her to walk with him. It was too cold.

When the rain paused, Emyn played outside with Cesua and Sinia, sisters who were her best friends. They chased white-faced black ducks and dangled worms to tease Sinia, who hated crawly things.

Cesua nodded toward the headman's house. Two figures crouched outside the door. "Bet he's hungry."

Emyn looked closer and saw a third person. A toddler rested in Almer's lap as he sat next to his father. Last summer the man had helped A'er build a cart. . . Hentios, that was his name. He was a cousin to her brothers, though not to her.

"Why is he hungry?" Sinia asked while Emyn was puzzling this out.

"He can't eat."

"Why not?"

"He can't eat because he's doing troscad. Troscad means you can't eat till you get justice."

"Can Almer eat?"

"Of course. So can Micco." Cesua, a year older than Emyn, knew almost as much as Iomat about the goings-on in the village.

"Why—"

"It's simple, goose." Her tone made Emyn glad she'd kept silent and let Sinia ask the questions. "Headman Volio took Hentios' mallet and tools because he owed him work that he never finished. So Hentios can't work even if he wants to, because he's got no tools. Now Hentios sits at the headman's door all day. He won't leave and won't eat until the headman says he'll do what a judge says. That's troscad." Cesua took a deep breath.

"A'er says Hentios is a drunk and wouldn't be working anyway," said Sinia.

"That doesn't matter. Troscad is sacred."

Emyn stared above Hentios where three skulls sat on a shelf over the door of the headman's house. One whispered to her, "Your people need water."

"What are you looking at?"

Emyn shrugged. "Who gets to be the judge?"

"A druid, silly. He has to come from far away. What are you looking at?"

Iomat spoke of druids as skilled healers; Emyn didn't realize they were also judges.

"The well has nothing left to give," said another skull.

"They're ugly, aren't they?" Cesua followed Emyn's gaze towards the skulls but Emyn knew she couldn't hear them. It began to rain again, hard, and everyone ran to their homes.

Hentios grinned up at Emyn as she passed. "Tell the headman I am still here."

* * *

INSIDE, WOMEN TALKED AND rain pattered on the thatch. Ghosts murmured too. Iomat put Emyn to work shaking and thumping thick stalks, coaxing the seeds in them to fall on a cloth spread out before her.

"I wait to be asked," the dead king announced suddenly.

Emyn straightened; she could see his outline before her. "For what?"

"For help. Your people need water." The image wavered though his voice remained strong. "I am a king. The chief must ask."

Did he mean the headman? "But he can't see you."

"You will tell him. I wish a sacrifice. He has several bulls. One of them will serve."

Emyn giggled. "You can't eat a bull!"

"The aroma is mine, insolent child. The meat may be shared."

He faded as Emyn said, "I have to ask Iomat."

"Ask me what?"

Emyn jumped. She'd spoken too loudly; men and women stared at her. Some looked angry.

"Ask me what?" Iomat left the cookfire and took the dried branch out of Emyn's hand. "Tell me what you heard. You'll have no peace till you do."

Emyn repeated what the ghost wanted.

Iomat seemed unimpressed. "Is he listening, this king?"

Emyn looked around as the women at the cookfire turned away. "I don't know."

"No headman is going to butcher a good bull on the word of a little girl." Iomat spoke loudly, her hands on her hips. "If your ghost was a king, he should know that. A headman is no different."

Women gasped when Iomat said the word *ghost*; she ignored them.

"No one else sees or hears him. When he was a living king, did he listen to children?" Iomat shook her head. "If he wants a sacrifice, he'll have to prove himself first. Tell him to refill the well or find us a new one and he'll get his bull."

The ghost was angry; Emyn could feel it. Shadows grew and pressed around Iomat, pulling darkness from the corners and roof beams. Emyn held her breath . . . but the shadows did nothing.

"I won't be shamed by a drunk!" The door flew open and the headman stomped toward the fire.

"If you'll let me—" Volio's sons huddled close and their voices dropped.

Iomat exchanged looks with the other women.

"Don't!" Volio's voice cracked through the house like the snap of a whip. "I tell you: no. You touch Hentios and I'll be blamed."

"Petty fools," the dead king whispered, suddenly very close. "Tell him now!"

Emyn looked up at Iomat. "The dead king—"

"Shhh."

There was no question of whom to obey. Iomat was solid; the dead king a noisy shadow. Emyn hummed softly to drown out his voice.

"HE'S GONE," Emyn said in the morning as she followed Iomat out of the house. Emyn held a basket for the mushrooms they hoped to find while the sun shone.

"Hentios? He got his tools back," Iomat said. "Volio is too smart to let that troscad go on."

"Hentios can eat now?"

"Eat and drink and wasting no time about it, either. Look at him, laughing like a crazy man."

Hentios stood in the doorway of Cesua's house, inviting two other men inside as they passed. Iomat sighed. "I'll tell headman Volio what your ghost said today."

Hentios was often at Cesua's house. Cesua's parents brewed ale and called Hentios a drunk. It made sense in an unpleasant way.

The headman's big voice startled Emyn. "So you talk to ghosts?"

"Yes."

"Do you see them?"

Emyn had been dozing by the fire and jumped to her feet. "Sometimes."

"What does this ghost say?"

Emyn knew better than to announce he wanted a bull sacrificed. "He says there is water that moves in the rock. He will show us where."

"If . . ." The headman raised his eyebrows and winked at Iomat.

"Lead him," the dead king commanded. "Toward the white horse."

"He'll show us now!" Emyn ran to the door and pushed it open. The rain drizzled beyond the overhanging thatch.

The only white horse Emyn knew of was the fallen marker near the ruins, so she pointed in that direction "That road behind Cesua's house—"

"Sonios' house," Iomat corrected, naming Cesua's father.

"There's water that way?" The headman squinted. "How far?"

The land sloped gently behind Cesua's house and wound eventually to the ruined and burned iron works.

"Water flows along it all," said the king.

White shapes beckoned from Cesua's doorway. Emyn's legs propelled her forward before Iomat could holler, "Wait!" She kept going, then huddled under the thatch outside Cesua's home until the headman and Iomat caught her.

Iomat started to scold just as the rain surged and began to pound.

Cesua's mother opened her door and looked at them all, confused. "Where's Hentios?"

"Hentios?" Iomat sounded puzzled.

"Hentios. He said he—"

A long, wailing cry rose over the noise of the rain. They all turned in time to see Hentios slide off the thatched roof as if he were trying to fly like a bird. A mallet and knife flew out of his hands as he slammed onto the ground.

Iomat's fingers dug into Emyn's shoulder and held her as she tried to run forward. Cesua's mother screamed; Hentios did not move.

The headman said a word Emyn did not expect as they all stared. "Now I'll be blamed for his murder," he muttered, pulling his cloak over his head.

He shouted for help and plunged into the downpour. Cesua's father and uncle burst forward; the three men carried Hentios by the shoulders and legs back into Cesua's house.

"Drunken fool," Sonios growled as he passed.

Iomat followed the men inside. Left alone, Emyn peered through the rain to where Hentios' mallet had flown. In spite of the wetness, light paler than fire shone at the spot.

Emyn walked toward it, her feet sinking deep into the mud. The mallet had broken into several pieces after striking a large rock.

"Here," the dead king boomed.

"Emyn!"

She bent to look at the mark left by the mallet and smiled. Above her the sky spilled out enough water to fill a well.

"Here," the ghost said again.

She was hoisted and carried into the house. Cesua's mother pulled Emyn's dress away, wrapped her in a dry blanket, and set her by the fire, flanked by the two sisters. Across the flames, the adults clustered around Hentios, now awake. Their voices made Emyn think of honking geese.

"Hentios said he would fix the roof," Sinia whispered.

"Where it dips," Cesua added and leaned very close. "A'er wouldn't give him any more ale so he said he'd earn it." The girl shook with laughter. "Now A'er says he won't be able to sit on his butt for a month!"

For this afternoon, at least, Hentios got his ale. Sonios filled and refilled a large cup as it passed from hand to hand. As the scolding voices softened and everyone—even Hentios—began to make jokes, Emyn held the blanket tight around her and stood.

"I know right where the well should be," she told the headman.

HENTIOS' TROSCAD WAS FORGOTTEN and the new well dug by the time a druid arrived. He'd come to judge a troscad; instead he presided over the slaughter of the headman's bull. Everyone told him their version of how the well was found and why the water was so sweet. Time and ale turned it into a tale of marvels that Emyn barely recognized.

After that, druids visited the small village regularly.

 3

"Dead trees!"

Emyn's screams sliced through the quiet of the night. Iomat calmed and shushed her as the rest of the household grumbled. A nightmare, they all agreed, and not the first.

She was sent outside the next morning as the headman listened and talked. It was a silly ruse; she heard the grownups clearly from outside. No one bothered to lower their voices.

"The girl talks half the night, Volio," shouted one man.

"Or sings," said another. "All hours!"

Emyn kicked at the dirt. She didn't sing. She hummed, and it was as quiet as she could make it. The others would hum too if ghosts chattered at them night and day.

"She's not the only person with nightmares," Volio's son said. "The dead creep in to all our dreams since she came to live here!"

"You can't blame the child for your bad dreams!" Iomat snapped.

How far would Iomat go to defend her? Maybe Emyn would be sent back to A'er's house. That wouldn't be so bad; Iomat could come too.

Emyn did not hear Volio's wife, even though she could shout as loudly as any of the men when provoked. Two days ago, Emyn had seen her grandmother standing by the woman as she cooked. "She likes the smell," Emyn told her. "She's always right there when you cook."

Why didn't Volio's wife join Iomat in defending Emyn? Didn't people *want* to hear from their grandparents?

"Men arrive." The dead king interrupted her thoughts. "Men of importance."

Emyn stepped away from the house so she could look down the path. The sky was a brighter blue than ever before. The trees were shorter, the grass disappeared, and a road made of stone stretched before her.

The overly bright sky reminded her of the nightmare. But she was not dreaming now, and roads were not made of stone. It could not be real. If Emyn was seeing things that weren't real, the ghosts were to blame.

Her grandfather wouldn't think much of a girl that cried over something that wasn't even there. He had returned home months ago, but his lessons remained. Emyn was brave; she was half Nervian.

She stepped onto the stone road and took a few steps. The rocks felt smooth beneath her feet. The air was heavy with the scent of sweet and unfamiliar flowers but she caught a whiff of something unpleasant as well. She knew the smell.

Throughout the summer, a piglet and a pup from each litter born was tossed into a pit to rot until Samhain when they were brought up, mixed with other offerings, and fed to the fields. The children dared each other to look into the pit at the dead animals. On hot days the stench soaked into their skin and made Emyn sick. Decaying flesh; that was the smell that flowers couldn't disguise.

The dirt on either side of the stone road was dry and covered with stubby bushes. A beam of wood sprouted from the ground as if it had been planted there.

"Look up," ordered the dead king, and she did.

High above, another beam crossed the first, like two thick branches sticking out on either side of a trunk. Emyn used every bit of courage she owned to hold back a scream.

A dead man hung from the beam, held there by nails and ropes. His clothes, streaked with dried blood, were as ragged as his flesh. Blonde hair sparkled in the sun the way Nonicos' hair did. The man's arms stretched over the crossbeam and were tied so that his wrists hid behind the wood. His shoulders and head leaned out, right over her.

Emyn didn't scream but she couldn't stop herself from vomiting. She turned and ran. Another post rose before her but she stared straight ahead, refusing to look up. That didn't help; right in front of her eyes, iron spikes drove through a dead man's ankles, one on each side of the trunk, nailing them to the wood.

"Crassus did this," the dead king said. "Pray he never comes here."

Emyn threw her arms over her eyes and ears and ran until she hit something hard. Her mouth exploded; she wondered if the ghosts could throw rocks. Arms held her up. A'er spoke and Iomat pressed a cool, wet cloth against her mouth.

"Open your eyes."

She wouldn't. She mumbled into the cloth, trying to tell them that dead men hung from trees.

"That was a dream, child," Iomat reminded her.

"No," Emyn shrieked. "They're here!"

They promised there were no dead men but Emyn couldn't trust their words. They didn't know. Finally, she squinted at the ground with one eye, saw dirt instead of stone, and looked at her father. The sky above him was white, not blue.

"You're going to have quite a bruise."

Emyn realized that the cloth was full of blood, and then she cried. Only a little, only until her A'er held her.

"Are they still mad at me?" she asked Iomat.

"Who? Oh, them." Iomat waved her hand toward the headman's house. "Nothing is decided. Volio has visitors."

Men of importance, the ghost had said. Emyn knew without being told that she had to talk to them. If the visitors had come yesterday, the vision would have happened yesterday.

She wiped her face clean with the cloth then stood with her father until the headman's door opened. The visitors emerged: two men wearing fine, striped cloaks.

Every family in Samarnum owned sheep and spun wool. Emyn knew these cloaks were costly. The thread was tightly woven and dyed in bright colors. She liked the way the stripes rippled as they draped and fell.

"Speak!" the dead king roared.

She ran forward and bowed. Before anyone could stop her, she described the rock road with wooden trees and the corpses hanging from them.

No one interrupted. The dead king whispered more words and Emyn repeated them: a Roman named Crassus had tortured thousands of men this way.

"Thousands?" One man turned to the other, as if he might make sense of this. He did not sound angry but hurt—as if her news were painful. "Thousands?"

"Tell us the name again," said the other visitor. "The name of the leader."

"Spartacus."

"Little girl," said the second man sternly, "who told you these tales?"

"The dead king."

"She hears voices," the headman began as Emyn's father pulled her away. The dead king whipped up a flurry of pale, tiny petals from the ground.

"Isminos!" Volio called to her father.

A'er pushed her toward Iomat and walked back to the men.

"IF YOU WANT TO keep what you have, keep it to yourself," Iomat muttered as Emyn woke.

"Women's fears," the headman snorted at her.

"Never mind," Iomat said when Emyn asked about her words. "Too late for that, anyway."

For once, most whispers around Emyn came from real people, not ghosts, but they were no easier to understand. She spent her time outside in the sun as A'er and Nonicos worked behind the headman's house for three days.

"Do not fret," cooed the white ladies but Emyn had learned over the past year how silly their advice was. One by one they began to chant. "Men will come."

"They'll bring you pretty gifts."

"They'll sing songs."

Emyn waved at them the same way she waved at buzzing insects.

"It's settled. We'll have our own hearth," Iomat announced at the end of the third day. "You and I. Your father built real walls around the shelter in back of Volio's house and we've swept out the geese and their smell. The roof is new; it'll be a fine place."

"I'm sorry," Emyn mumbled.

"For what?"

Emyn looked at her small pile of clothes next to Iomat's pots and baskets. "It's my fault. They don't want me here, so you have to leave too."

"Leave? We'll be behind his house. He even thinks it was his idea." Iomat's voice was low but cheerful; she kept her eyes on the thread she spun. "We'll still be eating from his pot, if you want to know. And we won't have to listen to his snoring. This is a gift."

"A'er has room for us—"

"Your A'er isn't the headman. Volio wants you under his protection, just as he does me. Even if you do scare his sons. I've scared his sons, too, you know."

Emyn watched the spindle twirl as it hovered over the ground. Did Iomat mean last winter when everyone whispered about her prediction? Emyn knew the words so well they sat like a memory in her head.

"None of you here assembled will die in your homes. Samarnum will perish before any one of you."

Emyn hadn't really heard the words; she'd fallen asleep after the story of her great grandmother. Nonicos had carried her home as the sun rose, home to A'er who was sick and could not leave his own hearth, not even for the solstice feast.

Iomat set down her spinning and made Emyn look at her. She was more than a healer and midwife. She saw the future in quick peeks and could read the signs left by magical beings.

Her face was stern. "We have a quiet little home to ourselves. This is a gift but there's a warning too. Listen to me: men hate what scares them."

Emyn was confused. "Should I be afraid of the ghosts?"

"When you see them every day? Of course not. Neither should anyone else. A life lived afraid is no life."

* * *

BY THE TIME SHE TURNED TEN, Emyn sat quietly at the headman's hearth whenever he had visitors. She listened to arguments over debts and boundaries, insults, feuds, and gossip, and knew better than to fidget or interrupt. On occasion, the dead king offered news, or other ghosts put forward a word to visitors. Emyn the child had nothing to say at such gatherings; Emyn the Gutumaros could speak at will.

Today, a druid and two companions sat before the hearth. They came from the Viromanduan king in the east and had spent four days traveling along the river on horseback. Their journey, from the sound of it, had been full of fine weather, races, songs, and generous meetings.

Visitors often gave the headman or even A'er a gift, but these men brought something for Emyn: a linen dress with a bit of fringe on the sleeves. She had never worn anything but wool before; she was used to the way it clung and warmed her body. This fabric slid all over her arms and trunk and chilled her skin as if she were naked. The guests were pleased that she wore it though, and told her she looked pretty.

The headman served choice mutton and wine from the south to his visitors. If the Viromanduan king ever decided that it would be easier to house Emyn himself rather than send men to hear her words, Volio would lose his oracle and the prestige and trade she brought. Worse for Emyn, she might never see her A'er or Iomat again.

Everyone made sure that visitors enjoyed their stay. Samarnum was a small place; any aggressive tribe could seize it. Generous hospitality and secrets from the dead were Volio's defenses.

Even the dead king cooperated, divulging his best news after the visitors had eaten their full.

"Alliances are made," he hissed, and Emyn repeated his words. "Kings promise land to warriors from across the Rhenus River. Land—green fields and pastures. Thus they entice foreigners to fight with them against their ancient enemy, the Aedui."

"Who? Who hires these mercenaries?" the druid asked. They all leaned forward to hear more.

"Sequani."

The visitors hung on every syllable. Emyn supposed that being the first to announce news—especially news of war—gave them stature before their king.

"And the Sequani will pay them with land?" the druid asked. "Sequani land, or land taken from the Aedui?"

"The Sequani promise much, but hope to give little," the ghost answered. "The foreigners bring their wives and their children across the great river. They come to stay."

"Are the foreigners German or Celt? What tribe?"

"They come to stay, to own the land promised by the Sequani."

Emyn repeated the words, and then waited for the ghost to say more. The Aedui and Sequani were large, important tribes, but they lived far away. Why did it matter what they did?

After a few long seconds, she sighed. "That is all the spirits say."

The druid watched her without speaking.

"Do not move. He is clever, that one." Emyn recognized the bard ghost, though he rarely appeared as more than a light and a clear voice. "He creates silence. Men will say anything to fill such a void. He learns much this way."

Emyn stared into the fire. Could the druid tell she heard more than silence? Volio coughed and clapped his hands. "The cup is empty. More wine!"

* * *

EMYN KNEW—as all children did—that the fate of each individual was controlled by the stars. Even the patterns in the sky at one's birth were important. The stars gave strength, virtues and weaknesses, and also determined which deities would watch over a person.

Iomat taught her to calculate the predictable movements of important stars, and what was meant when paths crossed. Stars told of meetings, health, marriages, and partings, but their routes were complicated to figure. They frustrated Emyn.

"You'll learn." Iomat, who carped and yelled when Emyn burned the morning cereal, showed unusual patience as the girl counted up months, got lost, and had to start over again. "Stars don't change and they don't lie. They'll be there every night for you to watch."

The stars could be a refuge against nightmares, Emyn found. On clear nights, seeing them sparkle over the quiet houses comforted her, whether she could understand their meaning or not.

Seasons passed and Emyn's dreams grew worse. She saw the Sequani and their fur-clad allies tear through homes, their swords drawn and bloody.

At farms and villages, Emyn saw the strangers take what they wanted and burn the rest. How much of it was real? Once they barred the doors and left a family trapped within to die in flames; the screams were horrible.

"You are weak," the dead king mocked, as she stood outside, shivering beneath a blanket and staring up at the stars. "Warriors fight."

"Those were not warriors," she whispered.

Nothing Emyn saw in dreams was anything like the tales told of warriors during feasts. There were no chariots or armored heroes, only men swinging desperately with axes and sticks.

Nervian or not, if these were battles, Emyn hated them. "Why don't the tribes choose a hero from each side to fight alone, the way stories tell?"

"Your head is full of women's tales!" the dead king's voice echoed in the still night, then softened a little. "That was once the way, long ago. But men are weak. There are no more heroes."

EMYN ENTERED THE HEADMAN'S house to find a young man by the glowing hearth. His companions stood behind him. They were important enough to be granted privacy for their meeting with the oracle.

Cesua had said he was handsome and strong; she hadn't exaggerated. Brown, glossy hair fell over his shoulders. A serpent's egg as well as a heavy torque circled his neck, marking him as both druid and warrior. His loose tunic left his muscled arms bare; no doubt he swung a sword around frequently.

Dumnocos. He was a prince of the Aeduan tribe—the ones who fought the Sequani and the foreigners. Maybe meeting this prince would sort out the different tribes in her mind and make their fights and alliances less confusing.

Dumnocos barely glanced at Emyn when she entered, but when she planted her feet before him, his brows arched over gray eyes. "You cannot be the one I came to see."

Laughter erupted behind him. The warriors sputtered like children. Dumnocos' eyes flashed as he uncrossed his arms and turned.

"You find this amusing? Three days out of our way and three days' ride back for a few moments of snickering?"

His glare settled on a bearded, blond man who stood as tall as the prince. "Yes," the other managed between snorts. "Amusing it is."

Dumnocos clenched his fists and set his mouth. The two men

stared at each other for as long as it would take Emyn to walk out the door, go to the well, and come back. In the end, though, Dumnocos' jaw and cheek started to quiver, and finally he burst into long hoots of laughter.

"Oh, Camulos, serves me right!"

"Sir, you did say a maiden—"

"I never doubted you, damn you! Oh, I'll be revenged for this one . . . ."

Forgotten entirely, Emyn watched the men slap each other on the back and laugh till there were tears in their eyes.

"He will be consecrated king." The soft voice—a man's—emanated from the wall where a red shield sat propped up, a serpent embossed on it. "He is chosen for this time."

There were rituals that went with kingship, Emyn knew: a man must couple with the goddess. She could be any age, but to consecrate a chosen prince such as this, the goddess would certainly be beautiful and young. Did Dumnocos expect to meet such a goddess here? Was that why he came?

Emyn smarted. If she had curves like Cesua's and if she were a little taller, he might not laugh so hard.

The men finally calmed and wiped their eyes. Dumnocos bent to smile at Emyn, his hands on his thighs. "Well played, little one. I hope my friends gave you something pretty for your part."

"I haven't told you what the dead have to say."

"Oh?" Dumnocos winked at the blond man. "Tell me, by all means."

He thought his friends had given her words. The dead king's message was not funny, and no one was here to defend her if Dumnocos got mad.

The shield with the serpent now leaned against her shoulder. No one had moved it.

"Speak," said the soft voice. But Emyn knew the shield was a ghost image and could not protect her.

"Speak!" commanded the dead king in his scratchy tone.

Emyn began. "The ghosts name your brother Divi . . . Divico—"

The dead king screamed the name at her at the same time the prince pronounced it: "Diviciacos."

"Diviciacos." She took a deep breath. "Diviciacos envies your position. The desire for power burns in him though you have been chosen."

The smile faded from his face. Emyn plunged on. The shield's weight pressed on her; she touched the wood and the leather strap. It felt real. "Great battles lie before the Aedui. Your enemies are strong; many of your kings will fall. Your brother watches for his chance. He binds the Aedui to strange gods and death."

Only Dumnocos had the sense to keep his mouth closed; the other men gaped and one touched his sword. Emyn's voice wavered. "The dead tell me this."

"Do they indeed?"

Dumnocos grabbed her wrist, yanked her arm up and pressed her hand against his serpent's egg. The shield fell to the ground. "Who gave you these words, girl?"

Her small fingers poked through strands of wire to rest against the stone itself. No one could lie while touching a druid's amulet.

"The ghosts." Emyn watched him; if she was going to be hit, she'd just as soon see it coming.

Dumnocos released her arm and turned to his friend. "I see no humor in these words. Explain yourself."

"I . . . I don't know what to say, lord," the blond man stammered.

"She *is* a Gutumaros, my prince," said a man behind Dumnocos.

"Is she?"

"Yes, sir, but we didn't think she had anything to say. We just thought it would be funny—after what you said the other night—"

"This has gone too far." The last man pulled a knife out of his belt. "She'll tell us—"

"Put that down!" Dumnocos snapped. "Do you think a child threatens me?"

The man tried to apologize, but Dumnocos waved him away and turned back to Emyn. "Tell me again what this ghost says. And stop shaking; I'm not going to hurt you."

Emyn felt empty like a hollow, burnt log, ready to collapse. "Great battles lie before the Aedui—"

"When?"

"I don't know."

"Will my father fall?"

"I don't . . ." The dead king hissed at her and Emyn listened. "Your father is brave and his chariot will be first in any fight. It is likely that he will fall in battle."

"And then what?"

"Your brother envies your position," she repeated the earlier words. "The dead king tells me Diviciacos seeks allies, but his judgment is flawed. He binds your people to death."

Dumnocos knelt so that his eyes were level with hers. "Can I change this?"

There was no sound. Emyn waited and wished desperately for an answer; it was a wise question.

The ghosts gave her no more words; she could only describe what she saw. "A red shield with a serpent in the center is lifted onto your arm."

"Your father's shield?" The blond man stepped forward. "What kind of an answer is that?"

"It's clear enough." Dumnocos' voice rang with authority, but his face was calm. "Go find the headman or her family and make decent payment, all of you."

The prince sat on the bench as his companions left. For the first time he spoke gently. "Is there anything else you have to tell me, little Gutumaros?"

"No, sir."

"Then I will tell you something. Before the Morrigu who watches us all, I am sorry we mocked you. I've seen many faces of that great goddess, but truly, she has surprised me here."

THROUGH MANY SEASONS, Iomat taught Emyn about the deities that aided healing, that touched certain plants with powerful magic, or that responded to the helpless. Emyn knew who to thank when she found a rare plant and who received the offerings that she and Iomat tossed into the Samar River.

Dirona and Ancamna were especially kind to the young. Briginda watched over women when they gave birth. Borvo, Dirona's son, protected warriors, and even in quiet Samarnum he helped men who got cut in fights or accidents. There were many others.

When Iomat had done all she could though, and her patient lay on the crossroads between worlds, it was the Morrigu who brought death. She sent a raven or shrieked in the wind till the blood of mortals froze. The Morrigu was violence and pain, picking the flesh from the dead before it could rot.

Iomat scolded Emyn when the girl shied from praying to such a goddess. "The Morrigu guides us through change. Death is change. You can't be afraid of her, not if you expect to do good for anyone."

The changes the Morrigu brought were imbued with suffering; to avoid them seemed good common sense to Emyn—like ducking when someone threw a rock. Emyn prayed that the Morrigu would ignore her and her village.

The Morrigu was a beautiful girl with a nose just like Emyn's, but her hair spread like dark wings in the wind.

The Morrigu was a loving mother and a leathery crone as well. Like all powerful deities, she changed appearance at will.

When Dumnocos chased his chosen goddess through a summer's evening, which face would the Aeduan prince see?

4

A young man with dark, lank hair and a face almost too narrow for his mouth emerged from Cesua's doorway to stand in the bright morning sun. Emyn stared. He shook his hair back from his eyes: a movement of unbearable grace. Emyn burned inside with something like embarrassment, as if he knew her secrets.

He turned; did he look at her directly? Emyn averted her eyes, nearly dropping her bucket as the door creaked open and banged shut again.

Her father had given her a new dress for her fifteenth birthday; she wished she had it on. Bright blue stripes would catch his eye—

Cesua nudged her. "Your turn."

Emyn looked toward the man; his face was still and distant. Cesua pinched her arm. "Emyn, fill your bucket."

Two pails rested at Cesua's feet, already full of water. Emyn glanced back at the man; his back was turned. She dipped her own bucket into the well.

Cesua sighed audibly. "For once I know what you're staring at and it's no ghost."

Emyn forced herself to watch the bucket as she pulled it toward her. Other figures approached. They must be real because the dead didn't like water. Spirits were no more than mist around the well and disappeared altogether at the river's edge.

She needed both hands to lift the bucket and set it on the ground. When she finally looked up, a second youth, taller, with golden hair that fell in curves and curls stood by the first.

A short man with a wild brown beard joined them, and the three walked towards the headman's house. The blond sent a dazzling smile their way as he turned; Emyn heard Tulia, the headman's niece, squeal.

Rustling branches and birdsong were the only other sounds as the trio skirted the old well and disappeared into shadows. The dark-haired man was last; Emyn studied the movement of the leather belt that rode on his hips and bit her lip. None of the local boys walked with such sure steps; they swaggered and strutted by comparison.

"Oh, my eyes have eaten well today," Cesua moaned, and a collective giggle broke the tension.

"That hair," Tulia breathed. "Did you ever see such hair?"

"On those shoulders . . . ."

"You were drooling, Ludula."

"I was not!" Ludula, who had married during the spring, sounded properly indignant.

"You were! Very impressive."

They were smitten with the blond man, Emyn realized. Smitten and as silly as the white ladies, all talking at once.

"Who are they?"

"Did they just stop for the night?"

"How long will they stay?"

The girls turned to Cesua; the men had come out of her house, after all. Cesua shrugged. "They arrived late. I didn't hear what they told A'er."

Tulia was bold. "I don't believe you. Sinia?"

"I was asleep."

"The old man's a druid; I saw his serpent's egg," Ludula said.

"Why were you looking at him?" Cesua giggled. "I only saw one man."

"There were two others," her sister offered.

Emyn could not contain herself. "One had dark hair."

Tulia jumped at Emyn's voice; she was not used to including her in conversations.

"He looked mean," said Ludula.

"For once I agree with Cesua. There was only one man worth looking at." Tulia grinned. "But if there's a druid, you won't get a second night with them. You know they'll stay in my uncle's house tonight."

"Does *anyone* know why they're here?"

Eyes traveled around the small circle. Cesua voiced the most obvious possibility. "Maybe they've come to see the all-knowing oracle."

Sinia snorted.

"I'll learn soon enough." Tulia shifted her pitcher from her hip and took a few steps towards her uncle's house, where she lived. "Emyn, if you want to be useful, get sick. That way they'll have to stay here longer to see you."

WHY WAS VOLIO'S DOOR shut on such a warm day? Emyn walked past it for the fourth time, or perhaps the fifth, circling the old well and spinning out thread. Surely the men wouldn't stay inside for long, not with the heat and fumes of the cooking pots saturating the air. She hummed and watched her spindle dance to the ground like a drunk. They had to come out eventually.

Unless they'd never gone in. Emyn snatched up the spindle and wound the thread around it, then caught the thread in a notch and sent it twirling again. She hadn't actually *seen* them enter the house. The three men could be anywhere . . . they could be back on the road, a league away.

Five times—or was it six? Suddenly Volio's door opened.

Emyn turned her head so quickly that her braid whipped her in the face. The dark-haired young man emerged, and the sun sent red sparks off loose strands of his hair.

He raised an eyebrow when he saw her; she said nothing. His brow was heavy and his nose had suffered at least one break. Emyn was enchanted.

"Wrong one?" He swept by. "Sorry to disappoint you. *He'll* be out later."

Her face burned but her tongue wouldn't move. The man vanished into Cesua's house.

He assumed she waited for the golden man! Geese honked as Emyn backed into the yard that surrounded Iomat's little shelter. In the dirt, a crooked line followed her spindle.

The other girls drooled over yellow curls. If he grouped Emyn with them, then he thought her as brainless as these honking geese. She had to do something. She flung the distaff and spindle onto Iomat's stool and marched to Cesua's house.

The dark-haired youth parted from the deep shadow of the doorway as she approached, cloaks draped over one arm and leather bags in his hands. He would bring these to the headman's house, but he was no servant. Emyn was sure of that.

Her mouth went dry and stupid once more.

"Do you want to ask me something?"

His low voice thrilled her. But his tone was resigned, reminding her that she must speak.

"You do!" mocked the white ladies.

"Ask him—"

"He'll give you pretty beads for your kisses."

"He'll give you this!" Shadows formed into a man, thrusting obscenely with his hips.

"Ask him," the white ladies repeated together.

Emyn swung her arm at the ghosts. Too late, she saw Cesua standing beside the path, rolling her eyes at the wild gesture.

He must think her touched. Emyn had no dignity left to lose, so she forced herself to look up.

"I did not wait for the other man, that's all."

"Emyn!" Iomat's call stopped any reply; grateful, the girl ran home.

SMALL MOUNDS OF DOUGH waited to be punched down and carried to the oven. Emyn threw herself into the task.

Volio's wife s squeezed her arm. "Who're you mad at?"

Everyone, Emyn wanted to scream, but instead smiled through clenched teeth. She could've slapped any person in Samarnum and didn't know why.

Iomat had been summoned to a house several leagues away to deliver a baby. That was her message when she called to Emyn earlier. The boy who fetched Iomat brought a horse. One horse; he would walk home.

Emyn tried to follow. The boy stopped and made a small

speech as he rocked back and forth on his feet, not lifting his eyes from the ground. The family did not want ghosts in their home, not at a birth. He begged Iomat and Emyn not to be angry at his mother; she had lost two babies in three years. "Please. Please do not frighten her."

Emyn stayed behind. What good were her skills if women didn't want her near?

She should be glad. If she'd gone with Iomat she might never see the dark-haired man who so enthralled her. But he would know by now that she was the Gutumaros and was probably avoiding her.

She picked up the board with the unbaked loaves and walked outside to the oven. Just a few weeks ago, Nonicos, newly married and giddy, warned A'er that boys would soon be following Emyn everywhere she went.

That hadn't happened.

As she rounded the corner of the house she nearly ran into Volio's youngest son.

"Bitch!" He jumped back as if she carried fire, not bread. "Watch where you're going!"

Men hate what scares them, Iomat had said long ago. *That's* what would follow Emyn wherever she went: hatred and fear.

VOLIO WAITED UNTIL EVERYONE had eaten their fill before calling Emyn toward the hearth to bow to the wild-haired druid.

"This is our Gutumaros, Honored Master Bodocnos. May her spirits provide the wisdom you seek."

The younger men sat behind the druid on mats. Emyn deliberately avoided the face of the dark-haired one, though she could see his hands resting on his legs, his fingers long and strong.

They had small scars, the kind her brothers got when they were learning to whittle.

If she raised her eyes to his face, she might go limp and stupid like a rabbit before a weasel. She stared instead at the basket between the two younger men, half full of cold bread.

They were students, according to Cesua. She even knew the name of the blond one: Coath. He'd looked away as Emyn stepped forward, as most boys did.

The master, a short, middle-aged man with a bronze and leather band around his head, glanced at her, grabbed a rag, and wiped fat from his fingers. "If you are the oracle who foretold the slave rebellion in Rome, you must be older than you look."

"No, Honored Master."

Bodocnos lifted an eyebrow exactly as his student had done earlier. "No?"

"I only saw the punishments, not the rebellion," Emyn explained. "I saw the crucifixions along the Appian Way. And I did not foretell it. I saw it when it happened."

"Ah." Bodocnos accepted a cup from Volio, drank, and handed it to Emyn. Then he turned away and began talking of his travels. He seemed to forget she was there.

To Emyn, Bodocnos presented an incongruous sight. His hair thinned on top but his beard stuck out at all angles, coiled and thick. Except for the bronze band and his serpent's egg, he looked a bit silly. He could be a beggar or a fool, or even tend sheep, just as Micco did—Hentios' youngest, addled son.

Bodocnos looked like anything but a druid.

She recalled the druid who'd come to question her about the crucified men—an especially nice man with red hair and a beard: Nanto. He'd sat and talked with her, counting her fingers and toes. He'd even let Emyn sit on his lap and ask him questions.

Did all druids have two faces: one to intimidate, and one to amuse and disarm?

Nanto had explained what slaves were, and how the Romans treated slaves who were once warriors. How they forced them to fight and kill before a crowd of gamblers, then locked them up to kill again another day. "That is wicked, is it not—to pervert courage, and punish skill?"

Emyn had nodded. Nanto told her that the slaves revolted but were finally caught and defeated by Crassus, a Roman general. To set an example, Crassus had crucified six thousand of the rebellious slaves along a stone road leading to Rome.

"I would never want to tell a little girl about such a terrible thing as crucifixion," Nanto had said. "Crassus won't let anyone take the bodies down. He wants them to hang here so all the other slaves will see them and be afraid."

Bodocnos uttered the word "Gutuatri," snapping Emyn back to the present.

Gutuatris heard and passed on the words of the gods, as Emyn heard and spoke for the dead.

"This Gutuatri, this holy man far to the south, fears the Latin speakers. Rome's frontiers are very near. Perhaps he listens more to his own worries than to words from the mighty, hmm?" Bodocnos smiled at Emyn, but his eyes did not relax with the rest of his face.

She said nothing; she could not know the Gutuatri's reasons.

Bodocnos had been talking of Rome; maybe that's why her mind dug up the slave revolt and its details. Back then, she'd wondered why the dead king showed her horrible sights from a land so far away. She still wondered, but now Bodocnos seemed concerned with the gossip of Rome as well. Why?

"Another wise man, reading omens and the stars, sees great

threats from across the Rhenus." Bodocnos paused again, but she could not see his face this time. Did he hope to draw out her ghosts with these predictions?

"Threats to whom?" Volio asked. "We heard of the Germani crossing the river years ago. Pigs, they are. The spirits said they fought for the Sequani." He shrugged. "It's too far away to touch us."

"Perhaps," Bodocnos sighed. "The Germani raid without restraint to this day and their numbers increase. They are no longer satisfied with the land they got; they want more, and other mercenaries cross the river." He turned to Emyn "Do your voices warn of them?"

The dead king hung like a shadow over Bodocnos.

Emyn said, "There are ghosts here but they give me no words."

The blond man shuddered and Volio crossed his arms.

"I wonder," Bodocnos said slowly, "if spirit messages might ring more clearly when heard in a sacred place. Have you been to the heroes' temple north of here, on the very edge of Viromanduan lands? Where warriors' skeletons, draped in their armor, hang from the outer wall?"

Emyn nodded. "My father took me once."

"Would you consider making the journey again? With your father, if you like."

He was suggesting a long absence from Samarnum. Emyn knew the decision was not hers to make.

"The Gutumaros lives under my roof and answers to our healer." Volio glanced pointedly at the blond man. "I could not approve her leaving, though I intend no offense against a learned master."

Bodocnos waved his hand as if his proposal were nothing

more than a passing thought. "I take no offense. You protect her as you would your own daughter; that is admirable."

The men believed no maiden could be safe from Coath's smile, apparently. Was the dark-haired student amused? He might raise an eyebrow if she looked—but while thinking of him, she lost track of Bodocnos' words. Now he waited for an answer . . . to what?

"Master, if the spirits do not wish to speak, why force them?" Coath spoke for the first time. His words were cowardly, but his voice sounded like a hero's: confident and strong.

Suddenly Emyn remembered the oak grove where she'd first met the ghosts. "I know of a sacred cluster of oak trees on a hill nearby, Honored Master. An hour's walk from here. Would that do?"

The idea pleased Bodocnos. "We will walk there together before the sun sets again, so that we hear your spirits in the darkness."

Coath began a word and Bodocnos cut him off. "It is fitting. Our day starts as darkness falls. What is heard then will be illumined by dreams and then the sun."

The master looked around and smiled at a cluster of children. "Now, who would like to hear a story?"

EMYN LAY STILL ON HER MATTRESS, facing west to honor the long-gone sun. Nothing stirred the air.

On most nights, she fell asleep telling herself the same sort of story Bodocnos had recited earlier for the children: the tale of a noble son driven from his own tribe by trickery and forced to live as an outlaw. She imagined herself an outlaw; it was her favorite daydream.

She'd heard many old stories of boys and even a few girls, compelled to live in the wild until they found their true place. She could do that. She was strong and could cook and brew medicines, and the ghosts would warn her of danger. Any group would fare better with Emyn looking out for them.

Eventually—as in the tales—her outlaw adventures would end. A prince like Dumnocos would reward her heroic deeds with a fine house and land, or maybe fall in love with her himself. By the time she got to that part of her fantasy though, sleep was close and the details blended into dreams.

Tonight, the story seemed childish. What group would want her? Boys and men feared her ghosts. Even outlaws would send her away.

Useless, that's what she was, except as an oracle. But as a woman? Useless.

Emyn snorted, got up and shoved hard on the door. It swung wide open and hit the wall. She stepped outside and wedged a piece of firewood under it.

The room was stuffy. Why did she need a closed door? No one would intrude on the Death Speaker.

 5

Golden light and tall shadows spilled across Sadonu's wreckage as Emyn and the druid walked quietly from ruins to the surrounding trees. Their steps drove the tiny, pale petals of pear and apple blossoms into the mulch.

"How sad that the fruit trees go untended here," Bodocnos murmured.

"Iomat says it's best to leave the land of the dead to the dead," Emyn said.

"She is right, but I am a sentimental old man."

The trees swallowed them up, blocking most light. Birds called from every direction. Emyn had not been to the grove since she was six and didn't know what to expect when they arrived.

Bodocnos spoke after a long silence. "Gutumaros, when were you born?"

"Close to Beltane, fifteen years ago."

"So you are just fifteen. What day exactly?"

"The sixth after Beltane, four hours after darkness fell."

The master hummed to himself as he worked through

calculations far more complex than the simple rules Emyn learned from Iomat. He would know all the paths of the stars and every nuance of their meaning. As a midwife, Emyn had learned only enough to give a few words of promise to new parents when settling an infant into their arms.

What had Iomat said to Emyn's own A'er, fifteen years ago? "Isminos, your new daughter will find death wherever she turns in her short life. Already, her mother has died."

That was what the stars promised, but Iomat would never burden a father with such cruel words.

"Isminos, the Morrigu watches over your daughter and marks her for a special purpose." Yes, that was probably what she said. Softer to the ears, though it hinted at the same thing.

Bodocnos strolled ahead of her as if he knew the path. "Master, have you been here before?"

"Yes, earlier today." When he turned to answer, the sun flashed against the bronze circlet on his head. "Your headman told me the way. I've sent Rialos and Cothuacos ahead to prepare and invoke blessings—"

"Who?"

"My students. Coath, you probably call him."

Rialos. She repeated the name to herself several times. "What tribes are you from, sir?"

"I am Dellovaci, to the west." Each time Bodocnos turned his head, the light hit the band; it dazzled her. "Rialos has no tribe, though that will no doubt change once he is a druid. Coath's family is Carnute...."

No tribe? Was Rialos an outlaw, then? Emyn let her breath out slowly, afraid the master would notice.

"He cannot walk away, this druid." The bard ghost was beside her. "He served the lords of the skull temple."

Bodocnos prattled on about the blond student but Emyn didn't follow his words.

Spirit whispers filled the air. "Such service never ends."

"He craves peace."

"Peace of the mind."

"Peace for the land."

"He cannot have both."

"He heard the dead."

"Emyn!" Bodocnos' voice struck her like a slap. "Emyn, take my arm."

She lifted her hand, not sure where his arm was. The bronze band blinded her. She felt his larger hand take hers and guide it to his arm as if tethering her.

"Why do you stare at my forehead?"

"It is bright with the sun."

"The sun is over there, Emyn." Her spoken name was warm. Like the arm that she held, it steadied her.

"No, the sun . . . reflects from the band."

"What band?"

"The bronze band on your brow."

"I wear no band." Bodocnos' voice was as quiet as the breeze that ruffled the willow branches before them.

"He cannot remove it," a ghost said.

"He took it up in the twelfth year."

"He took up the knife in the twelfth year."

"I wore such a band once, at a temple," Bodocnos sighed. "Do you often see things that aren't there?"

"I see visions." Emyn shook with the implications of this question. How would she know if little things weren't real?

He patted her hand where she held him. "Perhaps your spirits wish to remind me of the service I performed when I wore that band. Do not worry. We'll keep walking; we are near. I can tell by the bluebells. See? They are thick through the entire grove; it is a lovely place."

The twelfth year, Emyn remembered, was one of great sacrifice. Such a year approached; it would begin in the fall after Samhain. Bodocnos' bright clothes, his wild beard, his quick and merry smiles, were all a sham. They hid the druid's true nature. The service performed in a twelfth year was to offer sacrifice.

Why had he come to see her?

BLUEBELLS FLOODED THE GROVE and Emyn sank into them. She had no chance to look for the dark-haired student and no time to think. The press of bodies nearby was sudden and warm and she slipped down, watching the bluebells shake, wondering if the ground would stay the same.

It didn't. Oak leaves crunched in her hands and an icy chill surrounded her. How could the ghosts drop her into another season?

"You were born to us here," whispered the white ladies, and for once they did not giggle or sing. "Will you die here as well?"

"*He* would like that." The dead king joined them, pointing a long arm towards Bodocnos. The ghost had not seemed so real, so near to flesh and blood, since she was six years old. "His knife craves blood."

Bodocnos' voice rang out. "What is revealed, Gutumaros?"

"I am not here, not at the grove I walked into." Emyn looked up and around. "The moon is in the wrong place. The dampness feels like autumn. The people I see wear serpent's eggs and rich clothes, beautiful clothes. Fur . . . antlers on some heads. The grove is large," she counted quickly, "three handfuls of tall trees, three handfuls on each side. The wise assemble. They wait. You are among them."

"All of us?"

Emyn hesitated. She did see all three, the druid and his students, but Coath stood alone in this large grove, dazed. He'd been pushed to the center of the gathering, and a woman offered a cup to him. "Someone drinks from a goblet. A cup etched in spirals—the moonlight dances in them."

"Prettiness." The word came from Coath's mouth but in her father's voice. Emyn leaned away as Coath offered the cup to her.

The dead king still pointed. "He would deliver you to the dead if he could find one imperfection."

"What do you see?" the druid asked.

"I hear the dead king. He says you wish to sacrifice me. Is that why you've come?"

"Your ghosts play with us," Bodocnos said. "I am warned, then. Tell me what they show you."

Coath was gone; Rialos stood in the center of the grove holding the cup. Emyn gasped.

"Ah. . . ." The dead king croaked out his laugh. "This one, then."

"Gutumaros," Bodocnos prompted her.

"A man drinks from the cup," she told him.

"Young or old?"

"Young." Bodocnos was too eager. She would not name the man in the center. "A fair man, with red hair."

The dead king made a sound of disgust behind her. "Liar."

"He drinks and falls to his knees. No. . . he is lifted up." Emyn closed her eyes. What should she say? How could she think this through with so many people whispering and shuffling around her?

When she looked again, Rialos' clothes were being carried past. He stood naked until Bodocnos helped him to kneel. Rialos' hair looked soft and clean, as if he'd just come from bathing. Moonlight glistened on every muscle and sparkled on the dark hair that covered his chest, hair that narrowed to a single line below his navel, leading her eyes down.

Emyn had never seen a young, healthy man naked before. She didn't now, she told herself. This wasn't real; the ghosts teased her. They enjoyed teasing her.

"Gutumaros, what do you see?"

"Master, I see lies. The ghosts have never shown me what the future holds; I do not believe them."

"Let me judge their stories, girl!" Bodocnos snapped. "Give us the words."

Emyn shivered. "A fog creeps through the crowd. The man is on his knees now, naked. A knotted cord falls around his neck. Some of the masters back away and others come close." Emyn shook her head, unwilling to watch. "This is enough—"

"We are not finished!" The dead king's voice screeched.

Before her eyes, torchlight glinted off the blade of a knife. A pale hand flexed and adjusted itself around the bone handle. The smallest finger vanished beneath a sleeve but not before Emyn saw a second, stunted fingertip growing from beside the nail.

Such a deformity marked a man. How could he hold a sacrificial knife? He was marred, judged by the gods themselves.

"The wrong man holds the knife!" Emyn's breath came fast.

"What do you mean?" Bodocnos' voice rang from her right, but she could see him before her in a different place, holding his student steady as the knife came closer. He wasn't going to save Rialos, just the opposite.

"He is the wrong man! He is marked! The knife . . . ."

In the illusory grove, someone handed Bodocnos a thick branch; he pushed it through the cord around Rialos' neck and began to twist. Rialos, perched on his knees, did not fight. He seemed asleep.

The cord tightened. Rialos jerked and fell forward, but Bodocnos caught him and forced him upright. The other man slashed with the knife and blood sprayed over the ground.

Emyn choked and covered her eyes.

"Master, stop this."

The male voice was soft and Bodocnos outshouted it. "Gutumaros, tell me what you see!"

"You must tell him!" The dead king hissed.

"Then show me truth!" Emyn demanded.

Bright daylight stunned her eyes, pouring through the doors of a stable. The smells of hay and dung filled her nose. Rialos saddled a horse as the man with the knife ran up behind him, striking. She saw the deformed finger again as the knife cut deeply into Rialos' neck.

Emyn covered her face while the dead king's laughter scratched at her ears.

She opened her eyes to bluebells. Rialos' body lay on the ground, white in the moonlight. He was dead; his blood soaked into the ground. No basins had caught it, no fields or rivers would be blessed by it. A waste.

"Tell them—" the ghost said.

"Tell them what?" Emyn turned towards the voice. "What do you want in return for this death?"

"Nothing!" The dead king roared, triumphant.

"Gutumaros, you must—"

"Then why?" Emyn ignored Bodocnos' voice; she wanted answers. Hands clutched at her and she pushed them away.

"Because this must be done."

"No! It won't do any good, that's what you mean!"

"It still must be done," said the dead king.

Bodocnos shouted, "Gutumaros, we do not barter with such a death! It is offered without conditions. Tell us what you see."

Emyn held her head, unable to think. The flowers were gone. She was in a stable again; daylight filtered in around loose boards. Rialos had been left to lie face down on the straw and dirt.

"Stop this or let me—" That was Rialos' voice. He wasn't dead; this wasn't real.

"No!" Frustration shot through Bodocnos' words. "We must know: should there be a sacrifice?"

"If there is, it will be the wrong man." Emyn shut her eyes tight. "The man marked at birth holds the knife. The blood spilled is wasted on the ground, no sacred vessel catches it."

"Nothing can be changed," the dead king said. "You will all die, and your bones will be scattered on the ground."

"Nothing will change, sacrifice or no," Emyn repeated for Bodocnos, then screamed at the dead king. "Is that the worst of your threats, that our bones will be scattered?"

"Such insolence from a puny child! Do you question—"

"Shut up!" Arguing with the ghost never did any good. Only one threat might sway him: "I will not give out your words!"

"You cannot withhold them!" Bodocnos cried. Emyn felt his hand on her arm at the same moment that the ghosts–all of the ghosts, all of their visions and sounds–evaporated around her. "You are their messenger."

She stared into the blessed darkness, then bowed her head. "They lie. You know they lie."

"Men lie as well. Lies mix with truth, and they're damned

hard to pick apart. Deliver your messages, Gutumaros, and let the wise puzzle over which parts are true."

Only Bodocnos' voice sounded in the grove. What had driven away the ghosts?

A sea of bluebells rippled in the moonlight. The breeze was cool against her face; Emyn's pulse slowed as she took deep breaths.

"And you," Bodocnos spat above her. "How dare you disobey me?"

Emyn looked up at Rialos' face—his real face, lit only by the moon. Why was the master angry with him?

"She asked—"

"Yes, and I ordered! Who is your master?"

"You teach us never to ignore those who plead for help."

"I've taught you—" Bodocnos' tirade ended abruptly as all three men turned toward the far edge of the grove, alerted by a squeal too high-pitched to be an animal.

"Who is there? Stop!" The druid jumped forward and waded through the bluebells to the edge of the grove, where two figures cowered. "Run away now and you will face greater dangers than my anger. Don't you know where you are?"

A girl burst into tears. In spite of the distance and darkness, Emyn recognized Sinia.

6

Emyn stood wearily in the center of the grove, alone. The moon was high and bright and in its light she could see Sinia, Cesua, the druid and his students standing in a clearing. Soon, Bodocnos high-stepped through the bluebells back to Emyn. The others stayed where they were, a healthy distance from the tall oaks.

The druid took her arm, pulling her into the shadows. He spoke in a low and urgent voice. "Tell me the truth. You saw a sacrifice tonight, didn't you? You saw a man purified and offered to the gods. The man who performed the ritual was marked."

"Yes."

"How?"

"He had an extra finger growing from here," Emyn touched the side of her little finger.

"And how did the victim die? By the knife?"

"No . . . I don't know. The cord was tightened and the knife fell, all at once."

"Two gods claimed him, then."

"Or—"

Bodocnos cut her off. "You recognized the victim, didn't you? Who was it?"

Emyn balled her fists and looked down; the druid sighed. "You are young; you want assurances that those you love will not suffer. I cannot give you that."

He turned abruptly and called out. "We must leave. Coath, I want you to stay ahead of me where I can watch you. Let's go . . . before these girls' parents come out to cut you into pieces."

Sinia and Cesua followed the druid. Cesua pushed her sister away when she tried to cling to her and skipped ahead.

The miserable Sinia fell back, and Emyn put an arm around her. "How long were you watching?"

"We just got there. You hollered at someone to shut up. Cesua wanted . . ." The girl began to hiccup and cry.

"We all know what Cesua wants," Emyn sighed.

Cesua pestered Emyn for samples of every love potion and charm Iomat made—all new faces drew her attention. But Sinia was as timid as her sister was exuberant. Dragging her along to the sacred grove to spy on Coath was just mean.

"How did she talk you into this?"

"She said the ghosts wouldn't hurt us because you're our friend," Sinia whimpered, leaning on Emyn's shoulder. "But I knew she was afraid to come alone. She said you'd get me home."

Emyn managed a small laugh. "She was right then."

Cesua, walking ahead of them on the path, tried to match her pace to Coath's. As he carried the torch, no movement near him went unnoticed by Bodocnos, who intercepted Cesua.

Sinia groaned aloud. "My A'er will kill me."

"He won't," Emyn assured her. "Maybe he'll wallop Cesua."

"Wish he would," Sinia mumbled. Emyn squeezed her shoulder. There were handfuls of jokes to make over Cesua's foolishness tonight, but no one was in the mood for jokes.

It was late and the trek back to the village long. Emyn, exhausted, dozed as she walked; once a strong arm caught her and kept her from falling. Rialos strode at her side after that, but said nothing.

The vision sprang back into her mind, and she held onto Sinia. If the gods granted her a wish, it would be to keep him alive. She didn't believe the ghosts. They'd shown her different scenes tonight; they couldn't even make up their minds what tricks to play. They couldn't see the future.

They couldn't.

THE TWO LARGE HOUSES near the well were quiet and dark; clearly, Sonios did not know his daughters had snuck away. Bodocnos motioned Rialos forward and whispered to him. Emyn hoped the druid would simply send the girls home. No one stood to benefit if he woke their parents . . . but Bodocnos rapped sharply on the door.

Sinia began to cry again, and soon her parents were demanding answers and threatening dire punishments. The sisters were taken inside; the druid followed.

"The master will explain what he can here." Rialos' low voice was warm in Emyn's ear. "He asked me to take you home."

Rialos held a small lamp in his hand. In its light his eyes looked golden, like an animal's. His arm touched hers as they walked toward the old well.

"Where do you live?"

"Behind the headman's house, in a smaller . . ." Her voice, barely a whisper at first, faded as she realized this might be her only chance to warn him. "A year of sacrifice is coming."

"Do not worry. No one will take you." Was he smiling?

"No, I worry for you! Do not go to any gathering. It was you the ghosts showed me."

"Silly little girl!" The dead king cackled.

Emyn pleaded. "Do not trust the wise. They want a sacrifice."

Rialos set the lamp on the edge of the old well and faced her. "Gutumaros . . . Emyn?" She nodded, happy to hear her name from his lips. "Emyn, listen to me. The wise want nothing other than animal sacrifices. No man has been killed, not for generations."

"But the ghosts—"

"They are shadows. What do they know?"

The ghosts tittered nearby.

"He is afraid," sneered the dead king.

Emyn waved at the ghost and Rialos caught her hand in midair. "What is it?"

"Not of us," the bard ghost whispered. "Of you."

"The ghosts taunt me," said Emyn.

Rialos covered her hand with his own, pressing it to his chest. "Perhaps they are only jealous. You are alive. They are not." His heart beat furiously beneath her palm. "Are you never free of them?"

"No."

"Now?"

The ghosts were gone. What power did he have?

His face was near. "They *are* jealous. They have no form while you are beautiful. You are. In the grove, even as the light faded, your eyes were brighter than all those bluebells."

He had an accent that she hadn't heard before, and Emyn's knees weakened. No man had ever poured flattery on the Gutumaros.

"Come." Rialos stepped back and pulled her along. The lamp was left behind as they slipped into the blackness between Volio's house and his stable.

The first kiss was warm and soft, but so unexpected that it was over before Emyn could respond.

Fingers wove through her hair as Rialos steadied her for a second kiss. She could not see anything; surely he couldn't either, but they were too close for that to matter. Lips partly open, just as Cesua had described to Emyn several times. A tease of a kiss, Cesua called it. If Cesua ever told her what such kisses did to a girl's insides, Emyn hadn't understood.

Rialos bit at her lips, and everything Emyn thought she knew slid away. Her blood turned into fire. She kissed back, parting her lips, and the fire became a torrent tossing her off balance.

Nothing else mattered but the light scrape of his teeth against hers and the strength of his arms when he pulled her to him. For a moment, no more, they pressed against each other without restraint, the angles of his body hard against her skin as if they could merge into one being.

Then it was over. Rialos sighed, though he did not let go. "This is wrong. I can't stay."

"I don't care."

"You are young and—"

"Emyn?"

Her name was not a shout but a question, loudly whispered through the night. Iomat called for her.

"In the morning . . ." Rialos kissed her forehead and pulled her away from the shadows.

Iomat stood by the old well. "There you are! I worried."

Her eyes, lit from below by the lamp she'd picked up, opened wide when she saw the young man behind Emyn. "It's late.

"Master Bodocnos sent me to see the Gutumaros home." Rialos bowed. "I may leave her with you then?"

"You'd better. We should all be asleep. What was your master thinking?"

Rialos' hand had touched her back; Emyn felt its absence like a rush of cold air. He was gone. Whatever he'd muttered to Iomat in apology was done. Emyn stumbled home and fell onto a mattress stuffed with straw and feathers, aching to feel his body against hers again.

VOLIO'S YOUNGEST SON ENTERED the stable to feed the horses the next morning and found blond Coath wrapped around Ludula. The youth had enough sense not to cry out, but he told his father about the pair within the hearing of Tulia, his cousin.

Tulia had no sense, at least not where handsome men were concerned. Soon all of Samarnum roiled over the shameful behavior of Volio's guests. The women sulked and Ludula's husband shouted threats, but Emyn didn't learn of that until later. As she rose and stumbled outside to feed the geese, she saw the Honored Master Bodocnos shoving his students back to the road: one looked sated and sheepish, the other solemn as a raven.

Emyn tried to bolt from the yard. Iomat grabbed her arm. "Don't embarrass yourself."

"Let me go!"

"Did he *ask* you to chase after him?"

Emyn stared at the backs of the three men. Rialos never turned around to look. If he had, she would have shaken off Iomat's hand and run, waved, screamed, done anything. She centered her thoughts on Rialos' back like an arrow on a racing deer, careening into him—but it did no good. He never turned.

Emyn's life shriveled before her. She had no more say in her own future than she did in the ghosts' visions.

"Here," Iomat pushed the spindle and distaff into the girl's hands. "Work."

Her fingers started the thread as they did every day, rolling and twisting a strong strand to tie to the spindle. Her hands knew how to work; her mind told her nothing.

"He is dead."

The ghostly king mocked Emyn with the claim and repeated it throughout the summer. His voice was gleeful, as if a hated rival were eliminated.

"I don't believe you."

"Would you rather die yourself?" he sneered, and the white ladies joined him, all chattering at once.

"Such a pretty girl!"

"Untouched."

"Your eyes and ears are with the spirits already."

"The twelfth year comes."

"You would make a fine offering!"

"What good would that do you?" Emyn snapped and waved them away. "Who would speak for you then?"

Once, she stepped into Iomat's house to see the dark-haired student lying lifeless in the corner, his neck twisted in an impossible angle. The dead king delighted in her tears and made them fall often with his tricks. Iomat called Emyn silly and selfish when she cried or cursed the ghosts.

After Lugnasad, another druid visited Samarnum. "What words do the spirits have for me?" he asked, as all visitors did.

"For the Sequani princes I advise? What borders are weak? What fields will grow bountiful next year?"

Emyn repeated the answers she heard and saw, then begged a moment of his time for herself. "The twelfth year comes before us all, Master. What sacrifice will the wise make?"

"He cannot tell you!" The dead king jeered.

"How is that your affair?" The druid waved his hand, dismissing her. "Leave that to the wise."

Emyn's face burned. "Then let the wise answer their own questions!"

Once sparked, the anger in her spread like fire, and every word from the spirits fanned the flames. The ghosts might take over her eyes and fill her ears, but they couldn't force her to speak.

The next time a visitor came to see the Death Speaker, Emyn refused to meet with him. The ghosts sniped at her all that night and the next, but Emyn would not bend.

Iomat scolded. "The gods give you gifts and you waste them!"

Emyn looked up, stupid with weariness. So now she set herself against the gods as well as the ghosts? Fine. Let them smash her. Death was better than living as their slave.

"Your messages give strength," the bard ghost reminded her after several days had passed. "Many come into this world simply to die with valor."

"Then they do not need to hear from spirits."

He sounded sad as he replied, "How do you know what they need?"

"I know that they do not need lies," Emyn's voice rasped.

She sickened. Iomat brewed medicines for her throat. Emyn tasted many herbs in them and knew that some would make her sleep. She didn't mind; she welcomed sleep.

Heavy snows fell that winter. The dead king claimed the

weather was both her fault and her punishment. She called him a liar, coughed, and frequently grew feverish.

She passed on only one message from the spirits that season: one that could be tested and that did not come from the dead king. "Spirits say the ground weakens under the old tree that shades your stable," she told Volio. "The snow will melt and the tree may topple. The stable could be damaged."

The headman nodded and thanked her and set his sons to work, cutting branches and digging out roots. "The spirits were right," he told Iomat later. "When will the girl make her peace with them?"

Iomat shook her head.

"MY WORDS ARE NEEDED." The dead king was like a fly buzzing at her ear.

Emyn held a fur tight around her shoulders as she sat before the small fire. The world warmed and days lengthened, but she hadn't changed her mind. She didn't answer the ghost; she was tired of calling him a liar and had no other words. She fell asleep and days passed.

"How does the dead king reign?"

Firelight and shadows fell on walls hung with woven patterns. Emyn did not recognize the house though she found comfort here, just as she did not know the woman who held her as a mother would.

"He is strong," the woman said as she touched Emyn's hand. Her face was young, her hair loose, her dress simple and dark. "No other is stronger . . . except perhaps you."

They had been visiting a long time, but Emyn couldn't remember what else they'd talked about. "He lies," she heard herself mumble.

"You have taught him not to lie."

It seemed simple. The woman's nose was like a hawk's, larger than Emyn's, and her black hair billowed up like wings.

"We choose strange partners, don't we?"

The Morrigu smiled at Emyn's joke, and the girl fell asleep once more.

SHE OPENED HER EYES; the dead king hovered beside her. "I have many truths," he said. "I don't need lies."

Emyn nodded.

When she woke again, spring had come and she was hungry.

7

"You don't have to be married," Cesua declared.

She had been giggling and leaning on Emyn just a moment earlier, seemingly tipsy. But now her old friend laid hands on either side of Emyn's head so that their eyes met.

"Volio says if I'm married—"

Cesua cut her off. "Volio is guessing. You don't have to."

Laughter intruded, drifting from the river's edge as couples paired off for the night. Weddings brought the lust out in everyone. Emyn had been surprised that Cesua chose to stay inside drinking mead and now walked back to Iomat's hut with her, when she could have her pick of the available men.

"Tulia and Esmios last summer, now this," Cesua groaned. "I don't want to be the only unmarried woman left."

"There's always Iomat."

Cesua snorted. "Sinia's a traitor."

"It's a good match. You know it is."

Cesua didn't answer. They both knew that sweet little Sinia had a way with Volio's hot-headed son. Even the stars said the union would be strong and joyous.

"Stay unmarried." Cesua wrapped her arm around Emyn's waist and the two began walking once more. "You don't have to marry to be safe."

"I know," said Emyn, though she didn't. Volio hinted otherwise; he worried about losing his oracle to an ambitious merchant or druid. Emyn might be a peasant, but she had value and she could be stolen. A marriage would make abduction a criminal offense, discouraging all but the most reckless men.

Cesua shook her head. "Too much death this year. That makes everyone think about babies. Just wait."

Emyn gave her friend a hug; maybe she was right. Death after death had filled the seasons lately. Her father, Nonicos' son and his unborn child . . . the home she'd known as a child reeked of sadness.

"Do you know who Almer looks like?" Cesua asked abruptly.

Emyn's stomach twisted. Almer must be the reason Cesua wanted to walk Emyn home. They had left him behind with other guests and the honeyed mead that Sonios had prepared especially for his younger daughter's wedding.

After a few flirtatious words and visits, Almer had stunned all in Samarnum by voicing a willingness to marry the Gutumaros. Volio cheered the idea; Iomat hated it. The ghosts offered no real advice and Emyn would not trust it anyway. Her insides churned with the knowledge that she must decide, one way or another.

"Did you hear me?"

"Yes. Who does Almer look like?" Emyn sighed.

"Do you remember that golden-haired student?"

"Ludula's golden stud bull, you mean?"

Cesua fell against Emyn. "Oh, he was beautiful! But do you remember his friend?"

"Of course I do."

"Well?"

"Well what?"

"Don't you think he looked like Almer?"

Emyn froze and Cesua's arm fell away. She did, she realized.

For a moment, Emyn felt as if Cesua had ripped her dress off and left her exposed for everyone to jeer at.

The dark hair that hung below his shoulders didn't shine quite the same in the sun, but nearly so. He was as tall, his shoulders as broad. Almer didn't walk with identical grace and his voice was not as deep, but when he stood still and silent. . . . it was all close enough.

"Emyn? Are the ghosts bothering you?" Cesua lifted Emyn's limp right arm and waved it around. "Go away! Leave her alone!"

Giggling, Cesua staggered through Iomat's door, pulling Emyn behind her.

A FEW DAYS LATER, Emyn slipped out of her home to deliver a pot of seeds to Cesua. Gathered from flowers that collapsed on their delicate stems to look like birds' nests, the seeds prevented pregnancy, and Emyn supplied Cesua and other women with them regularly.

Cesua sat in back of her house, mending a dress for colder weather. It was the sort of work that usually invited talk and help, but Cesua was scowling and in a foul mood. Emyn handed the pot over and left.

Her own thoughts draped round her like a veil.

Almer's father, Hentios, had died nearly three years before, during the winter that Emyn passed in fevers. His mother never left their house, and his only brother could not think. Emyn often saw Micco at the well with Almer; he was not trusted to lower the bucket into the water himself. He could only push the cart to carry water home.

Still, Almer was a man. Emyn could have children, a family, a home.

Or she could turn him down. She imagined herself in ten or fifteen years, gathering and sorting and crushing the same plants every season, just like Iomat, growing older and wiser, always alone.

Were those her choices? Emyn paused beneath a sycamore tree that shaded the middle space between her brothers' house and Cesua's. "Almer or nothing," she said aloud, but quietly. Put that way, Almer seemed more attractive.

"A crossroads is a dangerous place to tarry," the bard ghost whispered.

She was not ready to go home yet. Iomat cackled off criticisms whenever the chance arose. According to her, Almer drank too much and worked too little. "He needs a woman to feed the half-wits he's saddled with while he goes his own way, just like his father."

So what if he did? Emyn wondered. She was still the Gutumaros. Travelers would continue to visit, ask their questions and bestow their gifts, guaranteeing that her family would never go hungry.

Drunk or sober, Almer made her laugh. And she could raise her own children once she had them, no matter what Almer did.

Maybe Iomat was right. Maybe Almer needed a woman so he could do what he wanted. But Emyn needed a man to get what she wanted: a family. It seemed a fair trade.

If Almer hadn't come up behind Emyn at that very moment, pinning her arms to her sides as he kissed her up and down her neck, his tongue teasing and warm, she might have pursued other thoughts.

But he held her arms down and kissed her neck, and when she sighed he slid his hands up to caress her breasts until she moaned.

"Marry me," he whispered. "Don't keep me waiting."

She wanted him so badly she ached. "Yes."

"We can shut ourselves away before a fire. Just us."

Emyn knew it could never be *just them*. At that moment, though, it was, and she closed her mind to intrusions.

"Yes."

That simply, it was settled.

"EMYN! WHERE HAVE YOU BEEN?"

Emyn jumped at Cesua's voice. The early spring morning had been silent, save for the steady, gentle patter of rain as she approached the well.

Micco jumped too, spilling much of the water. Emyn cooed and calmed her brother-in-law before answering Cesua. "I've been at home, of course. Where else?"

Cesua gave the boy her biggest smile. "Visitors came and went, two days ago."

Emyn shrugged and dipped the bucket into the well again. If visitors wanted to see her, they could have waited or sent a messenger. She lived too far from the well to walk the distance each morning. Jugs and buckets lined the small cart that Micco pushed; they would hold enough water for at least three days.

"Micco, do you want to see Sinia? Do you? Can you push the cart to the headman's house? Come on, then. We'll all go see Sinia." Cesua winked at Emyn. Micco loved Sinia's soft voice and gentle ways; his eyes sparkled as he tried to say her name.

The large house was dark enough that they all stopped just after entering.

"Sinia's grinding flour. I'll take Micco over there," Cesua whispered to Emyn. "Go see Iomat; she has news."

Iomat had moved from the little hut back into Volio's house when Emyn married. Now she rose from her seat at the fire for a hug. Emyn pretended not to notice as the old eyes studied the shape and color of her face. There had been a bruise once; Iomat's gaze never let her forget it.

Iomat dropped some dried leaves into a cup; Emyn filled it with steaming water and followed Iomat to a bench in the corner. The cup smelled of the rose hips and petals they'd collected last summer.

Since she was six years old, Emyn had listened as women poured out their woes before Iomat. They cried and moaned about the men they wouldn't leave, the problems they'd never fix. The same women came back month after month, year after year, for medicines, calming brews, and a sympathetic ear.

Emyn had vowed that she would never fill Iomat's ears with her troubles. Other women did that; not her.

No distaff was tucked into Iomat's belt. "You are not spinning?"

The ghosts began to chant, drowning out Iomat's answer.

"The time for spinning is over."

"No more weaving."

"The looms will burn."

"The ghosts are noisy." Emyn slid a hand under Iomat's. She didn't dare squeeze; Iomat's knuckles were swollen and her fingers slanted at painful angles. "What goes on at Volio's house?"

"The same as ever. His sons get into trouble, they all drink too much. I'm glad winter is done. They can run themselves ragged outside, the men and the children. . . ."

Emyn lowered her head and let the woman's voice wrap

around her. She was a child again, safe in her home, with a fearless and wise woman looking out for her. The gossip, the pettiness of the living and the dead, never changed. With a sudden pang, Emyn missed the rhythms of life here in Volio's home.

"That druid came by for a night. The one who caused such an uproar with his students."

Emyn straightened up. "Bodocnos."

"Yes, that one. He asked after you and wished you all blessings. He seems to think there is unfinished business between you and him."

"A strange man." Emyn reached for the cup and drank.

"He has a new student now, very young. They came north from Bibracte. Do you know where that is?"

"No."

"Bibracte is an Aeduan town. Hundreds live there, the boy said. More now, driven from their homes. Their enemies came at them from the east. Many battles were fought, chiefs and kings died. Your ghosts told you about that, and it's happened."

Emyn nodded; the news of Aeduan losses had been drifting north for months. If that was all Bodocnos had to relate, no wonder he hadn't waited to see her.

Iomat warmed her palms around the cup. "Some tribes treat land like a carcass, to be cut up between warriors, I said that, and the master agreed. 'Good kings are overthrown,' he said."

"Your great heroes are dust!" hissed the dead king.

"Their shining helmets fall," sighed the white ladies together.

Emyn waved at them. "Did you tell Master Bodocnos about Diviciacos? The Aeduan prince that traveled to Rome?"

"I told him. That was at the beginning of the month, wasn't it?"

"Yes." The brother of Dumnocos had set out for Rome to ask its rulers for aid, according to the dead king.

Iomat chuckled as she handed the cup back to Emyn. "I told him your ghosts were not happy with that prince."

"No, they weren't." The ghosts had kept her up all night, scolding as Emyn paced around the fire and spun thread. This winter had taught Almer what it meant to be married to the Death Speaker; he was not pleased. "Did the druid bring other news?"

"His students won their eggs, if that's what you want to hear. The handsome one just last summer."

"The golden-haired man? That must have thrilled Cesua."

"Oh, all the women sigh when I tell them." Iomat nudged her and laughed "But—what is this?"

Emyn choked on a sob that broke out without warning. The tears bubbled from her like a fresh spring from the ground. She covered her face with her hands in embarrassment and sobbed as Iomat patted her shoulder.

"I'm sorry . . . ." Emyn's voice cracked.

Feeling foolish did nothing to stem the flood, and Iomat's arm went around her back, pulling her close. When her tears ran out, Emyn continued to lean against Iomat, catching her breath, afraid to talk or look around.

"Do you know what's wrong?" the woman whispered.

Emyn pulled soggy strands of hair away from her face. Most of her life was wrong. She spent her days with ghosts and idiots. Her husband had to be drunk to touch her; the thought of ghosts watching them rut drove him mad.

Her home. She'd walked into it on an evil day, against good advice. What answer did Iomat wait for?

"Emyn?" Sinia touched her shoulder. "Do you want some food?"

"I think that's a good idea." Iomat wiped Emyn's face with a cloth that smelled of the rosehip brew. When Sinia turned away to get bread, Iomat whispered, "What would you think if a young bride came to you and burst into tears for no reason?"

Emyn stared and Iomat laughed. "Oh, yes, a baby. Crying like that . . . . I'd bet gold on it, if I had any."

IOMAT DELIVERED EMYN'S SON exactly one moon after Samhain, on a quiet and cold morning. The dead responded to Emyn's screams with both scorn and comfort. Almer paced through the darkness inside and out, and his mother slept undisturbed by the fire. Micco hid in the shed with the two cows that were Emyn's dowry.

When it was over, Emyn stared at the tiny red face, drinking it in. Aumios. He'd come early by all their reckoning and was small, but healthy and ready to grow. Iomat picked him up and put him into Almer's arms.

"A philosopher," she announced. "They make wonderful sons. Nothing at home truly bothers them. It's the whole world they fret over."

Fascinated, Almer stared at his son. His own birthday fell in two nights. Someone, maybe even Iomat, had said much the same thing over him twenty-three years ago. Maybe he was meant not to worry; maybe that was why he drank so much. Emyn fell into an exhausted sleep.

NEITHER BABIES NOR OLD folks ventured out of doors over the next few months, and Emyn missed Iomat more than ever. The weather was not enough to confine Almer to a home with ghosts, though.

He tore out of the house before sunrise one morning after

shaking Emyn awake from another dream of the Germani. A foul man had grabbed her, hit her, forced her down; his breath smelled of rot. Emyn slapped at Almer's arms when he woke her.

"Shut up!" Something—maybe a fist—hit the wall and Micco whimpered. Almer's feet stomped as the door opened and shut.

Although he brought water from the well every few days, chopped wood, and kept sporadic watch over his family, Almer stayed away often after that. Questions only invited lies. Emyn held her baby through long, cold nights, telling herself that the house was more peaceful and life much easier with her husband gone.

CESUA ARRIVED IN THE SPRING, full of news. She'd moved into a man's house with her bundled clothes and little else. Her parents had protested—not against the man; Lausos had sheep and cows and worked hard. But they'd wanted a celebration for their wild daughter.

"I told them when Sinia married," Cesua grinned. "No wedding, just a good man for me."

Her new home sat beyond the best fields; two old aunts and an uncle lived with them. Three days ago, the men had taken a cart upriver to barter cloth for supplies. Cesua rode the horse in the opposite direction to see Emyn.

"What are you making?" Cesua pointed to the bundles of green stems with yellow flowers on the floor.

"Medicine," Emyn said. "Can't you smell it?"

"I smell drunk sheep plants. Are you making medicine for sheep now?" When they were children, they'd watched sheep eat the branches until the animals got dizzy and walked into each other.

"The juice is good for fevers," Emyn said.

"Then I won't get any fevers." Cesua poked her nose in the baskets of herbs and other plants that hung from nails, and groaned. "I miss Lausos."

Emyn laughed ruefully; it struck her that Almer's absence had become more comfortable than his presence.

"What's funny?"

"You." She didn't want to tell Cesua the truth. "You, content."

"Me? Look at yourself!"

Emyn shuddered. She was far from content, but where else could she live? No one wanted her ghosts. And who would feed Micco and his mother? They weren't much company, but at least they weren't afraid of her. Micco even liked her humming.

"Emyn!" Cesua waved her arm. "Are you?"

When Emyn didn't answer, Cesua rolled her eyes. "I asked if you're ever bored. You're not, are you? Those voices never let you alone long enough to be bored. The rest of us were always looking for someone—anyone—who would make the night different. I think you needed someone to hold you down and give you peace."

Emyn nodded and hugged Aumios close: a little ball of fire, an ember in a woolen blanket. "A baby does that. You'll see."

"Let me see now." Cesua bent over her. "Please? Go eat something and let me hold him."

Emyn handed Aumios over and moved the cooking pot closer to the fire. The old day was ending; she lit her clay lamp and set it on the table.

Light flickered against the wood. Too much light, she realized. No small lamp could cast such a glow.

Torchlight.

Emyn looked up and into a large room, larger than any in Samarnum. Ornate vessels and plates lined the table before her, and the smell of roasting meat hung on the air. Shields lined the walls; including one she'd seen before: red with an embossed serpent on it.

"A bride," whispered the dead king. The crowd gave way so that Emyn could see her: a girl, perhaps sixteen. She wore a thick blue gown edged in gold thread.

This was a cold celebration, though: no excitement shone in the girl's eyes. She was property. She'd just changed hands.

"Dumnorix gave his own mother in marriage to seal an alliance," the ghost continued. "Now he takes a second wife for himself."

Dumnorix?

"Dumnocos," Emyn breathed, recognizing the man as he turned. His hair cascaded over broad shoulders and fell against the fox fur that trimmed his robe. Gold sparkled on his hands and at his throat. How could his bride not be impressed?

"Emyn!" Cesua called as if from a distance.

"Hold my son! I cannot see—"

"Pay attention!" Emyn jumped at the dead king's command. "Aedui marries Helveti. Both tribes will be strengthened."

The Helvetians lived very far south. She'd heard gossip from visitors last fall: the Helvetians were driven west from their villages and farms, and even from large towns. Germanic tribes, like the ones who'd cross the Rhenus River years ago, invaded. Why would Dumnocos marry into *that* tribe?

If Dumnocos now bore a new, kingly name that probably meant that he'd replaced the many Aeduan leaders who were slain battling the Sequani. Two tribes with great losses might join to form one strong front.

She looked at the sullen bride again. Dumnorix might be a king, but in marriage he seemed no luckier than Emyn herself. Did that matter to a king and a warrior?

"Dumnorix builds his alliances with marriage bonds. His brother courts Rome instead," the dead king announced.

"Diviciacos." Emyn remembered the words she'd spoken years before. "He binds his people to death."

The ghost grunted. "Diviciacos, the pretender . . . he does not fight as warriors do. His weapon is his tongue."

The ghost rumbled on. Who was that near the door, standing beyond the warriors? Emyn took a step forward. Long swords poked from beneath their heavy cloaks. Armed men at a wedding?

"His courage is tied to ambition," the dead king said, but Emyn no longer paid attention. "When such men take power. . . ."

The sword-carriers clustered around a man who distributed coins. Once they had their money, they nodded to each other and left until only one was left, the man with the leather pouch. Emyn watched as he tied the near-empty bag to his belt and adjusted his cloak, nearly covering his thin, bearded face . . . Rialos.

Cesua screamed as a line of fire erupted and raced towards Emyn's head.

 8

Emyn shrieked and raised her hands, then screamed again as icy water splashed over her head and face, drenching her.

Almer stood before her, the sizzled remains of her braid in one hand. His eyes were wide and brilliantly green. "Not burned?"

"No." What was real?

Cesua blotted at Emyn's face with a rag. "I was so scared. Almer, thank Briginda you ran in. Oh, Emyn."

Aumios slept on Cesua's shoulder. A bucket lay on its side next to the table, and the little lamp had fallen over as well. Her braid must have caught fire as Almer entered. A bucket of fresh water always sat by the door.

Emyn tallied these facts as if they were star paths, far away. She would drop her stone necklace—a gift from the Viromanduan druids—into the river as an offering of thanks to Briginda and the gods who preserved her.

Almer put his arms around Emyn and touched the remains of her hair, trying to force a laugh out of his throat. Which of them was shaking more?

"How did this happen? Your hair is gone. It doesn't hurt?"

"The lamp. . . . My braid must have touched it when I turned." She caught Cesua's eye. There was no reason to tell Almer about ghosts and visions.

"Emyn, you are so featherbrained." Almer swallowed hard but kept smiling. "You must pay attention to what you're doing. Please."

"You *should* pay attention," the dead king hissed from behind her. "You are easily distracted."

She shivered in Almer's arms as he wrapped his cloak around her. "Here. Please, for the baby. Be more careful."

In retrospect, it was one of the tenderest moments of their marriage.

WITH THE RETURN OF light and warmth, Emyn could visit Iomat and her brothers again. She warned Almer when she'd be gone so that his mother was not left alone. The woman tended to sleep too close to the fire when she was cold.

Through the summer, the dead king talked more about the Helveti than any other tribe. Always a nasty gossip, the ghost reveled in the worst news, that the Helvetian king schemed beyond what was honorable. He swore oaths with other chieftains, true, but to sway powerful men to his side, he also paid thieves and outlaws. Their tools were threats and assassination, and no one could hold the Helvetian king accountable for their actions . . . or so he thought.

By the hottest days of the year, a message went out with every traveler who passed through Samarnum and with the farmers and weavers who pushed their carts to larger villages to trade: the Gutumaros had news for the wise.

* * *

"NONICOS' WIFE IS MISSING!"

Emyn stared stupidly from the door and Esmios ran closer, out of breath. "She's missing! Ask your ghosts where she is."

Emyn did; they didn't answer. "What happened?"

"She walked toward the river with a basket. Hours ago, toward the fruit trees, but she hasn't come back."

"Maybe she took a nap?"

Emyn knew it was a silly idea and Esmios waved it away. "You know how she's been. Can your ghosts help?"

Months before, Nonicos and his wife had lost their last child, a little girl, to fever. Since then the woman sat at her loom and watched the world through inconsolable eyes. Had she found a way to end her sorrow?

Emyn shook her head. "They're not helping now. Are you all at the river?"

"Most of us. Tulia is at home with the babies."

"I'll go there. If I learn anything, I'll come tell you."

In the fading light of the old day, Emyn led her small family to her brothers' house and sat up most of the night begging the ghosts for help but getting no response. All in the village rose early to continue the search; Emyn stayed behind with the babies.

That day, of all days, a foreign druid appeared in Samarnum, brought by Emyn's message. The man came from the furthest island and carried a strange name, Ferdiath, and an even stranger appearance.

He stood near the well and called for hospitality. Tulia rolled her eyes and Emyn grimaced. The news of a distant king and tribe paled beside the tragedy in their lives. The family's home was out of kilter, as surely as if a wall had collapsed.

Yet there stood the druid; they had no choice but to attend him. Emyn warmed fresh water and spread out cloth to clean his hands and feet while Tulia brought food and drink to the man.

His sleeveless shirt and long pants were striped in shades of green and yellow that Emyn had never seen on wool, and his skin was tinted and patterned as well. Blue dyes swirled up the length of his arms and clustered in patterns over the back of his hands, even running up the side of his smallest fingers.

The white ladies found Ferdiath alluring and sighed as they traced the designs that slid along his muscles. Emyn had never seen a man so decorated; she didn't know where to look. Beside the tattoos on his arms, half the hair on his head was missing—the front part, up to a line that spanned ear to ear. Beyond that, his hair grew thick and brown, tinged with sunshine.

Ferdiath caught her staring and extended his arms, flexing the muscles. "This is proper habit in Eire, really," he said in a heavy accent that struck Emyn as added ornamentation. "I can't even call it a fashion. We have always done this."

Emyn nodded as he talked, distracted but polite. She told him that her sister-in-law was missing, possibly drowned, but he seemed unconcerned and prattled on about the islands and trade routes.

Once he was refreshed, Emyn led Ferdiath outside to the shade of a large sycamore tree and unrolled a mat. It didn't matter who received the ghosts' words or how exotic they looked, she told herself. *Deliver the message.* Then the druid would leave—or at least, go to Volio's house and pester Iomat and whoever happened to be there.

"We bring you men. We could bring more," the dead king said. "You could have many gifts."

Was the ghost offering to set her up as a whore? Emyn hissed, then flushed as she realized Ferdiath heard her. There were women, both east and west along the Samar's banks, who welcomed men in trade for food or coins; Almer found himself a bed there at times.

Almer . . . his house had become hers. Emyn had what she needed for herself and her child, everything but a husband to lie beside her. Maybe she *should* let the ghosts bring her men.

"I know all the ways of divination," Ferdiath was saying. "I follow the stars and trace the birds across the morning sky. I can interpret the throwing of stones and sticks, the turning of wheels, and the messages whispered in dreams."

His lilting voice made everything sound like a poem, but his frank stare unnerved Emyn. "It's not divination," she said. "It's not the future I see."

"The present, then?" He sat cross-legged before her.

Emyn knelt. "Yes, only . . . now it's the past. Ten days past."

"I have met other oracles, though none as lovely as you. You have the face of the goddess we call the Mor Riorgan when she appears as a young girl." His arms moved like snakes with their weird patterns, and he twirled his fingertips into the fringe around her face.

"He would bring us acclaim, this one," the dead king whispered. "He would drape you in gold to stand before kings."

Emyn sat very still, pretending not to notice the brush of Ferdiath's hand against her cheek.

"Your hair—is there a reason you've cut it so short?"

"My braid caught fire."

"He will carry you from here to lands filled with wealth," the dead king urged.

Her family needed her today. She scooted back a hand's breadth.

"Here is what the spirits showed me," Emyn said, and she looked past Ferdiath to the smooth tree trunk behind him. She would watch the unremarkable tree.

"I stood in the courts of the Helvetians. More than a dozen druids gathered. They were young and old, bearded and clean-shaven; one a woman. All were solemn. I saw serpent's eggs of every hue, golden torques and chains. A wall of brilliant clothes and furs curved in an arc around me."

"Do you know why they gathered?"

Emyn shut her eyes; a faint breeze carried the smell of summer fruit. "To judge a king."

Ferdiath was from an island, so the politics of this land might seem strange to him. Emyn tried to explain; she'd learned a lot from this vision.

The king of the Helveti tribe had overreached himself. He grabbed for too much power. One daughter bought him an alliance to the Aeduans through her marriage with Dumnorix; another wed a prince of the Triboci. Sisters, sons, nieces—the king wove a fine net of alliances as he married off his kin.

"Not all with kings, though," Ferdiath interrupted. "With those who wished to rule. Some of his allies planned to overthrow father and lord with his support."

"Yes."

Ferdiath laughed at her surprise. "I have heard of this ambitious king. But there must be more news for you to call a druid here. What has happened?"

"The king forgot. His first duty was to his own people."

"Ah."

"He did not protect them, not on the frontiers where the Germani tribes have raided for years. Not in their towns, where wild armies attack and plunder. Instead, he plotted to lead his people away from these troubles, into lands offered them by his many allies.

"That was how he thought to save his people eventually." The dead king had told Emyn this story so many times that his words came to mind as if he were speaking. "But he kept them waiting while he contracted marriages and alliances. His plan was too distant to satisfy the chiefs and princes of the Helveti."

"The Helveti tribe is large, is it not?"

"Yes. One ghost says, 'How many fish fill the seas?'" Emyn shrugged. "The Helvetians were not content to wait for their king."

"A strong man finds waiting more difficult than damming the sea." Ferdiath uncrossed his legs and stretched them out; one rested against Emyn's.

She ignored the leg. She had words to deliver.

"His people turned on the king and he was brought before their judges in chains. A king in chains." Ferdiath's leg moved, and the fabric between them slid along her thigh.

"That was what I saw, the judges assembled. But the king's own army was strong and camped nearby. Many nobles still loyal to him sat behind the judges at the trial. They rose up before judgment could be given. They rose and drew weapons."

Ferdiath was shocked, as any man would be. "Against druids?"

"No, not against them. They were not that foolish." Emyn looked at his face; a mistake. Ferdiath smiled. Misty forms of women played with his hair. Emyn clamped her eyes shut.

"The nobles held their swords and shields up as barriers. A path was forced through the crowd. The nobles pushed and swarmed around the king until they'd gotten him away."

She breathed heavily. Ferdiath slid his hand over hers, and she pulled away. "No, don't. The ghosts are teasing you. You must remember my words."

"I listen carefully. I could repeat your words exactly if you'd like."

"No." Emyn opened her eyes and stared at the woven mat between them. "Listen, please. The Helvetian king is now dead. I was not shown how or why, but I know he did not kill himself. Why arrange to escape if he meant to do that?"

"Are some saying he killed himself?"

"The ghosts repeat that to me, and say that many princes hid their parts in his death." Her ears followed the sighs and giggles of the ghosts, and she fumbled for words again. "No one . . . no one would want to be blamed for a king's death."

The white ladies stroked Ferdiath's arms and chest and even reached down below the silver-tipped belt that he wore. Could he sense them? His eyes sparkled; clearly, he was aroused. Emyn shut her eyes again.

"The Helvetian chieftains have decided to move with all their people. They harvest their crops and say that over the next month they will burn their homes and fields, even their forts, and march. They swear this with sacred vows to bind them."

"So it will be, then."

"So it will be," Emyn nodded. "My ghosts do not see the future, but they are insistent upon this: From these events comes a terrible danger.

"There is a Roman warrior named Caesar, a very ambitious man. He desires power. Now he sees an excuse to take it. He will conquer tribal lands and add to Rome's wealth."

Ferdiath's voice was soft as fur. "The Romans already have what they took three generations ago. Their province, as they call it."

His hand rested on hers once more.

"That only whets his appetite. That land, far to the south, is Roman now. No one disputes it. He wonders why he should not claim more. Caesar's hunger has no limits. He might destroy us; he might even destroy his own Rome to satisfy it.

"That is why I asked you to come here—you, an Honored Master. Something terrible has begun, the ghosts say. Take these words back to the wise. This man, Caesar, comes with an army to subdue the Helveti. But he won't leave."

"I will remember." Ferdiath's hand moved up her arm, dangerously close to her breast. Emyn had a ridiculous thought, of milk dribbling over his fingers. She had nursed Aumios before leaving her brothers' house, but time had passed since then. "I take your words, do not worry—"

Ferdiath's lips pressed against hers. His mouth was hot and delicious, and for a moment she let herself enjoy it.

The kiss threw Emyn off balance; Ferdiath wrapped an arm around her waist as she fell back. Damp weeds cushioned them. Ferdiath's free hand slid along her arm to her wrist, then into her own waiting hand. Her back arched. How did it look, his tattooed arms against her pale skin? She opened her eyes, seeing the blue swirls through the sweep of his hair.

The white ladies licked at his ears with their smoky tongues.

Emyn shuddered and sat up, pushing Ferdiath away. He was being tricked; maybe they both were. "The ghosts tease you."

"No. I know all you've said. I've drunk in every movement and blush with the words—"

"Honored Ferdiath, I see them. Women—dead women—surround you. They play with you. This is not right."

The druid pushed himself back and muttered. Emyn rose to her knees. The white ladies ceased their twittering and departed.

"Please forgive me, Gutumaros."

Ferdiath stood; Emyn accepted his hand and let him pull her up. He did not let go as he steadied her.

Her face grew hot. With a smile or her smallest gesture, he would lead her from this half-deserted cluster of houses. Emyn's mind divided and argued with itself.

Could she be delighted while most of the villagers searched for a waterlogged corpse? Yet how did that matter? The woman died or ran off yesterday. Emyn lived with the dead . . . but she lived. If pleasures were thrown onto her path, why should she ignore them?

She looked down and studied the blue lines that webbed the edge of Ferdiath's hand. All she had to do was squeeze it gently. She didn't.

"Again, I ask forgiveness. You are a married woman," Ferdiath said finally. "We respect that on my island, as here."

"It was the ghosts. I understand."

He smiled. "I will pass on your warning as you ask, but it was not entirely the ghosts. You are beautiful, Gutumaros."

Emyn stood in the shade as he left, confused and full of dread. His flattery meant nothing. She forgot the missing woman as well.

Instead, she pictured the blue lines along Ferdiath's little finger.

She could still see them in her mind, and the hump that the blue web disguised. A growth, perhaps no more. Maybe a second fingertip, maybe something else.

Five years had passed since she'd met with Bodocnos and his students in the sacred grove, yet her stomach still clenched with the horror of that vision.

She hadn't seen the man who held the knife; only that second fingertip. Was Ferdiath that man and if he was, what did this mean? The year of sacrifice was over. For once, no ghostly voice whispered to her, either to advise or taunt.

"Fairy aunt!" Esmios' son wrapped his arms around her legs

and looked up, laughing at the sunlit fringe of her hair. "Fairy aunt!"

She smiled and scooped the boy up. "Is Aumios still sleeping?"

"Babies sleep. Play with me?"

Emyn set him down and raced him to her brothers' house where Aumios lay nestled next to Tulia's new baby. She tied thread to a pine cone so the child could pull it after him like a dog, then she and Tulia chased him around the house. When he finally grew tired and slept, the women waited.

The searchers returned after dusk. They'd found no body, but a family downriver, badly shaken, had seen a woman's bloated corpse flow by as they threw offerings from a short dock.

9

esua visited Emyn's home again just as Aumios was learning to walk. The weather was clear and bright; it seemed that the sun had snuck away from the land of promise and wedged its way into the middle of winter. Two full moons had passed since Samhain, so fair days were too precious to waste. Emyn propped her door open and left her silent mother-in-law to enjoy the breeze while everyone else went for a walk.

Emyn carried a basket of bread, hoping she would find something to gather after the bread was eaten. Micco followed them, mouthing sounds that might be "Almer" or "Aumios" or even "Emyn."

Aumios tottered ahead, picking up rocks to taste, laughing when Emyn pried them out of his hand. The women giggled and talked as they followed the river east from Emyn's home; they did not think about what might hide in the trees.

Should they have?

Had she missed a warning, a noise that would have alerted her?

Something shuffled through the leaves on the ground.

Aumios lurched into a shadow on his unsteady legs, and his head twisted in a way that made no sense to Emyn.

Her heart stopped. She thought of snakes, wolves, boars, monsters, all in a flash. She didn't see arms or a man looming over her; only Aumios' little body falling onto the ground. He didn't curl or squat, he didn't make any of his usual movements, didn't tuck his arms in or call her name. He just . . . fell.

Cesua screamed, "Run!" Emyn couldn't move.

It was the ghosts, throwing her into visions of things that couldn't be. Aumios couldn't be lying on the ground. He was her life, her joy; he could not lie like that, not so still.

Emyn was pushed and grabbed. Something tugged her short clumps of hair and snorted in disgust. She heard her clothes rip and lost sight of Aumios; the ground hit her. She tried to move away, but hands gripped her arms and wrenched hard. She wanted this creature out of her way so she could get to her son.

The truth reached her slowly. She couldn't get to Aumios. Aumios was dead, and his killer pinned her to the dank, gritty earth. The bruising pain between her legs was him, shoving into her with drunken fury. Ugly sounds and the stench of garbage came from him. Cesua sobbed. Emyn snapped to attention as it all sunk in. Her child was dead and his murderer was raping her.

She shrieked and struck, wriggling an arm up to claw at his face while she kicked and tried to push. It did no good. The man was large and on top. He yelped at her scratching and struck her face. Her hand was forced back easily and twisted. All the while the man kept up his horrid rhythm, every thrust an outrage. Emyn screamed.

He hit her again, slurred something like a curse, then grinned and dropped his bearded face to her breast. She felt his teeth tear into her and fainted.

* * *

SECONDS PASSED, NO MORE. He was still ramming, unaware that she'd become conscious. So much noise, huffing and sweating, kept his dull mind from noticing anything but his own urgency. Emyn watched through slitted eyelids.

A short sword was strapped to his waist; its sheath poked her leg repeatedly. Next to it, she saw a shorter blade tucked loosely into his belt. A sensible man would have removed the belt and weapons, but pigs had more sense than this brute.

Emyn flicked her left hand at his face to distract him. Slow to respond, he blinked at the fingers near his eyes. He never saw her other hand and probably never felt the knife slide away from his waist.

She stabbed him in the neck, her arm as strong and sure as if she'd trained for this act. For an instant, he seemed not to notice. She jerked the knife away, and blood vomited out of the wound. He dropped like a dead tree onto Emyn, almost suffocating her.

She spat out blood, gasped for air, and turned her face away. Moments passed without connecting to each other.

Had Aumios fallen, had she really seen that? She lay beneath a corpse. The beast was dead: good. Loathsome as his bulk was, she didn't try to move him at first. Why should she? She could stab him ten times more, but he wouldn't be any more dead. What else was there to be done?

She did not want to breathe in his stench or die beneath him.

She pushed then cried out in pain as he fell back onto her. Maybe she should use the knife to cut him into smaller pieces and remove him bit by bit—

Cesua screamed.

Emyn struggled harder against the weight. How many men were there? She could kill more. She could kill a hundred more! Her legs squirmed under the corpse, and she worked them free, pushing and kicking. The foul weight shifted and settled on the ground. Her hand still gripped the knife. She snatched the short sword from his belt, rolled away, and stood.

Blood dripped from the burning wound in her breast. She tasted more in her mouth as she crawled towards Cesua's sobs, a blade in each hand. She wouldn't let herself look towards Aumios. Cesua hadn't lost her son; Cesua didn't want to die. Emyn had to help her.

The second monster sprawled over Cesua. Emyn didn't trust her legs and didn't want to cast a shadow. But how could she kill him if she didn't stand?

She set the knife down and grabbed hold of a tree trunk to pull herself up. Only a few steps . . . when she was close enough, she braced the sword hilt against her belly and threw herself at the man's back, driving the point in below his ribs, pushing it toward his heart.

He screeched like an animal and reared. His elbow hit Emyn's jaw, knocking her away. She raised herself on hands and knees in time to see him turning towards her, the sword still buried in his flesh. Why didn't he fall?

The man grabbed an axe from the ground and ran at Emyn. She cried out to Cesua; she wanted to tell her to run and hide. Something came out of her mouth, then she fell into darkness.

THE WORLD BEGAN WITH RIVERS, filling the land as blood fills the body.

With the rivers came the gods, the great ancestors: Danus, the first mother, then others who displayed the skills of living well and wisely to those who followed.

That was the tale told in deep winter when the longest night began. Dimly, Emyn began to wonder if she dreamed. Who spoke?

We are Viromandui, the People of the White Horse.

Her eyes would not open. A fire roared and crackled, and Iomat whispered soothing words to her. But it was not Iomat who recited the tale.

Emyn had been dreaming for a long time. Now her body tried to wake, and pain burned like fire.

She heard conversation: Nonicos' soft tones and Esmios' sharper ones, Tulia, the headman, Iomat . . . and at least one stranger. The unknown voice sang quietly, just for her. She knew the song; Iomat taught it to her years ago. "Come, sweet mother and son. Come Dirona with your balm, come Borvo. . . ."

An unexpected voice: Bodocnos. Emyn picked his words out of the stew of noise that bubbled beyond the healing song. The sound of the druid talking made no sense, but Emyn listened. She had nothing else to do. She couldn't move . . . at least, she didn't think she could move. She didn't feel like trying.

"For months, they've been ravaging in fields, cutting through forests, taking what they find . . . that they came so far north is surprising, but not unbelievable."

"I'm not convinced they were Germani," said Iomat.

"What else? Iomat, you can't think—"

That was Esmios. He sounded angry and Tulia shushed him.

"Does it matter?" Bodocnos whispered.

Emyn slept again.

WHEN SHE WOKE NEXT, her eyes opened easily, though light and darkness dizzied her as she looked around. She lay beside her father's hearth in the same place she'd slept as a child. Did she live here now? Had she ever left?

Emyn saw another familiar sight: the dead king perched on a table like a spider web spun of smoke and dust.

Perhaps she was dead and part of his world now. The others might see nothing more than a shadow where Emyn lay. She heard Bodocnos again, reciting a poem.

Germani raiders. She remembered his voice; he said they cut through forests. They were the ones she had seen in nightmares: men who took what they wanted and gave nothing back to the gods. She'd seen them run by houses, throw torches on the thatch, grab young girls and rip their clothes away while they screamed.

Cesua had screamed, but Emyn knew no one would hear them. A boy's voice repeated the poem after Bodocnos.

Why had Cesua screamed? The Germani—the horrible men! Emyn tried to think, but there was a crack in her mind and everything spilled through it like a broken jug that dripped all over. A bad dream, the worst possible nightmare, that's what it was. She slept in her father's house with the druid Bodocnos reciting poetry over her. Maybe she'd dreamed her entire life.

A shadow fell across her face as the song began again: "Come, sweet mother and son . . . ."

A monster had been on top of her when Cesua screamed. Had he killed her? Was that what happened? He had killed Aumios. If Emyn were dead too, her baby should be near. She tried to say his name. It came out like a groan with no beginning and no end.

This was foolish, Emyn decided. If they were both dead, she shouldn't be so helpless. There was no sickness in the land of promise. And if they weren't dead, Aumios was probably making Iomat crazy now that he could walk. How could the poor woman keep up with him?

Emyn shifted her arms and tried to roll over.

Iomat said, "Hold her," very sharply, as if she had been standing by, waiting for Emyn to move.

Her entire side exploded with pain, as if a hot knife ripped into her hip and jabbed its way around. Strong arms held her down. She was the one who was screaming, not Cesua. The man had swung his axe at her. As he fell his last, dying act had been to smash her bones.

Cesua held her, Emyn remembered. She'd used their torn clothes and river water to mop blood from the bite, and she cradled Emyn's head. Aumios' little body was near but Cesua chanted, "Don't look, don't look, don't."

"Don't fight, dear, don't—" Iomat said as a warm liquid coursed down Emyn's throat. She began to pant like a dog and felt herself separating from her body again, leaving all pain behind.

DURING THOSE FIRST FEW nights at her brothers' house, Emyn never remembered from one hour to the next that Aumios was gone. Someone always had to tell her, and if she had not been immobilized by pain and drugs she would have cut out the tongue from every mouth. Soon enough, though, she woke aware of the loss. It sat like a rock on her chest.

Other isolated truths appeared and reappeared.

Her face was bruised and swollen beyond recognition. Esmios turned from her to ask Iomat more than once, "When is *that* going to go down?" Tulia's youngest sister broke into hysterical tears when she visited. Emyn guessed that she must look as grotesque as the *nains*, whose glowing eyes peeked out of black, distorted flesh.

Bones were broken. She heard the stranger speculate aloud if she would walk again, ever. The back of the axe had struck her hip. Any bone would break under an iron and wood haft brought down with such force. Emyn wondered if her jaw or head were cracked as well.

She was brave. Her brothers told her so and no one doubted it. Emyn had killed two drunken brutes twice her size. All were amazed at her strength. She was never completely sure later how much of the story came from her own memory and how much was filled in by what others told her.

She remembered killing the first man. She knew where to stab in the neck; the dead king had shown her years ago in the sacred grove. Other scenes were dim or missing from her mind, but everyone else seemed very certain of what happened.

The ghosts had not warned or saved her. Had they even watched as she fought for her life? Emyn could not remember any ghosts present, only Cesua.

Cesua had not left her. Even though other marauders might lurk nearby, and days could pass before anyone came to look for them, Cesua stayed. One memory was clear: Cesua kicking and spitting at the ugly corpse on her way to the river for more water.

Emyn wished Cesua were there so she could hold onto her hand, and one afternoon she was. Emyn squeezed until Cesua laughed and begged her to loosen her grip. Her face and neck were bruised, but she was healing. "Are you home?" Emyn managed to say.

"I've come to visit. We're staying at my father's house."

Emyn murmured Lausos' name and Cesua understood. She put her face close to Emyn's ear. "Lausos is a good man. Almer is not. Don't go back to his house. As soon as you are on your feet, walk away from him."

Emyn tried to smile, but her mouth felt lopsided. Almer had

not come to see her; she assumed she lay at her brother's house because he didn't want her in theirs.

"No one will drink with him," Cesua added. Given how little effort it took to find a drinking partner in Samarnum, those were damning words.

Emyn saw Micco churning butter one dark evening and tried to say his name.

Nonicos sat down next to Emyn. "He led us to you, you know."

She'd forgotten; Micco was there. He probably fled when Cesua first cried out.

"Ran all the way here and fell on his knees in front of Sinia, wailing and keening."

"Like the Morrigu chased him." Esmios joined in. "Never heard such a racket."

"We knew something scared him—"

Micco turned away when Emyn said his name again. He would not look at her misshapen face, but he would not leave her either.

One other thing Emyn knew: it was Nonicos who carried Aumios' body to the sacred place to be reclaimed by the earth, not Almer. Nonicos promised to dig a tiny grave for the bones in spring near that of his own children. Would Nonicos ever be done with grieving?

How did he bear such sadness? How could she?

"The boy has taken to calling you Chiomara."

"Boy?"

"Moradag. Emyn, you insult him. You have known him for days." Bodocnos sighed at Emyn's blank look. "My student, Moradag. How do you think he feels, so easily forgotten by a Nervian warrior like yourself?"

She could see a boy, twelve or thirteen years old, standing behind Bodocnos. He grinned, and he did look familiar. She said his name.

"That's better."

"Who is . . . Chio . . . a?"

"Oh, I know you've heard the story. Tell her, Moradag."

The boy stepped toward Emyn, spreading his arms. He grew larger with his words until he filled the room.

"Chiomara was a queen of fierce beauty, who lived three generations ago and more with her husband, a strong and wise king. When Rome invaded their land—Galacia, on the other side of Greece—they rallied and united the Celtic tribes of the far east to fight. Chiomara was captured by the Romans and fell into the hands of a centurion—that's a high-ranking warrior. He tried seducing her, but she wouldn't have him. So he took her by force. Only after that did he learn her husband was a king.

"The audacious soldier sent word to Chiomara's husband, demanding a high price to ransom her back. The money was gathered and all parties met on a riverbank. Chiomara was released. When the centurion bent down to pick up his gold, Chiomara grabbed a sword and with her own arms, chopped off his head."

Moradag, caught up in his story, swung an invisible sword down with both hands, then lifted the centurion's head and spat on it.

"She covered the head in a cloth and walked up to her husband. There, she pulled the cloth away and threw the head at his feet. The king, shamed that she'd killed a man once a contract had been made, said to her, 'Woman, a fine thing is good faith!'

"And she met his eyes and said, 'A better thing, that only one man live who's lain with me!'"

Moradag ended with a flourish, and Iomat, Tulia, and Bodocnos applauded along with a strange man Emyn had never seen before.

"You must admit," Bodocnos whispered, bending close to Emyn, "That my students are truly exceptional."

"Yes." She wanted to say more, but felt as if her mouth were full of rocks.

"Worthy Chiomara." The boy took her hand and kissed it. "My first true poem will be of your strength and courage."

"Then . . . a new ending," Emyn mumbled, wondering if he could understand her words. "My husband . . . won't ransom me . . . but . . . I got two heads." She held up two fingers for emphasis.

Moradag winked at her. "Turn your back then, lady, and find yourself a better man."

WARM WATER BATHED HER FACE; the touch was gentle.

"Bibracte," a young voice breathed, very close. Moradag again. And Bibracte was an Aeduan city, far away. "How odd, isn't it, that I went all that way to find my teacher—and then learned he was a man of my own tribe?"

Emyn drifted in and out of lucid thought. Her life had been overthrown; she knew better than to dwell on that. Bodocnos' student must be Bellovaci like the master. And they were here because . . . she tried to pull together the bits of conversation she'd heard.

Bodocnos had been near, wintering in Virmandum with his student. News of the attack on the oracle traveled quickly, and they realized a healer might be needed in Samarnum. Bodocnos disparaged his own skills in that area, so he had urged another druid to come with him . . . Omullos? Emyn tried to say the name.

"You are awake, Chiomara." Hands lifted her head slightly as a new bandage wrapped around it. She kept her eyes closed. "Omullos returned home yesterday. Do not worry; Iomat watches me carefully. You are healing quickly. You did not need Omullos' hands and eyes any longer."

"Now this one," Iomat said, pulling back the fur that covered Emyn.

Emyn felt the bandage on her breast pulled away. Moradag murmured an apology for stinging her, and soothing water washed off the pain.

"Borvo guides and inspires you, Moradag," Bodocnos said.

His voice came from near the hearth. "Between Omullos and Iomat, you learn a great deal, and I see your path more clearly."

Emyn tried to nod but her head felt heavy. She slept again.

IN THE DARKNESS, men shouted. Each time the door opened, wind rushed in and the fire leapt high, but someone held her hand through all of it.

The voices of her brothers came and went. Once Moradag, all out of breath, gasped, "There's nothing left."

Cesua whispered, "Have you told her?"

The gray morning crept in through cracks and a half-open door. Iomat brought Emyn cereal in one bowl and a brew smelling of bark in another. Emyn waited while Moradag piled furs and blankets at her back, raising her so that she could eat. She saw bloodshot eyes and weary, grim mouths on the others. "What happened?"

"Almer is gone," Iomat said.

"Gone?" Emyn mouthed. "Where?"

Iomat didn't answer. Emyn raised her eyes to Moradag. "I heard shouting."

"We saw a fire, far off," the student said. "The shouting was us, calling for help."

"Almer burned the house down," Iomat sighed. "I don't think he meant to. I think he was drinking and fell asleep."

A fair guess, Emyn thought. She could count on one hand the nights he'd been sober over the last few months. He'd lost his son, too: another reason to stay drunk.

She was surprised but not really sorry. What was the house to her? She never wanted to go back to it. She managed to ask, "Where did he go?"

Iomat exchanged a look with Moradag. "Almer didn't get out of the house, Emyn. Neither did his mother. You're a widow."

"Oh." Emyn couldn't think of anything to say. Almer was dead, burned up. Her baby was gone. Wife and mother no longer described her; those roles had been wiped away.

The baby began to cry and Emyn flinched. It wasn't hers; it was Tulia's daughter. More than anything in the world, Emyn wished she could pick the infant up and hold her. How was Tulia managing such a full household?

"It's a bad ending and no one's fault." Iomat picked up the bowl. "Drink this."

"No," Emyn put her hand over Iomat's. Her brews were heavy with potions to deaden pain. Emyn was suddenly tired of lying down half alive, half grieving, half aware. Had the last two years even happened?

DAYS PASSED. Emyn's pain was real and sharpened her mind. Only at sunset did she ask Iomat for the numbing drinks that would help her sleep. She dreamt of Aumios then; he lay in her arms and pressed kisses against her cheek.

Without the anodyne, Emyn could follow conversations and speak clearly. Moradag spent much of each day listening to his teacher and reciting long poems. Emyn listened to a strange teaching rhyme she'd never heard before in which the wise praised their favorite trees. Double meanings hung on each line, she was sure, but they were beyond her understanding.

Lulled by the warm room and soft voices, Emyn's eyes wanted to drift closed, but she fought the urge. She would not doze today; she felt the time had come to sleep through the night without help.

Her eye tracked a motion: holly branches, hung on the door

to celebrate midwinter. They shook as if someone were knocking hard outside, but there was no sound. Suddenly they stilled.

"He leaves out a line," the bard ghost whispered.

Words from the ghosts were rare in this house; Emyn suspected that Bodocnos kept them away. The druid was fully occupied with his student at the moment, though, as they chanted about the powers of different trees: the oak, the holly, the birch.

"Tell him," the ghost urged.

"Master, the bard ghost says there is another tree in your poem."

"Bard ghost?" Bodocnos looked over. "His claim is unlikely. That would make eight. If they tease—"

"There is yet another tree at the end of the verse. That makes nine: three threes, a sacred number." Emyn talked fast; the ghost tossed many words at her. "He says that describes the nine heroes as well, each with their own tree."

The druid jumped and hurried to Emyn's side. His face was pale, almost yellow in the firelight. "Tell me every word."

The rhymes were built of poetic images and made no sense to Emyn, but she repeated the entire poem as Bodocnos fingered a knotted cord that hung from his belt. She'd seen such a cord in Moradag's hand as he studied. Did the knots help him remember words?

"What is his name?" Bodocnos asked when Emyn fell silent.

"The ghost?"

"Yes. He must have a name."

"Must I?" the spirit, now a strong white glow near the fire, laughed. "No, I think not."

"He is amused," Emyn said. "He gives no name."

"Do any of them have names, Chiomara?" asked Moradag.

"They've never given me any."

"We have none to give," said the bard ghost.

"I suppose," Bodocnos said when she repeated the words, "That is what they relinquish to live on in shadows."

THE STABS AND ACHES of mending bones distracted Emyn from her loss, but tears remained near. Esmios' little son wanted to play, but all Emyn could do was talk to him while he sat on the floor. Even the baby could not lean against her.

Nothing useful could be done while lying on her back, so Emyn was glad on the day that her brothers lifted her to her feet. Under Iomat's watchful eye she moved her legs carefully, one arm on each of their shoulders. She slept that night without the help of Iomat's potion, utterly exhausted.

Bodocnos announced that he would return to Virmandum with Moradag.

"Master, it is so cold. Please stay."

"You don't need me."

Emyn sighed. "Would I send you into the snow because I'm better? Samarnum is generous. Headman Volio offers you his hearth; I heard him."

"And such generosity is appreciated. We'll stay at his house tonight, in fact. He promised a farewell feast." Bodocnos motioned to Moradag, who sat across the room. "A druid knows when it is time to leave. We spend our lives learning that. I have a student, and Omullos waits to instruct him in Virmandum.

"Moradag, make your goodbyes. We'll leave early in the morning."

The youth took her hand; even a simple farewell sounded like poetry from him. "My master promises that we'll see you again, and I will hold him to that. You will dance with me one day, Chiomara."

"Off, then, to the headman's." Bodocnos sat on the stool by Emyn's bed as soon as Moradag vacated it.

Her mattress rested on a wooden frame strung with ropes. Sturdy benches supported the frame so that Iomat could reach her without bending over, and now the druid's eyes were level with Emyn's. "Now. Some things we must discuss. Gutumaros, your ghosts have not pestered you much of late, have they?"

"No, Master." Even the dead king had been silent, and Emyn did not believe for a moment that kindness or sympathy quieted him.

"You may find them a bit noisier once I leave."

She took the druid's hand and touched it to her forehead. "Master, thank you for all you've done. You have given me peace greater than any drug."

"Peace?" Bodocnos frowned. "I do not give peace. Choose your words more carefully."

"Rest?"

"Rest is better. That was my intent."

"Master." Emyn still held his hand; she wished she could reach the serpent's egg. "Is there any way I could learn to keep the ghosts quiet?"

"Such skills take years to command." Bodocnos pulled his hand away gently. "Even some of the wise are unable to banish spirits. Coath—I'm sure you remember him—lacked the concentration. He was too easily . . . distracted."

Emyn smiled; it was pretty girls that distracted Coath. But if concentration was required, she would never manage it either.

"Emyn, have you thought about what you want to do when you're able to get up and move around?"

"No." Emyn shifted her gaze to the fire. There was nothing she wanted to do, nothing at all. No doubt there were things required of her; ghosts and dreams would reveal those.

* * *

"YOU MUST THINK ABOUT IT. Here is a question to start. Where will you live?"

Her eyes swept the room. This was her brothers' house. Tulia was a good wife, but sharing her home with ghosts was too much to ask. "Maybe . . . when I can walk, the small house that Iomat and I once shared . . . ."

Bodocnos nodded. "Volio would gladly offer it again if you decide to stay. You can leave Samarnum, though. Have you thought of that? As an oracle, and even as a midwife or healer, you would be welcomed in more places than you could count. Virmandum, Bibracte, Bibrax?"

"Leave?" The idea shocked her. Her family lived here and nowhere else. Her ancestors were here. She was part of Samarnum; what gods would she know in a strange place?

"Nonicos is a decent carpenter; he could find work anywhere."

Emyn gaped at Bodocnos. "Nonicos?"

"He hasn't told you that he thinks of leaving at times, has he?"

"No." Had she been blind, lying here without seeing? Nonicos must ache as badly as Emyn. Every corner of Samarnum held a memory of what was lost; she knew that now. Did Nonicos expect to see his wife and children every time he walked into this house?

"Talk to him, Emyn. Pray, and consider the possibilities. Walking away could be the wisest course. In Samarnum, you may find that you've lost more than you've kept."

Possibilities? Emyn's mind lurched ahead. Broken bones healed. Leave Samarnum . . . how much of her sorrow could she abandon, or would it follow her?

"Moradag and I will stay in Virmandum until spring, then we'll journey south. At Midsummer in the center of the land, the wise gather to exchange news and form alliances. Did you know that?"

"No."

"They do. I invite you and Nonicos to travel there with us. Druids arrive from every part of this land and many tribes will be represented. You may find a new home with those who can promise protection, and who will honor you." Bodocnos rose. "Think on it. Come to Virmandum by the end of Cutios if you wish to go with us."

Emyn reached her hand to him once more. "What of the ghosts? Are they tied to this place?"

"A good question." Bodocnos closed his eyes. "One of them is very strong and bound to you, rather than this place. I think the rest may drop away once you leave . . . but you will never be free of spirits, Emyn. You will find new ones wherever you go. Does that disappoint you?"

She tried to shrug. "It is the way I am."

"It is. And you are still alive and quite sane." The curls of Bodocnos' beard shifted as his mouth widened into a smile. "You have a fierce spirit, Gutumaros. More than a match for anyone, living or dead."

BOOK TWO

Crossroads

 **11**

The sun had not set on their first day of travel when Nonicos stopped the mule and walked back to where Emyn sat on a pile of furs in the cart. He looked past her to the side of the road and spoke softly. "Micco has followed us. He may run away if I chase after him."

Emyn groaned as Nonicos continued. "We are half a league from a meal and a warm hearth. I know he'll come to us for food."

"And . . ." Emyn's voice faded. They had put several leagues between them and home. If they returned, she would never find the strength to leave again.

"I can't think of anything but to keep him with us." Nonicos shrugged. "We should have expected it."

Not all ties to the past could be severed.

Traveling was difficult those first days. Emyn could not walk on mud or rain-slicked grass; she huddled in the cart while Nonicos guided the mule. Once they reached the planked road that led to Virmandum she forced herself to walk a little each day, even though it slowed their pace. Micco scampered off the road, gathering grasses for the mule.

The landscape changed. Beyond the quiet, constant sound of drizzle, Emyn heard strange whispers. The dead king did not leave her, though, and day after day he harangued her with news.

On her first night in Virmandum, she poured out his words to Bodocnos. They shared the fire with several students in Omullos' comfortable home. Bodocnos swore the boys to secrecy, forbidding them to repeat spirit words throughout the town like gossip.

"A NERVIAN DEATH SPEAKER? This should be amusing."

Emyn hammered her walking stick onto the wood floor and pushed herself up from the bench. Bodocnos blocked her as the stranger disappeared beyond the cookfire.

They both spoke at once. "He talks as if I were a hired dancer."

"He is a sycophant and not worth your time."

While Emyn glowered, Bodocnos added, "Any fool can see that you're not a dancer. You wear no bracelets."

Emyn's anger flared quickly these days, but a joke washed it away just as fast. She lowered herself back to the bench and grinned. "If bracelets would make me dance, let me wear your serpent's egg for an hour so that I may be wise."

Bodocnos shouted for ale. When it arrived he handed the cup to Emyn.

"Have this instead," the druid said. "You won't be the first to feel wiser after a bit of ale."

Emyn tasted the ale and watched the wide room. Shields lined the farthest wall, their metal bosses glinting with firelight. Emyn had seen houses like this in visions, but found it hard to believe she sat in one—in a king's house, sipping a king's ale. Omullos had brought them here, and now conferred with the Viromanduan king and his druids. He would summon Emyn forward when the king wished to receive her counsel.

A crowd of men sat around a smaller fire near the shields. They tore into roasted pork as they laughed and called out to each other. Emyn judged that two houses the size of Volio's would fit in the space between her and them.

Her stomach rumbled. Was the druid as hungry as she was?

"Do I keep you from your usual seat in that company, Master?"

"There? With idle warriors and courtiers?" Bodocnos snorted. "I avoid such creatures, and so does Omullos. You keep us from our usual seat at a humbler hearth where our students relax now. Once you deliver your news, we—Ha!" He whirled and caught a girl by the elbow, pulling two loaves of bread from the basket she carried. "May the Morrigu take note of how your king treats a guest!"

Emyn set down the cup and accepted the bread. The loaf warmed and satisfied her inside, though it was nothing like the bread baked in Samarnum. It seemed she'd eaten one bread her entire life, and now in the course of a month, she'd tasted whole handfuls of new flavors.

The small things changed daily, but not the large. The same stars watched over her. She was still Emyn; still grieved. Waking or asleep, she heard ghosts and delivered their words.

Before leaving Samarnum, Emyn had dreamed of towns on fire. Somewhere, she knew, real towns burned. Somewhere, people loaded their beds and looms and harvests onto wagons, preparing to leave. In dreams, she saw women sob as roiling, black balls of smoke rose in a moonlit sky to hide the stars.

One day as Emyn napped, she saw these strangers through a dirty haze. The wheels of their wagons cut tracks through the ashes that layered their frosted fields.

The stars said that now was the time to walk away from unfulfilled hopes and build on new plans. The Helvetians had done that. So had she.

"Gutumaros."

Emyn jumped, and Omullos patted her shoulder. "The king invites you to speak."

She rose and dusted crumbs from her dress. The two druids flanked her as they walked to the end of the hall where the warriors and nobles sat. Bodocnos held her stick as she sat on a cushioned stool, then they both stepped away.

Alone, Emyn faced a grove of richly clothed men. Which was her king? Was he even present?

The dead king should know. Emyn grunted, "Who?"

The hazy ghost circled a florid man of commanding height. The enameled pin that held his cloak bore a graceful white horse. His eyes were unfocused and weary. Drunk?

"Sir? Shall I speak?"

The dead king nodded; the living one seemed not to have heard.

"Sir, so that I do not fill your ears with what you already know, I ask if you have heard of the migration of a great tribe, the Helveti."

"We have heard much," a gray-haired druid to the king's left answered. "We know of the overthrow of their king and their vow to seek new lands."

Emyn nodded. "My spirits have shown me that as the snow began to melt, the clans of that tribe destroyed their towns and farms. They slaughtered animals to poison their wells, threw torches onto their homes, and have left nothing behind for their enemies."

"We know of that as well," the druid said. "Only this morning, a runner told us that the Helvetians have traveled south to Genava, and gather on the bank of the Rhodanus River."

"Honored Master, they do. They wish to cross the river, and there was a bridge at Genava."

Emyn took a deep breath. Genava did not belong to the Helvetians, but sat in the territory of a yet another tribe, a tribe allied with Rome. But Bodocnos had warned Emyn against appearing to instruct the king.

"Thousands of tents rose in meadows and fields where the Helvetians camped," she said. "Genava feared invasion and asked for help from their allies. A Roman legion raced there. They tore down the bridge."

"Why would they do that?" the druid asked.

"They claim they are defending their province to the south," Emyn answered.

"They provoke war!" the dead king hissed.

Emyn waved at the ghost. "The Helvetians are now forced to ask permission of Rome to cross the territory."

"What arrogance!" said a man who wore a warrior's torque. "The Romans tell an ancient tribe where they may walk?"

"Yes—"

"Arrogance, if it is true," said another man, the one Bodocnos had called a sycophant. He chuckled. "Personally, I—"

Emyn ignored him and turned back to the oldest druid. King or not, he seemed to command the most respect. "My spirits listen at the councils of the Roman general, Caesar. The Helvetians came to him, asking to cross the land and he promised to consider their request. He told their emissaries to return when the moon is new. He knows that more Roman troops will arrive by then.

"Caesar will refuse their request," Emyn asserted. "He has told his trusted warriors this."

"So the Helveti tribe will be turned aside," the older druid said impassively. "I know the land there, and the mountains. The Helvetians can go west into Sequani territory or they can fight the Romans for passage south. Either way, why should we concern ourselves with a distant squabble?"

"Honored Master, the Helvetians may fight—"

"Your spirits predict this?"

"No," Emyn flushed. "The spirits reason from clear signs, just as the wise read the stars. They have judged both forces, and say the Helvetians will fight and be beaten. Rome will send as many armies as it needs; they breed soldiers as we breed sheep."

"What is that to us?" a younger druid asked. "If the Helvetians have put themselves in a subordinate position, that is their folly."

"We do not fret over Rome!" a warrior bellowed, and others laughed. "We looted their fine city. They should fret over us!"

Men cheered and banged cups against the table.

"You are not the people you once were!" The dead king's voice was the only one Emyn could distinguish in the din. "Try to defeat Rome now. You will be destroyed!"

"We looted their city a long time ago," Emyn said, raising her voice. She did not dare repeat the ghost's insult, but she could not hold back his warning. "Rome is stronger than it was. Led by this general, Rome takes its first steps against us."

"Us?" the younger druid smiled. "We are not the Helveti, Gutumaros."

"Do your spirits suggest that Roman armies will march across rivers and mountains to come to Virmandum?" the gray-haired master asked. Men close enough to hear laughed in derision and hit their cups against anything that would ring with noise.

"I am only the voice of the dead, Honored Master." Emyn

bowed her head before the druid. "I do not interpret what they say or add my poor words to theirs. The dead watch Caesar and worry. They say that we should prepare to meet him."

12

Moradag flopped loudly onto his backside for the third time, then lay in the dirt and laughed until a bulky man extended a hand to help him up. The pair began to wrestle again.

Emyn took a deep breath, ready to protest. Nonicos placed his hand on her shoulder. "Don't," he whispered. "You will embarrass him."

She resettled herself on the bench.

"He's getting better," Nonicos offered. He wrestled with Moradag often but he was not as rough as this man. Micco crouched close to Emyn, covering his eyes.

"Micco, let's go see Mule," she said, gripping her stick and leaning on her brother to stand. "Let's see if Mule needs food."

"Mule is getting fat," Nonicos muttered. "Micco, brush Mule. No food. Just brush him."

Emyn held the boy's hand as they skirted the dirt ring cleared of rock and debris. Moradag was thrown once again, and Micco fled to Emyn's other side to hide behind her.

In the stable, she handed Micco the brush and reminded him, as she always did, to stay away from Mule's backside. No animal ever received such loving attention; Micco would brush until Nonicos brought him inside to sleep. Emyn pulled a shawl out of their cart and tied it around her shoulders before limping away.

She had not expected traveling to be so easy; they might all get fat soon. Now that they journeyed through Bellovaci territory, a relative of Bodocnos or his student seemed to live around every bend in the road and their hospitality could not be refused. Folks welcomed the travelers with rich food and wine and spread mattresses in raised beds for them at night. Little gods of stone and wood watched over Emyn's broken sleep just as they had at home.

As she passed the ring, the big man handed a sword to Moradag. "Let's see if you remember anything useful."

He attacked suddenly and Emyn gasped. Nonicos sprang in front of her, grinning and waving her into the house. Moradag yelped with glee as he bounded into a grassy meadow, ducking and swinging.

"He's at it every night," the man's wife giggled, and pushed a cup into Emyn's hands. "Tarugos knows what he's about. No one will be hurt."

"Men fight," the dead king cut in. "*Your* people are weak."

Emyn took a drink of rich, dark ale and handed the cup back. "Tarugos is a teacher?"

"A good teacher." The woman patted Emyn's arm. "He's trained many fine swordsmen. Moradag will be one of them."

"Men fight," the dead king repeated.

In the fading light, ghostly warriors stood around them. "Kings must be whole."

"They are first in battle."

"Their arms are strong and deadly."

"Kings?" Emyn asked softly.

"King? Oh, one day, perhaps," the woman laughed and then grew solemn. "King or not, Moradag needs to practice each day so that his muscles grow right. Remind the druid if he forgets. Each day."

"I'll remember," Bodocnos called from the door.

"Take his sword and make him use it. You know who he is. There are things he must know. He can't just study the stars." Emyn looked from the woman to Bodocnos, wondering how many years ago this conversation had started. "Stars don't win battles. He needs a strong arm."

The druid touched his serpent's egg. "My oath: he will practice daily. Emyn, you are my witness."

She nodded. "The ghosts listen too. They respect strength."

"There. Are you satisfied?" Bodocnos asked.

The woman took a gulp of ale. "I'll be satisfied when I see a grown man with a good arm before me."

EMYN WOKE IN THE DARKNESS, sure that she heard her baby cry. She crawled on her knees looking for Aumios until her brother shook her and pushed her back to her fur. Her baby did not cry. Her baby was gone, and she would never hold him in this world again.

They left Tarugos' house early the next morning and Emyn walked until her feet were numb. When the sun was high Nonicos led the mule off the wooden road.

"You walked all morning, Chiomara!" Moradag took her arm as Emyn stepped onto soft grass still damp with mist. "Tomorrow we'll race each other."

He was gone before she could answer, grabbing a bucket and running through the trees. Bluebells were beginning to appear and Emyn heard a brook gurgling in the shadows.

"Ride this afternoon," Nonicos said as he pulled chips and branches of dry wood from the cart, handing them to Micco. "At least for a while."

Nonicos built a fire. Tarugos' wife had filled their small cauldron with stew and packed loaves of bread that softened when dipped in broth. They ate well. If a drizzling rain had not started, they all might have fallen asleep.

Once she was in the moving cart, Emyn held a pelt over her head but let it fall like a veil when her arms tired. The moisture came and went, never very heavy. She drifted into sleep, lulled by the steady motion and rattle of the road.

She woke in a room made of cloth. The cloying aroma of roses wafted from a tall man who paced to and fro. He was alone.

Emyn sniffed as the man passed her. "Perfumed?"

"An unworthy habit, acquired in Rome." The dead king's voice rumbled in the quiet room. "Diviciacos."

His features were much like Dumnorix': gray eyes, a proud face, thick hair the color of polished oak, but his demeanor was nervous and unsure.

"Why does he pace? Is he worried?"

"He has cause." The ghost laughed. "He promised grain to the Romans. When snow covered the ground, he pledged this. He never thought he'd have to deliver so much. What will his people eat?"

"*His* people? Does Diviciacos lead the Aedui now?"

"He has bound them to Rome."

The room changed. Emyn sat near walls draped with lengths of wool. Mystic designs and stories were embroidered into the cloth; she recognized the horned god as well as Dirona and Epona. Before she could decipher their pictures, though, voices drew her attention to the hearth.

She needed no ghost to proclaim Dumnorix' name. The prince sat among supplicants who presented gifts.

"Your wisdom overflows its banks, dispersing your enemies in the flood," babbled one man.

Emyn didn't move as the courtiers poured flattery on the prince. The room was warm, more real to her than the dampness that surrounded the cart. She began to doze. At the sound of a woman's voice, she jerked awake

The other men had vanished. The bored princess of the Helvetians, the wife of Dumnorix, stood in front of her. Emyn knew her titles, but not her name.

From the wall, the horned god posed as if giving a blessing. Emyn stretched her fingers, searching for the rough boards of the cart. She felt nothing.

"You will go, won't you?" The princess pouted like a child pleading for a trinket.

"Of course," said Dumnorix.

The princess' face relaxed. She turned her attention to the design etched on the back of a silver mirror. An attendant stepped forward; Dumnorix waved him away and sat on a bench. Alone, he and his wife looked everywhere but at each other.

"This means I must visit Sequanni chieftains," Dumnorix said at last. "You should return with your cousins."

"To wagons and tents!" She wrinkled her nose "If—"

"To your people." Dumnorix' voice reverberated against the wall.

The princess bent over her mirror and asked with deliberate nonchalance, "Does your brother have a geis?"

Dumnorix stood and stared at his wife.

Emyn held her breath. A geis was a rule: a personal, unbreakable law laid upon one by a druid. Only men of destiny or criminals were burdened with them. She'd never met anyone who admitted to having a geis.

The princess smiled as if she discussed the weather. "You cannot cross the sea. I wonder if your brother had a geis pronounced over him as well."

"You were cautioned not to speak of that."

"There's no one else here. Why do you worry?"

"I'll tell your cousins that you will journey with them." Dumnorix' voice frosted the room like the icy surface of the river in winter.

"Emyn." Bodocnos' sing-song voice accompanied a light shake. "Come down from the cart. We are stopping."

She looked around, confused. The sun was far in the west. Nonicos had unhitched the mule. He and Micco led it away to graze.

Moradag hopped up to help Emyn scoot to the edge of the cart. "We sleep under the stars tonight, Chiomara. And we have fresh fish to cook; I'm surprised the smell didn't wake you."

"Fish?"

Moradag jumped down. "Yes, from a lucky man who was happy to share his bounty with an Honored Master. Now—" he and Bodocnos caught her arms and waist and lifted her to the ground. To her surprise, Moradag was taller than she. When they'd met again in Virmandum he was her same height, she was certain. How had he grown in less than one cycle of the moon?

EMYN LEANED BACK AGAINST A TREE, watching her brother. He held her walking stick in his lap, whittling away while the golden light filtered through the trees. Mustaches and eyes were emerging from the wood.

She turned to Bodocnos. "How long has it been since you lived among the Bellovaci, Master?"

"Years. Perhaps as long as Moradag has lived on this earth."

"Do you miss your people?"

"Do you hope I can give you a magic word to stop the ache? There is none." The druid scowled. "Many druids live apart from their tribes. Most, in fact. As you will. Why do you suppose that is?"

Emyn didn't dare guess.

"Wisdom comes from outside. All chiefs know this—they seek outside their borders for guidance. And druids find the greatest secrets beyond the boundaries of this world."

Bodocnos sipped from a cup of wine—a gift of the Bellovaci —as it was passed around the fire. Without thinking he handed it to Micco who took a big gulp, expecting water. Micco squealed, spat out the wine, and tried to rub the taste from his tongue.

Nonicos and Moradag jumped up laughing, then took the boy to the brook to rinse his mouth.

"Has he always been like that?" Bodocnos asked. "Does he ever speak?"

"He tries once in a while. He says Emmm, or No-ee." The first time Emyn had seen Micco, Hentios was holding him up, drinking to his new son while Almer grinned. That was just before Emyn met the ghosts and the last time Hentios had shown off Micco.

"I've heard something like Orra from him too," Bodocnos sighed. "I suppose that's Moradag."

"What spirit guides him?" Emyn asked.

"You would know better than I, Gutumaros."

Emyn didn't know Micco's birthday, but she was sure that no one in Samarnum had bothered to study his stars or his path. She often saw lights around him, though. They seemed no less intense and doting than the lights around everyone else.

The boy was a puzzle. Micco had loved Almer but stayed with Emyn after the attack. If he hadn't curled up in a corner of her brothers' house last winter, refusing to be lured away, he would have died in the fire that killed Almer and their mother.

A month ago Micco followed Emyn into a strange, cold world. Why? Nonicos thought the boy was attached to Emyn, but it could as easily be Nonicos' kindness that held him, or Moradag's bright humor and songs.

No one really understood Micco's reasons.

"There is a dreadful beauty in endings," Bodocnos said. How long had he been talking? "The taste for many things sours as one ages, but not this. Are the trees and their leaves ever more lovely than when the sun is setting, and the day dies?"

He could not expect her to answer that. Emyn watched while darkness grew and a new day began. Finally she asked, "Has Dumnorix been made king of the Aedui?"

"He has," Bodocnos nodded without surprise, as if they had been speaking of the man all afternoon. To him, questions were meant to be answered. "He was trained for that role since birth; the stars and signs were clear. But not all of the Aedui accepts him. His brother Diviciacos leads several clans by election."

"The friend of Rome."

"They are an unlikely pair, aren't they?" Bodocnos picked up the cup. "I'll refill this. Micco spilled more than we drank."

"Our two Aeduan brothers," the druid mused as he sat back down. "I wonder what happened to their father's seed. It is clear to me that they were meant to be one person, one great leader. Split apart, they are each diminished."

Emyn took the cup, wondering if he was serious.

Bodocnos went on. "The pity is that they love each other.

They have the same goal: the continuance of the Aedui. But in pursuit of that—"

"Men's love withers when power is to be gained," said the dead king, drowning out the druid's words.

Bodocnos waited for Emyn to speak.

"I saw both brothers today," she began, then told him of her visions, withholding only the exchange about Dumnorix' geis. No one should hear that; she wished she hadn't.

The others returned as she spoke. Quietly, Nonicos arranged furs and blankets around the fire. Moradag settled next to Micco, singing as he would to a child.

"So Dumnorix visits the Sequani." The druid held the cup before him. "Their largest city is Vesontio, so I imagine he will go there first."

"I didn't hear why he must visit them."

"The Helvetians—his wife's people—wish to cross Sequani land. They have no other way to turn, do they? They must either fight Rome or treat with the Sequani. Perhaps those visitors—Helvetians, I am sure, and probably his wife's cousins—asked Dumnorix to negotiate for them. He is a druid and a king, doubly skilled at oratory and diplomacy."

"But—bargain with the Sequani?" Emyn kept her voice low. "I don't understand. The Sequani killed Dumnorix' father."

"His father fell in battle. There is an honorable difference between that and murder." The druid drained the cup. "The kings of the Aedui and the Helveti forged alliances through marriages. Aedui, Helveti, and Sequani and more are now bound together."

Emyn pulled a fur around her shoulders as she listened. The Sequani had invited barbarians across the river years ago to help them battle the Aedui. Did they still stand with those mercenaries?

"And the Sequani . . . well, this is another story altogether. A new king overthrew the old, with help." Bodocnos sighed and leaned back, arranging himself for sleep. "Leadership is a tangled mess these days and far from what the gods intended. To be a king was once a sacred charge."

"Kings are first in battle, the ghosts say," Emyn recalled.

"First in the charge and in the fight," Moradag sang from across the dying fire. "In famine, first to hunger. First to rise when work beckons."

"I'm glad you remember," Bodocnos observed. "Even if it is only to impress your Chiomara."

Moradag laughed and rolled into a ball.

"A sacred charge," Bodocnos repeated. "Once, but no more. There are times when I despair."

Emyn had seen Dumnorix in battle and in thought; she did not share the druid's pessimism.

HER SLEEP FILLED WITH TROUBLING IMAGES. Almer's face, dead, pale, and bloated, rose to the top of the well in Samarnum as Emyn woke with a gasp. She dozed again, but Aumios slipped on the wet grass and began to cry. Her eyes flew open but she saw only the outline of trees blocking the stars. The moon hadn't risen; she'd only slept an hour or two.

Her baby's wail sounded so real . . . a nightmare with Aumios alive was better than the emptiness that came with waking. This time she didn't try to fight the tears.

When she next woke, a figure stood by the fire. He leaned against his red shield; a bronze serpent stretched into a spiral on it.

A sliver of moon cast faint light, but Emyn could see the warrior's eyes watching in the night. She slept well after that.

13

The weeks passed. On a morning when the nearly-full moon set as the sun rose, Emyn prayed for Esmios, Iomat, and her friends. A month and a half had passed since leaving her home; she wondered if Samarnum's little gods could still hear her distant voice.

Tall broom plants lined the road, their bright yellow flowers in full bloom. Broom plants had to be cut within a moon of Beltane, Iomat always said. If Emyn could arrange a place in the cart to stack the branches—

"Hold on." Nonicos held up his hand then pointed down the road. "Is that a wagon?"

He led the mule to the side, getting the wagon off the planks and out of the way.

"Moradag, what do you see?" the master demanded.

"A chariot . . . four horses."

"Emyn, hide!"

Together, Nonicos and Moradag half-carried her up a slope to huddle behind a screen of bushes that included the broom plants.

"He is near!" the dead king cried as the others ran back down the hill. "You will give him my words."

The rumbling of chariot wheels and horses' hooves grew to a deafening racket then stopped. Shouts from the road mixed with Nonicos' angry yells.

"Go, fool!" the dead king urged. "They will take you to Diviciacos."

"Outlaw," strange ghosts began to chant. "Outlaw, no law!"

"They come for you!"

"No law binds them."

Micco ran past her up the slope, terrified.

With or without the ghost's encouragement, Emyn could not leave the others to face outlaws on her behalf. She stumbled to the road, grabbing at tree trunks to check herself as she descended.

Bodocnos and Moradag were pushing Nonicos back. Two warriors faced them, their backs to Emyn. The taller man shouted; his tone was full of bluster. "Keep that oaf away if you don't want him run through!"

"Where is she?" the other man demanded. He waved his drawn sword towards Nonicos.

"You cannot ride up and lay claim to a woman, no matter who you think she is!" Bodocnos' voice was strong as he held up his serpent's egg, but the men he faced were not intimidated.

"We know who she is and who you are." The tall man crossed his arms. "We are outlaws, outside your orders, old man. Where is the oracle?"

"The oracle is here!" Emyn hobbled from the trees as straight as she could. "That is my brother you threaten. If he is harmed, you will explain to Diviciacos why the only words he'll get from me are curses."

"Tell him not to interfere, then," the warrior barked.

Emyn loaded indignation into her voice. "Where is your honored prince?"

"A day's ride west, near the forest of the Carnutes."

"And how many days' walk?" demanded Bodocnos.

"You'll let us know how long a walk it is when you catch up, I suppose." The leader drew a sword and grinned.

Her brother tried to push past Bodocnos again.

"Don't, Nonicos, please!" Emyn cried. Having a woman stolen from their protection did not sit well with any of the males. Emyn tried to sound convincing as she added, "They won't hurt me. The dead king is certain of it—"

"Back!" the leader shouted. He was twice Emyn's size, but when she faced him he took a step away. "Adio, get her in the chariot."

"All men fear me!" cackled the dead king.

Adio did not touch her. These men might face death fearlessly in battle, but they were as frightened as children in the dark when it came to ghosts. Worse: as outlaws they lacked the protection of powerful tribal gods.

Emyn leaned heavily on her stick as she walked by the leader. A crone shadowed him, whispering words that only she could hear.

"Have you forgotten your grandmother?" Emyn asked quietly, looking directly into his eyes. "She led your clan. What twists your mind that you snatch free women from the road for coins and wine?"

"Adio!" The tall man blanched and gripped his sword more tightly. "Get her!"

"Put it away, grandson," Emyn's voice quavered like an old woman's. "You have your prize. Leave these people alone."

The man sheathed his sword as Adio stepped between them.

"Tell me what injuries you suffer, Gutumaros," Adio asked, walking toward the chariot. "For your own comfort."

"My hip was broken. My left hip."

"Your arms are strong?"

"Yes."

The man bent and arranged blankets into a pile inside the chariot box, then clenched his teeth and scooped Emyn up. He leaned into the box and set her on the blankets. "That's the best I can do. Hang on tight to the ropes."

"I'll take the reins." The leader jumped in. "Adio, you watch her."

"Unworthy coward," the dead king mocked. "He will die an outlaw."

Adio slid his weapon into a sheath that hung from knots inside the chariot. The other man cried out to the horses. Emyn glanced up and grabbed the ropes over her head as the box jumped forward and seemed to fly off the ground.

Two pairs of legs positioned themselves, flexing and swaying with the chariot's motion. She turned her head and looked out the open back. Nonicos and the others grew smaller as they scurried around. Too late, she saw her half-carved stick slide to the back of the chariot and pitch away. Would the others find it as they rushed after her?

The wood box vibrated and jerked; Emyn stretched up for a better grip on the ropes. Beyond her reach, spears and axes were bound tight to the inside of the chariot, but the rope nearest her hung loose. She looped her arm through it as branches flashed dizzily overhead.

At a turn in the road she was thrown off-balance and lost her grip, Adio reached down in time to stop her slide across the leather floor, then moved to stand behind her so she wouldn't fall out the back. Diviciacos would not reward them for a damaged oracle.

* * *

During their one stop, Adio warmed rabbit stew in a pot that had been strapped and loosely covered inside the chariot. It did not smell or taste very wholesome, but Emyn was hungry and ate. She learned from their talk that travelers spread gossip, including the fact that a Gutumaros traveled south and west with the druid Bodocnos. She was not surprised; the first question asked at any meeting on the road was always, "What news?"

Adio kicked dirt over their fire, then lifted Emyn back into the chariot. They flew forward and veered onto a road heading west, toward bright gray clouds that obscured the sun.

Much later, when the chariot slowed, Emyn could neither move nor look up. Every joint, even her teeth, ached as if her bones had been shaken apart, fractured from the inside.

"We've arrived," Adio announced.

Emyn's hands had petrified around the rope. The abrupt stillness of the chariot was not enough to get her blood moving again. Adio lifted her arm and slid it out of the loops, then let it fall to her lap.

"Shake it around," he suggested and hopped to the ground.

Emyn tried to flex her fingers; they were unresponsive.

"Up, lady," the leader grunted. "Diviciacos is waiting."

Her arms would not move properly, and her legs were no better. The tall man did not wait. He bent, slung his hand around her waist and lifted Emyn, carrying her under his arm as he stepped down into a field of bluebells.

"There." He stood her on her feet but her legs were still numb. She could no more stand upright than a fish could, and flopped onto her side.

Bluebells bounced before her. She heard laughter from several directions. "Coward!" she shouted to the outlaw's back.

"Is she for us to share?" a man called.

Nauseous, sore, and angry, Emyn found the strength to kick a man who grabbed at her. "Get away!"

Her dress tore loudly along its seam as more laughter erupted. She twisted and pushed herself onto her right knee, pawing at the fabric, trying to make it cover her legs.

The men around her hooted. Beyond them, juniper trees and thick bushes marked the edge of their camp. A cloth tent filled half of the clearing, flattening the bluebells. Painted on each of its sides was the circling snake of the Aedui.

"Gutumaros?" A blond head separated from the crowd and suddenly, a familiar face stood before her.

Emyn stared, stunned. Coath, Bodocnos' handsome student who had stirred such a commotion in Samarnum one summer . . . was this a trick of the ghosts?

Coath looked around, unsmiling. "Is this the way you treat an oracle?" Fixing the tall outlaw with his eyes, he spat. "Did her ghosts scare you so badly that you had to drop her?"

The outlaw warrior made a move; Coath put his hand on a knife hilt at his waist. His serpent's egg sparkled on his chest.

The warrior hesitated, then squared his shoulders. "You mistake me, Honored Master, if you think I would attack you. Never! I bring the Death Speaker to Diviciacos." He raised his voice on the last part, as if he thought someone might dispute his right to the reward.

Coath extended a hand to help Emyn up. Before she could grab hold, a voice called for order.

"Diviciacos!" the dead king screamed.

Emyn forgot Coath; her blood, so recently hot, now froze.

"Have we forsaken hospitality in this camp? Fetch a bench for the Gutumaros!" The prince's voice sang out, sure of approval.

Gray eyes lit on her; his smile tried to charm. "My apologies, lady. Allow us to show you the respect you deserve—"

"Respect from animals?" Still on her knee, Emyn met his eyes. He was a druid, but a thief and a liar as well. She would not bow to a man who'd kidnapped her! "Is this how you hope to please your ancestors, Diviciacos? By dragging their voice through the dirt? Do you think you can command them to speak that way?"

"If you have been ill-used, Gutumaros, all will be made right. I promise you that."

A bench and cushions appeared, but Emyn ignored them. "Why did you bring me here?"

"To hear the advice of the dead, knowing well that it may be flawed."

"So." The dead king whispered words and Emyn repeated them loudly. "Even before hearing it, you've prepared an excuse for ignoring their counsel?"

Emyn felt the ghost behind her, so close that if he had physical form, he would be embracing her. Other spirits stood near, suffused with the same rage. She could give them clear voice, they told her. "Let us in. Once. Now. This time."

Diviciacos mouthed more pretty words. He wouldn't listen, but was that a good reason for not speaking?

The ghosts pressed closer. Should she allow this? It was only a step into darkness, after all—no worse than a step into a dark room . . . She shut her eyes and said, "Yes."

Emyn felt the jerk as she was yanked from the inside, sucked out of her own skin to float like smoke in the air. Below, the shell of Emyn, pale in a sea of deep blues and greens, stood and began to walk with long, stiff strides.

Words rang out: "The cuckoo hides its egg in another bird's

nest. When the egg hatches, the birds feed it. But the baby cuckoo is large and needs more food. If there are young birds in the nest, it pushes them out, so it can have all the food.

"Your friend Caesar sits in your nest, Diviciacos. How will you feed him?"

"Do your ghosts compare the Roman commander to a fledgling?" the prince asked.

She could not see Diviciacos' face from above, only his body. His cloak, made of light wool lined with dark stripes, spread from arm to arm. He looked like a cuckoo with a striped breast, and the shadows that wavered with the bluebells were his wings.

Emyn-above giggled and Emyn-below giggled as well. Emyn-below reflected her spirit like an image in water.

"You do not care that he shoves your rivals out of the nest, do you?" Was that her voice, rumbling like a man's? "What happens when Caesar grows so fat that there is no room for the Aedui? Who will help you then? Everyone else will be smashed on the ground, starving."

Diviciacos circled Emyn-below. "Such brutality is not the Roman way. Your analogy doesn't fit, Gutumaros. Rome is our strong ally, not a cuckoo. The Aedui remain in their own land."

"For how long? You are blinded by promises. Rome is not a cuckoo chick, oh no. He is an eagle. He will take what he chooses, not what you give him."

The sky began to drop, not in pieces, but all at once to cover the earth, falling with such force that Emyn could feel the ground tremble, even up here, high above it. Men assembled for battle: warriors, Romans, mercenaries.

"Look." Emyn recognized the Morrigu's voice; dark hair—or wings—wrapped around her. "Now see what comes. You may not live long enough to see it again."

A different world lay below: a world of the dead, stretching as far as Emyn could see. The earth did not hold enough dirt to cover all the corpses. Warriors, hacked and soaked in blood, lay scattered across the landscape. Scavengers tore at the bodies; they stripped away the armor and cut black fingers from hands to steal rings.

Men perished slowly on battlefields, begging for water or death. Druids and chiefs were pushed to their knees and executed before crowds of Roman soldiers. Women were raped as men jeered and fought for their turns. In a swamp far to the north, children huddled in fear. Esmios' little boy, the one who called Emyn "fairy aunt," sat among them. They were being separated, the strong who could walk from those to be left. Thousands of ordinary people were loaded into carts, their hands bound and their feet weighted, to be sold as slaves far away.

This was not war like the bards celebrated; no heroes claimed victory.

Diviciacos marked a crossroads, Emyn realized. The past led to this moment and the future branched before them. The path of every tribe bent with his choice.

She heard a voice: brutal and hoarse—was it hers? "Your own tribe is your greatest strength, but you've cut it in half."

"The division is not my doing. My brother Dumnorix is stubborn; he does not know the meaning of compromise."

They were still arguing, Emyn-below and Diviciacos. It seemed that hours had passed. She'd seen the sky fall and the world end, and still they argued.

Emyn-below said, "You do not ask for compromise. You are as stubborn as your brother."

The Aeduan laughed at that. "What do the spirits advise, then? How do we mend what is torn between us?"

"You have asked and I answer." Even from her own throat, Emyn recognized the grating laugh of the dead king. "Your brother is right, Diviciacos, and you are wrong."

Emyn slipped back into her body as a large hand stretched around her entire neck. The dead king may have gone too far.

Diviciacos shouted inches from her face. "You are in Dumnorix' service, then. What has he promised you to cloud my vision?"

She had no control over her rasping voice. "These are the words you want to ignore, aren't they? How many others have tried to make you listen?"

Would he snap her neck? Every child knew that those who heard the Morrigu's voice faced death shortly after.

Words gurgled up. She could stop them now, if she wanted— but she didn't.

"Here is what your ancestors say to you, Diviciacos of the Aedui. Your people will not honor you, but Rome will praise your name for the wealth you bring them. In Rome, find your reward. The lands you love will be given to strangers."

"Lies and sacrilege!" Diviciacos roared. "I see that even the voices of our ancestors are not above the manipulations of my brother!"

Pain hit her knees. The ghosts were still beside Emyn, and more words formed . . . but she was on her hands and knees, vomiting and panting.

"Honored Diviciacos." Coath's voice floated above her. "I have met this sad creature before, near Nervian lands. This woman is clearly possessed. She is ignorant and at the mercy of her ghosts. I will take her out of your sight."

"Do that! Before—"

"I didn't come here by choice!" Emyn spat out.

"Shut up," Coath grunted in her ear. He lifted her to her feet, but she could not feel solid ground beneath them. "Shut up or you'll be as dead as your ghosts."

Her legs were useless. Coath picked her up like a child, hoisted her over his shoulder, and took long strides away from the hooting crowd.

 **14**

"Some advice for you, Gutumaros. Your village is far away. If you intend to insult powerful men in front of their followers, you should hire bodyguards."

Coath had carried Emyn through the trees as far as he could, then lowered her onto a patch of bluebells as he doubled over, gasping. When he recovered, he held out a hand to her.

Emyn stared at it. Everything before her swirled like an eddy in a pond.

"You angered him past reason. We really should keep moving." When she did not respond he added, "Gutumaros? Are you hurt?"

"No . . . I don't know." Her head was heavy. In spite of the danger, all Emyn wanted to do was sleep. "I don't think I can walk."

"You walked in front of Diviciacos."

"That was the dead king."

"Then . . . you really were possessed?" Coath's voice lost its fullness for a moment. "I only said that to get you away. Is it true?"

"It is true." Emyn shut her eyes, but even the darkness moved in sickening circles.

"Gutumaros, we must get further away from those outlaws. They respect nothing." As she opened her eyes, Coath stretched his arm out to her.

That was brave. Offering his arm to the Death Speaker probably took more courage than defying Diviciacos. How could she loll dizzily on the ground? He was right; they couldn't stay here.

Emyn grabbed Coath's arm and stood. She tried to take steps. Her arms flailed and he caught her.

"My hip was broken—"

"Hold tight to my arm." Coath tried different poses to support her, on one side, then the other. After a few steps they found a rhythm. Progress would be slow, but they could move.

"Where did you come from today?" He guided Emyn out of the small clearing. Shadows fell on them from behind; sunset was at least an hour away, maybe more.

"Outlaws took me from my brother and Bodocnos—"

"Bodocnos?" Coath sounded delighted.

"Yes. He brings us south for the gathering of druids. I'm not sure where we were when the outlaws came." Emyn forced her feet to move. Coath would have to carry her if she slipped back to the ground.

"Tell me what you can. I know the land well; I'll get you back to Bodocnos and your brother." His voice was full of confidence. "From Samarnum, did you go south?"

"No. East to Virmandum." Emyn tried to think of useful information. "Then south. We entered Bellovaci territory and followed the Isara River through the forests all the way to the Valley of the Swallows. It was a longer route, but the master wanted to keep me far from the skull temple at Coboneton."

"Coboneton . . . all those bones and armor." She felt Coath

shudder. "The master served there once. I don't think he enjoyed it."

Emyn had the same impression. She felt better now; talking took her mind off the dizziness and her weak body. "We veered west after that, but stayed out of the great forest. From there we walked in the lands of several tribes until we reached the Parisi. They all welcomed us because we traveled with an Honored Master. We crossed the Sequana River just after Beltane."

"Where on the river?"

"At an island with a village."

"There are several of those," Coath said. "Luteca?"

They had tossed offerings into the great river, but that was all Emyn could remember. Her birthday had passed there, barely noticed: she was twenty-one: three sevens, a propitious number. "We followed the Sequana south for three more days, and struck west only two days ago."

Coath nodded. "I know the road you were on, then. We'll head north for a bit to meet that road and go east. Very simple."

"Won't they follow us?"

He glanced back at the footpath and the westering sun and bit his lower lip. "I suspect Diviciacos prefers not to see you again. We must avoid meeting him by accident, but that shouldn't be hard. He's already made camp for the night and plans to travel west in the morning." Coath abruptly cast off his own fretful expression. "So, tell me. You cannot walk without help. Why are you traveling?"

Emyn talked. Coath lowered his voice to express sympathy, raised it when surprised. By the time she told her story, shadows had lengthened to resemble wide, gaping holes across their path. Emyn tensed, ready to swing from Coath's arm at any misstep.

They reached the east-west road. Emyn must have been half-conscious when the chariot rode over it earlier. A post and a heap of pebbles marked the place as a crossroads.

Coath bent down and picked up two stones, handing one to Emyn. Neither of them said a word; crossroads could be dangerous.

Lugh protected such junctions; he was a god powerful enough to hold spirits in their own realm—most of the time. The moon was full tonight, though, the boundaries between worlds strained. And the sun would be setting soon. She and Coath stood on the border of a new day as well as a new road.

Coath added his rock to the pile, then held Emyn steady as she bent to offer hers.

Diviciacos was the crossroad. What horrors from the worlds of shadow did he let loose? She'd seen sights today that she would never forget.

"Emyn?" Coath urged her to rise.

A woman's voice shook the ground beneath them. "Do not turn back. That way is closed."

The voice was strong; Emyn's quivered. "I hear the Morrigu."

Coath blanched. No face had ever looked more terrified and less like a hero's. His bravado was damaged but he did not abandon Emyn. They walked on.

"Why were you in Diviciacos' camp?" she asked, hoping to distract him.

"What?"

She repeated her question.

"Curiosity." He turned to glance at the road behind. "My father hosted him only a few nights ago, along with his . . . retinue —the legitimate ones, at least."

That made sense to Emyn; outlaws were not entitled to hospitality. She was glad that Adio and his partner had been left outside. "Your father's lands are near?"

Coath's voice regained some confidence. "Two days south and east, at least by my pace. I wonder if Bodocnos meant to stop there. Did he mention me as you traveled?"

"No," Emyn said.

"Probably he meant to surprise you, then."

"I could not be more surprised," she grinned. "Did Diviciacos stay long at your father's house?"

"Only a few days. He said he intended to visit many kings and clans, so I tagged along. I thought it might be interesting to travel with the prince, but I doubt they'll miss me."

In the gold light of the lowering sun, Coath flashed a smile that would have knocked Cesua's legs from under her. "I'm glad I was there to rescue you. I never had the opportunity to carry off a woman before."

"Are many of his men outlaws?"

Coath shook his head. Too late, Emyn realized that he probably expected words of gratitude instead of a question. "At least half of the men back there are outlaws. They'll serve any prince who pays them."

"Why?"

"Chariots and matched teams aren't for the poor."

"Of course." Emyn gave a little laugh; that was not what she'd meant. "Why would strong men become outlaws, though?"

"It pays well, if you have no other prospects." Coath seemed to be picking his words carefully. "Men . . . or boys . . . escape. They leave something behind to become an outlaw, some part of themselves they no longer want."

Emyn stumbled over an unseen root; not much daylight remained. Best not to say anything about that, she decided. "I've heard outlaws can't be punished."

"They aren't equal to free men, so—" Coath pushed through

bushes; the path had nearly disappeared. For a few moments neither spoke as they watched the ground, separating rocks from shadows. Before Emyn could ask another question, Coath said, "Rialos is the one you should ask about outlaws."

"What?"

"Rialos." Coath squinted, looking ahead through the gloom. "Bodocnos' other student, years ago? He came to your village with me. Dark hair, a crooked nose? I think I see smoke."

She held her breath; he didn't notice.

"Yes, smoke. Do you see? We can rest soon."

Emyn could feel the relief in his stride and in the arm she held. Well-marked fields lay between them and the smoke he'd seen; their path was clear again, though the light was nearly gone. "So the other student—"

"Was an outlaw, yes. When we first met him, the master and I, he lived with a band of thieves."

"Was he born to thieves?"

"I don't think so. He ran away. Unless he's managed to make peace somehow or buy his way back, he remains an outlaw—even as a druid. He has no family or tribe. . . . I can see the house now, just ahead."

Coath walked faster. Emyn could not see his face; maybe that was just as well. Gallantry and fear were likely battling it out there. She stumbled, trying to keep up, and knew he would answer no more questions now.

When they were close enough to the farmhouse, Coath called out a greeting, declaring himself a druid. A young couple with little to spare offered Coath and Emyn what they had: stale, coarse bread, ripe pears, and a vegetable stew flavored with old bones. The fire was enough; Emyn reeled when she smelled the stew and left it for Coath.

The day had been too full. Only when she lay still on the dirt floor did the Morrigu's vision come back to haunt her, keeping her from sleep. Not for the first time, Emyn was glad that the stars foretold a short life for her.

She guessed the moon was at its zenith when small panting noises billowed from the corner. Their hosts were making love.

Coath heard too; his arm slid around Emyn's waist. Was he so used to having whatever woman happened to be near? She shoved him away, and he rolled onto his back. Within minutes, he was snoring.

15

"My lord." Coath—Cothuacos, here—bowed toward his father, a chief of the Carnute tribe. "Your hearth has never warmed more grateful souls than those here today."

Emyn basked in the firelight and left the fine words to the men. A cup was handed to her; the liquid swirled in shadows. She smelled Roman wine, touched her lips politely to the edge and passed the cup to her brother.

Several handfuls of men and women sat on mats in the large house. Ten shields, as tall as Emyn and painted with brilliant colors, leaned against the wall. The spirits of warriors and ancestors crowded near the shields, promising safety and rest—exactly what Emyn's group craved, at least for a few days.

She sat up straight as she realized Coath was telling his father the story of their daring escape from Diviciacos' camp.

"He lies to all!" the dead king scolded, but Emyn ignored the ghost. Why should a handsome hero not exaggerate and make the tale more memorable? Five days ago, when Coath first described the rescue to his old teacher, he'd added a few drawn swords and threats. The ghost kept silent then. Why criticize now?

Truly, Coath had saved her, and he could say what he liked to impress his father. Maybe all stories were built this way, with bits added as events were retold.

The proud father handed Coath the choicest chunk of roast before distributing meat to the rest of his guests. Only then, when it was polite to do so, did he ask their names.

The chief knew the druid, of course; they'd met years before when Coath became his student. Moradag was introduced as the son of a Bellovaci king. Emyn bent forward in a bow when Coath presented her as "the beauteous and bold oracle of Samarnum."

She hardly knew whom he meant. "The crippled and homeless big mouth" might be a more fitting title.

A delicate gray hand distracted Emyn; it stroked the fabric she wore with fondness and care, as if smoothing out wrinkles. This soft gown, richer than anything she'd worn before, would make any woman look beautiful.

That morning Emyn and the others were pampered by the chief's slaves as if they were visiting royalty themselves. Attendants helped her bathe in warm water. Afterward, a girl cleaned her nails, while another dried and brushed her short hair and pinned a linen veil to it. Flowery oils clung to her skin as she was wrapped in the gown. No doubt slaves beat the dirt of travel out of Emyn's faded clothes while she sat here, eating and drinking.

A name brought her attention back to the conversation: Coath was describing how he'd broken Rialos' nose many years ago. "Not that it had been straight before," the young druid laughed.

Bodocnos, who held the cup, leaned towards Emyn and whispered, "Coath never mentions that he actually lost that fight, in spite of breaking Rialos' nose."

Emyn was sure she flushed, remembering the shape of Rialos' nose as if she'd met him yesterday—as well as the taste of his lips and the color of his eyes. How could a chance encounter still heat her blood? She took the cup from the druid, touched her mouth to it once more, and passed it to Nonicos as their host asked where they would venture next.

"Several paths stretch before us, so the choice is not yet made," Bodocnos replied. "Travelers tell of flooding in some areas."

He turned to an ancient, fragile man whose druidic amulet hid beneath an ice-white beard. "Tiacos, I honor your skill in translating the signs of Carnute's ancestors. Perhaps when the sun rises, I may sit with you and discuss the flow of wind and water?"

Emyn wiped grease from her hands and broke apart a loaf of bread, handing some to her brother. Nonicos turned often to check on Micco, who sat by the door with the dogs, quite happy. Her mind drifted as the men talked.

She had expected new adventures and surroundings to jar her from her past; that had been the point of this journey. To cross rivers, ride in a chariot, sit with kings and chieftains in lands made famous by the heroes of ages past . . . thirty times thirty surprises had fallen on Emyn since leaving Samarnum. On most days the gods kept her mind busy. Only at night did sadness refill it.

What would happen when the journey ended?

Around the hearth, the subject switched back to Diviciacos. Other visitors described the Aeduan prince's travels. "He sends messengers to the Lemoti and Parisi," one man told Coath's father.

"And southwest as well. I heard he might visit the Tueboii," the talk continued.

"The Tueboii? No, he's on the road north—"

"He lies to all!" the dead king screamed.

The fragrance of roses overwhelmed Emyn, and she waved

her hand before her face. The first time she'd seen Diviciacos, he'd smelled like that. He'd been pacing in a tent, considering how he could deliver the food demanded by Caesar's armies. How many weeks had passed since that vision?

"That was the first I heard of shortages," a man reported.

"He said much the same here, didn't he?" someone asked Coath. "His clans need food."

"Everywhere he goes—"

Tiacos bent toward Bodocnos. "Our crops are fine. Strange that Aeduan fields alone were flooded."

Diviciacos must be asking for food for his tribe as he visited these neighbors, but that itself struck Emyn as odd. With so much happening in the south between Rome and the Helvetians, how could Diviciacos spend the summer traveling, moving his painted tent from land to land as if he indulged in a hunt?

He lies to all . . .

"He lies!" Emyn cried, indignant with sudden understanding.

In the following silence, she stared up at Coath. "The ghosts speak. Did Diviciacos ask about your father's crops?"

"He did, Gutumaros," Coath answered slowly.

"Diviciacos promised food for the Romans armies. More food than he can afford. His own people will suffer—"

Coath caught her meaning. "How long since he promised this food to Rome?"

"A month ago, and now the Roman general raises more legions. Thousands more men must be fed."

"He tells the tribes that the Aedui face grave hunger because of flooded rivers, and he pleads for aid." Coath raised his eyebrows at his father. "We promised to share our harvest."

"As did our allies," said Tiacos. "Lady Gutumaros, do your spirits judge the truth of his words?"

"My spirits say that Diviciacos lies to all."

"At last you speak for me!" the dead king hissed. "You are dull and slow."

She did not argue; too many people sat near.

COATH RODE OUT THE NEXT MORNING, eager to warn neighboring clans about Diviciacos' false pleas for aid. Not all would be warned; Coath's father took delight in repaying old offenses by withholding the news from a few clans.

Emyn and her traveling companions remained as guests while Bodocnos gathered information and mulled over their course. "My conceit blinded me to danger," the druid muttered one evening. "I led you into a hornets' nest, ignoring small warnings."

Their goal had been the land of the Carnutes, and here they were. Now, though, Bodocnos wanted to leave Carnute territory as quickly as they could. Emyn was glad, but kept her relief to herself.

AFTER TWO NIGHTS AND DAYS spent watching the stars and consulting with Tiacos, Bodocnos confronted Emyn. "Do your ghosts offer advice? Tell me now if they do; I am close to a decision."

No voices came to her. She heard only shouts from outside where Moradag sparred with Carnute warriors.

Ignoring the command at the crossroads would be foolish, though. "I cannot turn back."

Bodocnos raised an eyebrow. "When did the ghosts say that?"

"While we were separated, and I walked with Coath. And it wasn't a ghost."

"Who, then?"

"The Morrigu spoke to me."

Bodocnos let his breath out with a snort, held up his fingers in a warding sign, and left the house.

Nonicos walked over and picked up Emyn's stick. Three bearded, smiling faces now emerged from the knob where Emyn gripped it daily. "Let me work on this for a bit. It's almost done."

No one else rested near enough to hear while Nonicos spoke and whittled. "Moradag told me this morning that the master cannot bring us to the gathering in Carnute, not after what happened. He thinks Diviciacos or his agents will be there, as well as the followers of Dumnorix. They'll fight and argue. He said they'd brawl over you like drunks at midwinter, each trying to claim an oracle for their own purposes."

Nonicos' knife and fingers danced over the wood, deepening the carved eyes. He lowered his voice. "When the master offered to bring you to Carnute . . . I don't know what sort of reward matters to a druid, but he hoped for something. Now he is disappointed."

Her brother paused in his work. "He is an honorable man. I don't mean—"

"I know." Why shouldn't Bodocnos expect compensation or honor for delivering an oracle to a chieftain?

What would the druid do now, saddled with a cripple, an idiot, and one strong man? Emyn had likely dashed his hopes for a quick return to the hospitable Bellovaci lands when she relayed the Morrigu's advice: do not turn back.

"Where do you suppose we'll go?" Emyn asked her brother.

The fire before her vanished. Gray daylight replaced the dark and fragrant room. Emyn gripped Nonicos' arm as the ground vibrated beneath her. He said her name, but wild noises buried his voice. Emyn shut her eyes tightly.

When she opened them she saw Caesar's army.

Thousands of men ran past her on all sides—not with flying, loose strides, full of exuberance, the way normal men ran. These soldiers ran with measured steps, row after row of them, always maintaining the same space between one man and the next. They were like even lines of plants in a field, shining in the sun.

"Emyn!" Bodocnos' shout came from far away.

"Rows and rows . . . marching west. I see them." She mouthed the words but couldn't hear her voice.

Everything about the Romans bore a horrible sameness. Their short dark hair, their clean-shaven faces, the curved shape of their shields—all held at the same angle, all with the same leather covers—their javelins, helmets, and swords, even their clothes. These graven men, without souls, trampled a sacred land.

"More come," the dead king said. "From the south."

"Emyn!" Bodocnos' voice shattered the racket of stomping feet, and the vision faded. "I am guided. Rows and rows, marching west, you answered. Good."

Emyn gaped at the druid. "Master?"

"I led you into the troubles of this land, and I will lead you from them. I have been given a destination. To avoid the gathering of the wise in Carnute, we will go south, but only as far as the Liger River. Once we reach the Liger we'll turn west, and follow the water. We leave in two days."

MORADAG DECIDED THAT EMYN must learn to defend herself by using her stick. Before leaving Carnute land he'd sought out warriors and their wives for advice. Each day as they traveled, he made time to lurch and grab at Emyn while she tried to trip and upset him. He had a few bruises to show for his work, and she regained some of the balance she'd known before her injury.

After one long practice, she fell to her knees, set a hand on the ground, and leaned on it till her weight settled on the grass.

"No more, Chiomara?"

"You've worn me out!" She grinned up at Moradag's silhouette and wiped sweat from her brow. "But you fell twice. Don't deny it!"

The boy smiled, dipped a cup into the bucket, and handed it to her. "My master calls me."

Left alone, Emyn sat on the grass and stared across the wide Liger. The midday sun shone like polished metal on the water, and a light wind rippled the surface. Beyond the river lay a forest full of color and calm. That calm was an illusion: she knew that squirrels, mice, foxes, and all sorts of creatures large and tiny hid there. The trees were home to hundreds of birds that could explode out to skim across the sky in complex patterns, and the river was full of eels and fish. Insects buzzed and explored, seeking damp, shady glens . . . all that was present, but hidden.

Her breathing slowed. So many things appeared calm on the surface. The world was full of spirits that touched and prodded folks, alerting and protecting them all without being seen. Emyn knew better than to be fooled by appearances, but there were times when she needed a picture of peacefulness, real or not. The deceptive vista across the river soothed her spirit.

"You dislike crowds." Bodocnos sank to the ground beside her, picking crumbs from the coils of his beard. The bronze band rested on his head today; she hadn't noticed it lately.

She supposed he was right. Did anyone enjoy being jostled among strangers? In Samarnum, she had seen more ghosts than people on most days. Crowds were a new phenomena of the wide and strange world.

"I know that tune. It's a Bellovaci song," he said.

Emyn smiled; she hadn't realized she hummed. Bodocnos tossed out a question. "The Roman legion you saw—were they setting up their camp?"

"I only saw men running, all with the same clothes and weapons." Emyn shuddered. "I think they stamp warriors out of molds in Rome, the way coins are struck in Virmandum."

"Soldiers, not warriors." Bodocnos held up his hands, one open, one shut. "A warrior's courage burns bright in battle as he releases his strength. Ask, if you ever have the chance! Warriors will tell you about the fire that fills them." His open palm lifted, and a flame danced on it.

The druid squeezed his closed hand hard. "But these men that Rome sends to our land are soldiers, not warriors. You are right, they are pressed from molds like metal, cold and soulless. They don't believe in an afterlife, so I suppose they see little reason to fight gloriously in this one."

A shout and creaking from the nearby road drew their attention. Moradag hollered and ran toward a farmer who pulled his own cart, piled with bundles of green asparagus. He traveled toward the busy markets of Cenabum, but Bodocnos led his group in the opposite direction.

Emyn started to rise, but the druid placed a hand on her shoulder. "Your brother can be trusted with the stew pot for one day."

She waited. No ghosts were near; if the druid had pushed them off, he must have more to discuss with her. After a moment, he spoke slowly; she knew she was meant to listen well.

"I was not always a teacher. I once held a position of obligation and esteem in the sanctuary at Coboneton. While at that temple, spirits filled my dreams and even intruded on my waking moments. I know the dead. Not as well as you, of course. I was able to walk away from them as you never can." The druid's voice was for once flat and dispassionate. What did it hide?

"There were times of sacrifice at Coboneton. Animals, not men—at least, not during my service—were killed there. The bones and armaments on display remind us of the god Camulos, who brings strength in war. The temple is dedicated to him, of course.

"There was an altar dug into the earth to receive sacrifices." Bodocnos closed his eyes for a moment. "There are reasons for all things. The blood replenishes the earth, so in the dark season the carcass lies there. First the gods take their part, and then the bones are buried to restore the soil.

"When an animal was sacrificed, one of the wise would speak for the dead. They chose me. Their messages were . . . overwhelming."

"Did you see the future?" Emyn asked.

"I saw possibilities," the druid said sharply, and his tone forbade more questions. "At the time I thought I saw the future, but much of it did not come to pass."

Yet. Emyn wanted to say the word, but bit her lip instead.

"I was not alone in that temple. Having others with whom to share my visions relieved me greatly."

The sharp flap of a hundred wings startled them. A flock of waterfowl rose from a sandbar as one, turning and forming a double wedge in the sky. Now it was Bodocnos' turn to wait.

Emyn had not hesitated to speak before Diviciacos. Why withhold words from a wise man that would make better use of them? She realized that she held her breath and let it out slowly. "I allowed the spirits to take over my body."

"Why?" Bodocnos whispered.

"They had so much to tell Diviciacos, and I was in the way."

"Are you satisfied that this was right?"

Emyn nodded. "Diviciacos bent the words, but I know he heard them."

After another long silence, she said, "I didn't know that I would see things while the spirits talked. I was like a hawk, circling."

"What did you see, Gutumaros?"

Gutumaros . . . Death Speaker. Would Emyn have been given such a vision to keep to herself?

"The Morrigu told me, 'See what comes. You may not live long enough to see it again.'" Emyn swallowed hard, pushing back useless tears. "I hope I don't."

"A burden sits lighter on two shoulders than on one."

Iomat used to say that. Emyn took another deep breath. "I saw warfare and destruction spread across the plains, along the rivers, in valleys between hills, all the way to the sea. The great battle horns blew. Fear must have filled our enemies; the noise was terrible! But it was not enough. I saw the war; I saw the land afterward."

Emyn related all that she could remember. Details rose in her mind about emblems and helmets, and formations of Romans like lines in the dirt, waiting their turn to move forward. When the battles ended, the horns lay broken and crushed by wagon wheels. The victors collected weapons—not for the tribal gods, but to barter over, like traders in a marketplace. Most of the victors—but not all—wore Roman skirts and kept their hair short.

Emyn talked the day away. Bodocnos waved off the others each time someone approached, telling them to make camp.

Some of Emyn's memories sounded ridiculous to her ears as she voiced them: the felling of entire forests as the Romans moved through tribal territories, erecting towers and palisades; or the intervention of ancient kings, shielding the wounded from the spears of centurions when they could. She held no sight back; she told him all.

In the end, she cried out of relief.

Bodocnos hummed and patted her shoulder. As she quieted, he whispered, "Listen carefully. Can you?"

"Yes." Emyn sniffed, wiped her face, and looked around. The sun was lowering after a long day; the river and sand shone with bronze fire. "No more crying."

"Emyn, you will never be done crying. I've charted your course, and you know it yourself. The fifth day in the month of Gianon, twenty-one years ago. Did you think I would forget?" He sounded petulant.

"I don't think you ever forget anything, Master."

"Of course not. Listen. We are the sum of all our moments. When you consider the meaning of your life and what it has taught you, take all of it into account. Do not leave out a memory, no matter how bitter. If you do you will be lessened."

16

"Murderers!" Emyn's bones vibrated with the sound of screams.

"What happened?"

"They strike in darkness!" she shrieked. Near her, Romans stabbed at bodies on the ground.

"Strike at whom? Who strikes?"

The din quieted. Emyn pushed herself up then looked around. She was further away from the dead. The half-moon in the west reflected off a slow, wide river—not the Liger—separating two camps. A group on one side was under attack by skirted men wielding swords. In the distance, men on horseback ran down and trampled those who tried to escape. Barges tied near the riverbank were in flames; thick black smoke burned her eyes.

Familiar faces emerged from the darkness and the vision faded.

Emyn took a deep breath. "The Romans attacked a Helvetian clan as they slept."

"Now? This night?"

She nodded, listening to whispers. "The ghosts say the

Helvetians crossed the river on barges. One clan, this one clan alone, stayed behind. Everyone else crossed, over several days. Only these were left, all from the same region, many families. They were tired, so they waited till morning."

She choked and shook her head. The Helvetians had obeyed Caesar's order. With no strong leader to rally them, they left the borders of the Roman province. They did not want war, only fertile lands and pasture for their thinning stock.

"This is Rome's revenge," the dead king hissed.

Emyn sighed and wiped her eyes. "The ghost says they take revenge."

"For what?" asked Moradag.

"Caesar says they raid Aeduan land," Emyn cried, repeating the ghost's accusations. "All lies! You see Caesar's tactics. He lies; he makes up excuses to attack! He kills the weak, the stragglers."

"In the middle of the night?" She recognized Nonicos' voice.

"The Romans have no honor." In her mind she still saw the dead around her, curled on their sides with their blankets and furs askew. Some of the bodies were very small. "The clan was not defying Rome. They were sleeping."

The ghost began to list blood feuds and ancient battles. Emyn waved him away, and someone caught her arm.

"The Romans humiliate themselves in the darkness." Moradag's voice held an edge Emyn hadn't heard before. "A fine victory to boast of: sneaking up on the helpless while they sleep!"

"Do you see, Bodocnos?" Emyn covered her eyes. "They will wage war no matter what is done. There is no right course for any tribe."

EMYN AND HER COMPANIONS now walked a route south and west of Carnute lands. As the sun reached its high point that day,

Moradag's sharp eyes noted a group walking toward them on the road—a group that soon sorted itself into two druids, each with a young student and a slave in attendance. The time of the druid's gathering approached; these travelers were bound for Carnute lands.

Soon, everyone sat together in the shade, enjoying a meal that the slaves had prepared. Bodocnos told the other druids of Emyn's latest vision. The men were impressed.

"Caesar summons his pet Aeduan to his side," the dead king announced. His shadowy form circled the masters like a dog hoping for scraps. "He wants the promised food and grain."

Emyn repeated the words, and Bodocnos explained who the "pet Aeduan" was, and what he had promised to Caesar. There was more: far to the south, Diviciacos invented an elaborate pattern of excuses about where the grain was in order to stall the Romans. Emyn repeated every word.

From that day on, druids dotted the road, coming from every land and tribe. Some accents fell so strangely on her ears that Emyn couldn't decipher their questions—but the ghosts always understood and answered.

The longest day of the year would fall on a moonless night, and this, the druids said as they passed, boded well for their coming assembly. Plans made when the moon began to grow always flourished; even more so in conjunction with the solstice.

"THE HELVETIANS SEND AN ancient and honored warrior as envoy to Caesar. Caesar is too proud to listen."

Emyn spoke from the center of a crowded house, Bodocnos behind her. She sat on a wooden board balanced over the cold ashes of the firepit, now covered with a mat. The householder didn't need a fire in such warm weather; she cooked outside. Men had stacked bricks to support the board and Nonicos lifted Emyn up to sit on it so that all could see her.

She had described the night attack again. Bodocnos called for quiet several times as travelers jeered in disgust over Latin lies and cowardice. Now she repeated news passed on to her by the ghost earlier in the afternoon.

"The Roman soldiers strut and puff themselves up with pride as if—"

Emyn smiled wearily as Bodocnos raised his hand once more. Buckets of ale on a warm night did not help men's hearing. She could not be angry though; one of the visitors insisted on paying for her party's food and ale when he heard that Emyn would speak for the dead tonight.

"The Romans strut as if their actions are brave," she went on. The dead king whispered phrases in her ear. "The Helvetians send their envoy to Caesar: a hero of two generations past, who once defeated Roman soldiers in battle.

"But Romans are ignorant. They esteem no man for his years or his courage. Instead of treating him with respect, Caesar pretends offense and impugns the man's honesty." Emyn paused while the men shouted insults, then raised her voice, matching the dead king's tone.

"The ghosts tell me this. Caesar accuses the Helvetians of marauding through Aeduan lands. He declares, this Roman general, that he will oversee and judge their actions.

"He, speaking for Rome, will tell the tribes where they may walk or live. Not in Rome does he decide, but here, between the fruit trees that our grandmothers tended and the homes that our grandfathers built.

"Caesar decides who stays and who will be cast out! He, a trespasser himself in Aeduan territory, expects obedience. He demands hostages from the Helvetians."

"Hostages!" Several men shouted the word. Bodocnos stood again and there was quiet.

"The ancient warrior told Caesar that his people are more accustomed to taking hostages than surrendering them. He left the Roman fort, and the Helvetians have struck camp and departed."

Cheers erupted and cups were passed around. Bodocnos didn't bother to restore order; Emyn had told them all she could for tonight.

Men rose to wander outside or claim a place to sleep. Several stepped around the benches to thank Emyn for her words and set a coin or a token beside her. One woman, who wore a heavy serpent's egg carved from bloodstone, held out her hand. "Do you know what this is?"

"A healing stone." Emyn touched the pebble, well-rubbed but not polished. Iomat owned such a stone; Emyn had squeezed it the night Aumios was born.

"It is yours, then." She pulled open Emyn's palm and dropped the warm stone into it.

Stunned by the rare gift, Emyn tried to thank the woman, but she'd already turned away. Emyn caught a glimpse of a gray braid as she passed through the door.

Nonicos tapped her shoulder, his eyes wide. Seven coins lay in his hand—more than either of them had ever gathered together in their lives. More bronze coins rested on the board beside Emyn, along with two tin pins. Nonicos scooped them up and into a leather pouch. "There's food too. Moradag holds it. Mostly fruit and dried fish.

"Men were giving Bodocnos coins for you. Then they started putting coins in my hand as well." He helped her down and shook his head. "Emyn, when you were little, visitors gave Ater coins. He traded them for cloth or geese—whatever Iomat needed. I never thought about it much."

"The ghost has never had so many powerful men to address before," Emyn said.

"Sister, you could make a man rich." Nonicos let loose a laugh. "All this time I thought I'd be taking care of you! The world is a strange place."

"CAESAR'S CAVALRY IS IN DISARRAY; the Helvetians have routed them."

Two nights later, in a clearing under the stars, men cheered as Emyn described mounted warriors who spooked the Roman cavalry and sent them running from a Helvetian force only a tenth their size.

Dumnorix was the man responsible for that brief, dazzling triumph, Emyn announced. He led his warriors into a Roman scouting party, infiltrating Caesar's horsemen. This had not been hard; many of Caesar's best cavalry officers were southern Celts mixed with mercenaries from other lands. Dumnorix looked no different to them than any other Celtic commander. He tricked the Romans, leading them into an unwise attack against the Helvetians that scattered their forces.

All agreed that the Aeduan was a daring prince to think of such a plan.

"Anyone else would have charged up to Caesar's warriors and lost men doing it," said an older voice.

"He's a canny one. Like a fox."

"Fooled the Romans. They thought they followed their own centurions!"

"He should toss his brother out. Dumnorix was chosen to rule, after all. If his brother hadn't gone off to Rome—"

"Licking their feet—"

"Licking their Latin asses!"

More words were drowned in the rude laughter, the jangle of cups banging against each other, and feet stomping on the ground.

THE PLANKED ROAD WEST was raised to protect it from the Liger's frequent flooding. With so much traffic headed against them, Nonicos led the mule and cart off the main road whenever he saw decent pathways alongside. Today they walked a quarter league north of the main road.

Two nights and days had passed since Dumnorix' brave ride. Since that encounter the Romans followed the Helvetians like cowed but hungry dogs, not daring to venture close.

"Pear trees," Nonicos observed and Emyn inhaled deeply. Her brother waved to the druid. "Good resting place, Master?"

Bodocnos nodded. Nonicos unhitched the mule, then led Micco into the trees to search the branches for ripe fruit. Bodocnos started a fire and Moradag went for water. They'd fallen into a rhythm; all knew their tasks.

Emyn's cauldron boiled with fresh onions and cut turnips; there was dried salted pork as well, and stale bread warmed in the steam from the pot. All were gifts of the men who'd listened to her talk under the stars. When Nonicos and Micco returned with their arms full of wood and fruit, she quartered a cabbage and tossed that into the stew as well.

"Those paths," her brother said, pointing toward the trees where the mule munched half-rotted fruit. "You can't see the dirt for all the petals and leaves on the ground. Pears and cherries, just like home."

As they ate, the talk was of plants and weather: a peaceful respite from the words of the ghosts. Afterward, though, Emyn raised a question from the previous night that had been nagging at her: why *didn't* Dumnorix take over leadership of all the Aedui? As rightful king he was as popular as his brother within his tribe, and even more so with his neighbors. He commanded men and arms. The good of his people—

A ghost approached their dying cookfire and leaned against a red shield. It spoke in a sonorous voice. "Dumnorix walks along the edge of the waning moon."

"He does indeed. Your ghost is a poet," Bodocnos chuckled when Emyn repeated the words.

"Why a waning moon?" Nonicos asked.

"It grows thinner every night, disappearing beneath his feet." The druid's face drooped. "The Aedui are no longer a powerful tribe. They've suffered in war over the years and were further weakened when Diviciacos split the clans. A ruler protects his people, stands fast for them—but not Diviciacos. He trades favors for power. In his ignorance he trades with vipers.

"Why does Dumnorix not take his tribe back, you ask? His brother Diviciacos has sworn oaths with Rome. He had no right to do so, but in Rome's eyes the Aedui are bound. Dumnorix can't undo that. Rome is a dangerous friend when crossed, as other tribes have learned. Whatever he plans, Dumnorix battles time."

"Because the Romans now camp in tribal lands," Moradag said.

"Yes," Bodocnos agreed. "He walks along a waning moon. How long can he hold his balance?"

A light breeze ruffled their clothes. The ghost, who had been nodding as he listened, disappeared like mist in the sunshine.

"What is most intriguing to me is that Diviciacos calls his brother 'Dumnorix.'" The druid looked at Emyn. "Not Dumnocos, his old name, but Dumnorix. You said he did when you were at his camp."

"He did," Emyn nodded.

"Dumnorix is a king's name. The Romans use almost the same syllable for king: *rex*. So simply by naming him, Diviciacos acknowledges his brother's right to leadership. And by using Dumnorix' name, the Roman Caesar admits that he aids a usurper. Odd, isn't it?"

Emyn remembered the young prince who'd come to Samarnum years ago. He'd laughed heartily and held onto his wits before spirits and surprises. She liked him.

She imagined Dumnorix leading his horsemen into the Roman ranks, a fire in his pale eyes. She let her mind drift and pictured *herself* a warrior: riding fast through the wind and hollering until her throat wore out, feeling the strength in her arms and holding nothing back, nothing at all, so if she died there would be nothing left unspent.

No wonder men loved battle. In a fight for life or death, tomorrow didn't matter, and its problems didn't have to be solved. The victory was as simple as surviving . . . or waking in the land of promise.

"Dumnorix has caught Caesar's eye; he can no longer move in secrecy against Rome."

The dead king's news created a commotion as Emyn announced it at a house full of farmers and traders. Fewer druids passed Emyn and her group. The gathering of the wise would start in just a few days. Only local folks gathered around Emyn now—but just like the druids, they disagreed over whether the Romans could be trusted. All praised Dumnorix for his courage, however.

One stout, redheaded man proclaimed that allowing Rome to march through foreign lands—by which he meant lands not his own—was smart. "They'll keep things in order."

"In order?" a grandfather shouted. "By burning farms and turning tribesmen into slaves?"

"Not here! In the south—" The redheaded man glared at his neighbors as they jeered. "What's wrong with that? The farms would burn anyway; they're always squabbling over land in the south! Better that soldiers under the Roman eagle die for it, right? Instead of just those who speak our language."

Fists banged approval on tables. What were they applauding, Emyn wondered. Death?

The old man bristled and stood. "And just why is that better?"

"I think it's obvious. Do we care about their lives? Our own warriors—"

"Celtic warriors never fear death!" The old man spat. "Those Roman savages aren't even reborn. Their deaths mean nothing!"

"Exactly my point. Let them all die far away."

The argument wound on. Emyn sat on a cushion of bundled hay; she closed her eyes and leaned back against the wall. The hot room was full of drunken bravado, and she could not block it out.

These men talked, but knew nothing of warfare. They'd never ridden in a chariot like Dumnorix or carried swords. Emyn had seen and heard enough from ghosts to know that the glorious fights men dreamt of were rare. In a real battle the crowd here, armed with farm tools and knives, would be smashed like insects.

The thought of needless, violent death sickened her. She'd

had a son; once, she'd hoped to see him grow up. Why did men think that their lives—the end result of years of love and guidance —should be tossed aside whenever they saw a chance to show off?

Men were stupid; they could never know what it meant to carry a child! Anger spouted in her like a fountain. In Almer's house, Emyn had held her son so closely that she forgot they were no longer connected. Sometimes at night, even now, she was sure she felt Aumios moving inside her.

"Are you tired?" Nonicos' voice was close. "Do you want to lie down?"

Emyn turned towards the wall, and a draft brushed her face. "Men don't know what they're talking about," she muttered.

"Well," Nonicos pushed himself up and away from her. "This one learned a long time ago never to argue with a woman about that."

Some of the wisest men of their clan, now loud and sloppy with ale, sat in this room. They did what every man, even the poorest, did when he could do nothing else: they talked as if they were as strong and potent as they wished they were.

"**R**ome and the Helveti tribe will fight at last!" The harsh voice of the ghost thrummed with excitement. "The families of the Helvetian warriors travel with them. Both armies are vast. Many will die today."

"What is it?" Bodocnos asked, stopping with Emyn along the road.

"Caesar chose favorable ground—" the ghost continued without pause.

"Caesar chose favorable ground and will fight the Helveti tribe today," Emyn repeated.

The druid took her arm. "Do you see them?"

"No."

Nonicos' voice rose over the rest. "Ride on the cart, Emyn, before you walk into a tree."

The sun rose higher behind the group as they traveled west along an empty road. Emyn had just repeated to Bodocnos that she saw no visions when the sight of a hilltop covered with uncountable Roman soldiers struck her eyes without warning, as if the hill were before them and their road led to it. "There!"

She did not hear the druid but knew he must be near. She described the hill that the Romans held, and how the Helvetians crept up toward the Romans. "They lift their shields high over their bodies, forming one great shield to protect them all! They climb together, no one lags behind. The Romans cannot stand against them—"

"What do you know, foolish girl?" the dead king snapped.

"The Helvetian warriors do not weaken," Emyn insisted. "These are my words, I see them! The ghost mocks me but there are so many—"

A bellowed command split the air, then another. Thirty times thirty Roman javelins arced overhead in unison. Emyn expected them to glance off the shell that the Helvetian shields formed. Instead, the descending javelins pierced the shields, driving through them the length of a hand before crumpling.

She rose, as frustrated as the warriors, and hands yanked her back.

"The javelins bend!" Emyn called out. "They can't be pulled from the shields! The javelins pin shields together, two, three at a time, and dangle from them . . . they are as tall as men, these javelins. The warriors throw their shields down; they cannot use them."

Without shields covering them, Emyn saw that women as well as men stood armed for battle.

The site faded; the sun cast a shadow before her and the cart. Bodocnos sat beside her.

"Did you stop them?" she asked. "The ghosts, I mean?"

"I? Not while a battle rages," he said. "They released you of their own accord, leaving us to wonder why."

Were the ghosts weary? Emyn didn't know how visions worked, even though she'd had so many. Was her mind taken to another place while her body remained behind, or did the ghosts set a scene before her, like a mirror reflecting action elsewhere? Which way made more sense, and how exhausting would either method be for spirits? She had no answers.

"So the fight begins at last, and you felt the Helvetians had the advantage," Bodocons said, after a few minutes passed.

"I don't know. There were so many warriors," Emyn sighed. "The Helvetians looked strong, but the Romans forced them to throw down their shields. How will we know what happened next?"

"Either the ghosts will tell you, or we will hear in days to come as the news spreads." The druid pushed Emyn's head down and ducked his as well as they passed beneath low branches.

"I think you should ride today, just in case the spirits decide to show you more," he said. "I'll stay near. If they take you or tell you anything more, shout it out to me."

THE MULE WAS UNHITCHED, and the cart sat balanced on piles of rocks. Nonicos had already retrieved the bucket and a small fishing net and waded into the river.

Emyn hobbled to the river bank and splashed water on her face. Nonicos called to Micco, handing a full bucket to the boy and pointing him toward the student and a small fire.

The sun was high. Moradag poured water into the cauldron and cut up carrots, turnips, and an onion for the stew. No one spoke; it seemed that they all waited. Emyn was aware, as always, of the cheerful spirits tied to this place, but she heard no voices.

The druid stood by the stream, silent. What did he watch?

Bodocnos had a destination in mind for their group. The ancestors guided him; that was beyond question. She and the others fell silent when they saw the druid studying the stars or the morning flights of birds. Eddies in streams, the fall of the druid's rock onto the pile at a crossroads, the track water followed as it drained from their path, and even the patterns of clouds in the sky —all were interpreted by his watchful eyes.

Bodocnos could be sharp or kind, often intentionally funny —but he was a druid and no one pestered him. When the time was right, he would unveil his plan.

Now, he turned to her expectantly.

"Shall I ask?" she asked and Bodocnos nodded.

She muttered a question and a few prayer-like words to the dead king. He did not come, but other ghosts spoke up. They told her that the tide of battle turned often, that luck crested and receded as rivers did, that swords and axes sang like the strings of lyres as they split the air.

In short, they said nothing that couldn't be said of any fight. By the time Emyn and her friends had eaten, cleaned up, and attached the cart to the mule, she knew no more of the battle than she had that morning.

Only when they made their camp for the night and the sun lowered, turning the sky to gold, did the dead king return.

"The warriors are dead!" His shout startled Emyn. "Piled on the battlefield, while women and old men fight from their wagons."

Emyn called Bodocnos and began repeating what the ghost told her. "They stand atop their wagons and boxes to throw stones at the Romans."

"Is that all that's left?" the druid said sadly. "The old? No one else?"

"The dead cover the ground," Emyn said. "Many Helvetians escape, hoping to hide till darkness. The Romans do not pursue."

"They are weary with battle," the dead king added. "They have time to rest before pursuing."

Emyn moaned. She was grateful not to see the battlefield or the bodies; she knew no commander would simply let enemies escape.

"There will be slaves for Rome," the ghost hissed, and Emyn mouthed the words dutifully: "It is not the warriors who flee but families, children. The Romans think they cannot go far."

"So it is over," Bodocnos whispered.

"For many, yes," Emyn replied, then listened again. "The Romans have captives they will not kill. The ghost wishes me to see one. I will—"

"Hostages?" Moradag suggested.

"I know this woman!" Emyn sat up straight.

The princess had not changed much, nor had she dirtied her hands or dress in the fighting. A gold chain and green stones looped around her slender neck and bordered an expression Emyn had seen her wear before, on her wedding day. It asked clearly and without caring, "What now?"

"Run away!" Emyn shouted. Could the woman hear her? Emyn strained toward the image, hoping for action. The skirted men who guarded the princess were tired and already drinking to their victory. She had a chance. "Run!"

"She will not," sneered the dead king.

"To whom do you speak?" asked Bodocnos.

"The wife of Dumnorix," said Emyn. Why did this woman's eyes reflect no pride?

"You are dazzled," the dead king mocked. "What do fine bloodlines matter?"

"How could she let herself be captured?" Emyn shouted. "She is daughter and wife to kings!"

The woman's face twisted petulantly as she was pushed.

"Fight," Emyn hissed. The princess was young and quick. She could grab a weapon, spit, kick, anything. Her husband defied the Romans. Her lineage carried responsibilities.

She heard the druid's voice; had he been talking long? "Perhaps Dumnorix will ransom her."

One of the Roman commanders laughed and pulled the princess to him. Emyn didn't know their insignia, but this man's cloak was of a finer weave than the others. He stroked the princess, caressed her breasts, then moved his hand down between her legs. He spoke and the soldiers laughed. The princess looked up at the man who fondled her . . . and smiled.

"Enough!" Emyn closed her eyes and heard the druid chant. The ghosts were gone, along with their visions. Bodocnos looked at her and raised one eyebrow. What could she say?

"She should not have let herself be captured."

AT THE NEXT TOWN ALONG THE LIGER, Emyn listened while Bodocnos described the battle to a small crowd that stood beneath wide sycamore trees. Two men noticed Emyn as she sat in the shade. They smiled and spoke lightly, muttering their charm. She smiled back and drank when one offered her a cup.

Bodocnos glowered, the dead king pointed out. From the corner of her eye she saw that the ghost was right: the druid's face was rigid with disapproval. Micco rocked on his heels beside her as one fellow left to refill the cup.

"He keeps you for himself, the old man," the dead king taunted.

"Ridiculous," Emyn muttered.

The other man had been watching his friend; he turned back to Emyn. "What?"

"Nothing. Is it always so warm here in summer?"

"Is this warm to you?" The man winked at her.

"Very warm. Isn't it to you?"

"He hoards you," the ghost continued to hiss. "Like a treasure to ease his old age. Is that what you want?"

"You'll never go back to your cold land then, once you've spent a season here!" the man laughed. Beyond him, the druid pulled his friend aside and spoke. The fellow glanced at Emyn as if he expected her to spit blood and—with growing urgency—called the other's name several times.

Within heartbeats, Emyn was alone. She stood as Bodocnos came close. "What did you say to him?"

"You cannot hear the Morrigu's voice one day and smile and flirt with men on another." The druid met her stare. "I told him what you are."

Her blood turned cold. She was a woman; she would not let the druid name her otherwise! "And what would you know of that?"

"As much as any—"

"As much as a pig knows of weaving!"

She marched away, stabbing her stick into the ground and ignoring his calls to return.

Emyn had rarely been rude to a druid before, not since she was fifteen. She expected curses to follow. Words formed in her mind; she would curse him right back even if the gods struck her down for it!

As the trees slipped past and a gaggle of geese honked in alarm, Emyn kept walking. She closed her ears to the taunts of the dead king and perfected the curse she'd fling back at Bodocnos if he said a word more—one single, smug, dismissive, huffy word.

She walked and walked, sweating out the rage inside. It had been growing a long time. The druid held her fate, leading her through strange lands without offering explanations or hope, and she let him. She let him! She handed over not only her own life but Micco's and Nonicos' as well. She trusted him—but she was sick of trusting blindly.

Now the druid warned men away from Emyn as if she were a mean bitch that might bite. Well, maybe she would. A stitch in her side finally halted her and she doubled over, catching her breath.

Someone coughed behind her, waiting. Emyn wouldn't turn to acknowledge the person. She stared straight ahead. The blood still pounded in her throat; let someone else make the first move.

"Chiomara, are you angry with me as well?"

Moradag, of course. He would follow when the master said to, and she could not be mean to him. Emyn stared at the tree before her, its trunk hidden behind weeds and bushes. "I am angry, but not at you."

"Good. I could not bear your fierce glances." He waited a few moments more, but she did not turn. "My master's duty is to protect you. He intends no hurt."

"I do not need protection from men who are courteous!"

"Of course not—" the student began.

"What does he think then, telling those men . . . whatever he told them?"

"Can I know what he thinks?" She could hear the smile in Moradag's voice. "A druid does not explain himself, Chiomara. Certainly not to a lowly student like me. But I know absolutely that he does what is right, for your protection and to interpret the gods' wishes."

"I do what is right as well."

"No one doubts that."

"I am not his student or a child or witless like Micco! I won't be treated as if I were! And I won't be told who to talk to. The ghosts nag me day and night. They push me here and there until I say what they want. I know my duty inside and out! How . . ." Emyn rounded on the youth, and her voiced faded. Why should he have to listen to this tirade? What good would it do?

Emyn stomped her stick into the ground. "He should not have said anything to those men, that's all."

"Perhaps not. I cannot answer for him. He is used to students who must be watched and goaded, not to heroes like you." Moradag put his arm around her shoulder and hugged Emyn as if she were his dear friend. Maybe she was; who else did he have right now? "Can you forgive him for being blunt?"

Did her forgiveness matter at all to the druid? For Moradag's sake, Emyn muttered "yes," and embraced him.

A plant caught her eye as they turned to leave; a stalk that emerged from grass and yarrow at the foot of a rocky slope. Blue petals drooped from the stalk like a helmet made to fit a tiny head.

The plant stood as tall as she did. What did it smell like? Different plants grew in this warm land; would she need to learn a healer's skills all over again?

"No!" Moradag ran forward and blocked her arm as she reached. "This is poison, Chiomara. Even to touch—"

"Even to touch." Bodocnos echoed.

She turned too quickly and nearly fell.

The druid stood on the path behind Moradag. He narrowed his eyes at the stalk as if he faced an enemy. "It will paralyze you to your core so that your heart can't beat and your lungs won't draw air. The poison soaks right through your skin, seeping from every part: the flower, the root, the leaf. You've never seen such plants before?"

"No." Was he going to pretend nothing had happened, and that she'd just wandered away and stumbled across a new flower?

"Aconitum," Bodocnos continued. "At the temple in Coboneton we bought such lethal plants from a half-crazed merchant who harvested them in the south. I've met some healers who swear it is useful. Aconitum dulls pain, they say.

"I do not trust it. The same dose that spares one patient will kill another. It is the Morrigu's herb, and she is a trickster."

"What did you use it for in the temple?" Emyn asked.

"We didn't use aconitum." His brow arched as if offended. Emyn glared right back at him, and he took a deep, long breath. "We kept it, though. A tradition, I suppose. In the time of our ancestors when men were sacrificed there, the victim drank aconitum to numb himself to pain. I'm told any dosage will do if one is not concerned about recovering. And there is no antidote.

"The colors vary. Remember the shape." Bodocnos pivoted on one foot and walked away.

EMYN'S OUTBURST WAS NEVER MENTIONED.

The weather held fair and sunny. They slept under the stars and stopped at homes only to accept food in exchange for a druid's advice or words from local ancestors. At times Emyn wondered if they would walk until their shoes wore out, their clothes grew threadbare, or the mule died. Their shoes had already been replaced once, by leatherworkers in Carnute. Emyn's two shifts were dingy and worn. But the mule thrived, and so did Emyn and her companions.

They left the Liger and struck north along a smaller river,

skirting towns of the Namnete tribe. From here, Bodocnos told them, the land stretched northwest into a vast peninsula that reached toward Britain. It was called Aremorica, and each tribe on it counted the sea as a boundary.

"Will we see the ocean, Master?" Emyn asked.

"Undoubtedly. I lead you to a holy place very near the sea."

Nonicos whipped around, his eyes bright. Emyn was sure hers shone with curiosity as well. "A temple?"

"No." The druid smiled, inviting more questions.

"A grove?"

"A grove of stones. No, forests of stones! Hundreds, raised and set in rows by an ancient race. The stones stand as if ready to march toward the western sea. The site humbles all who visit, and my arts tell me to bring you there."

The druid took Emyn's stick and began to draw a circle in the dirt, leaving a bit of it open. "This is the great bay of the Veneti. The ocean is here." He tapped the ground outside the incomplete circle. "Inside the great bay is a smaller gulf. Smaller but wide enough. In that gulf, islands appear and disappear with the tide. From one bank, the opposite shore lies too distant for sight."

Emyn exchanged a puzzled look with Nonicos. She had never seen the sea or waters wider than the Liger. She supposed they'd understand the master's words when they arrived at this great bay.

"We are south and east of Aremorica." He tapped the ground several steps from the incomplete circle. "We will travel along inland rivers then west to the holy place. Beyond that, an arm of land stretches out into the sea embracing the bay."

Nonicos peered at the scratches. "Will there be farms there, so close to the sea?"

"Many, and great trading centers as well." The druid nodded, then looked up and beamed at Nonicos. "The journey has been long. You must ache to find a home."

Emyn had grown strong on this trip, though she still limped. The thought of living in a place permanently now seemed as strange to her as the idea of traveling had, months ago. Every road and glen rang with the voices of different spirits, pulling her attention away from aches and memories.

But the druid spoke to Nonicos, who stood like the trees. His roots needed to spread into soil.

"Veneti lands are rich," the master continued. "There are farms, yes, and pastures, but many villages are full of men who fish the seas. No one goes hungry. You will find work wherever you turn; skilled carpenters are in high demand.

"Gods ancient and unknowable bless the Veneti, but Dirona and Lugh watch over the land as well. And the sea—oh, the sea will creep into your prayers and your dreams!

"That is all I will tell you for now. You do not have to stay there. Perhaps I have clothed you in my own wanderlust, and you wish to explore the roads and forests of this land for as long as your legs will bear you." Bodocnos laughed and handed Emyn her stick. "See this place, though. Smell it, listen to the gulls. The gods guide us there for a purpose."

 18

Before another full month had passed, Emyn stood among the ancient stones raised by ancestors in the earliest days of the world. Just as the master said—just as he claimed *she* said though she didn't remember—rows and rows of them, marching to the sea.

The stones grew taller toward the west, but many had fallen. All sprouted from the heather as if they'd grown from seeds . . . rock seeds, producing a hardy rock crop. Did they guide souls from one world to the next?

Clouds as gray as the stones hung down from the sky, looking near enough to touch. The world throbbed with life here. Emyn could feel the ancient spirits.

A raven flapped and thumped onto the stone an arm's length from her. Its eye met Emyn's as if to challenge her. The others must be astounded; the raven was the Morrigu's messenger. But Emyn heard no voice. She stared stupidly at the black eye; it mocked her.

"GRAAAAK!"

The bird hopped and turned, fixing her with the other eye.

Nothing? it seemed to ask. Wasn't there a thought in her

head to be drawn out, like a worm from the ground?

"We are near the end of our journey." The words became true as they left her mouth and rang in the air.

Bodocnos' shadow fell on the next stone in line. He seemed suddenly frail, with much work before him. The words rushed out of her. "You are always welcome, always leaving, always beginning something new. Not every journey can be completed."

The raven spread its wings. Emyn stared beyond the stone at the spot where its eye had been, as if she could *see* emptiness.

After a long silence Bodocnos whispered, "Have you other guidance, Gutumaros?"

Guidance? She sensed the spirits like a field mouse sensed her when it darted across her path. She could no more guide men than that mouse could.

The druid took her arm and led her to the small fire Nonicos had started.

THEY CAMPED WITHIN SIGHT of the stones. Emyn dreamed of whispers that told her about grand and multicolored truths waiting just outside her reach. They were near the end of their journey, a good place to be.

The next morning Emyn, Nonicos, and Micco touched the ocean for the first time. The hiss and draw of waves were the sounds of her dreams, noises she couldn't identify though she'd been hearing them for a day and more.

It had never occurred to Emyn that the sea released a sound as regular as breathing. She wondered if birds heard heartbeats from the clouds as they moved through the sky.

They spent the morning wading on the beach, laughing as the sea sucked sand and rocks from beneath their feet. She didn't know it that day, but the taste of salt on her lips, the dampness in her bones, and the constant surge of water to shore would be part of her for the rest of her life.

Bodocnos threw back his head and laughed suddenly. "Lugnasad! Did you all forget that the great feast starts tonight?"

"Food!" Moradag lifted Emyn just as a small wave broke at their ankles.

Were they near the end of their journey? It felt more like a beginning.

THE BEAT OF DRUMS and the aroma of roasting pig led them to a nearby town. Only friends, not strangers, visited on Lugnasad. Although sundown was hours away, the dancing had already started. A pretty girl pulled Moradag into a circle while Micco clapped his hands and pealed "Ah," over and over.

Emyn stood with Micco and watched, until her brother took the boy off in search of food.

"Ariovistus."

The voice sounded close. Emyn looked around, though she knew no one stood behind her. The name was repeated. She shut her eyes, wondering what the ghosts planned for her now.

Foreign words followed, then a shout: "Caesar!" Emyn clenched her teeth; was this his voice? Someone translated: "I have heard that name before."

"—the most evil of men. He tortures women."

"—children—"

"Great general, he is a savage!"

"He raids our land!"

"He drinks the blood of his enemies out of a cup made from a skull."

"The skull of our ancestor, honored Caesar—"

Emyn grinned at the pretended indignation in the voices. Every king drank from a cup made of an ancestor's skull. Were the Romans ignorant of that?

Who spoke and where were they? Emyn had no way of knowing, but she should tell the druid. She wandered away from the dancing.

The path before her tumbled gently down to a cluster of houses. Bodocnos stood near the village well and waved his arms at someone on the road.

Through the trees came four men carrying a woman in an open litter. They stopped and carefully lowered their burden before Bodocnos. Emyn could not hear their words, but clearly the druid was busy. She would tell him about the voices later.

Damp pine trees scented the air as she walked along another path and strong breezes blew dust at her eyes. The sun broke through the clouds at last. Emyn stumbled into a clearing dappled with light that fell on handfuls of faces. An older man jumped up and caught her arm, then helped her sit on the ground. "Well! What paths have you traveled to come here?"

"From the east—" A cup was pressed into her hand.

"How far east?"

"Far. Almost as far as Cenabum," Emyn said.

Heads turned towards her and shouted questions. "You must have passed some of the druids. Any news from their gathering?"

"What about the Romans?"

"And the Helvetians? Is it true the Romans enslaved them all?"

"Not all—" Emyn tried to answer, but more questions came fast.

"What do they say about the Germani?"

"Are they still fighting?"

"They . . . ," Emyn tried to make sense of the weird voices she'd heard earlier. "Different tribes—Celtic tribes, the Aedui and others—beg Caesar to lead his army against the Germani."

"Caesar!" The old man chortled beside her. "Why doesn't he just go home?"

A woman handed Emyn bread dripping with honey. "What about prices?"

"Prices?" Emyn asked, and bit into the bread. Bits of leaves and dirt clung to it.

"How much is wine selling for in Cenabum?"

"Good wine," the old man clarified. "Not the watered juice the Romans drink." If people knew about Roman wine and customs, Emyn was not the only stranger to visit.

The dead king's voice sounded at her ear. "Caesar pursues Ariovistus."

Emyn swatted at the ghost. "I don't know the price of wine anywhere," she admitted, and the old man sighed.

"There is no wisdom left in this land," the dead king hissed. "Your past is glorious, but your future is dust!"

Two younger men emerged from the trees, took off their shirts, and began to wrestle. They were evenly matched and maybe equally drunk. Men and women called insults and encouragement as the wrestlers ducked, feinted, and grabbed at each other. Eventually, one fell badly and cradled his elbow as he sat up.

"Damn, that better not be broken!" The leathery man next to Emyn jumped up. "My grandson," he offered in explanation and was gone.

Another fellow strode forward to challenge the uninjured man. As he lifted his arm for a swig of ale, the sun sparkled off curls of hair on his chest. The crowd resumed its shouts as the two began circling.

A redheaded woman lit on the ground beside Emyn in a flutter of yellow and orange. Her clothes looked too fine to risk dirt and grass stains. Shouts pulled Emyn's eyes back to the match.

"Cheat!" the woman beside her bellowed, and others echoed the charge. A third man tore off his tunic and jumped into the contest. Emyn rose on her good knee to see better.

"I like watching half-naked men, too," the woman trilled. Her bracelets jingled as she leaned close to Emyn's ear. "But I prefer them less sweaty."

Emyn laughed out loud. The match became a melee, and Bodocnos appeared from nowhere. "Up! Before one of those louts crashes into you."

"But—" One hand was around her waist, the other on her arm. Bodocnos had a grip like iron. What had sparked his temper this time?

Emyn swung down to catch her stick as the woman stood up. She was tall, beautiful, and flashy like a whore. Was that what annoyed Bodocnos? Now that Emyn thought about it . . . had she ever seen the master look fondly at a pretty girl?

"I've been searching all over," the druid fussed, lifting and pushing her. "Watching men brawl, Emyn? What—"

"Why were you looking for me, Master?"

"Because no one could find you!" he sputtered, then pointed past trees to several thatch-topped buildings. "A noblewoman wishes to meet you. Don't keep her waiting any longer."

BODOCNOS LED EMYN DOWN the path to the houses she'd seen earlier. Pine trees lined the dirt road, and slaves had draped a sheet of canvas over branches to protect the lady Vinnia from the sun, which blazed behind her.

"Where are you from?" she said, before Bodocnos could finish a proper introduction. "I've just heard the most extraordinary stories about you."

The voice was sharp and demanding. Emyn could see nothing but a silhouette with active arms; this was much like facing a ghost. "A village on the Samar—"

"So you are Nervian, then?"

"My mother—" Emyn tried to answer.

"Do you eat raw meat?"

"No."

"Is it true that Nervians are descended from the Greeks of Sparta?"

Emyn had never heard that. She stared beyond the woman to a far hill as Bodocnos said, "Our Gutumaros was raised in a Belgic village, but she hears spirits in every land. In this place, the ancestors of the Veneti speak to her."

"My ancestors?"

"Assuredly." Bodocnos caught Emyn's eye. "Lady Vinnia is a niece of King Gundori, who lives on that island."

"Mad spirits rest there," the dead king observed.

"Has your family always lived there, lady?" Emyn asked.

"Oh, no. We are prominent all over the great bay." The woman's hands spread and waved to indicate directions. "My father owned many fields inland and six ships that sailed from Venetona. Have you been there?"

"Venetona? No—"

"No?" Her voice lifted in excitement. "Then I will invite the druids from Venetona to visit. The high king lives there; my father ate in his hall more than once. Promise me you'll let no one else on the island host you."

Emyn watched the hill beyond. She didn't need to listen; the dead king would answer the woman. He *wanted* more druids to hear his words.

Was that hill an island? She could see the blue ocean beyond it.

"Attend!" the dead king snapped as a gust flew into her face.

"I had three brothers. Two are lost to me." Vinnia sighed.

The dead king withdrew as other spirits interrupted, touching the woman's silhouette.

"The spirits say you are mistaken." Emyn straightened and tried to find Vinnia's eyes in the shadows. "Of your three brothers, only one is lost to you."

"What?"

"A man is near, closer than you can imagine. You will see him soon. Vael. His name is Vael."

Bodocnos' mouth dropped open, and an incomplete word escaped. The silhouette burst into loud sobs.

ONLY LATER, after Morodag had shown Emyn the house where they would spend the night, did Emyn see the island Bodocnos spoke of.

She and the student passed the well and the spot where Vinnia had stopped. Ahead of them, several footpaths converged, becoming a wider road that rose and crested as it led south. Vinnia's litter had swept along that route to disappear beyond the ridge. Now Bodocnos waved them forward to join him at the top of the ridge and look beyond.

Emyn gasped. To her eyes, the village bordered another realm, one built of myth. The sea spread out on either side of the road to break on sand and rock beaches. Directly before her, the road sloped slightly, and then ran straight out over the sea at least a quarter-league. What giants could have piled and leveled boulders that would stand above the waters?

If the road had risen into the sky it could not have astounded Emyn more. Truly, where the land ended and the sea began marked an entrance to nether worlds, as all the stories said.

The road spanned the sea between the shore and the hill Bodocnos had pointed to earlier—the hill where a king lived. Once across the sea, the road became a path again, winding up the green hill. Scattered homes with thatched roofs peeked from behind pine trees and shrubs.

So this was an island. Emyn had heard of islands where druids retreated to study, confer, and conduct their rituals without interference. "Is that . . . one of the isles of the wise?"

The druid laughed behind her, his humor restored. "Oh, no. Those are farther out to sea, farther than sight. No, before you lies the island of King Gundori, who rules this small corner of the bay. There—you see?—our noble Vinnia returns home."

A speck like a beetle crawled along the road toward the greenery on the island. "Will we stay a few days?" Emyn asked. "Vinnia said she'd invite druids from Venetona."

"Vinnia is a vain, silly woman. Do not rely on her intentions." Bodocnos spat, then looked around and lowered his voice. "Gundori grew rich taxing ships that prefer the safer waters here to those further east, inside the gulf. He calls himself a king, though he bows to the real Veneti king at Venetona. Gundori's predecessor was not so ambitious; his title was chief. Kingship owes more to wealth than destiny these days."

Emyn knew by now what the master thought of the responsibilities of kingship, and growing rich was not one of them.

"No druid lives on the island," Bodocnos went on. "King

Gundori fancies himself wise. When his advisor died a few years ago he sought no replacement."

Emyn frowned. To rule without the advice of the learned seemed as foolish to her as it must to Bodocnos.

"Now you know the politics of the land as well as I," Bodocnos growled. "In an hour the sea will rise to cover that road, and Gundori's little hill will truly be an island."

"How—"

"The tides rise and fall with the moon. Stay and watch, if you wish."

"No, Chiomara," Moradag grinned. "The tides rise and fall every day. Let's go back to the music."

THE SUN SET IN A FIERY GLOW, streaked here and there with drifting gray clouds. For long minutes the clouds darkened to black shadows, and the entire world was bathed in orange.

Near the musicians, Micco slept at Emyn's feet as she rested on a bale of hay. Smudges of grease and dirt stuck to his chin.

The players set down their drums and strings as the dancers drifted away. One of the men bent near her to fetch the leather bag that fitted over his lyre. He grinned and nodded. "Look."

She turned. On a bare patch of dirt, Nonicos faced a tall, slender woman. He held both her hands up in the air and twirled her slowly in a circle. Emyn had never seen Nonicos dance before. His face passed between shadows and the last rays of sunlight as he turned with the woman, eyes fixed on hers.

When the light vanished, Emyn shook Micco awake and walked him back to the fire pits and the feast.

The signs were clear enough for her. The journey was over.

 **19**

Days later, Emyn saw the woman who had cried "Cheat!" at the wrestling match. She stood in the doorway of the house where Emyn and her family slept. The morning sun struck her hair like a copper helmet and outlined her figure through a finely-woven robe.

Two men approached the woman, but she stepped aside. Her bracelets jingled as she waved the men through the door.

Definitely, a whore. The woman posed her body the way a merchant exhibited his best wares: catching the light, drawing the eye to their beauty, angling for the highest price.

She looked directly at Emyn. "My name is Aruca. Come talk to me."

Emyn picked up her stick and walked outside, bracing herself for the wind.

"The old teacher and his student have left you," Aruca stated.

"He continues his travels, but we decided to stay," Emyn said. "We need a home."

"Your brother has found one, I think." The sun glittered off Aruca's bracelets as she pointed to the well, where Nonicos filled a bucket for the tall woman he'd danced with at Lugnasad. "Have you?"

"I do not seek the same comfort as my brother."

"No? Not even in your secret prayers?" Aruca's green eyes teased, but Emyn kept silent. She had few enough secrets; she'd have none if she answered every question asked of her.

The woman lifted Emyn's chin with her finger and frowned. "Why do you wear such a ragged dress?"

"We have been traveling. There hasn't been time—"

"Take time."

Emyn looked down; her dress had been the color of honey when she left Samarnum. Now it looked like the dirt.

"You are the Death Speaker, aren't you? Who knows what lofty audience you might face. You will embarrass us all, dressed like a beggar. Do you know Haebro?"

Haebro owned the alehouse, Emyn remembered. "I've heard his name."

"I am there most evenings. He does not thin his stew with water like *that* woman." She shot a glance at Emyn's house and wrinkled her nose. "Come visit me, but get a decent dress first."

Aruca turned and walked away. Her clothes were nearly as bright as her hair. They clung to her curves in a way that suggested nakedness more than bare skin would.

Why would she seek out Emyn's company? Maybe Aruca had heard that Emyn was a healer. She might need the seeds Emyn had once ground for Cesua. Pregnancy would ruin that beautiful figure.

A group of children clustered near a shed and pointed at Emyn, giggling. Aruca was right: she looked like a beggar, and there was no good reason for it. She had coins; the householder could tell her where to buy.

* * *

"THERE WERE TWO OF THEM, two pins." The older woman touched an enameled pin that spanned Emyn's palm. "She said they were too heavy for a dress. She used them to pin her cloak. Guess she was wearing the other one when she ran off."

The woman's eyes were red-rimmed; losing a grown child must be as hard as losing a little one.

"Keep this—" Emyn offered.

The woman sighed and curled Emyn's fingers over the pin. "No, take it. Does me no good." She nodded at the coins on the stool. "You paid a fair price. Take it."

Emyn wondered what was fair about cold metal, but the pin rested in her hand and the clothes were already bundled. She scooped them up with her left arm, feeling more like a thief then a visitor. "I should go while the sun is out."

"Her daughter's bones whiten in the pit," the dead king said. "She will not return."

Emyn shouldered the door open before the woman saw her face. What good would it do to tell *that* to the mother?

Micco jumped up and followed Emyn down the path back to the village.

SUTTIA, THE HOUSEHOLDER, had been the right person to ask about finding clothes. The woman knew everyone's business; Emyn could imagine the tales Suttia told about *her*. On her first night, the woman had watched Emyn undress and asked about the scar on her breast. "What happened? Your husband do that? No wonder you left him!"

Emyn checked to make sure the last coin was still tucked into her belt. Suttia had told her how much to bring and how to bargain. "Don't offer," she'd said. "Let *her* name a price."

Many coins remained in their bag; there would be more when Nonicos sold the cart and mule. How long would it last? Emyn was unused to pricing her needs and paying with coins. In Samarnum—

"Micco, carry this." She handed him the bundle of clothes and stretched her arms.

The Morrigu had led them here; fretting over money was unworthy. If the gods were watching over them they would thrive. If not, nothing would save them.

Comfrey, mint, pansies, berries, and handfuls of other plants peeked at her from behind bushes and ferns. She even saw the knee-high clusters of dead, white flowers as tiny as gnats, bending with the breezes. Aruca might not be the only woman who wished to avoid pregnancy; Emyn should collect those seeds while she could. Maybe Suttia would loan her a basket so she could start earning her place by the fire.

The dead king interrupted her thoughts with harsh tones. "Ariovistus taunts Caesar."

By now, Emyn knew Ariovistus led both Celtic warriors and the Germani who had crossed the great river years ago. "What does Ariovistus say?" she asked softly.

"He tells Caesar that he will not run to him like a dog that has been called. If Caesar has anything to say, *he* should come to Ariovistus."

"That is bold." Emyn smiled at Micco. The boy's steps faltered as he watched her.

"They mock each other. Soon they will fight. Who will hear?"

Emyn shrugged. Caesar seemed distant here; she didn't care about his boasting. Having conquered the Helveti, was he still a threat to other tribes?

"I will not be ignored!"

The ghost whipped up dust. Emyn pulled Micco to a fallen log and told him to shut his eyes as she hummed one of her grandfather's songs. It calmed Micco even if it didn't silence the dead king, not at first. Eventually, though—

"Lady Gutumaros?"

Emyn's eyes opened; two teenage girls stood in front of her.

"Please do not be angry," one said.

"Suttia told us where you went—"

"We need to talk to you."

"*Alone.*"

"Please don't tell anyone!"

Micco slipped from Emyn's arm to cower behind her.

She tried to raise a single eyebrow as Bodocnos did. "Don't tell anyone what?"

"We want . . ."

"There is a man." The girls looked at each other.

"Only one?" Emyn asked, and bit into her lip to keep from smiling. Love potions. As sure as Lugh brought the sun each morning, girls would dare anything for a love potion.

"Well . . . there's a boy, too."

"He'll be a man next spring!"

"Indeed? On what date, exactly?" Emyn committed to memory the birthdays of the girls and the fellows they hungered after. She would figure the stars later and pick her words carefully when they all met again.

The ghost stopped complaining as the girls voiced their half-thought wishes, begged, and squeezed each others' hands for courage. "If you could just make him look, that's all. Just once, to give us a start."

"And what will you give for such secret charms?" Emyn queried in a low voice.

"Give?"

"Pay," Emyn said.

"Oh."

"We don't have coins."

"I have pins—"

"A leather belt?"

"A basket," Emyn decided. She fixed her eyes on the pair; not a hint of amusement crossed her face. "And a spindle. In three days' time."

She watched the girls scamper away, then rose and stepped back onto the path with Micco.

Love potions. She had probably brewed one for every girl in Samarnum, once . . . except herself.

Never herself; there was only one fellow that she'd wanted badly enough to use a love potion. But Rialos had vanished so quickly that there wasn't time.

Emyn had come close to asking Bodocnos about Rialos many times. The words would shrivel in her mouth until the druid scowled or walked away, or talked about something else.

In the end, she decided it didn't matter. What could Bodocnos tell her anyway? That Rialos kissed girls in thirty times thirty villages? That he married? That he didn't?

Did it matter?

EYES TURNED AS EMYN entered the alehouse. She held the door open while she scanned the room, then let it shut, throwing all into firelit shadows.

Aruca sat next to a low table and leaned against the wall. As Emyn approached in her new blue skirt and shawl, the whore nodded. "Better."

Emyn grinned and lowered herself to a bench on the opposite side of the table. A large man set a cup of ale before them; Aruca called him Haebro. Emyn nodded her thanks before taking a gulp.

"Ah, so you drink. I heard you were Nervian."

"My mother was Nervian, but it's only wine they despise."

"The enfeebling liquor of Rome?" Aruca laughed.

"Rome." Emyn pronounced the word with distaste. Before she could say more, the bench jumped. A man sat down heavily on the wrong side of the leg and the bench flipped up.

Emyn slid, crashing into the man as they both fell.

A woman screeched; others laughed. Emyn tried to push herself up. Only one arm found the floor; the other pushed against the man's chest. With a loud yelp he shoved back, and her shoulder hit the floor.

Her entire side burned, and a hand snuck around her breast for a squeeze. Where did that come from? Emyn saw an arm before her eyes, heavily muscled, with a polished metal band circling it.

Fury sharpened her mind. She would not be made an invalid again because of this drunk! She pulled the knife out of his belt and had the point at his throat before anyone could stop her.

"Honey, don't. . . . It was an accident, I swear. Don't get excited—" He smiled and grabbed at her arm but she scooted away.

Now the knife was aimed at his groin. Was he still smiling?

"Maybe I'll slip and have an accident too," she growled. Sweat broke out on her forehead; she could not shift her weight from the side that burned.

"Emyn." Aruca's voice was calm. "Emyn, tell me: can you stand?"

"No." She didn't move the knife. "I can't get up."

"Haebro!"

"We'll help you, woman," a man said. "Haebro, on the other side. When I count to three, we both lift. One—"

"My hip," Emyn moaned.

"We've got your arms. Hold them stiff. Two . . . three."

Aruca counted with him and the room shifted dizzily. "Don't let her go!"

Both men kept a firm grip under her arms. Emyn put her weight on her good leg and gingerly moved the left. It hurt, but not too badly.

Her breathing slowed; the pain faded. Both men still held her; she nodded to Haebro and slipped her arm away. Her stick was pushed into her hand. When she felt balanced, the other man let go.

She stood on her own. Bruised, maybe, but not broken. "Thank you."

The men nodded. Eyes turned away and a few voices resumed conversation. Haebro set the bench back in place then stood by fretfully as Emyn sat.

A minute later the drunken man leaned heavily on the table and asked for his knife back, calling her "honey" once more.

Emyn stared at his armband, a warrior's prize. How had he won that? He was too stupid to be carrying a knife, let alone a sword.

She stabbed the blade into the table, barely missing his thumb. Aruca laughed as he jumped back.

"The knife is mine." Emyn looked up. "If my hip still hurts tomorrow, I'll come back and slice a piece of you off with it. If you want to argue, I can do that now."

The man blanched, then reddened and turned away. A few seconds later the door banged shut.

Emyn looked up at Haebro, still hovering over her. "I suppose by tomorrow every man near this village will know to stay away from me."

"More likely within the hour," Haebro sighed.

"We're not a very large place." Aruca pushed the cup towards Emyn. Half the ale had slopped out and over the table, but Emyn drank deeply as Aruca signaled for another cup.

"WHY WOULD YOU GO to an alehouse?" Nonicos groaned and shook his head.

"I wanted ale."

"You could have gone with me."

"I live here. I want to visit and walk around without fear."

Her brother sighed; he had come outside to look for her just as she left Haebro's. "No gods to protect us; no wonder this happened."

Nonicos was greatly bothered that homes here had none of the wooden statues he and Emyn had honored in Samarnum, and he blamed every problem on their lack. "We need our ancestors, and they need a place to rest."

He held Suttia's door open for her. They moved slowly through the gloom; most of the lodgers were already asleep. "I'm going to carve us a little god when the sun rises," he whispered. "To preserve us from gossip, if nothing else."

"That's good. Maybe it'll protect me from drunks."

Her brother grunted and fell onto his mattress next to Micco. Emyn shuffled to the other side of the fire by Suttia and the children, pulled off her shoes, and looked around.

She never had to wonder if her ancestors were watching. She felt their presence everywhere—even at this far border of the world. This was a strange land though; she'd take a friend wherever she could find one.

"Enjoy it while you can," Suttia said of the sunny and cloudless day. "Never more than a handful of such skies each year, I swear."

Emyn turned away before rolling her eyes. She'd already seen more such skies in the weeks since arriving but Suttia was the type to remember dark days, not sunny ones.

A wagon rolled along the road from King Gundori's island, and Emyn ambled down the path where it would be forced to pass her. Maybe the cart's driver would tell her some news of the island.

"Caesar pursues Ariovistus to Vesontio," the dead king announced.

"Why?" Vesontio was the great city of the Sequani. What had that tribe to do with Romans or Germani?

Ariovistus led the marauders that had been asked, years ago, to cross the Rhenus and fight for the Sequani—but he no longer honored ties with his old allies. Still for Ariovistus and Caesar to chase each other into Sequani territory seemed foolish.

"Vesontio crowns a rich land; it has much to offer hungry armies."

"They go to pillage?" Emyn glanced around; no one was near.

"They . . . secure provisions."

"From Vesontio?"

"They race to Vesontio. Whoever gets there first can hold the other off for months, perhaps even through the winter." The dead king was barely visible, a shadow in a patch of sunshine.

"They would fight the Sequani as well as each other?"

"Fight?" the ghost said impatiently. "Pay attention. They do not fight the Sequani!"

"How can they not?" Emyn hissed; the empty wagon she'd seen had nearly crossed to the shore. "The Sequani will protect their city! If the Romans and Germani race each other to Vesontio, won't the Sequani close their gates and keep both out?"

"The Sequani do not fight. They will stand with the victor." The ghost let out his ugly laugh. "Woe to the vanquished!"

Emyn shuddered in spite of the warm sun. Those were the words spoken in ages past when Celtic warriors sacked the city of Rome. Every child knew the story and its lesson: *Woe to the vanquished!*

She would sooner die than hear those words from an enemy's lips.

The creaking wagon stopped before her. A large woman with a gray braid sat atop it. "I know most folks here except for the oracle," she called. "Is that you?"

WITHIN MINUTES, Emyn had tossed her new basket into the back of the wagon and climbed up next to Darsa, who said she'd be glad of company.

"To the farms," the woman said with a snort when Emyn asked where she was going. "I collect taxes."

She burst into laughter at Emyn's shocked face. "I cook for the

Lady Vinnia. She owns the farmland." Darsa waved her arm to the north. "I ride out for food every few days. Eggs, vegetables . . . I call that paying a tax, but I'm just a cook." Darsa yanked on the reins, pulling the horses from the main road onto a smaller path. "I collect taxes, and you battle men in alehouses."

Emyn groaned. "How did you know that?"

"Oh, men talk. Men talk worse than women."

That was true enough; the dead king was the most gossipy creature in this world or his. "Did the lady tell you to look for me?"

Darsa nodded. "She's invited the druids of Venetona to visit and wants you to meet any who come. She'll send for you when they arrive."

"I am honored."

"I don't know what day or who she'll send for you, but it won't be me. I'll have my hands full. A druid's visit," Darsa shook her head. "I'll be busy, no doubt of that."

Darsa liked to talk, but didn't ask questions. As the wagon rolled inland, she rattled off the farmholders' names and the crops they grew, described the work waiting for her at Vinnia's home and the duties of the slaves and servants there. Emyn supposed she spoke to herself when she was alone.

They visited two farms, collecting eggs, sacks of wheat and millet, baskets of vegetables and fruit, and an assortment of brown, white, and yellow mushrooms. In one house, Emyn passed on words from a loved grandfather and was rewarded with a block of cheese as well.

No wonder Darsa drove two horses: when the sun was high, a much heavier wagon returned to the village. From the rise near the shoreline, Emyn looked out over the waves and whitecaps till they blurred into blue all the way to the horizon. Dark rocks poked above the water in spots. "Do people live on those far islands?"

"Not on most of them, no. Most, the land disappears when the sea rises." Darsa studied the road as it stretched beyond the shore. "Nothing lives there but moss. There's one island that has a fortress and stocks of food—or it used to. I remember going there when I was a little girl, and the Namnete threatened to attack. Nothing came of it, though."

"Are the Namnete and Veneti at peace now?"

"Who knows? Ask a druid when you see one." The woman set aside the reins and hopped off the wagon; her strength belied the gray hair. She kept talking as she walked round the horses to stand below Emyn and help her down. "We are on good terms with most tribes, even those out to sea. The large island, Britain—we trade metal with them. But the Namnete . . . there's always been fighting back and forth over the salt fields or the river ports. Nothing too serious.

"But you know, things can change. Just like that." Darsa snapped her fingers. "A new chief, a greedy one, or a small insult. Anyone might say, 'Those Veneti are getting rich and lazy. Why shouldn't we take a share of the wealth?'"

Darsa laughed to herself as she reached into the wagon for Emyn's basket and cheese, then shrugged and picked out a few of the vegetables for her as well. "Oh, we think things will never change, don't we? And that's just when the worst happens. But the gods, they bring what they bring."

Iomat used to say that. Emyn called to two children and loaded their arms with food as Darsa urged the horses onto the road; the sea was already rising.

The next day, Emyn jumped as the dead king announced, "Dumnorix resorts to sorcery against the Romans."

She walked alone on a path overlooking the shore. "What kind of sorcery?"

"Rituals of blood."

The news chilled her. She hobbled over to a moss-stained stone and leaned against it as the wind whipped her hair across her face.

The dead king's voice was full of delight. "His messengers seek supporters in all lands."

"Even this one?" she asked.

"All lands."

Since arriving here at the end of the earth, Emyn felt far from Caesar and his conflicts. But if Dumnorix threw himself into the Roman's path again, the confrontation touched her in a personal way. She had met the prince and looked into his eyes; she knew his secrets.

She hurried home and fetched the large enameled pin that she'd bought along with her clothes. A few days before, Nonicos had pointed out a spring hidden by thick ferns. "This is where the secret mother of this land rests," he had whispered reverently. "I didn't dare ask her name. Not yet."

Emyn didn't need her name; "Mother" would do. She whispered her prayers before the spring, then parted the ferns and dropped the pin into the water. "This is beautiful. This is for you. Add your strength to the ancestors of Dumnorix. He fights for all of us."

NONICOS TOOK EMYN TO the alehouse that evening, after settling Micco to sleep near his favorite dog. The pair nodded to Haebro and sat on a low bench, next to the shelves holding stacked cups and bowls.

Emyn spotted Aruca standing with two men across the firepit and lifted her hand in greeting. Nonicos turned to look.

"Tell me something," he began, but grew tongue-tied. Haebro put a cup on the bench between them, and Nonicos gulped ale.

Emyn waited. Was he finally ready to talk about Laurina? It hadn't been difficult to learn the woman's name. Everyone noticed that Nonicos waited at the well each morning to draw water for the woman while a little girl with the same chestnut hair clung to her skirts.

Two other women had whispered questions to Emyn about her tall brother. They'd noticed his strong arms and large blue eyes, his neat moustache. Laurina had better not keep him waiting. "What is it?"

"How do you know a ghost from a real person?"

Emyn gaped at him.

He fumbled for words. "When you were younger, you thought the ghosts were real."

"Little girls are easy to fool." She shook her head. "What do you want to talk about, really?"

"The ghosts. Tell me."

She shrugged and looked up at the rafters where so many spirits watched. "The dead are like smoke or firelight. Sometimes they look real, but not often. Their voices sound alive, though."

"What about the strong ones?"

"Like the dead king? I always know him, but he is shadowy too."

"The visions look real, though. The battles? I remember you broke your tooth once running from one."

Emyn grimaced; she had run from crucified corpses that day. "The visions are very real. If I had one now, I wouldn't even see you. The noises, the smell—everything changes."

Haebro pulled up a wide stool and sat with them, exchanging a look with Nonicos that implied agreement. Emyn looked from one man to the other, then glanced around the gloomy room. How many of these customers had been here when she sat with Aruca? Was she about to be scolded?

"What is wrong?" Emyn demanded, readying herself to argue. She would not apologize for defending herself!

"We need to explain," Nonicos began, and at the same time Haebro muttered, "You don't know this place—"

"Should I not come here?" Emyn blurted. "Is that what you're trying to tell me?"

"No!" Haebro's face fell, and he looked beseechingly at Nonicos.

"It's—it's who you talked to," her brother faltered.

"Aruca?" Emyn asked. Had she shamed them by sitting with her?

"Sometimes I see her too," Haebro smiled a little. "But no one else does."

His words echoed like the crack of thunder on a sunny day.

Nonicos spoke again. "Emyn, several people talked to me about what happened. They all thought it was pretty funny, you chasing off that loudmouthed fool. Just like you described—except no one mentioned another woman with you, even when I asked." He took a deep breath. "So I came in to meet Haebro, and we talked."

"We did," Haebro agreed, and a long silence fell again.

"Ask her," Nonicos prodded.

Haebro took a swallow of ale before voicing his question. "What does she look like?"

"Aruca?"

Haebro flinched when Emyn said the name.

"She has beautiful red hair, loose—not braided." Emyn looked across the firepit; the men were alone now. "She wears bracelets—"

"Little bracelets or wide ones?"

"Little ones, lots of them. Tin and bronze. They jingle."

Haebro stood abruptly and leaned against the wall beside them. His shoulders shook.

Nonicos let his breath out slowly. "I think she may be a ghost, Emyn. Haebro knew a woman named Aruca, but she disappeared last winter. He said she used to come in for a meal every day."

Emyn shut her eyes and heard the soft tones of metal rings shaking and clinking together.

"She lived here for awhile," Haebro muttered. "In back, in her own room . . . ." He turned and shuffled away.

"Poor Haebro," Aruca whispered. "He aches still."

"Haebro said you talked to yourself that night." Nonicos' voice was no louder than Aruca's. "You're used to ghosts. I know they don't scare you but . . . maybe this one fooled you."

Emyn's mouth was dry; she picked up the cup. A hand—a small hand, a woman's hand, squeezed her shoulder. It was warm.

It was real.

 **21**

Sea breezes swept the island, but the air in Vinnia's crowded house was thick and close.

A round, rouged face hovered over Emyn and squealed. "Did the Germans cut off your braid? Animals!" The plump woman turned from Emyn to Vinnia. "You didn't tell us that!"

Emyn tucked her loose hair behind her ear. Nothing, not even a veil, could hide the fact that it was still too short to pull into a braid.

"It caught fire," she began, but no one heard. Trying to explain anything to this noisy gaggle was useless. She just hoped they would not start wailing again.

"I could hardly tell you anything with all the excitement!" Vinnia fanned herself, and then motioned for a slave to take over. Several women spoke at the same time, their voices drowning out each other.

That morning a freckled youth in a slave's tunic had fetched Emyn and given her the news: one druid had responded to Lady Vinnia's invitation to come and meet her new oracle. Not the chief druid in Venetona, to be sure. That great man, the highest Master of the Veneti, did not come.

Emyn had hurried into the longhouse and thrown on the best of her clothes, the deep blue skirt and matching shawl, while the slave waited. "Who visits, then?" she asked as he helped her into the wagon.

"That question has many answers, honored guest," the slave replied with a smile. He told her that a young druid had arrived without announcement and without attendants, walking alone over the sea road. Still, he was an Honored Master so Lady Vinnia had greeted him with a cup and platter of summer fruit as slaves knelt to wash his hands and feet. After he was cleaned, the druid rose to kiss Vinnia's cheek and whisper in her ear.

"Then the lady cried out and collapsed into his arms, and tears of joy fell from her eyes!" The slave paused then dropped his voice to a whisper. "This druid, Vinnia announced with sweet sobs between her words, was none other than her younger brother, Vael, whom she had believed dead for three times five years and more."

The island's wealthy merchants and nobility came to celebrate. The slave mimicked Darsa, barking orders and dispatching slaves for more provisions. Then he grew solemn. "You are the most desired guest, honored oracle. Our dear lady says you prophesied this meeting weeks ago."

Emyn nodded; the freckled slave was adept at drama and flattery. How did slaves come by their learning?

By now they had crossed the sea road, and she heard no ghosts at all. The ocean lapped at the surface of the road and would soon cover it, keeping Emyn on the island for hours.

Vinnia's home, inside and out, seemed busy as a beehive. As Emyn walked through the doorway, a noise like a barnyard surrounded her. Some of the voices came from spirits, grating against Emyn's ears. The dead king had warned her that island-bound ghosts would spout only nonsense. She didn't believe him—how would he know? But it seemed that once again, he was right. Sorting out the sounds of living from the dead would not be easy.

Another woman entered the house to embrace Vinnia and meet Emyn. "You!" The newcomer took both Emyn's hands. "You're the oracle who foresaw all of this!"

"She won't see your ancestors here," the plump lady announced as slaves rearranged cushions to make room for the new guest. "The ghosts don't talk to her."

"Oh, no! Why not?"

Emyn smiled. "Spirits surrounded by water have no knowledge, lady. These are not your ancestors, only mad ghosts."

"The oracle lives in the village." A jeweled hand pointed in that direction.

"We'll have to visit her there."

"We can go together, you and I."

The women built plans, and their voices faded like the seagull cries outside. Ghosts clustered in corners, useless and deserving of the dead king's scorn. Some hissed obscenities; none were very strong.

The new arrival, wearing a yellow dress as bright as broom flowers, turned to Vinnia. "Is your brother the man talking with Lorsus and the other merchants?"

"I suppose," Vinnia said. "He's outside with them."

"My oldest son knows him!" Yellow wool twirled as the woman grabbed Vinnia's arm. "He says your brother won a horse race against an Irish druid last spring."

"Are you sure?"

"My son won a silver buckle, thanks to him!"

"Druids racing?" a woman giggled. "Who would bet against them?"

"But he was always rather wild, wasn't he, dear?" The last woman to address Vinnia wore a checked dress. Emyn forgot their names, and the ghosts weren't there to remind her.

She had not yet met the honored master Vael, but she envied him the fresh, salty air he enjoyed outside. This large house was dark, the brightest light coming from Darsa's cookfire. The scents of ten heavily oiled women and the smells of fish and vinegar mixed into a sickening brew.

A slave set two buckets on the ground near Darsa's feet, where she stood tending a large cauldron. Emyn jumped when water splashed out of one bucket, but Darsa ignored it. The slave used sticks to pull a giant insect from the steaming cauldron.

". . . his mother's blood," Vinnia was saying and the other women sighed in sympathy. "A slave, a dancing girl. What could we expect?"

"A slave?" the youngest in the group asked.

"Oh, my dear, you didn't know?" Vinnia sat up straight, wiped her eyes, and cleared her throat. "It was one of the savages, snatched right out of the forest!" She dropped her voice, "I hear men *like* such woman at times. My own mother had died, but still . . . we were mortified that Father took up with such a vulgar female."

"How awful for you, dear Vinnia."

The boiled bug was longer than Emyn's hand. She stared as another was lifted out; surely no one here ate bugs! Darsa dropped two more wiggling, clawed, antennaed creatures into the pot. They came out of the buckets, so they must be sea insects.

". . . and when her child—my brother—was no more than three she killed herself. Dreadful. Just cut open her veins and bled to death one night. . . ."

Which was worse, the story Vinnia recited or the battle going on behind her? Two muscular slaves now whacked and poked and twisted the wet, steaming things, breaking away armor and extracting strips of fatty meat from backs and limbs, then they cracked open the large, curved claws with metal tools.

"She was pregnant, too—did I say that already? Killed herself and her unborn child."

"How horrible!"

"What did you do?"

A different slave with an undirtied tunic offered a platter of insect meat to Vinnia, and she plopped several strips into her mouth. "I was already married and living here, so of course it was left to my brothers to handle. *My* mother's sons." Vinnia wiped her hands and waved the platter away. "That little whore unmanned my father! I can never forgive her. Never."

"Of course not!"

"Poor Vinnia."

Although no one looked at her, Emyn forced her face to appear sadder than she felt. Whatever quarrel had separated Vinnia from her half-brother, her sympathies were with the Honored Master Vael.

The slave pushed the platter in front of Emyn, and she shook her head, trying not to inhale.

"But I miscarried a child, and then another—"

Vinnia broke down into loud sobs, and a blur of blue, yellow, striped, and checked dresses threw their arms around her, offering solace and sharing her grief. Ghosts clustered around them too, their voices equally shrill:

"She sleeps with her slaves, you know."

"The handsome ones."

"They tell her she's pretty—"

"If they're smart."

"Or they're sold away!"

Emyn shivered. Flickering lights continued to dance around.

"She'd let you lie with one."

"They are strong and young!"

"Which one do you want?"

All eyes were on Vinnia. Emyn leaned on her stick and rose, creeping away from the group without making a sound. From across the sea she'd imagined this island a peaceful refuge—until today. Separated from the mainland, the place had rotted in its isolation. Its spirits were vile and cruel; who could live here without going mad?

SUNLIGHT FROM A WHITE sky bathed Emyn as she left the house, and she breathed deeply and looked around.

Clusters of well-dressed men stood or sat on cushions, laughing and drinking. Slaves wove through groups of guests, refilling cups and carrying Darsa's platters and baskets. Geese flapped and pecked near a stable. Her eyes traced paths that led up to rock fences or into trees that bent away from the constant wind. In a pasture to her right, empty litters sat idle, their bearers resting quietly under the shade of evergreens.

A well-dressed man nudged his friend. "Who—"

"Must be Vinnia's seer," the other grunted, and Emyn turned toward that crowd. She spotted the Honored Master immediately.

The druid stared back at her; his dark hair and beard glinting with auburn lights. His eyes took in everything: the stick, the cropped hair, the bewildered expression that must mirror his own. Emyn mouthed his name: Rialos.

*   *   *

HE RECOVERED BEFORE SHE DID. He was a druid and would not show confusion.

"Emyn." Time seemed to have skipped. Rialos had stood across a circle of men; now still as a rock, he was close enough to touch. "You are my sister's oracle?"

"Vinnia is your sister?"

"You are acquainted?" asked a man.

Rialos turned to the speaker. "The Gutumaros of Samarnum is known to many—although I suppose she uses a new title now." He smiled; perhaps "Vinnia's seer" crossed his mind. "When did you leave Belgic lands?"

Emyn's head spun, but she tried to match his polite tone. "In early spring. Master Bodocnos brought me here."

She wanted to say more, but swallowed instead.

"What news is there, oracle?" A man asked, and several more began to speak at once.

Rialos raised his hand, silencing them. He opened his mouth and clenched it shut again.

Emyn felt his eyes on her, his alone. She grasped for more to say. "I have words for you, Honored Master. The ghosts tell me of events in Sequani lands—"

"That affects us all," said one of the merchants. In spite of the summer's warmth he wore a cloak trimmed in fur. "Let's hear your words!"

The oldest man among them lifted his hand and stepped toward Rialos. "This is not village gossip! Our trade may rise and fall on such news."

Other men murmured; Emyn waited. Bodocnos would never allow others to force his decisions. Why was Rialos silent?

She leaned forward and whispered, "I can walk well, if you'd like to leave."

Did she imagine panic in his eyes, just for a moment? In the next heartbeat he nodded and took sure steps away from the crowd. At the first sound of protest he whipped back to glare and announce, "I will speak to the Gutumaros alone."

Rialos walked past Vinnia's stable and up a slight incline slowly, but without taking her arm or looking at her. Emyn felt thunder explode and echo in her head. If Rialos was Vael, then the stories Vinnia told were of him. His mother was the slave, the dancing girl that Vinnia hated.

They stopped before a short rock fence, wide enough for sitting. Beyond it the ground rose sharply, darkened by bushes and pine trees.

"Please sit. You look frail." Was his mind recapturing all of Vinnia's gossip about her? He could see that she limped. Did women talk about Emyn's scar, the bite mark sewn into puckered lines on her breast? Would Vinnia know of that?

"I am not frail. I've walked across many lands." She sat on the rocks; she could draw steadiness from them. "Did Bodocnos find you, Honored Master?"

"No. I was gone. He left a message but not. . . . " his voice trailed off.

Not about her? Why wouldn't Bodocnos mention her? The bright sun cast Rialos' eyes in shadow, and the short beard obscured any hint of his mood.

Rialos cleared his throat. "Vinnia said you lost much: your husband, your child. Is that what drove you from Samarnum?"

Emyn nodded.

"I am sorry. I've wished only happiness for you." Rialos' simple words removed the sting of imagining Vinnia's shrill descriptions of her sorrows. He watched her, though; she had to say something.

"I do have news." Emyn paused. When he didn't stop her, she plunged on. "You probably know that Caesar sent the remnants of the Helvetian tribe back to their old lands?"

"We've heard that. Do your ghosts foretell how far north the Romans will push?"

"My ghosts say there is no limit to Caesar's hunger for glory." The dead king's phrase came to her easily. Mouthing his words relieved her of the need to think; Emyn's mind still reeled at the sight of the man before her. "He outran the warriors of Ariovistus and now quarters in Vesontio. The Sequani opened their gates to him."

"To Caesar?"

"To whoever is strongest; today, it is Caesar. There is more. The ghosts say that Dumnorix used sorcery to confound the Romans. They tell me that the homes and byways of Vesontio echo with howls of terror."

"Howls," Rialos repeated. His hands shook—whether with anger, excitement, or another emotion, Emyn couldn't tell. "When? Now? Do your spirits tell you?"

"I hear nothing on this island, but the dead king said two days ago that the Romans screamed with fear." Her voice rose with excitement as the ghost's had. "Dumnorix raised the spirits of his ancestors against them. Not alone; the spirits say that many masters participated in blood rites in different lands. On a certain night they cast a mighty spell together. Now the Roman legions are in turmoil. Archers and soldiers flee shadows in terror, weeping. They will not obey their leaders. Centurions desert their men. All are afraid. They imagine that warriors and wild beasts fall upon them."

Rialos paced before her like a faithful hound who heard his owner returning. He had joined in those rites; she would bet all her coins on it! "Dumnorix . . . where is he?"

"Hidden, the ghosts say. His part in this is unknown to Rome."

"This began two days ago?"

"Yes. The dead king questions whether Dumnorix can sustain what he began."

"The same dead king?" Rialos looked away and breezes blew hair across his face. He smiled. "Dumnorix has great strength."

Emyn grinned back. He seemed less a compelling stranger, and more a friend. "You hope for his success."

"How could an honorable man want anything else?"

Below them, the group of men broke into pairs, and one fellow beckoned to his slaves.

"Will you tell them my news?" she asked Rialos.

"I will tell other druids and the king in Venetona." He gazed in another direction. "But your story is not finished, is it? Will our ancestors' spirits drive the Romans away? Do you know?"

His low voice thrilled her with a memory that was best left alone. "I don't."

"Your words are not meant for the merchants of this island. Those men aren't warriors. Blocked roads and closed ports are their concerns. They want news of war, so they can buy more iron to hammer into weapons to be sold."

Emyn's stick rolled away from the stone wall, and Rialos bent to pick it up. He studied the carvings for a moment before handing it to her: carefully, so that their fingers would not touch.

Emyn leaned on it to stand. Rialos made no move, and she followed his eyes as she stood beside him.

Near Vinnia's house, the slaves brought a litter to one man. Emyn squinted and frowned. The man who settled himself on the litter was young. "Why doesn't he walk?"

"Because he owns slaves," Rialos said without humor. "My sister calls you Nervian. Are you?"

"My mother was Nervian."

"They believe that slaves make men lazy, isn't that true?"

"Yes." Iomat had said those very words whenever men or women with slaves passed through Samarnum.

The merchant on the litter called out a command, and the slaves lifted him with smooth and balanced movements. "Go!" he shouted, and they stepped evenly in a well-practiced rhythm, running lightly down a path. Their grip was firm; the litter never tilted or jerked. It floated.

"Do your ghosts travel from other worlds to advise such men?" Rialos asked in a weary voice. "Truly?"

 22

The tramping of feet from the north heralded the coming of Gundori, Vinnia's uncle and king. The ghosts sang in excitement and circled the man as Emyn watched dubiously. Once off his litter, Gundori bore himself with authority and men deferred to him, but he was short, bald, and paunchy.

Emyn bowed when Vinnia pointed her out; Gundori stared but said nothing. Men followed him into the house. Emyn saw Rialos in the crowd as she backed away, glad no one invited her inside. The air in there was surely as stale and sickening as it had been earlier.

Vinnia's words carried through the walls and over the other voices. "Uncle, here is Vael, returned—"

Emyn edged closer to the door as the druid corrected his sister "Rialos, please."

"How will I ever remember?" Vinnia cried. "Couldn't you be Vael here?"

"Be mindful, Vinnia." Was that the king's voice? It boomed and did not match his appearance. "Vael is a slave's name."

Silence fell, sudden and complete. Those standing outside raised their eyebrows as they looked at each other. Not even a king could insult a druid! Would Rialos take offense?

But no; his voice was calm. If not for the sudden quiet, Emyn would not even have heard it. "Just so, and I am no slave. My name is Rialos."

Sighs and nervous laughter wafted outside. Emyn stepped away from the door and out of the shadow of the overhanging thatch.

"He watches!"

"Oh, he hates!"

"He wants to kill you."

"What did you do, pretty?"

Who hated her? Alarmed, Emyn scanned the meadows, the path, and the other buildings. Then she understood.

The stars balanced their surprises good and bad on this day. Glowering at her from the stable stood the man who'd knocked her down at the alehouse; the man whose knife now belonged to Emyn. She met his stare, pivoted on her stick, and walked inside. She shook, but he could not see that.

The room felt as if it would burst through its walls, spilling men and women out like floodwater. Emyn stood close to a wall, watching the bodies before her. Ghosts wove through them: gray, ugly, silent forms. Nauseous, Emyn moved toward Darsa. Something familiar, like a cookfire and simmering stew, might calm her soul.

Edging along the wall, she managed to get between Darsa and the back of the house, away from all the chatter and jewels. The air here, still heavy, smelled of the sea and food, not of perfume. She leaned against a post and sighed. Rialos stood near his sister, accepting and passing a cup. From here, Emyn was sure, no one would notice her watching the druid.

But she jumped and stifled a scream as a slave pulled away

wooden boards on the floor and hopped into a hole deep enough to hide him. "Darsa!" she hissed.

"What?" Darsa turned to look. The slave handed up a bucket filled with grain and another boy took it.

Emyn's voice trembled. "You keep food in the ground?"

"It's rock," Darsa motioned. "Just rock. See for yourself."

"But it's a pit," Emyn said, though Darsa wasn't listening anymore.

Pits were for the dead. Emyn stared into the darkness as the slave climbed out. "It's very dry, lady." He nodded politely and kicked the boards back into place, covering the hole.

Emyn's insides twisted. This could not be right! Sacrifices to gods of war and vengeance were thrown underground for insects and worms to feed on. "Isn't the food poisoned?" she asked.

No one answered her. She edged away.

The man in the fur-lined robe tapped her shoulder. "What of the Namnete?" he sputtered. "They claim all the salt fields as their territory. Who is going to protect our interests there? I need to know!"

"My ghosts have not spoken of them."

"Ask, please. My name is Lorsus, I will pay you well—"

"Lorsus. The salt fields." Emyn nodded; she felt eyes on her and heard her title called. Hands guided her toward the king. Gundori pointed to a stool before him and she sat. For a long while, he said nothing.

Emyn's mind, her stomach, and even her blood churned, and she wondered if she would explode, splattering the king and all the guests with bits of flesh. She sat alone in a mad house where people ate insects, food was stored underground, and neither ghosts nor men made sense. Her soul ached for home, but she had no home.

"Tribes to the north trouble me," Gundori muttered, finally.

"Young men are impetuous; they cross borders and steal. Do your ghosts speak of them?"

"The dead king talks only of Roman invaders lately." Emyn forced her voice to be as smooth and calm as the Samar on a still day.

The king bent close to her. "Then why are you here? Why are you sent to me? Am I to know more of Rome?"

Without her ghosts to advise her, Emyn had no answer. The king rose and left, joining a cluster of merchants near the fire. Emyn stayed on the stool, staring ahead where Gundori had sat.

The afternoon passed slowly as Emyn sought shelter in shade and shadows, praying not to be noticed. When the sea dropped to reveal the road to the village, she thanked Vinnia for her generosity and tried to leave.

"I'll call my litter for you," Vinnia announced. A slave ran off at her command.

"Oh, please, take mine." The lady in the checkered dress sidled next to Emyn. "It's so very comfortable."

"Gutumaros, *mine* will shield you from the sun."

Emyn wanted to walk, but her preference didn't matter. Vinnia and her friends argued over whose litter would bear her while the ghosts keened.

"Why do you leave, pretty?"

"Stay. We will drape you with jewels!"

"Like a statue—"

"White as chalk you will be, with garnets round your neck!"

"Va—Rialos, dear, help us!" Vinnia's voice rose over the din. "We need a druid's wisdom. I insist that the oracle ride in my litter."

"But mine has a canopy!" The squabbling began anew.

"Share the honor," Rialos laughed and pushed through the

pack of women. "The canopied litter and four men to carry it. This one is yours, isn't he, Vinnia?" With a charming smile, he pointed to the freckled youth who had driven the wagon earlier.

"And one of mine!" called an eager lady.

"*Stay—*" The spirit voices hummed like wind.

The litter waited in front of her. Emyn looked up at Rialos. "If I hear more news from the ghosts—"

"You will come to me, of course!" Vinnia answered as she kissed Emyn's cheek. "You are always welcome here."

"Yes, and Vinnia will send a messenger to the king." Rialos smiled at his sister, took the stick from Emyn, and held her arm steady as she sat and pulled her legs into the litter. "Or you may go directly to him, though I don't know if my generous sister will forgive you for neglecting her. Gundori is a wise ruler who will respect your words."

He had two faces, this druid. Earlier Emyn spoke to an earnest man who'd grown from the student she met in Samarnum. But now he charmed and teased the ladies; he was what everyone wanted him to be. Once Emyn arranged her legs in the litter, he handed her back her stick. "Where shall I tell them to go?"

Them? Emyn realized he meant the slaves who would carry the litter. "The village at the end of this rock road. I live in Suttia's house."

He lifted an eyebrow, and his voice dropped so low that Emyn doubted her ears. "A poor place from which to spread news. I will visit you there."

The litter shifted, and she grabbed at the air, then the curtain. Vinnia's home, Rialos, and dozens of voices faded as Emyn floated above the ground.

* * *

WITHIN TWO DAYS OF her visit to the island, the weather changed abruptly. Dampness drifted through Suttia's house like an aroma.

"It is over," the dead king announced as a misty rain filled the morning.

Emyn bent down to catch her spindle and wind the thread.

"Listen to me," the ghost insisted.

Emyn grunted, set aside the spindle and grabbed her shawl and stick. "Micco, let's go see the dog," she called to the boy, who rocked on his haunches by the fire. Happy for any chance to touch animals, he scampered before her as they stepped into Suttia's half-sheltered yard. The dog cowered from Emyn as dogs always did. She turned her back to it and leaned against a post. "What is over, dead king?"

"The spell of Dumnorix, and all who worked with him. The efforts of his ancestors."

Emyn's disappointment tasted bitter. Could nothing stand against Rome?

"Caesar gathered his centurions and upbraided them for their cowardice!" The dead king seemed to enjoy the awful news. "He shamed them. He roused them to his side once more. Listen: he challenges all his warriors to lift their standards and follow him to further victories. It is a mighty speech."

"Is it? I am glad I don't speak Latin."

"He is a great general. They will follow him. Dumnorix' spell is broken."

"What of those who fled?" The words were louder than she intended; tears and foolish hopes pressed against her eyes. "You said many snuck away. What of them?"

"They hide like insects fleeing the light! Yes . . . those cowards creep back. No one believes their excuses, but they are men of wealth and position. All pretend that they did not waver."

Micco watched her while the dead king spoke, but when Emyn made no more sounds, he turned his face back to the slobbering dog with fur the color of beach sand.

"There is more," the ghost said. "Do you want to hear?"

Emyn shook her head, knowing she had little choice. The dead king would play out his news like she played out wool for thread, a bit at a time.

"Diviciacos aids Caesar. He has chosen once and for all time and will not turn back. Diviciacos undid his brother's sorcery."

Emyn punched at the post. This was a small loss, not even a battle—but it pained her. So much hope rode on Dumnorix' efforts against Rome! His ancestors were powerful. How could Rome defeat them?

"WAKE, LITTLE GUTUMAROS." A shawl of scarlet butterfly wings swept over Emyn's face. Aruca giggled as Emyn tried to scratch at the tickling cloth.

A dream and all its memories slipped away. Why was she here, nestled against a tree? Its thick branches blocked the midday sun. Bodocnos, Moradag—were they nearby?

No. She didn't travel anymore; she lived in a house. Emyn shut her eyes, straightening her mind. She had walked all morning; now she rested perhaps a league from the village.

A woman had gone into labor two days ago. Emyn knew how to deliver babies, even if she got little practice. The couple was too poor to be picky about whether or not the midwife brought ghosts into their house. This was their first child; they lived alone except for the young sister who'd bought a love potion from Emyn, won a kiss from a boy, and now trusted Emyn in all things.

The woman had held Emyn's healing stone as her body worked to deliver a pink, healthy son. Emyn sat up into the night figuring his stars, but the dead king sneered at her efforts. "Rome steals your destinies and mocks your stars."

"Your son will surprise you with his talents," she'd told the parents, ignoring the ghost. "You will wonder—who taught him that?"

"Sleepyhead!"

Emyn opened her eyes halfway; the color red tinted the shadows and light around her. She'd seen such fabric once. It came from far away, beyond Greece. She remembered . . . the merchant would not let anyone touch it until he'd inspected their hands for dirt, calluses, and broken nails. "Silk?"

Aruca laughed and bunched the material under Emyn's nose. "You should wear this color."

Emyn pushed it away. Silk draped and floated around Aruca; the skin beneath it pulsed with life. *Seemed to* pulse with life. Aruca was illusion, like the silk.

"What is wrong? Surely I do not scare you?"

"I believed you were real."

The ghost sighed and settled next to Emyn. "It is your own judgment you mistrust, then. I am still Aruca."

Emyn could not argue. Which one of them lingered in the wrong world?

She felt affection for Aruca stronger than her bonds with Darsa or Suttia. The women of this coastal village had picked their friends years ago, and Emyn had no place among them. Aruca dabbed at Emyn's single tear and the silk soaked it up, turning several shades darker.

"Your shoes are worn," Aruca sighed. "Surely you can afford—"

"Are you my mother, now?" Emyn sniffled and laughed. Before she left this morning, the new father had used charcoal to mark the length and width of her feet on a piece of leather. A gift of thanks, he'd said. "I've earned new shoes and a sheath for my knife."

"Good." Silk blurred the air between them. "You have much to fear from one man. Keep your knife with you."

"Who?"

The ghost ignored the question and pointed to the bundle of food in Emyn's lap. "Eat, for strength."

Afterward, Aruca stayed with Emyn as she walked, holding her free arm. The tin bracelets chilled Emyn's arm where they touched her, but Aruca's skin felt warm. The wind blew her skirt tight against her legs as the path began its slow descent towards the village.

"When I was very young, very restless," the ghost said, "I was told to watch a little wolf cub. I liked the task better than cutting onions or feeding the geese."

"A wolf cub?"

"Yes, a wolf cub," Aruca sighed. "The lady's wolf cub."

"The lady?" No woman in the village or farms would be called 'the lady.' Emyn groped for an answer. "Where did you live?"

"Very near . . . I have always loved this tree. You can see it from almost anywhere." A grandfather oak spread its branches over the path. This was a sacred tree where ancestors gathered, where secrets had been whispered for generations. Piles of small rocks dotted the ground between it and the dirt road.

Emyn held a pebble in her hand to drop in tribute as she passed the tree, but now she stumbled over to lean against its trunk for strength. What was Aruca telling her?

"You lived on the island, didn't you?"

"Yes."

Aruca whispered the word from the path. Emyn turned to face the ghost. "As a servant or a slave?"

"My mother cooked for the lady."

Emyn dropped the pebble and her stick; her arms went limp like boiled leaves. "Your mother is Darsa?"

"I make her sad, even now." Aruca shook her head, and her red hair shimmered in the sunlight. But stepping into the shadows, her hair was suddenly not as bright nor her skin so smooth. As she towered over Emyn, Darsa's strong mouth and chin emerged: younger but unmistakable.

Emyn reached to touch her face. Aruca was again flawless: blue-veined skin beneath waves of bright copper. "Why do you change?"

"I like to be pretty. Vanity does not die, no more than the soul." She beckoned Emyn, urging her away from the tree.

Emyn, too full of this new secret to ask more, grabbed her stick and stumbled on. They were the same height now, their stride matching.

Suttia stood outside her house talking to another woman. She waved to Emyn just as the ghost tugged her arm. "My messages are for you alone."

"Girl or boy?" called Suttia.

"A boy!" Emyn turned to Aruca. "Why—"

"Do not ask more. You are home."

"Healthy?" Suttia had her hands on her hips, only a few feet away.

"Yes, mother and child."

"Red-haired?"

Emyn stared at Suttia; neither parent had red hair.

Suttia winked. "He looks like her husband, the baby? There's talk—well, come have some cider. Then you can help me cook."

"He came by," Suttia called out later.

Emyn looked up from the onions she was hacking into chunks. "Who? My brother?"

Suttia snorted; she'd been quick to tell Emyn that Nonicos stayed away while Emyn was gone, and that Micco had whimpered until Suttia let him sleep with the dogs. "No, the druid, the young one, on his way to Venetona."

The knife stopped in midair. Before leaving to deliver the baby, Emyn had given Suttia the dead king's news. She'd hoped to see Rialos herself, though.

"Told him just what you said, that Caesar had control of his men again, that Diviciacos undid his brother's sorcery." Suttia whacked the head off a large fish, and then slit its underside open. The woman could be trusted with messages. When it came to gossip, she had a prodigious memory. "And he thanked me, of course. Said something about sour news being more distasteful, with nothing to sweeten it. Do you think he insulted me?"

"How? The news *was* sour to him." Emyn forced a laugh. "What else did he say?"

"Nothing." Suttia ran her thumb along the fish's inside, pushing out its guts.

"Stupid woman!" the dead king bellowed and blew hot wind into Emyn's face. "I bring you the one you want, but you do nothing. You do not charm or tease, but I bring him here. And you run away."

Emyn cut the ends off another onion and quartered it.

"You could wriggle in gold from your neck to your ankles," the dead king taunted, "But you prefer the dirt. I weary of you."

She looked over at Suttia. "Did he say when he might come back, the druid?"

"No, nothing. That's enough onions. They're making you teary, aren't they?"

* * *

A CHILD SAT WITH DARSA the next time the wagon crossed the rock path between island and shore. No more than eight or nine, he wore a tattered, undyed tunic with a streak of paint that marked him as Vinnia's slave. Darsa waved him to the back of the cart as Emyn pulled herself up by one arm; only then did she notice that his eyes and hair were the same rich shade of brown, like good soil.

"Who is this?" she asked.

"Gorio, though he doesn't answer to it. Sit!"

The boy didn't obey until the horses started to move again. He lost his balance and Emyn grabbed the thin tunic, then his arm, to steady him.

"I'm to teach him to talk. Me! He's right out of the forest, that one. What am I supposed to do with him?" Darsa growled and spat.

"Does he belong to you?"

"To me? No, he's the lady's, like the rest of them. Who has to train them and see that their work is done, though? And now this. Teach a boy to talk. How do you teach a boy to talk if he can't understand you to begin with?"

"Gorio?" Emyn turned to the boy. A host of bright lights clung to him as he stared at his knees, avoiding her eyes.

"Why did the lady buy a slave that young?"

"Don't ask. I don't." Darsa continued to grumble as the horses plodded along. "He's stupid, if you ask me. Not that anyone does. How can he not know his own name?"

"What words does he know?"

"None. So can your ghosts talk to him?"

Emyn took a last look at the boy before sitting straight beside Darsa. "He is surrounded by his own ancestors, but they do not speak to me."

Darsa shrugged. "Thought I'd ask. They fought like dogs over him, the lady and her brother."

"Her brother . . . the druid?" Emyn asked. "He is still visiting?"

"Before he left. Days ago." Darsa shook her head back at Gorio. "The Lady Vinnia tried to give the boy to him. That's what started it."

"But . . . his own mother was a slave."

"She was."

"Then why—"

"Why do you think?" Darsa's hands reddened where they wrapped round and clenched the reins. She let lose an abrupt laugh. "Me, I don't think. Does no good."

By the time they returned home with a wagon full of food, Gorio knew the words for apple, cheese, millet, horse, wheel, eat, blue, hand, egg, stone, and pine tree. Emyn suspected he knew others as well, but as a slave, he'd also learned to keep his mouth shut. He jumped down as Darsa packed berries and vegetables into Emyn's basket, and handed a bag of apples to Micco, who'd been waiting for their return.

"Get back up, boy! Back!" Darsa hollered at Gorio.

"Up," Emyn patted the wagon seat. With a forlorn look, the child climbed into it. "I could teach him more if you leave him—"

"He's not mine to leave." Darsa looked Emyn straight in the eye for the first time. "We'll get along, I suppose."

NOT JUST SUTTIA, but all the villagers shared gossip freely. Emyn learned the place had been without a carpenter since before Lugnasad, when King Gundori began work on a new house and furnishings. Skilled men had moved to the island with their families, and no one knew when they'd return.

"I suppose you'll be moving Laurina in here, soon," Suttia said loudly one afternoon. "Is she stuffing a new mattress for you? Her old one must be worn out by now."

Nonicos' face turned as red as Aruca's silk. He rarely spent nights at Suttia's anymore. Emyn had moved her own mattress from the women's side of the hearth to a place in between where Micco could curl up safely at her feet at night.

Laurina's husband had been a fisherman, knocked off his ship and drowned in rough weather last year. She lived with her mother-in-law and the dead man's brothers and their wives. They allowed a passionate courtship under their roof, but eventually Laurina and her child would be expected to go live with Nonicos.

"Do something by Samhain," Emyn hissed to her brother when Suttia turned back to her cookfire.

"What?"

"You don't want to wait till the dark half of the year to marry, like I did."

Emyn picked up her spindle and limped away. The six months after Samhain were an unlucky time to begin anything new, but she didn't need to say that out loud.

 23

Days passed slowly. The harvests came in; apples were mashed and pressed for cider as bees swarmed into the sheds along with children, hoping for a taste. The weather grew colder and the wind was always present. Women in the village approached Emyn for brews to soothe throats and ease fevers, and a few of the ladies from Gundori's island sought the advice of their ancestors.

Emyn rode with Darsa and Gorio whenever they went to the farms, and soon learned all the paths near the village and along the beaches, and what grew along them. She absorbed the ebb and flow of the tide and stopped thinking about it. Like everyone else, she simply knew when the sea road was open or submerged, or if fishing boats were afloat or beached.

On the same day that the first chestnuts were stored in smokehouses to dry, a battle began. Caesar defeated Ariovistus, but there was no one for Emyn to tell.

"The armies fight!" the dead king shouted. Emyn's eyes saw nothing beyond the now-familiar trees, the paths, and the well, and she was glad for that. She stayed inside all afternoon, worried that the dead king would take her sight away. He never did. He must have decided that with no druid nearby to hear, transporting her spirit was not worth his effort.

In the evening he announced: "Ariovistus flees to the great river. Many try to follow."

Emyn sat on a bench, spinning. Her back was to the fire and Micco leaned against her leg. Over and over her fingers twisted the wool. When the spindle touched the ground Micco grabbed it, wound the thread, and handed it back so Emyn could set it spinning again. Other than those thoughtless motions, the dead king had her full attention.

"The Romans ride. Horses are faster than men, faster than women. Romans catch them easily. They do not reach the boats. Most die as they flee; the river is leagues away, and they are already tired. The women die, and the children. The wives of Ariovistus are cut apart like animals for slaughter."

He stopped talking. Emyn whispered, "Is it over?"

"Over?" the ghost asked. "For whom? It is over for the sons and daughters who died. For you who live, it only begins."

SLAVES CARRIED A LITTER from the island: wealthy Lorsus had come to consult the oracle. Suttia sent children with a bucket to get ale from Haebro, but Lorsus had brought his own wine. Emyn watched as a slave held the ewer high above a cup and poured; in the firelight it looked like garnets spilling out.

Lorsus spread himself onto the bench nearest the hearth, protected by his furs against any possible chill. He worried about the Namnete and the salt fields, but Emyn assured him, as the dead king had assured her, that the Namnete wanted no confrontations with the Veneti. "Your men work unmolested.

There is no reason to claim further territory."

"No reason? I have buyers—"

"Greedy pig!" the dead king screamed over Lorsus' words. "He has all he can ever sell in this world, but he wants more. He will be dead before he exhausts his supply! They can salt him and hang him from the beam!"

"Do you not have enough to satisfy your buyers now?" Emyn asked when both voices stilled.

"Now, yes. But—"

"That is all you should worry about." She dropped her voice; men listened with more respect to a low tone. "When you need more, when you have used up what you have, you may ask the spirits' advice again."

"Tell him of Rome!" the dead king demanded.

Emyn hesitated; Rialos had told her to go to Gundori. Still, Lorsus was here. Why miss an opportunity? "Do you ever travel to Venetona?"

"What do you care, little fool? Tell him of Rome!"

"I loathe travel." Lorsus waved his hand. "It requires far too many slaves to ensure my comfort . . . or are the spirits advising me to travel?" He leaned forward and offered Emyn the cup again. "*Should* I venture to Venetona?"

"No." Emyn touched her lips to the cup politely. "The ghosts have words about Caesar. I hoped you might carry them to Venetona. You could tell your king as well."

"I can send messengers. What are their words?"

Emyn looked at the slaves who stood behind Lorsus. Would they be the messengers? "Caesar and Ariovistus have fought at last," she said. "Do you wish to hear the tale?"

He did. Another cup of wine disappeared while she spoke.

Lorsus chuckled as she finished. "That general has made

himself rich. First the Helvetians, now the Suebi and Germani. It is the same general, this Caesar?"

Emyn nodded.

"Well, maybe he'll stay in Rome for awhile."

"He does not listen!" the dead king railed.

"Caesar will not return to Rome. He comes for conquest, not just to raid." Emyn dropped her voice so low that Lorsus had to bend closer to hear. "Caesar quarters his men at Vesontio, forcing many of the Sequani clans from their homes. They must go begging to neighbors for food while Rome's troops enjoy their harvest and slaughter their livestock. He will not leave."

"Vesontio, yes. You mentioned Vesontio earlier."

Emyn wanted to slap the man. "Will you send messengers to the king in Venetona? The ghosts insist," she added.

"This very evening, yes." Lorsus signaled for more wine. Emyn looked at the slave but he avoided her eyes. She hoped he paid attention. Lorsus was already too drunk to remember anything.

"You speak with a Belgic accent," Lorsus muttered. "I import wool from several Belgic tribes . . . the Bellovaci, and others. The quality is much better than that found locally."

"He is worthless, this pig."

Emyn nodded and Lorsus kept talking. Many slaves worked on Gundori's new house, he said, weaving tapestries, carving panels. "So much skilled work done by slaves seems strange to you, I suppose, being Nervian? You'll soon see the advantage of our enlightened ways!"

"Where does Gundori keep so many workers?" Emyn asked.

"To the west, beyond—" Lorsus swept his arm in that direction. "You've seen the island's fields . . . or maybe not."

"I saw only a little of the island. I thought it was all rock."

Lorsus laughed. "From here, you would never guess how large it is." Waving his arms, he launched into a long description of the island's geography. Emyn sat still, wishing she had told anyone but Lorsus about Caesar's latest battle. Would he remember any of the ghost's words?

"Between us, I don't mind saying that Gundori reads the stars as well as any druid," Lorsus droned on, his voice dropping to an inaudible mumble at times. "He marks the spring equinox as . . . as the most auspicious time to establish a new home. The true equinox, not our artificial holidays as he calls them. That's what he said when I shared a cup with him. So . . . his new house is begun, but sits empty through the dark months till that holiday."

A slave signaled from the doorway.

"The tide, yes! I must go." Lorsus drained his cup and stood. Slaves jumped forward, taking his arm to steady him.

"You will remember to send the spirits' message—"

Lorsus waved a hand at Emyn, muttering words meant to reassure. Slurred together, they had the opposite effect. Behind his back, Emyn pulled at her hair in frustration.

NONICOS MARRIED WITH A small celebration and Laurina and her daughter came to live in Suttia's home. Emyn's brother would have his own house one day; everyone knew that. Enough work waited to keep Nonicos busy through the winter, earning coins and goodwill. In spring he would build a well-framed house with smooth, painted walls for his family—which would include Emyn and Micco.

Samhain came, and Darsa's wagon, driven by slaves, made three trips on the last morning of the year to gather all the grain and produce due Vinnia. The holiday games and pranks began long before the sun lowered. Men raced along the beach, falling into the sand while their wives and friends yelled from the rocks. Emyn laughed at them, then thought of Rialos racing on horseback and her throat clenched. *"My son won a silver buckle. . . ."*

Bracelets jingled beside her. Aruca had a way of appearing when Emyn needed a word or distraction most. Below her, the younger men sped toward girls who held cups of mead for the finishers.

Emyn whispered, "You said once that you cared for a wolf cub."

"A long time ago."

"What is long to you?" Cheers drifted up to them. The men had run the course, grabbed the cups, and grabbed the girls as well. "The lady's wolf cub, you said. Why do you call him that?"

"Because he hid. He trusted no one. I had to trick him to make him laugh."

"How old was he then?"

"Like the boy that rides on the wagon." Wind blew Aruca's hair back as she smiled. How was that possible? "As old as him."

"So you took care of him—the lady's brother—and taught him to laugh."

"Did I?" The smile faded. "In the end, he learned he couldn't trust me either."

"Why not?"

Aruca's eyes watched the beach. "Everyone leaves."

Men, women, and children climbed back up the path to pile into Suttia's house, the largest in the village, to celebrate the new year while the ghosts and demons howled outside.

After the feast, Emyn spoke the words of the ancestors, making sure that a bit of advice or a word of comfort went to each person assembled. Then she sat between Micco and Oleda, her new niece, as the oldest stories were told. Soon the child slept in her lap as warm as fresh bread. Micco rubbed his face against a fur until he dozed as well.

"Here is one more tale for the night." Aruca whispered. "One for you alone."

Emyn nodded. Aruca's silk draped over the child.

"When he came to the island, my little wolf brought a goddess, no bigger than his hand. She was all that he brought. We do not keep such gods here, but it was a custom of his mother's people, as it is yours. He hid her in the crevice of a tree where no one else would find her. She was quite happy there.

"Then one day, she was gone. The cub said nothing. I heard him cry, and now I know why. He let her go, rather than seek help to find her."

Aruca kissed Emyn's cheek in the darkness and was gone.

The roof was black above her. Near the fire, voices muttered and a song began. A new year was a time to make promises, to right what was wrong and to end bad habits.

Emyn was no longer a girl, able to catch a man's eye as she swayed with her bucket toward the well. She limped like an old grandmother now. The scar on her breast was a mark of courage, yes, but it was still a scar, and ugly.

Women and men changed as they moved through life. That was why the Morrigu could be young or old: she taught by example.

Rialos had never returned to see her. He sent no word; he did not think of her.

And why should he? Imagining that he might was the pastime of an adolescent. Emyn decided she must stop wasting her thoughts on what she couldn't have.

The resolution brought no comfort.

* * *

WINTER SETTLED OVER THE village as Aumios' second birthday approached. Some days, sadness sucked the life out of Emyn. On the anniversary of her son's death, Nonicos and Laurina walked with her to a small dock a league from the village.

No boats were near the area. The platform was built over a rocky cove, an inlet to another world. Nonicos brought a wooden figure he'd carved; a few cuts marked it as male. Emyn twisted holly around it. They prayed, and Emyn held her arm out over the sea. She loosened her grip on the little man and let it fall.

She seemed to dissolve like salt in the drizzling rain. Nonicos caught her as she fell and pulled her away from the platform's edge. Oleda laughed; her mother hushed her and exchanged looks with Nonicos. Emyn sat until her legs were strong enough to carry her once more. Then they all walked back to the village that was not Samarnum, to the strangers she barely knew and the children that belonged to others.

A NIGHT LATER EMYN stumbled outside. Only the stars watched as she tottered up to the ancient oak tree.

Lately, Emyn was as oblivious to time as the ghosts were. She filled her days with naps and her nights with wakefulness. Now she wandered through darkness so cold she felt she'd plunged into an icy stream.

Spirits hovered near. Teeth chattering, she waved them away and staggered along the path till she touched the tree. Tears bubbled out before she was ready for them, and she threw herself against the trunk and slid to her knees. Sobs tore at her throat and took her breath away. She pulled the fur over her head and hid her face.

Her baby was gone. Her arms were empty. She was uprooted and alone, useless, and a fool. For as long as it took Emyn to wring herself out like an old rag, she wallowed in tears and hopelessness.

Then it was over. She didn't feel better, but she was too tired to cry any longer. Damp hair stuck to her face. Had she thought she could leave sorrow behind in Samarnum? Emyn huddled against the rough trunk, hungry for any comfort.

She had traveled thirty times thirty steps from her home, an uncountable number. As each league passed Emyn had busied herself with new sights and foods, different spirits, strange accents, all the while dreading the end of the journey. Dreading this moment.

She had come to the end of the world. There was nowhere else to go, nothing left to hope for. She felt old as if a life of sixty years lay behind her. If she looked in a pool tonight, a crone would stare back.

Like the Morrigu.

BOOK THREE

The Morrigu

 24

Emyn dreamed of the Morrigu. She flew with the raven goddess over lands and the sea, beyond mountains that rose sharp and icy, as far as summer. They dove and the smells of roses, grass, and ripening fruit drifted up to cling to her.

She jerked awake as the fire leapt; Suttia had tossed a fresh log onto it. Orange sparks splashed up and faded. Emyn looked around sheepishly, but others were dozing as well. The longest night of the year was about to start; folks napped so that they could stay awake for the stories.

The door was thrown open, shaking loose the holly branches that hung over it.

"King Gundori summons the Gutumaros!"

Emyn stared at the silhouette in the doorway as all other activity stopped. Did she know that voice?

"She is ill," Laurina announced from the cookfire.

Emyn pushed herself into a sitting position. Why would Laurina say that? Lazy, perhaps, but not ill—

"The king has a healer if she needs attention." The man stepped too close to Laurina; was he threatening her? The point of a sword stuck out from beneath his heavy cloak.

Emyn pushed herself to her feet as the warrior scanned the room. Their eyes met; he was the man from the alehouse. "The king waits for you."

"Take your knife," Aruca commanded.

"She has a fever," Laurina tried again. "She should not—"

"And the king has a healer! Are you deaf?" The man shrugged back his cloak, revealing the polished band that circled a muscular arm. He rested his hand on the hilt of his sword.

"She is only being kind." Emyn lurched forward and coughed, spewing spit. The man backed up. "I'll come, of course. Please give me a moment to wash my face."

"Be quick. The tide rises soon." He positioned himself at the door as if he were guarding the house.

"Insolent show-off!" the dead king roared.

"Keep your wits, little Gutumaros." That was Aruca's voice.

"Help me find my stick," Emyn said and leaned on Laurina's arm. As they turned away she dropped her voice to a whisper. "Do not push this man; he is evil."

"I know," Laurina moaned. "Emyn, don't go with him—"

"How can I not? It is the king who summons me."

"King!" Laurina snorted as she bent to pick up the stick. Emyn grabbed her knife and its sheath from the small box of clothes. She tied it around her thigh in a dark corner as Laurina stood between her and the armed man.

"Let me get Nonicos."

"That man will run him through!" Emyn gripped Laurina's arm. "Promise me you will not call Nonicos. Not till we're gone."

Laurina threw her arms around Emyn. "Be careful!"

"Kiss Oleda and Micco for me. I'll come back as soon as I can."

* * *

"YOU'VE COME TO JOIN US!"

"To be adorned . . ."

Mad spirits gathered and shrieked as slaves carried the litter and Emyn onto the island. In the fading daylight, smoke trailed from the house of Vinnia, half-hidden by trees. Emyn glimpsed a hearth fire; no doubt Vinnia's doors were open to welcome guests for the long night. But instead of ascending the road toward the homes, the slaves trudge along the beach.

Were they impervious to the wind? They kept up their rhythm and gave no sign that the frigid air bothered them. Gusts buffeted Emyn as if she were a thin branch high off the ground. A fur lay next to her and she tucked it around her for warmth, but never let go her hold on the side of the litter.

The sky grew darker. Wouldn't the king's house be near the top of the hill, giving him the most commanding view? Yet these slaves ran far below, keeping the ocean beside them. She felt helpless; where did they take her?

Aruca and the dead king could not guide her here. Emyn turned in the litter; behind her, the moon shone in the east, about to be swallowed by gathering clouds. Ahead, the sun fell beyond the edge of the world. The longest night was beginning. Her senses sharpened like an animal's in an open field.

"He waits for you."

"He waits, hard as iron."

"Sharp like a blade—"

Emyn could not shut them up. She sang one of her grandfather's songs, then another, repeating them over and over as the slaves ran on.

* * *

THEY STOPPED FINALLY BEFORE a tent painted with spirals. A lamp inside cast shadows against the canvas.

The last glow of day faded. Across a sloping meadow that stretched a quarter-league before her, Emyn saw torches burning near stone markers. Apparently Gundori planned a display; Emyn wondered who would be in his audience.

The same warrior who had fetched her stood by the tent opening. "You are to dress and anoint yourself. Inside."

His breathing was even, his voice impassive. He must have ridden here on a horse or another litter, arriving early to meet her at the door. If she didn't do as requested Emyn supposed he would force her. And even in a light and tipsy mood, the man was rough. She nodded without looking directly at him and entered the tent.

There was little to see inside. A small table held a lamp, a cup of wine and two delicate bottles, probably filled with scented oil. A wooden box the size of two fists waited on a bench. Emyn flipped open the lid; pins and jewels sparkled from within. She looked around; there was nothing else in the tent, nothing except a swath of black that spread around the tent pole like the opening to a fearsome cavern.

Dress, the man had said. In what? Emyn stretched her hand before her, half expecting it to vanish into the gaping patch of black. Instead she touched soft, brushed cloth. A gown? She had never seen or even heard of such a dark dye. Was she to clothe herself like a raven?

"Leave your own rags on the bench," the man called from outside. "Pick some ornaments and drink the wine. I'll take you to the king then."

"Fine!" she answered, worried that silence might bring the man inside. Emyn yanked off her shirt then pulled the raven dress from its peg and lifted it over her head. The sleeves were short and loose. Once the black cloth settled around her, she untied her own skirt and let it fall. A beaded yellow belt hung from the peg as well, so Emyn tied it tight around her waist.

The dress billowed over her legs where the knife was secured and hidden. Glancing at the tent opening, she bent and retied the sheath around her calf so it would be easier to reach.

She sipped the wine. Pulpy with berries, it made her lips tingle. A local brew, she supposed, like the distinctive cider of this land. She sat on the bench and opened the box.

What ornaments should be worn with a dress like the night sky? A silver pin shaped like a crescent moon? Emyn lifted a handful of trinkets from the box. Her fingers looped through bracelets, the sort Aruca wore. Emyn straightened her fingers and let them slide off. Bronze and iron pins fell away as well. An enameled brooch remained in her palm and she stared at it, puzzled.

How could this pin be here? Emyn had dropped it into the sacred pool.

It was the same. Months ago, she'd bought it along with clothes from the woman whose daughter had run away. There had been two such pins. When Emyn traded her coins the woman had said, "She must have been wearing the other one when she ran off."

This was the other pin. The daughter had run off . . . to King Gundori?

"Pick something."

Emyn jumped at the voice and dropped the brooch. She scooted around to face the man. "I see nothing that could adorn a dress of black."

He touched the cup. "You didn't drink."

"I don't want wine."

"Attend!" The shout brought two slaves inside. "Hold her arms down."

The men obeyed. Emyn screeched and twisted, but it did no good; the warrior picked up the cup, stepped behind her, and yanked her hair back. "Hold her nose," he commanded, and he poured the wine down her throat.

Some of it spilled, but Emyn swallowed most of the brew. A slave wiped at her neck with a rag; another poured oil into his palms and stroked her hair, rubbing it in. Emyn glared at the warrior, but he slammed the cup down and stomped out of the tent. "Follow."

BLUE-BLACK CLOUDS FILLED the sky like smoke and dipped toward the sea. Torches burned near the distant stones. Suddenly the wind died; the frigid air was still like that of a cave . . . or a pit. Emyn shuddered at the thought. Her mouth and throat thrummed like an insect, and her stomach clenched.

"Keep your wits," Aruca had said. This was no display she was being led toward. Emyn knew she was in danger, but could see no escape. The slaves might not give chase but two warriors flanked her: one she knew, and one a stranger. Both were strong. They could easily catch her if she ran.

Dampness from the grass soaked through her shoes. She gripped her stick; the men matched her pace but did not touch her. They walked toward standing stones; beyond them the meadow ended in rocks. She guessed the rocks led down to the shore. That would be the place to go if she could twist away; there might be caves. And if she did not get away?

She would die here, she realized, and shook against the nausea and numbing cold. A hand took her arm, and Emyn jerked away. She had a knife. She was not easy prey.

No breeze carried the sound of bells and harps, but their

notes filled the icy night as Emyn drew near. Holly branches lay across the three large stones which stood taller than the people around them. Young men held torches. They were dressed in undyed tunics like the musicians: slaves, all of them. None seemed bothered by the cold.

Gundori waited before the stones. His cloak was lined with fur and he wore a massive gold torque. Emyn looked past him to the rocks. If she could reach them and throw herself over the edge, how far would she tumble before reaching the beach?

"My Morrigu."

Gundori held her hand. His eyes were bright with madness. Every bone in her body screamed at her: Run now!

She whacked her stick against one man's shins and spun away. Before she could take three strides, though, an arm grabbed her waist and yanked her back. She was on the ground and the king shouted angrily; he did not want his goddess bruised!

The king's eyes filled with tears as she was pulled up to face him; veins of bright red throbbed in the torchlight. "You are perfect. So terrible, yet lovely."

The spirits began to keen, drowning the music with their wild voices.

"Sharp as a blade, he waits!"

"Jewels to adorn you—"

"You . . . you," the words wouldn't come; Emyn was caught in a nightmare. Her voice slurred, her mouth wouldn't move. She could think, though; she knew the law! She was a free woman who'd committed no crime; not even a king could hold her against her will. Emyn put all her strength into speaking until a word finally emerged: "Wrong!"

"Do not weary yourself, my dear." Gundori's voice was soothing as if he thought to calm her.

She flexed her hand, reaching for her knife. Her hand brushed something, but her fingers wouldn't bend to grab it.

"This will be done. On the Morrigu's night, on consecrated ground. Here is your cup. This will end your pain and bear you into the next world with my petitions."

A figure approached with deliberate steps. Horrified, Emyn recognized the freckled slave who had driven the wagon to Vinnia's house months before. Now his eyes were dull, focused only on the cup he bore. She twisted, but hands still held her, though she could no longer feel them. She tried to lift her leg and kick. Nothing moved—the wine had crippled her! Her throat was swelling, and no part of her body would obey.

"This meadow is your altar. Your blood will enrich my land; your body coupled to mine will bring the fruit in the spring, the wheat in the summer . . . "

Other women had died here: Aruca and the runaway daughter, perhaps many more. With so much dancing around the edge of her mind, how had she not guessed?

The cup was close. She fell back. Stars hid behind clouds, and Emyn saw only the dark.

"Graaaak!"

A raven bent over her, demanding attention, asking to be let in.

"My sacred Morrigu," the king murmured. His hands explored, lifting the dress.

"You can die now, if you like," the raven whispered. Emyn knew the voice; it strengthened her in dreams. "But this is no fitting end for you. Do you want to give up?"

Emyn's eyes began to close. Wings batted her face. "Let me in or die!"

With a last dizzy act of will, Emyn mouthed the word, "Come."

25

Arms struggled and crossed before her. One was ringed with a metal band. "Stop!" the king shouted.

Emyn heard an answering cry tear from her own throat. Did he dare command a goddess? Blood sprayed over them all.

She screamed and raised her arms as if dancing then brought them down with a powerful push that lifted her from the ground. She flapped her wings again and flew toward the beach.

Frigid, misty air woke her fully as if she'd been slapped. She flew! No one could harm her—no one could even touch her! She glided toward the rocks and bushes then rose above them. Why stop? Why not fly on and on as she did in dreams?

Men cried out in fear, their voices fading behind her. She lowered a wing to turn, delighted at how easily she moved. But she was curious. How had the puny king reacted to her triumph? Did he still worship his Morrigu once he'd seen her power with his own eyes? Did he wish to caress the raven now?

A dark figure ran beneath her; the shimmer of pale hair caught her attention. Emyn? Was that her self or a shadow? The raven dipped to look closer, but the king's hoarse shout diverted her. Why did he yell? She veered toward the torchlight.

The slaves stood listlessly as if nothing had happened; one continued to strike the rack of bells he held. A warrior was on the ground; a dead cold thing. Blood had leapt from his neck like a waterfall spilling over rocks. She'd seen it as she ascended . . . had she swung the knife?

Blood trickled down the king's face from a cut over his eye. He wiped his sleeve over his wound then bounded after the shadow. The other warrior followed him, the one Emyn recognized. She saw rage in his eyes. He wanted to catch this woman and hurt her. She was no goddess to him; only a creature to be brought down and gutted like a wild pig to a hunter. He would pass his king in a moment.

The raven dove, screeching. The king threw up his arm, and she swerved. He tried to protect himself, but fury guided her wings. She dove again. He had summoned the Morrigu; now he would face her!

Her talons struck flesh. Delicate tissue split beneath her claws. He fell, but she didn't let go till his frantic arms beat her away.

Emyn took to the air once more. The warrior had slowed, but still pursued the woman. She swept down, pecking at the king's face. One eye was swathed in furrowed, oozing scratches; she tore at it viciously until he screamed in terror.

The warrior gave up his chase and returned to his king, who lay weeping like a child. The raven flew on.

EMYN WOKE IN DARKNESS, vomiting and pushing herself away from the ground. She couldn't feel the earth or rocks that must be there beneath her; she felt nothing except the jerking motion of her heart. She pushed as hard as she could and rolled over . . . into bushes, rocks, a woodpile, an animal? Her senses couldn't tell.

She had flown. Not a dream, not madness: Emyn had flown and fought beside the Morrigu. That was a deed to carry into the next world and be proud of!

She tore into that memory as if her mind had talons. Not the pain, the triumph.

COLD ROUSED HER. Emyn shook and could not stop. Her stomach pumped violently. As she leaned to one side, twigs and branches poked at her. No longer numb, every bit of her body and bones throbbed with pain.

Her middle heaved, but nothing was left inside to come out. She crawled on her elbows to get away from the bushes that shrouded her, and then fell panting against the wet ground. Had it rained? Where was she?

She was alive. She might not stay alive, but she hadn't died at Gundori's hand like a slave or a criminal. The Morrigu had saved her. She had flown.

But she couldn't fly now; she couldn't even stand. . . . Could she? Emyn tried without success. In time she got to her knees; that was something. Now she could look up and around even though her body wanted to stay hunched over, fighting the pain. Clouds obscured the stars, but the bright half moon, just above the western horizon, shone under them.

Hours of darkness still protected her. Emyn's teeth rattled and the damp dress clung to her torso and legs. There was no place to turn for warmth, not tonight, but she needed shelter. Besides pine trees and bushes, she saw a fence outlining a yard. Still on her knees, she crawled to it and pulled herself to her feet.

She was alive. With the Morrigu's help she might stay that way.

*   *   *

"YOU CUT THE KING! You cut the king!"

   "He squeals like a pig!"

   "Mean little pig."

   "Someone will pay!"

   "Did you think of that?"

Emyn cringed under the assault of the voices, but didn't let them distract her. She willed her legs to move, wincing and biting back noises that tried to escape from her throat. Even when she fell or stepped on a jagged rock, and staggered from tree to tree in the moonlight, she kept silent and tried to judge the shadows and paths before her.

Through branches, she glimpsed light reflecting off the sea. The ocean coursed far below, and she realized that she wandered above most houses on the island. When she had escaped from Gundori, when the Morrigu forced her legs forward, she had run up the rocky hill of the island, not to the beaches. The king and his warriors would never expect to find her up here.

As near as Emyn could guess, she must have run three or four leagues, mostly uphill. No wonder every muscle and bone ached! She would not be safe until she got off this island, but she was too weak to walk to the shore by dawn. She needed a hiding place.

   "Blood for blood—"

   "Who will pay?"

   "Their knives are ready."

Emyn grabbed a tree as her stomach heaved once more; the cramps came as regularly as labor pains. They would stop. In a few heartbeats, she pushed away from the trunk and lurched ahead.

*   *   *

BY STARLIGHT, Emyn circled the large house twice: once while behind bushes and a second time leaning against the walls, trying to feel heat, smell food, or hear living voices. By now she was certain that the building stood empty and cold. Was it roofed? Nearby, rock foundations outlined a stable or perhaps a house for slaves, still to be built.

The king's grand new home. This could be no other place, so high above the sea. Across the water lay the rocky beach north of her village. She guessed—and hoped she was right—that Gundori's current home overlooked the sea road and its commerce. Probably the king sat there now while slaves applied sweet-smelling unguents to his eye. She would not find a better hiding place than this: far away, out of sight.

The mad ghosts had called her every name imaginable over the last few hours, but they quieted now. Emyn couldn't waste this chance; she hobbled to the door at the front of the house and pressed her ear against it. She heard nothing. She pulled on the door, yanked harder, then dug in her feet and tugged with all her might. Gasping in pain, she slumped to the ground, the door still shut tight.

"*You cut the king!*" The voices started up again.

There was another, smaller door near the back. She would try that. Surely it would open. First she needed a minute to rest.

Had she cut the king? Emyn's memory trapped odd images. The knife had arced in the torchlight and drawn blood, but mostly she remembered the softness of Gundori's flesh when she flew down to attack him. She might well have put his eye out. That would be worse than killing him; if a king was not whole, he could not rule.

Who would take his place? Lorsus the Wealthy?

She sidled away from the door and lowered herself to sit

leaning against the wall. Lorsus had told her about this house. Not finished for months, standing empty . . . many slaves worked on its furnishings. They wove tapestries, perhaps with images of the horned god on them . . .

EMYN WOKE WITH A START; the sky was gray. The sun was about to rise.

Pain shot through her like small knives as she pushed herself up and hurried to the smaller door. She winced and heard the ghosts giggling . . . were there other voices, were living men near? The dim light of dawn exposed her.

In a panic, she yanked at the door until she thought her shoulder would rip loose. Finally, bit by bit, the door scraped over the ground. Emyn squeezed herself into the opening, using her body to wedge and push until she had enough room—

She was inside; it was no darker here than without. Overhead, unthatched beams crossed the sky. The sun lit clouds from far away as it pushed over the edge of the earth. Emyn pulled the door shut behind her and looked around. She was inside, but where could she hide? What if slaves came here to work during the day? The few tools and piles of wood she saw would be no help.

She tripped and fell onto boards, cut roughly and bound together to form a pallet. Through the gaps in the wood, Emyn glimpsed the darkness of a pit. The boards covered a hole, just as they had at Vinnia's house. A storage pit. Not for sacrifices, not for the dead, but to keep the grain dry in this upside-down land.

Emyn moved the boards enough to stick her head into the hole and took deep breaths. Musty air rose. She reached her arm down and felt the rock along the side of the pit. It was uneven, and at the furthest point her fingertips touched, she was sure she felt a ledge wide enough for toes to balance on.

Did she dare?

She had flown with the Morrigu this night. She would dare anything.

Pulling the dress tight around her legs, Emyn pushed the boards aside and lowered herself into the hole. Four ledges, each a forearm's length below another, were carved in the rock. Her foot missed the last one, but she didn't fall far. When she stood straight she reached up and nudged the pallet back over the opening. Then she turned her back to the faint light and felt her way.

She crouched in a level tunnel twice as long as she was tall. The floor dropped away at the end, maybe into another pit. On the sides of the tunnel, more storage areas were being carved out. Tools rested in one depression; how long before workmen returned to use them?

Once she had her bearings, Emyn dozed in the tunnel, facing the shafts of light that filtered through the pallet above. Bouts of sleep were filled with nightmares. Each time she woke, the light reminded her that she wasn't trapped or dead. Rain splattered onto the floor above.

Before noon, she heard voices. Men pulled the heavy door open: the one she'd been unable to move. Between words and a few shouts came the scratchy sound of paws scampering throughout the house.

Dogs. They used dogs to search for her. Emyn stayed very still. No one could see her, but dogs didn't need sight. They sniffed to find their prey, and she reeked of vomit. If the men came near, they might smell her themselves.

"He looks for you, big raven."

"He'll make you pay!"

Emyn tried to listen beyond the voices. Where were the dogs? For once she was glad the spirits were near; dogs hated ghosts.

"Blackie! Duck! Enough, come!"

Emyn let out a slow, quivering breath as the man called from the doorway, "Nothing here!"

She heard the door close and suddenly, unrealistically, she wished for water. The men were gone, but someone would eventually come back. As soon as darkness arrived with a new day, she would leave.

HOURS LATER, moonlight showed her a path that wound downhill; Emyn stayed close but never walked on it. Instead, she limped behind bushes and rocks and trees alongside it. When her stomach convulsed again, she crumbled into a nest of ferns.

She drank water from a stone-lined spring on the long descending trek, but not even water would stay inside her. She slumped down and vomited, angry with her weakness. This had to stop. She could not live without water and food and could not move without strength. When she stopped heaving, she stood up and walked on, a hand over her mouth to muffle the labored breaths.

She was too cautious, she realized. No one would hear. Everyone within earshot, even slaves, sheltered in their homes out of the cold. The thought of women and men sitting near the warmth of their fires, living their lives normally, brought comfort.

The moon that guided her would be gone soon. She'd had two goals tonight: to get water and to walk to Darsa's wagon. She'd found water; now she had to find the wagon.

If Emyn was right about the date, Darsa would drive the wagon to the mainland by late morning. She might even stop at Suttia's house to ask for her. But Emyn intended to intercept

Darsa and test their friendship by begging for help.

She imagined Darsa's surprise when a black-clothed Emyn cried out: "Help me, I've attacked the king and his warriors want to kill me."

What would Darsa do?

That was for Darsa to decide; Emyn had no other hope. In her filthy state and bizarre dress, no sane person would let her approach. She could not cross the sea road without being seen, and then Gundori's men would drag her back to the king, no doubt to be killed.

Emyn walked, holding her hands out to grab any tree or fence for support. She had lost count of the times she'd wished for her stick, lost somewhere in the flight from Gundori. She knew she was close to Vinnia's estate but to recognize it at night . . . she glanced up again. The moon was in the west but not low—not yet. She still had time.

JUST BEFORE THE MOON RESTED, Emyn stretched to look over a rock wall, then crouched down and wept in relief. She knew where she was; she'd seen this view and the enclosures nearby months ago. This was where she sat when speaking to Rialos. She'd found Vinnia's home; somehow she'd find the wagon.

The door of the house opened, exposing scant light from the hearth. A slave ran to a ditch near the road and relieved himself.

"Do you want him?"

"He rides the loud woman all night!"

"Grunting, grunting—"

The young man ran back to the house. The geese honked and he hissed "Shut up!" before opening the door and slipping inside.

Geese. Emyn had forgotten about geese. Their racket would

be worse than any dogs . . . and what if Vinnia had dogs as well? The ghosts kept up their awful gossip, but Emyn ignored them. The sight of the slave brought another young man to mind: the freckled slave who'd carried the cup toward Emyn in the meadow. He had been drugged, she was sure. What had happened to him after Emyn escaped? What of the others?

She shuddered behind the rock wall and hugged herself. She would never take for granted the warmth of a fire again, not after two nights spent hiding in this bitter cold. Weariness allowed her to doze fitfully, but the frigid air and her own nervousness woke her often.

In the deepest darkness after the moon set, she crawled toward Darsa's wagon, anxious to get into it before the household stirred and began its work. As she passed the pigs' enclosure the smell of slop, garbage, and dung dizzied her. Once she reached the stable, tall walls hid her from the main house, so she stood and shuffled behind it. The wagon would be in the stable, most likely. How could she get inside without setting off the geese? Emyn contemplated this as she came to the end of the wall.

Nothing was visible, but her fingers gripped a thick post. Above it, thatch slanted down, black against the stars. The post supported a roofed shelter—for what? Emyn's eyes strained through the darkness; she was afraid to move closer until she was sure.

No geese honked, so she shuffled beyond the post, reaching in front of her. Waist high, where the top of the wheel should be, her palm brushed wood—curved wood. She could trace the shape of the wheel. The wagon rested in front of her, under the thatch.

She edged forward, her hands out, eager to touch the familiar shape. She felt her way around to the seat she had ridden on so many times. The wagon was steady enough to climb on; no doubt rocks wedged against its wheels. Emyn pulled herself into the bed just behind the seat and stretched her arms out, exploring. Her fingers touched empty baskets, a coil of rope, and canvas sacks for grain. She pulled them all toward her, covering herself as well as she could. For the moment, she was grateful for her black dress. She would look like a shadow under the seat.

Exhausted, Emyn rolled against the wagon's front boards, right under the seat, and shivered as she fell once more into a nervous sleep.

"Emyn?"

She woke to blinding light that outlined a silhouette overhead.

 26

Gorio repeated her name, and turned to shout the news to others.

"No!" Emyn choked, and her arm shot up to grab his hand. "No, please, shhh!"

Gorio leaned over the seat, and she could see his wide eyes and somber mouth in the shadow. "No?" He reached down to touch her cheek, wet with tears. Had she been dreaming? "Darsa," Gorio whispered. "Get Darsa?"

"Darsa. Yes, Darsa, shhhh." Emyn put a finger to her lips. "Only Darsa No one else."

The child bobbed his head and was gone.

Had she just handed away her life? The next face to peer over the wagon, the next touch she felt, might bring death. And she could do nothing but lie here, shivering and defenseless. Her heart pounded like a drum.

Shouting erupted from the yard; the noise stabbed Emyn like a knife. If she had a weapon, she would have killed herself in that moment. Her muscles tightened, ready to fight. No one would haul her before Gundori alive.

"Hitch up that wagon if you expect supper today," Darsa

hollered. "Damn fools, wasting my time! Get in the wagon, boy!"

Emyn breathed out—how long had she held it in? Gorio was at her back, dropping a small fur over her arms. He moved the baskets and the ropes, unfolded a strip of canvas and draped it over her. Crates, bleached and smelling of bird droppings, rattled near her head.

The wagon jerked. Gorio sat near her back. "Shhh," he whispered to her. "Sh, sh, sh."

Time passed; Darsa climbed into her seat. "All right back there?"

"Good," said Gorio. They were moving. Emyn's eyes burned. If anyone looked, if they noticed . . . she was now responsible for Gorio's life and Darsa's as well.

Gorio leaned against her as if she were a pile of rags. She still shook; as the wagon bumped along it was impossible to stay still. Even through the canvas, Emyn caught the stench of fresh fish, the taste of salt, and heard the calls of people crossing to and from the village, selling food and exchanging gossip.

"Big men," the boy murmured. Emyn heard Darsa laugh and ask about a woman. A man shouted "Ha!" like a blow falling, then another added to the joke in a low voice. They knew Darsa; she served Vinnia. The wagon slowed, but never stopped.

Voices receded, and soon the only sounds were the creaking of the wagon, the gulls' calls, and the lapping of waves. Emyn's fists unclenched for the first time since waking. There was still danger; she could not show herself in the village. With a start, like waking from a dream, Emyn realized that she had no idea where Darsa might take her.

"Shhh." Gorio patted her shoulder when she jerked. "Quiet, shhh."

The dead king railed and screamed, but from far away. Gorio stroked her matted hair . . . no, Aruca. Gorio still sat at her back, but Aruca's soft hands touched Emyn's face and hair just lightly enough to soothe, not tickle. "You're safe now," the ghost whispered. "Rest. You're safe."

Emyn believed her. Warm for the first time since Gundori's litter had arrived, and knowing that others stood watch, she gave in to her weariness. The poison, the running and climbing that she didn't remember, and the crawling and walking that she did, was over. The world spun away from her.

She was pulled up gently, and opened her eyes. Trees reeled overhead. Soft voices babbled like water, and then quieted, tumbling along another path. Aruca touched her cheek, reminding her to rest. Fear diminished; Emyn slept and slept.

SHE WOKE BURIED IN fur like a mouse in its nest. For a brief moment Emyn thought she was once again a child in her father's house, waking after the holiday and wondering if snow covered the fields. Whose roof sheltered her? Gaps overhead showed stars against a deep blue sky that slowly lightened.

She turned her head when someone snored and raised herself on her elbow. There was Nonicos across a near-dead fire, blonde hair bunched up. A heap of fur to his right would be Laurina and Oleda; Micco rested near their feet. Her stomach growled. She was hungry—no, starving.

Emyn got to her knees, pulling the fur with her as she edged closer to the stone ring where embers glowed. Plenty of wood was piled within reach, and she built the flame up, adding chips as she coaxed it with a branch the length of her stick. . . .

Her stick was gone. Emyn remembered everything at once and shut her eyes, falling back on her heels. Gundori's litter, the foul drink, the blood, the flight . . . and the nights of pain and weakness, the hiding. How long had she been on the island? Where had Darsa gone?

Home, hopefully. Home safely. Surely the gods of this land would watch over a woman who helped a friend.

Somehow Darsa got her to Nonicos. Emyn owed Darsa; in this or the next world she would repay. But where was Emyn now? So far from the coast that she couldn't smell the sea: in a farmhouse long abandoned from the look of it. Once again, the world had tipped over like a cup, and everything Emyn thought she knew spilled out.

The black dress was gone; a shirt—a boy's, softened from much wear—covered her. Fire warmed her hands and face. Emyn shut her eyes once more.

A warm fire. How many times in the last few days had she wished for this very thing? Maybe she should not ask for more than the moment offered.

She sat in silence, waiting for the light to wake the others. Eventually her brother rolled onto his back and Emyn gasped. She clapped a hand over her mouth and rose to her knees again.

Nonicos' swollen face had lain against a pile of rags stiffened with dried blood. A bandage wrapped round his head had shifted during sleep, and Emyn saw the worst immediately: he'd lost an eye.

"Shhh," Laurina's breath was hot in her ear. "Let him sleep. He's all right."

"Wha—" the word emerged like a puff of air.

Laurina forced Emyn to turn away; when their eyes met, she whispered again, "He's all right."

"His eye—"

Laurina nodded. "It's gone. He's healing."

"Who—"

"Can you stand?"

Rags were wrapped around her feet, Emyn noticed, and Laurina handed her a heavy wool skirt to tie at her waist.

Laurina walked her outside the little house. Somehow, knowing about the fire within made it less cold. "Gundori did this, didn't he? His men—"

Laurina nodded. "On midwinter's day. The tide went out late in the morning, and warriors rushed over the road. We were still sleeping. We'd been up the long night, you know. We heard them yelling. We thought raiders, at first. Maybe even pirates. People ran. But it was our own warriors."

Laurina shuddered. "Our own warriors. They charged into Suttia's house and demanded you. But you had gone with them! We—"

"Mama."

Laurina bent and scooped up the child. "We told the warriors that the king had sent for you, but they said terrible—"

"No." Oleda put her hand over her mother's mouth.

Laurina pulled it away. "They frightened her. They—"

"No!" The child was stubborn; she would not let her mother speak.

"It is your story we wait to hear," said a ghost.

"Tell me later," Emyn put her arm around the mother and child. "It's cold out here."

The ancestors of Laurina and Oleda surrounded them, and spirits hovered by Nonicos as well—but they could lift no sword or shield in defense; no spirit could. Emyn had always known that . . . but the Morrigu, a goddess, had saved her. Why?

When they'd all shared cereal and sun was high, Laurina took her daughter and Micco to gather firewood, pinecones, and whatever else they might find nearby. Her brother finally stirred, so Emyn used a stick to toast more millet over the fire then poured the grain into another pot filled with water as hot as they could get it.

Nonicos knelt across the fire from her and winced in pain.

"I don't know much about what happened," Emyn told him. "Your daughter objected."

"Oleda saw them hit me. She won't hear a word about warriors after what happened—cries and carries on."

Emyn smiled without mirth. Long ago, she thought she could block bad things by not looking. "Did Darsa leave this food?"

"The millet and eggs, yes. She said Vinnia would never miss it. The rest," he nodded toward clay pots with lids, and baskets, "Haebro brought. He got us out here. He said he'd bring more food."

Emyn glanced at her brother whenever she could, trying to build a picture of his new face. Half of it was familiar, the other half strange. Even his moustache seemed split: one side stretched across his swollen cheek.

"Does Suttia know we're here?"

He shrugged, and then gritted his teeth. "She doesn't want to know."

Emyn was sure that his ribs were bruised or broken. "This is my doing—"

"No. My own stupid fault. They said you'd stolen gold from Gundori."

"Gold is your due!" hissed the dead king.

Emyn stirred the millet as it swelled and softened. The ghost would have to wait.

"No one believed it, but I . . . could not stay quiet. My sister, a thief?" Nonicos laughed a little. "The warriors—five or six of them—they were looking for someone to hit. I called them liars, so they went after me. They didn't use their weapons. Just fists."

He tried to swing his arm out in front of him and winced again. "And feet."

She couldn't keep the heat out of her voice. "No one helped you?"

"No one could, Emyn. Against warriors? They do whatever they want. They threatened to burn the house to the ground if they found out that anyone hid you."

There were no bowls. Emyn used the stick and a folded hide to move the pot from the fire and push it toward Nonicos. "So Haebro brought you here?"

Nonicos blew on the cereal. "Brought a bucket of ale out to the warriors to start. That got them off me. Later he used his own cart to move us. Lots of men owe him favors. Now we do too."

Emyn watched him eat. Rescue always came from unexpected places, but she understood. Haebro helped them because he could not help Aruca.

"We can't go back," Nonicos said. "Ever. Even Laurina agrees and she lived there for five years."

Emyn nodded as he passed the pot back to her. There was still cereal in it. She had eaten some earlier, but a little more sounded good.

"Not for honor, not for revenge, not for property. Do you understand, Emyn?"

She looked at him sharply; the words began to sink in.

"No one knows you've come back," Nonicos said softly. "No one wants to know. Haebro's made them keep our secret, and we have to keep it too. To go back would put everyone in danger. Haebro, your friend Darsa, the boy. Do you see?"

"I do." She put the bowl down.

"I'll get better. You're already better. We'll find a new home."

Emyn stared at the pot. The world had tipped over, and everything spilled out.

They were alive; they would find a new home. The Morrigu had saved Emyn, and together they had attacked a king, maybe put his eye out. Her brother paid with his own eye for that. It wasn't fair, but it made strange sense.

She accepted it until she thought of her brother's tools. Nonicos had hauled those tools all the way from Samarnum. Someone else would use them now.

That small thing, Nonicos' tools . . . that made her angry.

A WOLF HOWLED IN the distance as Laurina plopped next to Emyn and heaved a sigh thick with weariness. "Tell me a story."

"About the magic doe?" Emyn grinned. That was Oleda's favorite tale; she had asked to hear it every night for the past week.

"No magic doe. And no ghosts. Tell me a story about Samarnum."

The fire crackled. Emyn told Laurina about the time Samarnum's well had dried up, and the ghosts showed Emyn where to find more water. She puffed her cheeks out like the headman, slurred her voice as if she were as drunk as Hentios, and imitated Iomat's sharp tones perfectly. Laurina and Nonicos laughed; Micco, who had been nearly asleep, crawled behind Nonicos. Hearing his father's name upset him perhaps—or was it Emyn's mimicry?

"Then we heard a holler from above, on the roof—Aaaahhhhhhoooooooo." Emyn's voice faded away. "And there lay the poor man on the hard ground, knocked out with his tail broken."

"Carried a bag of straw to sit on for a month." Nonicos slapped his leg.

The ghost interrupted. "My voice goes unheard while you tell stories."

Emyn waved him away and described how Hentios' mallet flew, marking the spot where the well was to be set.

"I kept my word," the dead king muttered. "Where is my reward?"

"Reward?" Emyn rolled her eyes at the others. "The ghost wishes a reward!"

"He got his bull," said Nonicos, and added for Laurina, "from the headman, in thanks for the well."

"You mock me?" The ghost bent near the fire, but could not stir the sparks or smoke. He was not as strong as he used to be.

"Sit troscad on the gods if you feel slighted," Emyn said.

"Don't tell him that!" Nonicos laughed. "He'll scream at you all night."

Laurina flushed and bit her lip, still not used to the idea of sharing a room with ghosts.

Troscad . . . Emyn's mind raced ahead of her story. A troscad could not be ignored. Anyone could start a troscad if they wanted justice; that was the point. Even a king had to submit.

"So did they dig where you said?" Laurina asked.

"What?"

"Finish the story!"

"Oh." Emyn breathed deeply. "They built the well where I said, once Nonicos and our father agreed to do the work. And eleven years later I married Hentios' son."

"She did," Nonicos snorted. "No one could stop her."

"You married the son of a drunk?" Laurina looked from Emyn to Nonicos and back. "Why weren't your ghosts looking out for you then?"

Emyn barely noticed the question. "Laurina, you recognize troscad here in the west, don't you?"

"Of course." Again, she looked to her husband and back to

Emyn, then her eyes widened. "Emyn, you can't begin a troscad against the king."

"The law says—" Emyn broke off when she saw her brother's twisted face. What did the law matter to Gundori? He bent it whatever way he wanted. Her idea fizzled like a falling star. "No. You're right."

"He would kill you if you even tried." Nonicos' voice was hoarse.

"I know. I won't do it. We'll never go back."

Laurina patted her hand. "My grandfather used to say that justice was for the next world, not this one."

Laurina's grandfather had lived on a river two days' walk beyond Venetona, the great port town of the Veneti. They hoped to find a home there, though Laurina had not visited since she was a child.

Emyn looked for a way to end the uneasy quiet that had descended. That afternoon, Haebro had brought a wheelbarrow laden with food and supplies. She reached for a large wedge of cheese. "Let's eat more. I've been hungry for days. Micco? Want cheese?" Nonicos handed her a small knife, the only tool he still possessed. The boy edged closer, his mouth hanging open, as Emyn sliced and passed wedges of cheese to the others.

Haebro had left the wheelbarrow with them, saying he would fetch it from the port city himself in spring. "Leave it with Nerrus when you stop in Venetona. He'll keep it for me. You can stay with him, too."

"We have no money," Nonicos pointed out.

Haebro had waved his hand as if that didn't matter. "You worry too much. Nerrus is old, and his house and woodwork need repair. This time of year, he gets lonely. You can earn a few days' keep and still have time to look around and price tools."

"How can I earn our keep if I have no tools?"

"Nerrus has a mallet and axe at least. Probably chisels, too, or he'd borrow them." Haebro was full of comfort. "He's a good soul. Don't worry."

They would load the wheelbarrow with their few ragged possessions and leave this ruined hut at first light.

Possessions?

Anger roiled up in Emyn when she least expected it, and now she nearly choked. What did they possess anymore? They wore rags, not clothes, and carried a few old baskets that Haebro had scavenged for them. Nonicos' tools, their box of coins, the healing stone, Oleda's doll—all these were gone. Suttia disposed of them, keeping what she wished. "She's within her rights," Haebro had growled.

What of *their* rights? Suttia could have helped them, could have given the box of coins to Haebro for them, but she didn't.

"Demand your due!" the dead king whispered, as if he knew her resentful thoughts.

"Did you see what Haebro brought?" Laurina pointed to a small pile. Rags, Emyn first thought until she saw a ribbon of yellow silk peaking out between folds of heavier cloth. "There are two good dresses in there and a fine shift. Made for a tall woman, but we can shorten the beige one for you. We won't have to look like beggars when we get to Venetona."

Emyn pulled out the dress; it was linen. These had to be Aruca's. How long had Haebro held onto them?

Nonicos raised his one good eyebrow when he saw the dress. "I forgot to tell you—Haebro said they found the black dress, the one you were wearing. Down on the shore by Gundori's pastures, caught up on some rocks."

"That should settle matters," Laurina said.

Emyn stared, unable to put together a question. The black

dress on the rocks near Gundori's pasture? She'd run so far from there . . . .

"Darsa took the dress back to the island," Nonicos explained. "She said she would throw it out to sea."

"And now they've found it?" Nonicos nodded and Emyn added, "Gundori thinks I drowned, then."

"He might, but no one else thinks so." Nonicos paused for a moment then shrugged. "Haebro didn't want to tell you this, Emyn, but you should know: There's a rumor that *you* threw the dress into the sea, once you had no use for it."

Laurina looked as confused as Emyn felt. "What do you mean?"

"Well, this is what Haebro says. Folks on the island—your lady Vinnia and her friends—think it was all a tease." Nonicos avoided looking at Emyn's face with his good eye. "That maybe you stole a gold necklace to get Gundori to come after you; that the whole uproar was just . . . to make him catch you."

"Gundori?" Emyn curled her lips in disgust.

"Well, since no one's seen him since that night, they're saying it could be because he's got a new woman."

"That's ridiculous!" Laurina hissed.

"It is." Nonicos looked apologetic, as if it were his fault. "But that's what they say."

"You see how craven your tribes have become," the ghost growled. "Wealth and power determine truth. Wisdom withers away."

"That's not true, ghost," Emyn said, but she choked on the words. "I will not believe it."

"Creature of blood and skin," the dead king said. "Why do you not confront living men as you do me?"

Nerrus' house proved a wise choice for a family wishing to avoid crowds and questions. His home stood just above the beach, far from the rowdier inns of Venetona where sailors drank and slept away the winter. From here, Emyn could hear rain and wind and the calls of gulls and seabirds. After living in the wild, the sound of the surf lulling her to sleep was more comforting than any music.

"You don't know anyone in town?" Nerrus asked the next morning when Nonicos talked about woodworkers and tools.

"No—"

"I do," Emyn spoke up. "I know the Honored Master Nanto and—"

"The druid Nanto?" Nerrus turned toward her. "Ah, now that's sad, that is. A master of words who cannot speak."

"Cannot speak? Why not?"

"Cannot speak or even move, from what I hear. Struck down months ago. Before Samhain, it was—yes, I'm sure of it. The younger one had to light the fires then."

Sad news—but it filled Emyn with hope. If Nanto were

paralyzed, Rialos would have taken over his duties. He had been busy; that's why he hadn't come back to see her.

"I want to visit the druids," Emyn told her brother. "Rialos will help us. I'm sure he will."

"Little Gutumaros," Aruca whispered. "You look for an excuse to see the man again. Is he worth the pain?"

Nerrus and her brother were watching; Emyn bit back a retort. "Can you tell me the way to the druid's house?" she asked Nerrus.

"I HAVE TO REST."

Near the top of the low hill, Emyn stumbled to a wide log and sank onto it. Close by, men and women sat on benches and rocks outside an inn enjoying the morning while heavier rains held back. They glanced toward the strangers and stared outright at Nonicos' scarred and battered face, but said nothing.

Emyn looked down the path. Tree branches sprinkled rainwater as the wind shook them. She spotted Nerrus' house below; Laurina and Oleda chased the gulls.

Nonicos looked out over the gulf where islands dotted the water. "We're protected from storms here, I guess."

A plainly-clothed man had emerged from the inn and sauntered near enough to overhear. "Not from all storms. The gulf makes her own weather sometimes. Where do you visit from, friend?"

"Very far, from Belgic lands. We travel to see cousins who live on the Visambu River."

Nonicos gave their names, and Emyn nodded when the man looked at her. She wore the linen dress that had been Aruca's and appeared more prosperous than she felt. But linen was no warmer than butterfly wings; Emyn shivered and clutched her shawl tighter.

"The currents are tricky," the man said. Other men edged closer, eager to add their opinions.

"Treacherous, they are."

"You wouldn't last long without knowing your business."

"Never been on a ship." Nonicos shook his head. "But I've caulked and mended a few and had no complaints about the work."

"Indeed? What sort of ships have you worked on?" The timbre of the talk changed and the voices grew warmer.

The men took to her brother as decent men usually did. Nonicos could find work here, but he wouldn't stay. The lure of living in a small village with family again hooked him.

She turned her attention to the sea. Only from this height by daylight could she appreciate the size of the gulf. The far shore was beyond her sight. More ships than she could count dotted the water and beach. All things here were beyond Emyn's ability to define. Some of the ships looked impossibly large; how could such heavy boats float on water?

Aruca appeared beside her. "There's an island in the center of the gulf where kings are taken after they die."

How could Emyn know which island was in the center when she could not see the other side?

She looked up the path. The houses were larger atop the slope where the king and the wealthy lived. "Can I see the house of the chief druid from here?"

"The chief druid?" A man raised his eyebrows. "Now, why—"

"It's none of your business why, is it?" His wife elbowed him. "You can almost see it, dear. Past the well, on your left. A quarter league, but it's flat from here."

"Thank you." Emyn knew that Nonicos had no wish to sit in a

druid's house. She turned to him. "I should go there first, out of respect."

"Do you want—"

She shook her head. It would be easier to ask for help alone.

NANTO'S DOOR OPENED AS soon as she knocked. No servant or slave stood there, but Rialos, covered in a dark cloak like a shadow. Emyn started, then smiled, but he did not smile back.

"This is unexpected." He looked past her.

"Honored Master." Was it her imagination, or would he not meet her eyes? "Is this Nanto's house?"

"It is. I live here too." He moved and she was forced to step backwards. He pulled the door shut behind him. "But I must leave."

Realization sank in slowly. He did not say her name. He did not invite her into his house. He withheld hospitality, a harsh insult.

For a moment Emyn felt poisoned once again. Emptiness grabbed at her, blocking light, air, and thought. The door shut; Rialos muttered something about returning before sunset.

He would not help her. He thought her foul and unworthy of welcome.

A roar like breaking waves filled her ears: the dead king, furious, screamed in anger. Emyn did not listen. Her mind raced along its own path. Gundori had taken everything from her family and her last hope for aid—a loan, a kind word, friendship, all were snatched away. Rialos had told her to go to Gundori if she had spirit words to share. Now he shut his door on her.

The ghost's words and Emyn's thoughts converged. "How dare he—"

She stabbed her stick into the dirt. "Honored Master Rialos," she called to his back and her voice echoed like a bell. "Take as long as you like. I will sit here in troscad until you return. I will sit here until you submit to judgment for what you have done to my family."

Aruca clapped her hands. "Good girl!"

Rialos stopped as if he'd hit a wall. Figures appeared in doorways, staring and silent. The druid turned and took a few steps back. "What? You'll what?" Emyn could not read his face, but his voice gave him away. She had truly surprised him.

"Troscad," she pronounced again.

"Troscad, against me? For what?"

Emyn took a deep breath. "Because of you, my family has no home and no livelihood. My brother has suffered injuries. No one will speak for us. I am slandered in every house and on every road in Gundori's land. Your words betrayed us, and I demand justice."

Her voice was strong; all the eavesdroppers heard. Rialos came closer and bent his head. "How is any of that my doing?" Emyn stood stiffly and didn't answer. She had stated the charges; the rest waited until a druid sat to judge them.

"This is ridiculous." Rialos looked about and noticed the curious stares that surrounded them. Suddenly his voice was smooth and cajoling. "Emyn, I must leave. I'm sorry. But there is no cause for troscad. We can discuss it all later . . . privately."

"I have declared troscad and told you why. I will sit here."

Anger crackled over him, changing his posture like a piece of meat charring over a fire. She saw it seep into the set of his jaw, his clenched fist; it curled through his entire body.

"Stay then, with your ghosts. Play your part." Rialos' cloak snapped as he turned and stomped away, disappearing beyond the corner of another house.

Emyn leaned back against the wall and let herself slide down it. There was nothing to do now but wait.

* * *

IT BEGAN TO RAIN. Thatch spared Emyn the worst of the wetness, but she shuddered with cold and pulled the shawl—the one shawl owned between her and Laurina—around her shoulders. Nonicos would assume she rested with the druids; he might not come looking for her for hours.

Her brother would not be pleased. A troscad could last for days; she would have to climb this hill before each dawn until it ended. When would that be? Emyn had seen a glimpse of Rialos' temper, and guessed that he was a stubborn man. His neighbors might talk, but he didn't have to listen. No one could force the druid to submit.

She sighed, and then straightened her back. She was better off than before. She had put her foot on a road and was bound to end up somewhere.

"COME IN OUT OF the rain, please. It does not help your brother." Rialos bent down and put his face close to hers. "We can discuss what you need."

Emyn jumped; he'd approached silently—or had she dozed? Beyond the druid's silhouette, she saw that the sun had not sunk low enough to release her for the night.

"I am the same person I was when I arrived," she said. "You did not want me in your house then. I will stay here."

Furious, he jerked erect and whipped past her, but in the next instant he stopped, as still as a serpent about to strike.

"Why prolong this, then?" He turned and raised his voice so that everyone standing in their own doorways could hear. "I submit to judgment!"

He held out his hand to her, but she ignored it. "When?"

"As soon as another druid can hear your case. Nanto cannot. We'll send for someone."

"Good." She poked with her stick; the ground was slick and muddy now, but it couldn't be helped. A wave of relief buoyed her when she recognized her brother's form on the path, hurrying toward them. "My family stays at Nerrus' house."

"You can rest by our fire. I have submitted. There's no rule that says you cannot accept hospitality from me."

The offer pained her; it came too late. Men never understood that a lost moment changed the world. "My brother is coming."

"Wait, Emyn." He growled the words; he wanted no one else to hear. "Why are you doing this? Troscad is not taken lightly. You damage yourself."

She glared as she walked past him. "I have not done the damage, druid."

No other guests beside Emyn's family boarded with Nerrus. In the warmth and quiet, Emyn felt it was as much her home as his. Nonicos worked daily on whatever needed doing while the women helped cook and mended clothes.

She tried not to think about a trial or how Rialos' anger blistered her, but the dead king brought it up constantly and urged her to visit the king. "He waits for my words."

"You've given me no words for him."

Nerrus looked up when Emyn muttered, and she smiled sheepishly.

The dead king snarled at her. "Why should I waste my voice when you pay no attention?"

Each day when the tide receded, Emyn took Oleda and waded out onto sand and rocks, looking for crabs and shellfish. What seemed like work to people who'd done it all their lives was as much fun for Emyn as it was for the toddler. Their feet were numb with cold by the time they'd filled Nerrus' bucket, but they never went hungry.

Five days passed. The month was ending and a new one

would begin soon, a lucky month. Lucky for whom, though? Either she or Rialos must lose to the other.

Emyn and Oleda walked along the exposed sand at low tide just before the sun set. Emyn struggled with the full bucket then sent the child to fetch Nonicos.

Orange light dazzled her. The setting sun reflected off the wet sand and tide pools and lit the western sky. Emyn could not pull her eyes away, even as a tall figure approached.

"That is heavy, Chiomara." A hand took the bucket from Emyn. Only when he spoke did she realize it was not her brother. "Let me carry it."

She threw herself into his arms, almost knocking the boy down. "You're so tall." The words were silly, but no others came to mind. "You're so tall!"

"I grow only to please you. Tell me when to stop."

"You can stop; you are perfect! Have you seen Nonicos?"

"I have, just now. I walked from the druid's house when I learned you were here."

Emyn let Moradag go, and he handed her the stick before picking up the bucket. She was relieved; Nonicos would have told him their story already, and he must know about the trial as well. "Will Bodocnos decide my troscad? Is that why you've come?"

Moradag caught his breath, set down the bucket, and faced her. "I have sad news, lady. I wish I did not." He took her free hand. "My master Bodocnos is no longer in this world. He left us behind to fend for ourselves."

MORADAG CLOSED HIS EYES, gathering his thoughts as the group sat before the fire. Emyn, Nonicos, Laurina, Micco, and Oleda watched him. Crumbs of bread had been brushed away, and Nerrus disappeared with a bucket of empty, drying shells. News had been exchanged, and Oleda asked for a song, but this most important story waited until they had all eaten and calmed.

"We came to see the Honored Master Rialos after leaving you, but he was not here," Moradag began. "My master left a message—not from us, but from the Lady Vinnia. She had invited Rialos to visit. After only two days, we left."

"Vinnia is half-sister to Rialos," Emyn said. "Did you know that?"

"No, I did not. I wondered why my master was so precise about the words of his message."

"They hadn't seen each other in a long time." She sighed. "I interrupt; please forgive me."

Moradag reached over to squeeze her hand. "I do not want to tell this tale any more than you want to hear it. But let me say the words then we can mourn.

"We went northwest, my master and I. We stayed near the sea much of the way. He joked that he could map the coast by the taste of the oysters in each cove. They are all different, you know. There were times when we cut away from the ocean and traveled along rivers. I thought he grew thin. Once I said he must pine for you, and he called me a brat.

"His face grew gaunt, and circles darkened his eyes. He could not hide his pain but he would not admit weakness. One night he raved. He insisted we return to Venetona. He said he was always too stubborn, and we should have waited for Rialos. By then, though, we were near the great harbor of the Ossismi peninsula, a port as busy as this one. Beyond that is the sea. Britain lies north, and the island sanctuary of wise women sits just west."

Micco hummed softly as he leaned against Moradag's arm, happy to have him back and ignorant of the meaning of his words.

"He was too weak to go back. Indeed, he was not even aware that I carried him the last few days of our journey.

"I sought healers. There were many in that busy place, but their faces fell when they rested their hands on the Honored Master and pressed their palms and fingers on his stomach. The tumors, by then, were large and unmistakable. Noble families and druids offered us every comfort. Soon he rested in a fine home on the softest mattress, but I do not know if it mattered to him."

They stared at the fire, unwilling to meet each other's eyes.

"At first he refused the medicines, saying he wished to keep his wits. In the end, though, pain stole his mind away. We did everything we could to ease his passage, and he died early in the month of Dumann."

"A hard month," Nonicos muttered.

"It was," Moradag whispered. Nonicos used Emyn's new stick to push a wedge of wood deeper into the fire.

After a few minutes, Moradag spoke again. "My master's last wish had been for me to return to Venetona and put myself under the tutelage of the Honored Master Rialos. I thought to wait until spring—there were three masters in that town, and all offered me a roof and training. Their kindness was my comfort. Unexpectedly, though, a druid of Eire arrived and said I could come south with him where he had business. And so . . ."

Moradag put his hands together and stared at his own fingertips, breathing deeply until he could speak again. "I have learned much since we parted, but not what I would have wished. Our travels last summer will remain in my mind as a time of joy that will never be matched in this lifetime."

Nonicos nodded. "We will remember the Honored Master Bodocnos as we do our own."

"Yes," the others murmured.

"It was the fourth day of the month," Moradag said.

"Then in the new year, on the fourth day of Dumann, we will make offerings, thanking the gods for the lives we are allowed to share."

"THE HONORED MASTER FERDIATH will decide your case, if you are willing," Moradag told Emyn later.

Ferdiath. She had suspected as much; how many Irish druids walked this land?

"I am willing. Do you practice your sword with the warriors each day?"

"I will. We only arrived yesterday." Moradag smiled. "I must stay stronger than my new teacher. If Ferdiath does not grant you justice, I'll have to challenge him." He held up his hand as Emyn started to speak. "Chiomara, I am not allowed to discuss the matter between you and the Honored Master. Anything else, but not that."

TWO DAYS LATER, Moradag brought a horse to carry Emyn up to the king's house. "The presence of an oracle cannot be ignored," he grinned, "whether his druid welcomes her or not. The Honored Masters Rialos and Ferdiath have gone to make sacrifices in honor of Bodocnos' life, so the king thought it a good day to invite you to his home."

Emyn had visited a king's house months before, when she first left Samarnum. The ruler of her own tribe had treated the Gutumaros as a messenger—to be heard then sent away. What should she expect from a stranger on this rainy day?

To her relief, King Vlidorix of the Veneti welcomed Emyn as a guest, sat her next to his wife, and waved slaves forward to wash her hands and feet.

She could not count the number of men and women who gathered in the king's warm and shadowy house. The sun passed from east to west as she spun and chatted with the women while the king held conversations with warriors, workmen, and nobles in fur-trimmed robes. Eventually, the king sent a slave to summon Emyn and the queen back to his presence. When she approached, Vlidorix indicated a carved stool.

"Sit, honored Gutumaros. Share with me the words of your spirits."

"Sir, they are as much your spirits as mine." Warm lights surrounded the king as they had all afternoon. "Your ancestors breathe their counsel into your dreams and thoughts. You are a wise ruler and need no words from me. They wish for you to know that they watch and are proud."

Vlidorix inclined his head in thanks. A spirit formed beside him and gave Emyn words to repeat.

"One great ancestor, one with lesions along his right leg—" she paused as the queen gasped. "He asks me to tell you this: Not every riddle has an answer."

The queen could not hold her words back. "Your grandfather loved riddles!"

Vlidorix nodded; the house had grown silent.

Emyn continued, "From the next world he brings those words. Not every riddle has an answer." Smoke from the sweet-smelling fire burned her eyes, and she blinked. The dead king appeared beside her. "A strong spirit who has always guided me now speaks. He has a message that concerns all kings.

"The general Caesar told his council in Rome that he has conquered the Celtic tribes here, and that we all pay him tribute." Men near enough to overhear shouted their outrage and Vlidorix lifted his hand, silencing them.

The dead king was already filling Emyn's ears with more news. "Caesar sends wagons of Helvetian bounty to Rome. Since he bragged of his conquest, he must now make his boast true. He studies his maps and consults with spies. He weaves many plans, some of air, some of strong thread. Be ready."

"For what?" more than one man shouted. "Where are his armies?"

"What does he plan?"

"He'll find no allies in the west!"

Emyn swiveled, looking at the tall men who spoke. Blades hung from their belts, and their ancestors stood beside them.

"He won't," she agreed. "No man of the Veneti will support Caesar! But other tribes are not as strong." She turned back to the king. "Caesar examines many roads. Not even the ghosts know which one he will take."

Moradag had not returned by dusk, so a polite but silent warrior guided Emyn's mount back down the path to Nerrus' house through darkness and the sound of distant thunder. A thick new cloak weighted her shoulders, woven in varying stripes of blue. It was a gift of the king—a generous gift. Emyn felt she owed Vlidorix more words whenever her ghosts delivered them.

ON THE MORNING SET for the trial, Moradag brought the same gentle red mare that had carried her up and down the hill to the king. Nonicos walked with them. Emyn settled herself on the thick blanket and listened as the boy and man talked. She was glad of the new cloak, though she still shivered a bit under Aruca's linen dress. The fabric wouldn't stay put like wool; it slid around and left her skin cool, as if she'd been stripped and exposed.

An escort of gray warriors walked ahead of them; one carried a red shield with a serpent painted on it. Why would the ghost of an Aeduan warrior guard her today? Their presence did not soothe her mind, and her questions could not stay inside for long.

"Moradag, what will happen?" Emyn twisted the reins in both her hands. "Do we go to the king's house?"

"We go to a smaller house, better suited for councils."

"I'LL WAIT AT THAT INN," Nonicos said. He'd already worked on a small boat owned by one of the men he'd met there.

"How many people will be at the trial?" She thought of another question before Moradag could answer. "When I talk, do I have to face—"

"Chiomara." Moradag reached up to put his hand over hers. "Do not worry. You will address the Honored Master Ferdiath. You do not have to look at anyone else if you don't want to. The room will be dark." After a moment, he added, "I should tell you that your ghosts will be barred from the house. The dead may not advise you at the trial."

"I wouldn't trust their words, anyway," Nonicos laughed.

"No one expects you to speak like a poet." Moradag patted her arm. "The Honored Master Ferdiath will ask you to state your case. Only he may ask you questions; ignore anyone else who speaks. When you are done, my own master, Rialos—who must answer to Ferdiath today, though it galls him—presents his side of the story."

"He is angry—"

"Ah, but he is a druid. He will speak the truth. And you must sit quietly, no matter what he says. Speak only when the judge— Master Ferdiath—asks you a question."

"I will." A simple instruction; would she remember it? Emyn

held herself rigid and bit back further queries: they were useless, after all. She would find out soon enough what waited for her.

Moradag knew she was not calmed. He and Nonicos tried to amuse her with jokes. The dead king grumbled, but the other spirits seemed to enjoy the silliness.

They passed the inn. After Nonicos left them, Moradag talked about the coming Imbolc celebration. Seven girls had already asked him to sit by them, he said, including the king's youngest daughter.

"The king's daughter? You must sit by her; you cannot offend the king."

"Yes, but I can dance with all of them, can't I?"

Her laugh was a little too high. "Are you trying to make me jealous?"

"I would rather dance with you, Chiomara. Anytime, holiday or not."

"You'll have to sneak down to Nerrus' house for that." They had arrived at the flat field that held the king's house, a stone-lined well, stables, storehouses, and other large buildings. All of Samarnum could fit in here.

"Look at them peering from their doorways." Moradag led the horse to the far end of the field. Emyn felt eyes on her and sat all the more erect. "They strain to see the beautiful Death Speaker. What secret passions have passed between you and the sober young master, they wonder?"

She shushed him as a boy ran forward to take the bridle. The horse shied and wheeled away. Moradag shouted in alarm as the runaway mare carried Emyn past the stable.

They didn't go far. When the mare stopped by a clump of berry bushes, Emyn jumped off. She fell too quickly to hold her balance and ended on all fours, staring into bushes and ferns.

Large rocks and a pool of water, all green with scum, hid beneath the plants.

"Are you all right?"

"Of course you are," an old man cackled. "Look, look!"

Emyn pushed up and scooted closer to where he pointed, pushing thorny branches aside. Amid the moss and algae, a thin chain, anchored to a rock, dipped into the water.

"Chiomara, are you—"

She ignored him, rolled back her sleeve, and stuck her arm into the bushes, far enough to catch the chain. Something weighted it. Emyn pulled a small cup with a pointed spout from the dirty water—a spout shaped exactly like a raven's beak.

She held it up for Moradag to see, but he shook his head, cursed the mare, and brushed leaves from her dress. "No one can stay clean long in this weather, Chiomara. Do not worry."

She wasn't worried. How could she be? The Morrigu had sent her a sign to show that she had found Emyn here in Venetona. Whatever happened now was part of her plan. Emyn almost laughed out loud.

She took Moradag's arm and let him lead her past a decrepit hut and the stable, back to a round house set between two oak trees.

Just before he pulled the door open, Moradag looked down and grinned. "This winter has been dreary. People will talk about this for months; give them a good story."

 29

They stepped into the gloom. Low orange flames lit the room before her and the sun shone through the doorway. Moradag let go of her arm and she stood alone in the shaft of light.

"Give them a good story," he'd said.

Emyn shook off her cloak, caught it as it fell, and tossed it toward Moradag. For a moment before the door closed, the light blazed around a form and shone through the linen dress. Aruca would have applauded.

Men sat on benches, but she could not see their faces in the darkness. A stranger asked Emyn if she'd like to sit; she said no. Ferdiath's musical voice summoned her forward and she walked around the fire pit, leaning on her stick.

"Emyn Gutumaros, you declared a troscad against the Honored Master Rialos. What compensation do you seek?"

"Twelve silver coins." That would pay for tools and a cauldron as well as clothes and food for several months, she and Nonicos had figured.

"And what is your accusation?"

Emyn took a deep breath. There were many ways to tell a

story, but she would not use pretty words. The memory of how Rialos had forced her back from his doorway as if she were garbage still stung. "I accuse the Honored Master of using my trust to lure me to his uncle's embrace, then abandoning me to death. I hold him responsible for the beating that left my brother with only one eye, and for the gossip that drove us from our homes and forced us to live as beggars."

Rialos stood and shouted, "None of that—"

"It is not your turn to speak!"

Emyn had not jumped at Rialos' outburst, and she stood unshaken as he stepped from the shadows. His eyes searched her face. What did he expect to find? Emyn stared right back. If he'd wanted the truth, he could have asked for it before this.

"Sit down!" Ferdiath's voice was harsh with warning. Rialos glared at him, but obeyed.

"Can you prove your charges?" Ferdiath asked Emyn in softer tones.

"Yes."

The Irish druid spread his hands as if giving Emyn time and space. His sleeves were long, falling over his hands. She took a few steps closer and gripped her stick.

"I am a widow, Honored Master. The druid Bodocnos brought me, my brother, and my brother-in-law to this coast last summer on Lugnasad itself. We settled in lands owned by King Gundori." Someone snorted loudly.

Emyn closed her eyes. This could be any inn or house. She was the Gutumaros, and she had flown with the Morrigu. The ghosts could not distract her here, and neither would living men.

"We began a new life." Her voice floated in the small room. "Hope filled us, especially when my brother found fortune in love and prepared to marry. The druid Rialos visited. He had been a student of Bodocnos, and I thought of him as a friend. His sister, niece to Gundori, invited me to her home."

She lowered her tone, and stood perfectly still. "I am a Gutumaros, as you know. I hear the dead. Rialos told me to bring their words to Gundori, and I trusted his advice.

"As the solstice began, Gundori—whom I respected as king —sent a litter to bear me to him. I expected to hear the stories of the long night in his house, but instead I was taken to the far side of the island where standing stones mark holy places. There," she allowed a tremble into her voice, "I was dressed, anointed, and given poisoned wine. I was forced in all these things and dragged into a ritual, one that ended in death."

Drafts whistled below the thatch and the door. Emyn looked at each shadow on the bench, turning slowly, imagining where their eyes would be. "I did not consent. I was forced. Gundori intended to pour his seed into me and feed my blood to the land. Many slaves were present, but they were drugged as well.

"Other women have been killed as I nearly was. Aruca the prostitute was one. This may not be the time for such accusations, but I make them. I cannot make them anywhere else."

She turned back to Ferdiath. "I escaped in the darkness and hid. My brother, who is a woodworker and has nothing to do with kings or druids, was beaten senseless the next morning—by warriors that Gundori sent to find me. My brother lives but lost an eye. Many witnessed this, but none will speak. The same warriors might beat them and burn their homes if they do.

"We hid, my family and I, while gossip spread that I had gone to Gundori willingly, that I lived in his home as his new whore. I thought no one would believe such lies, but I was wrong." Silence surrounded Emyn as she leaned on her stick and turned with deliberation towards Rialos.

"The Honored Master Rialos now learns the consequences of his words. I ask only for what my brother has lost so that he can replace his tools and feed and shelter his family."

That was enough. Emyn lowered her eyes and waited.

"What is your birthdate, Gutumaros?" Ferdiath asked, and she told him.

"One thing troubles me," Ferdiath began, after a moment spent calculating the import of her stars. "You use a stick. I assume you cannot run. How then did you escape from Gundori and his attendants?"

"The truth will seem strange, Honored Master, but it is the truth. Gundori called me his Morrigu, and that goddess saved me. I felt that I had wings and I flew. From above, I saw this poor body race over the ground. I was a raven when I saw this. With my talons, I clawed at the king's face. I trust my memories, but I realize that this makes an eerie tale."

"You ran, possessed?"

Emyn nodded. "My legs worked well when numbed, but I paid for that with days of pain. I ran far, and then I hid."

"Did you run from the island?"

"No, honored judge. But I hope you will understand that I wish to keep some parts of my escape secret to protect others from Gundori's vengeance."

"Ah." Ferdiath waited, and Emyn kept her face calm. Finally, he asked a last question. "What you have described is a crime, but it is Gundori's crime. Do you feel it is right to force payment from Rialos?"

Emyn sighed; this was a troubling point. But she could not confront Gundori. The ghosts had helped her frame an answer.

"If a man starts a fight, others may be injured. Doesn't the man bear some responsibility for that, even if he runs away after the fight starts?" She kept her eyes on Ferdiath, then twisted her head to include the other figures. "Gundori's lechery is known. Men talk, and women avoid the island. Yet Rialos sent me to him. I only ask for enough compensation to restart our lives. I think that is fair."

Ferdiath gave her a moment more. When she said nothing else, he nodded toward a bench near the fire. Then he turned and said, "Rialos, speak your defense."

Rialos stepped close to the glow of the fire, and his voice filled the room. "Gundori tells a different tale. He claims—"

The druid's eyes met Emyn's, and he faltered as if a look could steal away words. After a moment, he began again. "You had a stick that others know well."

Was that a question, and did he expect an answer? Moradag had told her to speak only to Ferdiath. Emyn stretched her fingers over the smooth knob of her new stick and said nothing.

"That stick, richly carved, leans against the door of one of Gundori's smaller homes for all to see. It is the house where he keeps his favorite whore."

Nonicos had put his soul into that stick! Emyn rose as an ember exploded.

"So he keeps a trophy?" she screamed. "King or not, he—"

"Gutumaros!" Ferdiath's holler hit her like a slap. "Sit down!"

Blood rushed to her face. Mortified, Emyn slipped back to the bench and tried to catch her breath. She had let the man bait her into behaving like a fool. Would this outburst decide the case?

"Rialos, that was unworthy of your position." Ferdiath's voice dripped with scorn.

"I am sorry."

The man sounded truly contrite, but Emyn didn't dare lift her eyelids to look.

"Continue with your defense," Ferdiath commanded.

"There is no need. I will pay what she asks."

Another trick. Emyn kept her eyes on the fire.

"Consider carefully, Honored Master." Ferdiath sounded almost amused. "There are those who will assume that payment without defense implies guilt. Is that what you wish?"

"I will pay what she asks."

Emyn watched little flames rise above the embers. Was he serious? Would he truly not defend himself or snatch the words back? The silence dragged on until Ferdiath muttered, "Well, then. Both parties have spoken."

Was that it? Her mind drifted. Emyn could hand her brother back his life. A minute ago she'd given into rage, and now, abruptly, she had won. How could that be? She felt like a pile of mud left in the sun, dried bits of her blowing away with each breeze.

Ferdiath cleared his throat loudly. "Gutumaros, again I ask: Does this satisfy you?"

'Satisfy' seemed a funny word for what she felt. "Yes."

"Lady, be certain. Once I pronounce the words, the case cannot be re-opened." Ferdiath leaned forward, and for the first time looked Emyn in the eyes. His brows rose, full of concern. "Is there nothing you would ask for yourself?"

She had won, but the rewards were like jewels tossed before a starving man. "I want nothing else."

"Then the judgment is made. Rialos will pay compensation for your brother's loss. The case is settled."

EMYN BLINKED AGAINST THE harsh light as she left the house. Moradag rushed to her side. "Please do not try to walk in this mud, Chiomara. I'll send for the horse."

"You are a dear friend," Emyn whispered, "but your master will not approve. You must stay with him."

"He gave me permission to bring you here and return you."

She nodded, grateful. The trial had drained the fight from her, and she felt weak. Her feet were numb with cold, the chill creeping up her legs. Moradag signaled the stable boy and waited beside her until the mare was brought out, a dry blanket over her back. Moradag helped Emyn mount, and then led her back to Nonicos at the inn.

"Ride the mare back to Nerrus' home," Moradog smiled. "I'll get her later when I bring my master's payment." Emyn watched him walk away. He could not be more than fourteen, but by most measures, he filled the form of a man.

Ghost warriors flanked them as she and Nonicos descended the hill and turned east along the road. Holding bright shields, the spirits positioned themselves by Nerrus' door. Micco ran out; Nonicos handed him a brush and guided his first strokes against the horse. Emyn paused before she entered the house and looked into a gray face. "Why are you here?"

"We watch," answered the ghost.

THREE NEW TRAVELERS STAYED with Nerrus this night; they had pooled their resources and intended to buy a fishing boat and sail it home. Emyn listened to them talk with her brother about the gulf and its rivers, and places where offerings were made.

Moradag returned. Oleda lifted her arms to him as light flooded the room through the doorway; the sky beyond was streaked with orange sunset. Oleda was going to marry the student, she told her mother. She would marry Ro-dak and they would sing songs together every night.

"My master keeps his word." Moradag pulled Emyn's hand

toward him and put a bag of coins onto her palm. "He conveys his apologies with the payment. Nothing, he says, is more shameful to a man than to be proved a false friend. He says this without resentment toward you, but with many regrets."

Emyn passed the pouch to her brother, smiling. Inside her soul rattled, in lose pieces like the coins.

"My master will supply anything else you need," Morodag added.

"Thank you," Nonicos answered for her. "This is settled. From now on, we will provide for ourselves."

"What will you do?" Moradag asked.

Emyn shrugged toward Nonicos, but didn't listen when he answered. She would go where the Morrigu drew her.

A sword hung from Moradag's belt. Had it been there earlier when they'd walked to her trial? She could not remember.

They sat by the fire sharing food and drink, but Emyn felt as empty after eating as she had before. The others watched her, probably wondering why she was not happy. The Morrigu filled her with strength this morning and she had won her case, but somehow she'd lost the thread that connected one event to another in her life.

"How is Caesar these days, Chiomara?"

"Far away," Emyn sighed. "Still far away."

"Too far for the dead king to see?"

The ghost could not resist such a dare. "He raises more armies! His eyes look north. When the weather warms he will test himself against the bravest tribes."

She repeated the words. The Nervians were the bravest tribe in the north, but no one said so. Emyn thought of her grandfather.

The house seemed suddenly confining. She stood and threw the cloak around her arms, picking up her stick as she walked out the door.

"Heroes live faster than farmers."

Emyn jumped; the door slammed behind her. That was her grandfather's voice. It came from above her as if she were still a little child. In all her conversations with the dead, Emyn had never before heard the voice of someone she'd known alive.

She looked around; the ghostly warriors accompanied her as she walked into the moonlit night.

"Why do you follow me?" she asked the ghosts. Waves crashed and washed away her voice. The tide was at its highest, but a wide beach still separated the water from the road.

"We watch," the warrior said as he had earlier. Emyn hugged her cloak as gusts shot through her thin skirt, soaking her with cold as if wind were water. Wavetops glittered under the crescent moon.

After several moments of silent hobbling, punching her stick into the sand and rocks for balance, Emyn said, "I heard my grandfather's voice."

"You hear many voices."

Coming toward her from the west were two silhouettes.

"You cannot fight them," said a ghost, and the silhouettes took on a menacing cast.

"Can you?" She squinted at the figures. They were large and clumsy on the sand.

"Hide, little fool!" screamed the dead king. His voice sounded far away.

Emyn halted and looked up at the warrior ghosts.

"You cannot run," said one, "but you can wait."

"Their blades thirst," said another.

The two figures were closer. Another figure ran along the road just behind them. "They come for me?" Emyn asked.

"They come to kill."

Emyn jerked her head from one side to the other. Where could she run? Back to the house, exposing Oleda and the others to danger? Into the sea to drown? Or up the rocks, climbing like a crab to the road? She could not move fast enough to seek safety beyond the road. The ghosts were correct; she could not run.

"They draw their blades."

"Good." Emyn swallowed hard. This was what her grandfather meant: live and die fast like a hero. She saw both a sword and an axe raised as the men hurried toward her. Death she could face, but she would never be dragged back to Gundori as a sacrifice or captive.

Emyn let her cloak slip from her shoulders. She stepped forward, but a ghost lifted his arm, blocking her. "Why go to them meekly?"

"I have nothing to fight with." The men were close enough now that she could see moonlight glinting off the familiar armband of one.

"No?" said the ghost. "Look."

The figure on the road passed the men below. "Run!" it screamed at her.

Her heart beat like thunder; she recognized Rialos' voice before the word sank in.

She ran. She ran toward the sea, but her steps were even clumsier than the warriors who pursued her. One caught her quickly; he reeked of ale.

"Now you'll pay, you bitch," he panted. "Now—"

She knew his voice and saw the armband again as she fell to her knees: Gundori's warrior. He grabbed her hair and yanked, pulling her back and forcing her head up.

Emyn shut her eyes. A sharp blade in a strong hand would kill quickly, probably before she even felt pain. For several heartbeats, though, nothing happened.

Blood splattered over her shoulders as the grip on her hair loosened. Emyn tottered sideways while the warrior fell straight back. His body made almost no sound as it hit the sand. A small knife protruded from his neck, the blade driven in to the hilt.

"Run!"

Rialos ducked as the other man swung an axe where his head had been. The druid was unarmed; how long could he avoid the axe?

Emyn dove at the corpse and wrenched the knife from its throat, but before she could act, a sword swept down in a bright arc. The second warrior's body split as the sword slashed through neck and collarbone. Blood sprayed like foam from the surf.

Rialos rolled away safely, and Moradag stood gasping at what he had done.

Moradag ran to the breaking surf and vomited.

"You're cut?" Rialos grabbed Emyn by the shoulder, using his sleeve to wipe blood from her neck and face.

"No," she managed; they were both gasping for breath. 'It's not my blood. It's his.'

He pulled her against him. "Thank . . . whoever looks after you."

Moradag returned. He said nothing about the master's arms being around Emyn, but his voice wobbled when he asked, "Could there be more of them?"

The three peered into the moonlit night. Figures ran along the road and the beach, but they were not warriors. They shouted to each other. A woman screamed and a child cried. Two boys were the first to reach the bodies, excited to see real heroes and villains.

"Who is it?" one asked. The other waved him silent, his eyes raised in awe to Moradag, who stood still and pale, his bloodied sword in his hand.

Emyn stared at the body, remembering the drunk who had

knocked her to the floor in front of Haebro. After all this, she didn't even know his name.

"Your strong arm saved us both," Rialos said.

"And your aim, Master." Moradag swallowed hard. "Chiomara, are you hurt?"

"No." She reached out to squeeze his arm. "Thank you both." Rialos still held her gently and her arm was around his waist as well. She didn't want him to let go.

Moradag glanced around, and then called to the boys. "Fetch that cloak, would you? It belongs to the lady. The stick too." He turned to Rialos. "You must have had a cloak as well—"

"I dropped it on the road." Rialos pulled back a little from Emyn to study the crowd that had gathered and pointed to a teenage boy. "Run to the king's warriors and tell them two men died on this beach when they attacked the Gutumaros. They were killed by Moradag, prince of the Bellovaci, and the Honored Master Rialos."

As the boy ran off, Rialos announced to the others, "We will rest at Nerrus' house for now. If you see a green cloak with a bronze pin, bring it to us there."

Moradag handed Emyn her stick, and then she turned with Rialos, relieved that he kept his arm around her shoulder. She averted her eyes from the curious stares and followed the movement of the druid's body as they walked back toward the inn. Nonicos ran to meet them, full of questions. She let the druid answer.

"I walked . . . I had some business, and passed several alehouses," Rialos said. "I heard the word "Gutumaros" from inside one. I went in, saw the two warriors, and stood near enough to hear their words. They had directions to Nerrus' house and said they would go see you." Rialos looked down at Emyn, dropping his arm so they could each pass through the doorway. "They were drunk, but said nothing about doing you harm. So I just followed."

"Gundori sent them," Emyn added. "One was the man who summoned me to Gundori's that night. He was rude to Laurina —" Her voice shook, so she stopped talking. Did it matter? The man was dead.

"Is that blood?" Laurina cried. "Are you hurt?" After a quick explanation from Nonicos, Laurina led Emyn to be cleaned up.

The hearth fire was bright, the house filled with commotion. In a corner, Laurina found the ragged clothes they'd worn in the wilderness: the old skirt and boy's shirt. She fussed at the blood on the linen dress and dipped it in water when Emyn removed it. "Maybe with lemon . . . the skirt isn't too bad. Maybe you can still wear it. . . ."

"We can buy new clothes now," Emyn reminded her, shivering as she pulled the faded shirt over her head. "Don't worry."

"Don't worry? Men just tried to chop you up!" Laurina burst into tears.

Emyn put her arms around her. "It's over," she said. "They're dead."

"More will come," Laurina sobbed.

"No one escapes," a ghost intoned.

Emyn waved away the spirit. Laurina wished for safety; any mother would. Emyn wanted to offer it, but knew her words were empty. "You will find a good place to live. You *will*. Gundori hates me, not you. Don't cry."

Laurina nodded and sniffed. As she bent and used the water to wipe her own tears away, Emyn caught a glance from Rialos, who looked away quickly. She tucked her shirt into the loose skirt.

A wail made both women jump; Oleda woke to an inn full of

noisy strangers. Laurina scurried off to calm her as Emyn limped toward the fire. It seemed that half of Venetona had followed them into Nerrus' home. She heard her title called, but ignored it. She had no news beyond what they already knew.

Rialos made room for Emyn next to him on a bench. His hands brushed the hair away from her face as a cup of milk was passed to her. Then, just as he had when she was fifteen, Rialos ordered the spirits to leave her alone, and one by one they drifted away. Soon, only his own low voice rose over the crackle and wind song of the flames. Safety, it promised, though she didn't follow the words. They didn't matter. As long he stayed near, she was safe.

Emyn let her eyes close. She thought she had dropped all her expectations into the sea as offerings, yet here she sat building up hopes again. His body—his side, at least—pressed against her now. That would be enough.

Sudden shouts announced the king's warriors. Rialos rose, and new bodies surrounded Emyn: Laurina and Micco. The ghosts came back; Aruca was near as well. "You are brave, little Gutumaros," she cooed. "The Veneti king must attend to his mad chieftain now. He cannot ignore this."

A warrior called Moradag's name, and the men cheered and laughed. He had killed; he was now one of them.

Emyn tried to pay attention to the conversations in the room. Nonicos and Laurina talked of the cousins who lived upriver. Travelers and fishermen exchanged stories of crimes around the gulf, of storms and shredded nets. A man complained about the lack of lawfulness and honor these days. Ancestors and warm lights pushed themselves before Emyn with odd images: an old woman with a basket of goose eggs; a man mending his net; a warrior with a sharp sword—

"Emyn."

She had buried her head in her arms as she huddled near the fire; now she raised her eyes.

"Warriors will stay here tonight." Rialos pushed hair from her face once again. "You and your family can rest easy."

"Thank you." Was it her imagination or did his hand linger against her cheek? No, she only wished for more.

"Tomorrow we'll bring you to the king. He should know all you can tell him about those killers."

Emyn nodded.

"I'll be here too," Rialos continued. "Just over there. In the morning we'll talk about your family and where you want to live. I think you should leave Nerrus', all of you. There are many places you could stay until you find a home. But that's for the morning." He smiled, looking as tired as she felt. "We should rest now. Sleep well."

She lifted her arm to touch his face, but he stood too quickly and was gone. Emyn crawled weakly onto the mattress that Nonicos shook out for her. No wonder most women stayed out of battles; her brush with danger left her too weary to move. The druid Rialos lay across the room, but she couldn't stay awake, not even to learn if he snored.

"One eye or not, woman, I'm whole where it counts!"

"Shhh," Laurina giggled as Nonicos muffled her laughter. Emyn had no idea how long she'd slept; there seemed to be no one else awake except for her brother and his wife.

Laurina sighed quietly and whispered; Emyn caught only a few words. "...good...our own house."

"And my sister?" Nonicos asked.

Emyn couldn't hear the answer. The dead king interrupted.

"No more farm houses! You have wasted enough time."

She lay awake for a long while, sorting through all that had happened. Would she and her brother part? He had a wife and child, and in-laws waited upriver. He should not be worrying about Emyn; she had caused him enough grief. He'd lost an eye for her! If he had been on the beach tonight—

Better that they travel separate paths.

Emyn sat up and ran her fingers through her hair. Venetona was a big town. The king might invite Emyn to live on the plain near his house. She would be protected there and close enough to visit Nonicos. She would be near Rialos, too. The druid had saved her life; he couldn't still be angry. He would not mind if she lived near him, would he?

And what of Micco? Who would he follow?

Emyn could see most of the room and all the bundles breathing around the fire. She knew Micco's form; he was not there. He would not be resting near Nonicos and Laurina. He had learned from Almer long ago never to linger near lovemaking.

Moradag was gone as well, but Emyn did not worry about him. Winks and comments from the warriors hinted at where he'd been taken. The many strangers, some with swords, may have scared Micco; he probably hid in the stable. The night was cold; did he have a fur with him?

Emyn pulled on her shoes, wrapped herself warmly, and leaned on her stick to pull herself up. She nodded to the wakeful warrior by the door. As she slipped outside, a gust of damp sea air pelted her face. She covered her head until she was inside the stable.

"Micco, wake." Emyn shook the boy. A horse's blanket clung to him in curls like a snail shell. "Come inside where it's warm."

She had to repeat the words several times; finally Micco rose and rubbed his eyes.

"Come sleep by the fire." She turned him toward the door where they both stopped. A man stood there, blocking the moonlight.

Emyn patted the boy's shoulder. "Micco, go inside. Go sleep by the fire."

Micco kept his head bowed as he staggered around Rialos and made long strides toward the house.

Emyn didn't follow, and Rialos pulled the stable door shut.

She stepped close. The dead king growled his amusement, but Emyn ignored him. In the darkness Rialos' body heated like embers, springing to life under a soft breath. She could sense the distance—a thumb's width, less—between her and him.

"Emyn . . . if you . . . ," His voice, weak for once, faded away.

Emyn didn't answer. She knew what she wished to hear, but not what he meant to say, so they stood as mute as Micco.

"A stable," the dead king sneered. "Animals!"

Did that matter? The darkness was a gift; she wouldn't dare look into Rialos' eyes. She had no idea what she would see.

His arms circled round and pulled her to him, pressing their bodies together. He shuddered; she felt every pulse.

"Do you want this?" Rialos' breath blew hot in her ear, and Emyn could only moan in answer.

Spirits crowded around; they brought the scent of damp earth to mingle with the smells of wool and sweat. The black air seemed rich and alive. She stood at a crossroad yet again, straddling different worlds.

Rialos' beard scratched but his lips were as warm and exciting as she remembered. Emyn sank and his arms caught her as they dropped to the floor together with only the horse blanket between them and the dirt. Rialos pulled at his pants, and then kicked them away while he pushed her skirt up to her waist. He stroked her thigh; she shivered. She tried to say that she wanted him now and always, but her words became garbled with gasps and sighs as he pushed himself inside her.

Emyn was part of the sea, rising and falling with the waves. Rialos' breaths came faster; his gasps echoed her own until they both cried out, exploding against one another.

WIND RATTLED THE RICKETY BUILDING. The cold woke and pestered them; they knew they had to return to the house and the fire. Rialos slipped away from her; she pushed herself up when she heard the stable door open. The moon had set and stars dotted the darkness. Her mind spun giddily as if she were fifteen again; the stars—the entire world—seemed new. The one man she wanted was hers. True, he had said few words, but he'd poured himself into her without restraint. She could not help but ask for a fact that any woman would want when planning her future. "When were you born?"

She passed beneath his arm as he held the door. The wind carried his words away; she heard only, "Does it matter?"

"What?"

"Go inside where it's warm," he muttered.

"But—"

"I'll follow in a few minutes."

"Why?"

"So no one will see us together." He stopped walking and in doing so parted from her.

The night stilled; even the tide paused. For the second time since the sun had set, Emyn shut her eyes, waiting for a blow to fall. Rialos wanted no one to know that he'd been with her.

Her blood felt as cold as the night. "You are ashamed!"

"Ashamed? Druids do not invite shame." He set his hand on her shoulder; she shook it off. "Much has happened since sunset and yesterday. You need time, perhaps."

"Time?" She had waited years for this night. She thought Rialos had, too—but what had he said, exactly? Nothing. This was a chance encounter to him, no more.

"Please go inside, Emyn. You must be cold."

She could not lie across the hearth from him and pretend to sleep! She took a step away. "I am naïve in these matters, Honored Master." His title emerged as a mocking hiss. "I *do* need time to think."

"Emyn!"

She walked toward the beach. The cold of a winter's night was nothing compared to the chill this man had cast on her soul. Emyn ignored the druid as he called her name again. She heard him curse. Within minutes a guard, not a ghost but a warrior holding a small lamp, stood behind her on the beach.

A guard. She did not ask who sent him or where the druid had gone.

"You have circles under your eyes, Chiomara," Moradag said when he returned with the first light.

"Your master is not here," the warrior Satto told Moradag. "He went home before the sun rose. Said you could see the Gutumaros and her family moved before you join him."

"Moved? You are leaving?" Several voices answered Moradag. He could not have gotten any more sleep than she had, but he seemed alert and full of good humor.

Emyn smiled and handed Moradag a bowl of millet.

"Why is *he* the one you want?" Aruca's question sounded curious, not scolding.

Emyn's mind overflowed with answers. Because Rialos' hair sparkled in the sunlight. Because he walked quietly. Because Rialos was not afraid of her or her ghosts. "He is brave," Emyn whispered as Moradag turned toward the others.

"Come and sit," Nonicos called. "We were just talking about the gulf. Satto knows it well."

"Walked most of it more than once," the man nodded. Emyn liked Satto: he was simple and plain-spoken, not like other warriors she'd met who were always boasting and showing off.

"Laurina has cousins up the Visambu." Nonicos began and was soon gathering information about the road and river at the eastern edge of the bay.

Aruca settled beside Emyn and rested a ghostly hand over hers. "A wolf is brave too, but you cannot caress it."

Laurina talked about the rich farmlands that her cousins worked. Her grandfather lived in a large house. A pier and another house had gone up when Laurina was a child; maybe more had been built since.

"Bah!" The dead king sounded like a sick man clearing his throat. "Farmhouses! Time ends; do not waste it."

"The river's not deep," said Satto. "But it's wide enough. Barges go up and down. You're a carpenter and a wheelwright, you said?"

"I've done both," Nonicos answered. "With another pair of strong arms I can make wheels."

"There's lots of traffic on the river. If there's a pier, men will stop to buy once they know your work. Or you could load wheels, maybe a small cart, on a barge. Probably be sold as soon as you passed another pier." Satto grinned at Nonicos. "Most wood-workers here are tied up with ships. You could live well."

"All I need are tools," Nonicos said.

"Easily bought. I know of two smiths who make axes and chisels as well as swords."

"Little Gutumaros," Aruca touched Emyn's cheek and urged her to turn from the conversation. "Would you be happy with a man who might love, but never trust you?"

Emyn looked down at her two hands clutching the ragged skirt. Did she have that choice?

What would make her happy? Only what she couldn't have. Oleda crawled into her lap then, smelling of milk. Best to think of the gods' gifts, rather than their tricks.

In what seemed like only a moment, Laurina was pulling the sleeping child from Emyn's lap. "We're ready to go. Moradag bridled the horse. Do you want to ride?"

"I'd better walk," Emyn mumbled as she yawned. "I'd fall off the horse." They were all the way to the main road before she thought to ask, "Where are we going?"

She didn't hear the answer. As soon as the question left her lips, Emyn remembered a dream with an immediacy that made her eyes dart around and led her to doubt her own wakefulness.

In the dream, Bodocnos had been sitting with her before a small campfire. "You know where you should be, Gutumaros. You always know. Why do you wait for others to tell you?"

They carried all that they owned, leaving the wheelbarrow with Nerrus so Haebro could pick it up on a future visit. When rain fell, everyone walked faster up the hill. Thunder cracked and Moradag scooped Emyn into his arms and ran with her for several feet. He ducked into a doorway where the sudden darkness jerked him to a stop.

The others, warriors included, crowded in after them and stomped their feet to shake off the rain. Moradag still held Emyn. She could not see a single empty place around the hearth, though a few of the hazy figures might have been ghosts. Moradag lowered her to a cushion.

"Move, child." Emyn waved her hand, sure that she was about to sit on someone.

"There is no child, Chiomara," Moradag laughed and pulled her wet cloak off her shoulders.

Emyn sighed; she could not trust sight or sound.

Satto's voice fell on her from above. "A good house, though it can get noisy. You will be safe here."

"This is where I stayed when Emyn started her troscad,"

Nonicos said as he set Oleda in her mother's lap. That seemed a long time ago: before the trial and the brutal attack on the beach; before every occurrence that fenced Emyn's life now.

"Your master wanted me to visit the king," Emyn told Moradag. "But I cannot enter his house in rags."

"Neither king nor master expects you to trudge through a rainstorm." Moradag smiled and bent to kiss her cheek. He had not removed his own cloak, and water dripped onto her lap and shoulders. "I will tell them both that you rest. With all you have endured since yesterday, you've earned a nap."

The fire was warm and the cushion wide; Emyn lay down and did not even hear the warriors leave. She slept until Laurina woke her, holding a steaming bowl before her face while Oleda giggled.

Her family sat around, passing milk, ale, stew, and bread. With luck and the gods' favors, Nonicos said—mostly to the innkeeper—they would leave in a few days, arriving at their new home in time to celebrate Imbolc. A chill gripped Emyn; this was the time.

When the meal was finished, Emyn faced her brother and told him that she would not travel up the river to live with Laurina's cousins. "My path is different. The ghosts insist, and I know they are right. A village is not the place for me any longer."

Nonicos tried to change her mind, but Emyn saw relief in Laurina's eyes. "We will be close enough to visit," Emyn reminded him.

When he realized he couldn't sway her, Nonicos patted her hand. "You do what is right. You will always be welcome in our home."

Nonicos spent the next days visiting smiths and other woodworkers, gathering the tools he needed. Emyn talked with visitors at the inn. No one believed that Gundori would send more men after her, but she made sure that the news spread: the Death Speaker would stay near the king, in Venetona.

When men and women approached Emyn and put pins, trinkets, and coins into her hands in exchange for a word from their ancestors, she had a question of her own: "Do you have a shrine sacred to the Morrigu here?"

No one knew of any. She asked them about the strange little well she'd found just before her troscad. "What of the spring behind the warriors' stables? Up by the king's house?" A cup shaped like a beak such as she'd seen on the day of the trial *had* to belong to the Morrigu.

"If there's a spring back there, it was never for the likes of us," a woman said. The others laughed as if that settled the matter.

Fortified with advice from the inn's customers, Laurina and Emyn visited merchants who sold cloth. With Micco following and Oleda holding a hand or skirt, they walked down the path to the main road, east and then back again. Both women lifted and shook dyed woolens, judging weight and fullness, looking for flaws, comparing colors. They returned home carrying lengths of beige and brown stripes, blue checks, a solid deep red, and a thinner piece of vivid scarlet, the color of currants.

"That's for girls," Oleda told Micco when he tried to touch the bright red cloth.

"Gutumaros?" A filthy old woman approached Emyn, who tried not to wrinkle her nose or frown. "I know about that spring, the one with the cup."

"Yes?" Emyn made room for her on the bench and signaled for ale.

"My old granny told me about it. She served under the rulers, years back, till she married and even then . . . , but her husband died, and she took her children . . . ." The hag rambled through family history as Emyn waited and tried not to breathe too deeply —the woman exhaled decay. If her granny remembered the spring, five generations must have passed since it was used.

"Here. Drink." The cup came round, and Emyn offered it to the woman.

"Well, bless you, that's kind. But all I meant to say was that they've forgotten the old ways, haven't they? If you remind them of that shrine and drink from the raven cup, it might go easier . . . or it might not. Who knows?" She laughed harshly. "No one escapes their fate in the end."

Her pale, knobby hands gripped the wooden cup. Emyn let it go. In the next moment it crashed to the ground and splashed ale onto her skirt. The bench was empty.

"Auntie dropped it!" Oleda squealed, and Micco clapped his hands.

MORADAG VISITED OFTEN. One day he told Emyn that the Irish master Ferdiath had announced that Emyn's spirits could tease and seduce; Ferdiath confessed he'd experienced that himself. "He was careful not to blame you, of course," Moradag added.

Emyn shrugged. How did that matter?

"Stand still." Laurina straightened a length of cloth draped over Emyn's shoulder, and then used charcoal to mark where it touched the floor. Emyn held Moradag's arm for balance as Laurina moved to her other side.

"I am only a student," Moradag sighed. "But I thought King Vlidorix would act against this Gundori, who calls himself a king. To seize free people for sacrifice is a grave violation of law. But Ferdiath's words add confusion."

"How?" Emyn asked.

"Well, if your spirits can seduce, then perhaps what happened on Gundori's island was more their fault than his."

"What?" Emyn shrieked and turned. Laurina caught the fabric and began to scold, but Emyn ignored her. "My spirits were not *on* the island!"

"I know—"

"You are a peasant," the dead king railed. "Who will listen to you? Only my voice carries authority!"

"My master argues with Ferdiath over every point," Moradag was saying. "Vlidorix knows this. Again, I am only a student, but I think the king seeks an excuse not to act. This is not a time to waste men and weapons against a chieftain who can barricade himself on an island."

Emyn fumed; so no one would rein in Gundori? She felt Aruca's hand on her shoulder and saw the ghost's sad smile. They'd done what they could, it implied.

"Ferdiath's tongue weaves stories like silk," Emyn growled. "Pretty and flattering, but too thin to serve any useful purpose."

"That is clever, Chiomara. You should learn the rules of poetry."

Emyn's jaw tightened. "We need sense and strength now, not poems."

THE NEXT DAY WAS BRIGHT, though cold. Emyn and Laurina took the cloth they had measured and cut the night before, and sewed in the sunlight. Nonicos had a new mallet and axe that he put to use, constructing a small cart to carry their possessions when they left Venetona. He bought two wheels with the last of the silver coins: a good investment, he said. Within days they would be at their new home and he would be turning out wheels of his own along with carts, tables, and benches.

The morning came when the new cart was loaded with tools, pots and bowls, food for the journey, the unfinished clothes, furs, and a small god that Nonicos had carved.

The clouds overhead moved and promised sun later. Emyn was grateful; she had dropped a tin coin into Venetona's sacred pool with prayers for an easy trek and rain-free skies over her brother.

She knew this would hurt. Slicing off an arm would be easier than cutting this last tie to all she loved. None of the words she wanted to say would come out of her throat. Nonicos would be leagues away before she could make any sound other than a sob.

"It doesn't matter." Her brother tried to laugh, but his own voice broke as he hugged her.

She held him tightly. The moment mattered, not the words.

They'd tried to tell Micco in several different ways that Nonicos was leaving and Emyn staying. The boy walked behind as the family started off. Before they reached the main road, he ran back to tug at Emyn's hand, trying to pull her onto the path with them. "No," she said and hugged him again. "Good-bye."

Micco whimpered and gazed back and forth between Emyn and the others until Nonicos walked back and gently pried him away. His life would run smoother on a farm with a small family, but no one knew how to explain that to him.

As IMBOLC BEGAN, the Honored Master Ferdiath appeared at the inn. He threw back his cloak with a flourish to reveal a yellow dress edged in blue, with embroidered sleeves as well as a beaded belt—all draped over his arm and hand.

"For your comfort, lady, so that you may enjoy the hospitality of King Vlidorix on this holiday." The gown rippled over his arm like sunlit water. "Your beauty, as I well remember, needs no adornment."

"Smile," Aruca urged Emyn.

"A better mate for you!" The dead king chortled at the same time. "You will glow like a flame at his side!"

"Smile!" Aruca shouted. Emyn smiled.

"Look up, blink," Aruca advised later, as Emyn emerged from the inn wearing the ornate dress. "Take his arm. Let him carry your stick. He is a big, strong man. Stand straight!"

Ferdiath's words were lost in Aruca's instructions, but the ghost gave Emyn a response: "Say: you have brought spring itself to clothe me, Honored Master."

Emyn repeated Aruca's intonation along with her words, though she thought she looked more like an overloaded branch on a lemon tree than the goddess of spring and fire that Ferdiath babbled about.

"Laugh!" commanded Aruca, and Emyn obeyed.

In the weird hours that followed, she was more aware of ghostly words than those of the living, including Ferdiath's. Emyn acted out Aruca's instructions while her mind wandered freely. Sitting in company while daydreaming reminded her of when she was a child at Volio's hearth, repeating what the ghosts said without comprehension and watching the grownup business. Now it was a king's hearth, but the business was still beyond her.

The food was savory; firelight flashed on the jewels and shadowed the rich fabrics that swirled through the huge tent. The Imbolc fire would be lit in the king's hearth later; for now, guests sat around smaller hearths, protected from wind and rain by temporary walls and a roof of decorated leather.

Emyn noticed the glares of other women as Ferdiath lavished

attention on her. When the Irish druid picked up a lyre and sang a song, filling the entire house with a bittersweet poem of lost love, Emyn was the envy of every woman present. For herself, she felt less a woman than a trained dog, minding Aruca's commands.

"Sigh . . . again, louder," Aruca coaxed. "Look at him. Do not let your eyes wander."

A long sleeve covered half the hand that held the lyre while the other brushed and plucked the strings. He was clever at concealing it, but Emyn remembered the hump on his little finger: the blemish that marked him. Ferdiath had seemed exotic once— was it only a year and a half ago? Emyn had picked up a bit of gossip that trickled down to the inn: that Ferdiath left a harsh and ugly wife behind in Eire. "He'd rather drift homeless than lie with her," a woman had snorted.

"Homeless?" another cackled. "He sleeps in kings' houses and eats their food. I'd wish such homelessness on my own sons!"

"But what does he have of his own?"

"As much as he wants!" the second woman sniffed. "His fortunes pile up with all those trades and boatloads of wine he arranges. Do you think he does that for nothing?" She'd glanced around the inn, then leaned close. "Someone's holding a fat pot of coins for him, mark my words!"

It was probably true. Once he put down the lyre, much of Ferdiath's talk seemed to be of wine and ships. The king's daughters and their friends approached Emyn, and she repeated spirit words to them.

As the sun sank, Rialos appeared with Moradag behind him. The druid hefted a bronze brazier that reflected the smaller fires as he circled the tent. Soon, everyone rose to follow him into the king's house where a newly built hearth sat, cold and waiting.

Rialos' deep voice sang out sacred words as he tossed embers onto the tinder. The fire crackled and blazed to life, and then he was gone. Was she relieved or angry that their eyes never met?

Once the house warmed, the Honored Master Nanto was carried near the flames. Emyn made her way to where he sat, propped on massive cushions.

"Do you remember me, Master?" She picked up a cold hand and held it between hers. "You came to Samarnum the summer after Rome's slave war. Your hair was red and beautiful like fire."

Nanto opened his mouth and grunted, but could not form words. Few spirits lingered near him; perhaps Nanto's soul spent more time in their world.

Ferdiath sat across the fire and began one of the great songs of Brigid. Like the Morrigu, the goddess Brigid wore three faces. Otherwise the two deities were different: Brigid valued learning over warfare, order over terror. Ferdiath claimed her as one of the most ancient mothers of Eire.

"She prefers the west, I suppose," Emyn whispered to Nanto, and his eyes watched her mouth. "We barely knew your Brigid in Samarnum."

The song ended. Moradag tapped Emyn's arm and led her to King Vlidorix, who asked her to repeat the charges she'd made against Gundori. She did; almost word for word—it was the truth, after all.

"He keeps your advice for himself," the dead king said, and Emyn nodded. Vlidorix had seated her where no warriors or guests could overhear.

"A wise man gathers tales like weapons and tests them," added another ghost.

Vlidorix asked about the attack on the beach as well. Did Emyn know the men? Where had she seen them before? She answered simply. She imagined that Rialos and Moradag had already told him what happened.

"Did they wear any token of Gundori's?" the king asked.

"I don't know. The man I recognized wore a warrior's torque and an armband," Emyn answered.

"Were they from Gundori, the torque and armband?"

Emyn could not say.

The king sighed and signaled to the queen, who moved closer. "My wife will make room for you in her house. A public inn is no fit place for the Gutumaros."

"Say, 'I prefer solitude.'"

Emyn's throat tightened at Aruca's command. The queen smiled at her. How could she speak so boldly to them?

"Say it! I prefer solitude."

"I prefer solitude."

The king raised an eyebrow. Emyn's face grew hot. "You are more generous than I deserve," she blurted, "but fear follows me. Your servants and slaves will not be able to sleep because of my ghosts. I would be an awful guest, upsetting your household."

"That was stupid!" Aruca hissed.

"You shame us, Gutumaros!" The king's tongue slurred a little. Like everyone else, he'd had plenty of ale. "Do you think I cannot control my own servants?"

"Or mine?" The queen added.

"Repeat my words." Aruca's voice blocked out all others. "You speak truly, King Vlidorix. I cannot stay in an inn, and I crave your hospitality. Please forgive a clumsy woman whose tongue is not trained to speak to the mighty."

Emyn fixed her eyes on the hammered gold ring that Vlidorix wore on his first finger as she echoed Aruca's voice. "I must have solitude; the spirits demand it. Is there not an ancient shrine and a spring on the other side of your stable?"

"A shrine?" The king looked to his wife: "Do you know of it?"

"There's half a tumbled down hut there. I would not call it a shrine."

"Its purpose has been forgotten then," Emyn said, still repeating what Aruca said. "A cup is chained to the rock, a cup shaped like a raven's beak. It should be cleaned and the water sipped once more for its wisdom."

"And so it shall be," said the queen.

"My spirits say the posts and lower walls of the hut are sound," said Emyn. "A new roof and plaster are all that is needed to make it a home."

"Your home?" The king lifted his cup and said loudly, "Gutumaros, if that is where you wish to live, the shrine is yours."

Emyn bowed her head and meekly followed Aruca's instructions when the ghost told her to thank him, rise, and walk away.

"Whether you trust us or not, do as we say," Aruca said, resting a hand on her shoulder. "Your life is not your own. No one's is. You must accept that."

Emyn nearly tripped as she looked up at her friend. "What sort of world is this that our lives are not ours to live?" she muttered. "Why—"

"You are far too morose, little Gutumaros. Here is Ferdiath with another cup to share with you." Aruca swept her hair from her face as if she could be bothered by it. "Pretend to drink and give the cup back to him. Smile!"

A few swallows were all the Irish druid had time for, and then he was singing once more, surrounded by adoring women, old and young.

The ghost giggled in Emyn's ear. "Rialos is beside himself! He cannot take his eyes off you."

Emyn glanced around the firelit room and saw Moradag slipping inside, holding the hand of a pretty redhead. It must be late indeed if the teenagers were done with kisses and ready to rejoin the crowd.

"Can I go sleep with the women now?" Emyn murmured.

"Go. Ferdiath is past remembering," Aruca squeezed Emyn's hand. "He will apologize to you later, but he won't be sure what he's sorry about."

TWO DAYS LATER SHE sat outside the inn, sheltered from drizzle by the overhanging thatch, and stitched in the uneven lamplight. A sleeved tunic of the soft red wool shifted in her lap as her fingers worked the needle.

"You'll have a new home soon." Aruca appeared beside her. "Will you be lonely there?"

"How can I be lonely?" Emyn whispered. There was no bench where Aruca sat, but the ghost didn't seem to mind. "You are always with me."

"Not for long." Aruca leaned to kiss her cheek.

"What? Don't leave."

"I must." Aruca blinked as if tears formed in her eyes. "But not today."

The barbed promise gave Emyn little comfort. She did not want to think of living anywhere without her friend. While Emyn stared, Aruca faded and disappeared.

Not today. She'd said "Not today," so she would return.

Emyn paused to stretch her hands and arms and walk outside, gripping a stick that would never be carved—not now, not with Nonicos gone. Below, fishing boats stayed close to shore, unsure of the weather. Bright paint and symbols adorned them. One was white with blue fish along its sides—a fisherman had painted exactly what he wished to receive. The gods must appreciate such frank entreaties, Emyn thought.

ON THE RAINY DAY that Emyn's new home was finished, slaves carried her clothes from the inn to the little hut. A small knob of a goddess with curved lines that might have been wings or breasts was set over the door. Nonicos had made it for her before leaving. The place was no bigger than the hut she'd shared with Iomat, which suited Emyn well.

It was the duty of the chief druid to bless all new structures on the king's land, and the stricken Nanto still held that title. A litter carried the silent man forward, while two slaves on either side held a leather sheet over his head for protection against the rain. Rialos and Moradag followed. Once they'd crowded inside, Rialos stood beside Nanto and said the words of blessing as he lifted the old man's arm. He knelt and lit the first fire, hung the cauldron over it, and once the water was boiling, added herbs to attract luck and banish misfortune. Emyn watched, satisfied. The trio of faces before her hearth—Nanto, Rialos, Moradag—sprang from myth: the sage, the man, the youth.

The next day Moradag brought a bucket that smelled of the sea to her home. A fish tried to jump out, and a splash of water sizzled on the hearth. "You'll get bread soon, judging by the smell when I passed the ovens." Moradag shook raindrops from his head. "Are you sure you'll not have a girl of your own to fetch for you, Chiomara?"

"To shiver in the corner, you mean?" Emyn waved the question away.

"Do you want no one?" Aruca's voice was barely audible.

She'd be leaving soon, she had reminded Emyn last night. Her time was done.

"This is the world of parting and forgetting," she'd said.

"Master Ferdiath wanted to call down the blessings on your home," Moradag informed Emyn as he accepted a cup of cider. The queen had provisioned Emyn well. "He and my master exchanged sharp words over it."

"Ask, silly girl," Aruca prodded.

"Please invite your master to drink the first water tomorrow," Emyn said to Moradag. She did not want to think of sitting by the fire without Aruca's laughter.

Moradag set down the cup, put his hands together and bowed his head. "He will be honored, voice of the ancients."

THE FIRST WATER OF a sacred spring, infused with moonlight and the rising sun, granted wisdom and surety. Although they'd ignored the spring for years, no one in Venetona would approach it now without Emyn's permission, and her invitation to drink from it would not be ignored. Emyn watched as the druid walked up just after sunrise, dropped to his knees before the rocky pool, and scooped water with the little cup.

Did Rialos know she watched? After drinking, he turned. His face was the mask he always wore. Seeing it hurt her like bumping a bruise.

Rialos put his hands together in thanks and bowed as Moradag had done. Ancestors clad in furs gathered near him: his mother's people.

"Please come in and warm yourself." She bowed back and followed him into the hut. "I have a favor to ask. But let me say first that, as druid of the Veneti, you are welcome to drink from the spring any morning, whether or not you grant my request."

"Ask, please. There is nothing I would withhold from you."

He withheld himself. Did he not see that?

The druid waited several heartbeats, then said again, "Ask."

"I fear to anger you. But I must." Emyn looked him in the eye. "Your sister has a young slave, a boy named Gorio. What I ask is that you get this child from her."

"You wish to own a slave?"

"No!" Emyn hadn't expected him to think that. "But if you . . . or even Moradag?" Her voice faded as she saw his solemn expression harden into stone. "I thought . . . maybe he could be bought or taken as a gift."

"You don't know what you ask." Rialos' voice ground out the words like a millstone crushing grain. "You grant the waters of wisdom one moment and burn a brand into me the next."

Emyn felt suddenly alone in a silent world and realized that he had banished her ghosts without even pausing in his speech. "You astonish me, woman. Have you no limits?"

"I ask you to bring the boy here, that's all."

"All?" Rialos paced before her. "Humiliate myself before my father's family and king, and that's all?"

"How would that humiliate you?"

"To go back to Vinnia and ask for her insulting gift? To keep a slave from the forest, a young boy made for Greek pleasures . . . is this a joke? Revenge? Some cruel game you and your ghosts have devised to taunt me?"

Emyn leaned on her stick. She would not be drawn into an argument about Rialos' dignity! "Give him away, if you don't want him. I only want him out of Gundori's reach."

"Why? He is a slave in another land."

"He is a friend. I used to see him often. I care about him."

"Do you? And yet you will not keep him." Rialos smirked. "A child . . . you ask me to pluck him up like a hawk swooping down on a mouse. Where would you like him dropped?"

"Anyplace is better than that island. Since no one will stop Gundori—"

"Do not presume to foresee our plans for Gundori!"

"The ghosts tell me enough to guess." Emyn drew herself up before the druid, stung by his haughty tone. "If Gundori offers another sacrifice, who will know? He performs his rituals in secret. Vinnia had a freckled slave, only a little older than your student. Do you remember? When you visited, you picked him to help carry me home in Vinnia's litter. He was there the night Gundori attacked me. He was drugged. He is probably dead. And Aruca—you knew her well. Her ghost was here a moment ago! She—"

"Enough!" Rialos' face twisted and he turned away. "Give me silence."

It was a direct order from a druid. She gulped back her words.

When he spoke next, his tone was controlled. "Slavery is a part of life here. You cannot build such friendships without hurting yourself. Learn that, if you intend to stay."

"It's too late," Emyn said. "I would buy Gorio if I could—"

"There are those I would buy back as well. But it cannot be done. Let him go."

Emyn had one last argument to make. He had made love to her and she kept that secret; she didn't have to. A debt existed.

She forced herself to look up into his eyes. "You said, 'Ask.' I ask. If you have any honor, do this for me."

"Honor." Rialos shook his head as if to laugh at himself. "I made a poor bargain when I went looking for that. I was better off without it."

The morning mist clung to his cloak as he walked from her hut.

Emyn sighed and huddled before her fire. The dead king formed at her side, a shadow with a familiar sense to him, like a rock under a damp overhang of moss. She heard his eerie laugh and asked, "What is funny?"

"How would a slave know the hour of his birth?"

The ghost's words hung in the air. Emyn was puzzled. She asked for Gorio's safety, not to know his future. What did the hour of his birth signify?

The memory hit her suddenly like a lone drumbeat. In Nerrus' stable, ducking under the druid's arm, happy for what seemed the last moment in this lifetime, she had asked Rialos, "When were you born?"

How would a slave know the hour of his birth?

Such an ordinary question for a woman to ask a man . . . but it had salted the open wound of his soul. And today she called on his honor.

 **32**

Cold, rainy days kept Emyn inside her little hut. She soon knew every finger's width of the dark place, but it changed. She paced from wall to wall; once it was eleven of her small steps, on another day, nine. The ghosts laughed at her efforts. They hung blue cloth from the walls one morning and yellow the next; sometimes they moved her bench or hid her belt.

Aruca never returned. Spirits wandered in and lingered, then left when they'd finished telling her a tale. Emyn barely listened.

Her grandfather talked to her in a dream. "Heroes live fast," he reminded her. "That makes for a better life."

"But heroes don't fight battles all the time, do they?" she asked. In this dream, Emyn was small, looking up at him. She saw stars overhead instead of thatch.

"No, not all the time. They have to rest so they can fight the next battle."

He sounded so real that she started and sat up. The embers in the hearth had nearly disappeared. As she stirred them and added wood, Grandfather adjusted a bearskin around her shoulders. He was truly there. Emyn didn't mention this to Moradag or anyone who might be troubled that she found warmth beneath invisible bearskins.

Although close to other buildings, the hut bred isolation. The stable hid her from most houses; she could not see the well or the children playing. She didn't watch the warriors wrestle or see who could throw a rock the farthest. She heard men lead horses out to exercise them, but the stable doors opened away from her so the voices were soon lost.

The first waters and daily delivery of Emyn's share of bread, fish, mussels, eggs, or whatever else the king provided, established a rhythm in her life. Otherwise she might have slept all her time away. Little else demanded her attention. At night the smell of mint or apples seeped into the air. Emyn was never alone, though the dead brought little comfort.

She remembered once, as if waking from illness, that spinning was how she used to fill her hours. Maybe that would restore her sense of usefulness. She asked the girl who brought bread to find her a spindle, distaff, and wool.

No spindle appeared the next day. "She forgot," Emyn muttered as she stood in her doorway and watched fog veil the retreating figure.

"Oh, no. She won't forget." The ghost of an old man sat by the spring. Emyn knew his voice—it had called "Look, look!" to her on the day of her trial. Now he rolled back on the stone, laughing.

"What is funny?"

"It's a different girl!" The ghost righted himself and slapped his knee. "You needed me to tell you that?"

It wasn't always the same girl who brought her food. How had she not noticed the varied hair, dress, posture, eyes? One always shared a little gossip when she stopped; another seemed as slow as Micco; the youngest averted her eyes and ran away once her errand was complete.

What else distinguished them? Was Emyn becoming spoiled like a slaveholder who couldn't tell one piece of human flesh from another? As long as her supper appeared . . . she shuddered and vowed to pay better attention.

As the absent moon began a new month, Moradag announced that he would accompany Rialos on a visit to Gundori's realm. "My master says I'm to display all my charm while we're there. Is his sister very pretty?"

Emyn groaned. "She is old enough to be his mother, but she roots out flattery like a pig."

Moradag accepted a cup of warm cider. "My master wants you to know that while snow rarely falls here, the wind and rain can wreck a house. He feels a storm coming."

"Feels a storm?"

"The Honored Master Rialos can predict the weather from the clouds and winds and the color of the sunset," Moradag said with pride. "He is teaching me what he learned as a child on this very gulf. Before I studied the night sky; now I learn the daylight. Soon I'll be able to foretell the weather as well as destinies."

"That is a skill to be prized," Emyn smiled. "But if a storm is coming, why travel into it?"

"According to my master, we have at least four days to get to Gundori's island; plenty of time. Satto promises to look in on you and ensure your safety while we're gone."

On the day after Rialos and Moradag left, Emyn sat as a guest in the queen's large house, between the weathered healer who tended Nanto and a thin man named Teuto. Ferdiath, to Emyn's relief, sat near the queen.

"We have Teuto to thank for the wine." The healer bobbed her head at the merchant as the cup came to her.

"As well as Ferdiath." Teuto smiled but his eyes were small and humorless. "With his help, my ships stay busy."

Emyn tried to imagine what Aruca would say but no clever words came to mind. Smile, the ghost would insist, so to honor Aruca's memory, Emyn smiled.

"Have you ordered them to stay in port for a few days?" called a man on the other side of the healer. "The Honored Master—"

"No." Teuto rolled his eyes as he cut the man off. "Druid or not, his knowledge of our seas is limited. I won't waste men and time on his fancy guesses about the weather."

Such disrespect sat ill with Emyn; she passed the cup without even pretending to drink. Teuto accepted it from her. "I don't trust the gods he hears," he muttered. "His mother's, no doubt."

Emyn stiffened but no one else seemed to hear. In a louder voice and with a false smile, Teuto raised the cup. "I put my faith in Lugh and make the proper sacrifices to Teutates, for whom I'm named. The gods have no reason to be cross with me!"

The vicious storm struck as Rialos had predicted. It broke branches off trees, uprooted saplings, and tore thatch from roofs. Satto checked on Emyn more than once as warriors ran from house to house assessing the damage. A few ships were wrecked, but most men had followed the druid's advice.

Teuto, however, lost two vessels, one heavy with cargo. The news gave Emyn secret satisfaction.

Ferdiath visited Emyn after the storm. He slept at Nanto's house and took his turn caring for the old master. The druid dropped many hints that Emyn's hearth seemed cozier but she did not invite him to stay the night.

* * *

"THE DRUID AND HIS student are back!" Eyes bright, *this* girl didn't wait for Emyn to ask for news. Quick fingers dug into the basket for a stone weight and spindle which she handed to Emyn. "You know him well, don't you, lady? Will you go see him?"

"I don't think the Honored Master would welcome another visit from me," Emyn said as the girl pulled a distaff and wool from her belt.

"The student, I meant, not the master. Oh—he lives with his master, I see. He'll come to visit you, though, won't he?"

Emyn smiled; the girl had a crush on Moradag. That she understood. "I'm sure he'll visit. Did they bring anyone back with them?"

"A slave, yes, everyone is wondering about that. The druid never kept a slave before, not for pleasure or work. Won-der which—" The girl put her hand in front of her mouth, suddenly aware that she spilled servants' chatter in front of an oracle. "I'm sorry, I talk too much; I always do."

"Don't fret. News in winter is a gift," Emyn said, just as Iomat used to. She was glad of the girl's embarrassment. It probably kept her from noticing Emyn's excitement at her news. "Do you have time to share a cup?"

It was a start. As the days passed Emyn began to make friends and find her place in the village that surrounded the Veneti king. Her hut sat apart from the other homes, but people found reasons to visit, and the druids or Moradag sent Gorio on errands to Emyn's hut almost daily. She told him stories, listened to him count, and took him with her to gather plants.

Spring arrived quietly as the days lengthened and warmed, bit by bit. Ferdiath visited to say good bye and make one last attempt to charm Emyn into his dyed and ornamented arms. His lies brightened a dull day. By that time she'd heard so many stories of his flirtations and late-night affairs that she wondered if Ferdiath was leaving Venetona because he'd run out of women to seduce.

On days when the sun broke through clouds, Emyn stood outside and spun. Sometimes the living came to see her, but always spirits settled round. The dead king gossiped about Caesar, who now rode in luxury from the south with even more men than last year.

When the visitors left, though, Emyn stared into her fire for far too long.

Emyn learned that Gorio tended the druid Nanto, and that the presence of the child enlivened the old man. "He had six children of his own, you know, all grown now," a woman who'd come to hear her ancestors' advice told Emyn. "I don't know why no one thought of this before."

As the moon grew and thinned and grew again, men, women, even warriors knocked hesitantly on Emyn's door. They held hurts inside that one more minute with a father or grandmother would ease, and secrets that needed to be whispered. They brought gifts as well as coins: belts and pins, honeyed chestnuts and other treats, pots, baskets and carved bowls, blue and red ribbons, and combs. Emyn realized her hair had now grown long enough to braid.

Women and girls—even one of the king's daughters—stole to her hut for love potions and charms. Eventually they came to sit and spin and gossip. Emyn presented a fresh pair of ears, and she could keep secrets. She soon knew as much as anyone else about the couplings and fights and insults that shaped the lives under the king's protection.

She lived as the wealthiest in Samarnum could only dream of living. Fields and livestock were tended by slaves in this land, so she was never asked to share in the work. The gardens were open to her; she could wander anywhere with her basket, picking up herbs and spring vegetables. Other food, water, and firewood were brought to her door. Slaves were sent to gut fish and carry away her garbage—such dirty work was beneath her dignity whether she liked it or not.

No invitation came from the house that held those she loved most, though Moradag and Gorio visited Emyn's hut often. On one day, the student sent Gorio home at sunset while he accepted another cup of cider.

"We hunt, Chiomara!" Moradag's smile was as bright as the fire, and Emyn remembered how harsh the dark months had been to him. "We'll be gone for days. The king leads us with several warriors."

"You'll outrun them all." She lifted the cup in tribute before passing it to him.

"We'll have to bring wagons to carry all the game home!" He drank deeply. "I am to tell you that while others will care for honored Nanto, my master says you are welcome to visit and even sleep at the house if you like."

"That is kind of him."

"He seeks reconciliation," the dead king hissed. "I do not forgive quickly. He must learn respect."

Moradag handed the cup to Emyn. "He guesses you might like to visit, but will not come while he is present. But the house belongs to Nanto. So you are welcome."

She drank and passed the cup; the student stared at it thoughtfully. "They speak a strange language, together, my master and Gorio. Did you know that? It sounds nothing like our tongue."

The dead king waited for an answer along with Moradag. Emyn remembered Teuto's mean comments. Who here knew about Rialos' past?

"It's dark already!" She pretended to be worried. "You'll anger your master by staying so late. I know what a temper he has."

"Temper? Oh, no. Compared to Master Bodocnos, he is the most patient of teachers. Except when the druid Ferdiath drew him into arguments. But he's long gone."

"Oh." No temper? "Is it just me that sets him on edge?"

"I think it is just you that *unsets* him." Moradag winked at her. "He even says so."

Emyn's throat was dry as dirt suddenly, so she sipped cider, while trying to frame a question that would not sound too eager. "I don't know that I like him talking about me to you. What does he say?"

"That he can talk to kings and princes, whores and scholars, but he cannot find a single word to please you." Moradag laughed and drained the cup when Emyn handed it back. "And when I protested, saying that you are not hard to please at all, he growled at me and walked away."

Emyn offered to refill the cup, but Moradag pushed himself up from the ground. "I said my master has no temper and it is true, but if I stumble into his house drunk, I'll pay tomorrow."

The doorway bordered a faint yellow glow that followed the setting sun. Emyn handed Moradag his cloak; his smile vanished as he looked at her. "My words have troubled you?"

"A little." She leaned on her stick with one hand and tossed the other in the air. "I sat troscad on your master and forced him to a trial. I should expect him to hate me."

"He does not hate you!" Moradag put his hands on her shoulders. "Don't think that. My master has never met a woman like you before, Chiomara. He does not know your ways."

"I have no ways—"

"You are honest and brave. Do you not know how rare that

is?" Moradag's voice rang like the low strings of a lyre. "Look at his sister and be fair. He's lived with men since leaving her home; he expects women to weave with the truth, pulling threads out to change the design or get their way. That is what he knows. You confound him."

Emyn had no words; she nodded and Moradag kissed her forehead lightly. The yellow light had faded to darkness.

"A new day begins," they both said at once.

EMYN SPENT TWO NIGHTS at Nanto's house, spinning and talking with the ancient healer who slept there. She learned of dank gullies where rare flowers and mushrooms grew. On the second morning, she brought the old woman to the Morrigu's pool to drink the first water. They lit a new fire to warm her little hut.

The sun was bright by the time the crone departed. Emyn took a basket and followed an uphill path, pausing over a clump of nettles. The leaves were useful . . . as she carefully bent her fingers around the stem, the path, nettles, trees, and the sea smells evaporated like fog.

She stood on the roofed, wooden platform of a temple, outside the building that housed the altars. A tall palisade surrounded her where armor and animal skulls hung. Beyond it she saw only clearings and forests.

Shouts rang from within the holy enclosure. Emyn jumped back as a druid ran out, wearing a leather and bronze band much like Bodocnos'. His arms cradled scabbards and swords, some with jeweled hilts. He dumped the treasure into a deep ditch just inside the palisade, and others began shoveling dirt over the weapons.

Figures with torches ran out of the temple as the roof burst in flames. Fire and thick smoke erupted from several places at once. Emyn coughed and threw her arms before her face. Smoke burned her throat, and a roar filled her ears.

Hands pushed her. She moved like the blind, falling more than once until she stumbled against a wall. Here the smoke cleared and the vision ended.

Emyn squinted up at the familiar stable. She limped to the Morrigu's spring and cupped icy water in her hands to toss into her face, and more for her eyes. Long minutes passed before she could draw a deep breath.

The old man ghost sat by the spring and grinned at her.

"Did you push me away from the fire?" Emyn asked.

He disappeared and hands shoved her backward. She landed with her behind in the spring, and the ghost was in front of her again.

"You see things, don't you?" He laughed before she could answer. "I know you do! That's why your eyes are so big, to see on both sides of that beak like a bird."

"I saw a fire," Emyn said. "A temple on fire."

"Ah," the ghost grinned; he had very few teeth. "They know Caesar's coming."

"Caesar seeks gold," said a weary voice behind her.

Emyn turned both ways, looking for the speaker. She rubbed her eyes as shadows moved and took on new forms.

"Our kings keep no gold," grunted one man as he sharpened his knife against a whet stone. Five ghostly warriors ringed a camp fire, tending their weapons. One polished a sword with a rag; Emyn could smell the oil.

"Caesar will learn soon enough where the gold is," said a warrior, peering down the straight line of his arrow, from feathers to its pointed tip.

"In the holy groves and rivers," Emyn whispered, horror growing in her.

The ghost with the whet stone nodded. "He'll sack the temples and take the gods' offerings."

Emyn crept closer and one man turned—the same warrior who had stood on the beach with her when Gundori's men ran forward. A shield lay tilted at his feet; a bronze serpent hammered into the boss of it.

"It is not enough that they shame our sons," he said. "They shame our grandfathers as well when they steal offerings won in battle."

"You are Aeduan," Emyn said.

The man lifted his eyebrows; she saw a resemblance to Dumnorix in the shape of his jaw and mouth. "Does it matter?"

EMYN HAD LOST HER new stick while escaping the temple fire. The healer walked with her to search for it in the afternoon, even though she was nervous about entering a haunted area. Twenty steps beyond the nettles, a stream trickled along a rocky gorge, thick with ferns and undergrowth. Emyn peered into its long shadows. If the stick fell there, it would have bounced off rocks until the stream carried it away. And if Emyn, caught up in her vision, had slipped into the gorge? "You're lucky only your stick was lost," the healer remarked.

The hunting party returned as darkness settled. Emyn heard horses snort and stomp as they approached the stable; men called to one another. She threw on her cloak and walked outside to see what she could in the feeble moonlight.

Slaves raced everywhere, carrying weapons to be repaired and clothes to be cleaned. Some held torches while others brought cups and buckets of ale. She caught the musty smell of red deer and other kills, hanging from horizontal poles shouldered by slaves.

By the next afternoon, the deer were skinned and roasting over a pit while the hunters drank ale and spun elaborate tales. The king laid out a generous feast, hosting the wealthy of Venetona as well as warriors, visiting captains, merchants, and traders.

When the meat was roasted to perfection, Vlidorix stood, and with a flourish, pulled out his knife. Emyn sat behind the queen and her daughters; they all craned their necks as the king walked to the pit. Who would receive the first portion? It belonged to the man who had brought down the largest buck, but none of the hunters had told their wives who that was.

The king handed the choice cut to Rialos. "And I'll ask again," he called out, "just how an Honored Master, of all men, aims with such a steady hand and eye?"

Rialos, now standing, grinned. "Like many a boy in winter, I learned long ago that if my aim was poor, I didn't eat."

The men cheered and the women applauded. Emyn felt a private thrill, as if she had some claim on his talent. Soon Moradag was surrounded by a pack of girls who elbowed and pinched each other for position as he told them how he'd helped his master bring down the deer.

Later, Emyn stepped forward to describe the burning temple and repeat the ghostly conversation she'd heard. She spoke out clearly, aware that the strong and the wealthy listened, though some sat in a stupor of rich food and drink.

"What does it mean?" asked a fur-clad man who sat on Vlidorix' left. He piloted one of Teuto's remaining ships and had brought the wine that flowed so generously today.

Emyn met his eyes. "I can only tell you what I saw and heard."

"I think the meaning is clear," Teuto called out as he stood. "Rome belittles our gods; they are sure that theirs are stronger. We deceive ourselves if we think we can hide from them—"

"We do not hide," Vlidorix bellowed.

"Hiding gold, I meant. Only that." Teuto's head bowed then bobbed up again. "The oracle spoke of hiding gold and offerings. Her spirits said Rome seeks such treasures. Why quibble? Rome is powerful and cannot be avoided. The question is: how will we negotiate with them?"

Moradag, sitting behind the druids, rolled his eyes upward.

"Negotiate?" Several voices repeated the word, inflecting it with scorn and disbelief.

A lively debate followed. One of Vlidorix' daughters took Emyn's arm and urged her to move back to a seat with the women. There she picked up a spindle and began to play out thread. The queen did likewise; other women kept their eyes on the shouting men.

"Who will use your thread?" the dead king growled. "Rome will burn your looms and your fine clothes!"

Emyn ignored the ghost. Her eyes flitted toward Rialos, who remained silent, at times smiling as the others argued. A dozen masks hid that man; he was teacher, adviser, a keen competitor, friend of Satto and other warriors . . . but did she know anymore of him than she had at fifteen? Even then he had seemed split in two: the student who kissed her and the condescending fellow who assumed that she longed for Coath and had snapped, "Wrong one?"

Emyn grabbed the spindle as it touched the floor and wrapped the thread furiously. She hoped the gods knew what to do with her; she could no more manage her mind than she could order the sun to rise in the west.

 **33**

Beltane's dusk was clear, a fitting welcome to summer. Emyn stood with the queen and matrons of Venetona and watched as Rialos lit the purifying fires. Crisp winds whipped up sparks from the fire and drove smoke throughout the fields, leaving the air scented with burning pine.

Once all the fires roared, wide gates were thrown open and the cattle were driven up the paths, between the flame, and into the verdant pastures beyond. People cheered and crowded around; the drums beat a rhythm to speed the heart.

"Where did the Honored Master go?" Emyn couldn't stop herself from asking.

"There are more pastures to be blessed." A woman waved her hand northward.

"But no more druids to help," said another. Emyn grew lost in the mix of voices, picking out only a few phrases.

"When I was a girl . . ."

"Three druids . . ."

"One here, one traveling north before the sun set—"

". . . never sing anymore . . ."

"He took that black horse. A black horse for a night ride, my husband says."

"He'll be back before midnight," a plump woman winked and elbowed Emyn. "But you'd better watch for the man, or someone else will sneak under him first!" Emyn laughed without sincerity at the harmless joke and ambled away, leaning on a pine stick that the stable master had sawed and whittled to the right height for her.

"No one sleeps alone on Beltane," so the saying went, but Emyn knew it was a lie. She'd spent every Beltane of her life alone, even when she was married.

"Will you lie like a dog at his feet?" the dead king hissed. "Then you deserve no better treatment than to be thrown scraps!"

"Even your advice can be right sometimes, ghost." Emyn glanced north. Smoke drifted over the road, lit by a fat creamy moon in the eastern sky.

"If you listened to me, you would be crowned with gold!"

She waved her hand at him as she walked toward the music and drums. Beltane was a night for running and dancing without care, but Emyn could not run or dance. Twice men approached from behind. One pinched her bottom; another snatched away her shawl. She turned, and the men turned pale when they realized they'd flirted with the Death Speaker.

By the time Emyn grew sleepy, the moon was smaller and high overhead. She had eaten all she could, sang songs with the children, answered questions from many women, and watched others drink and dance and jump over fires. Now she found herself a cozy nest beneath a pine tree. A mist crept over the land, dimming the fires. Shouts grew rare and farther away.

She was almost asleep when she heard her name called. "What?" Pine needles crackled beneath her as she pushed herself up. "I'm here."

"Emyn? I've been looking for you." Rialos dropped to his knees and took her hand. Did she dream? "Come with me tonight."

Emyn shivered and came fully awake. She didn't dream, but he smelled of ale and sweat. He stood, then bent to tug at her arm. "Come away."

She yanked her arm free. "No."

"Why not? Walk behind the trees at least."

Emyn scowled at him, felt around for her stick, and lifted herself up. Rialos tried to help but she pushed at him again.

"Emyn." Out of the pine tree's shadow, she could see the face he wore as he whispered her name. It was his most charming mask, the one he wore for Vinnia and her friends. She knew by his posture that he was not as drunk as he pretended. "It's Beltane. Let's be together this night."

For a heartbeat she imagined lying in his arms, then just as quickly anger doused the fire. "And tomorrow will not be Beltane so you will leave. Is that right?"

"Tomorrow's cares are for tomorrow. Tonight is made for joy."

Joy? She felt no joy, only fury. It rose in her like a flooding river. "And the night after tomorrow is not Beltane, is it? Or the night after that?" Her voice lifted; she could not dam it. "How many nights till you smile at me again, Rialos? Thirty? Three times thirty? Am I to lie alone all those nights, grateful that you thought of me on Beltane?"

He took a step back, but the flood carried her along like dead branches and debris, crashing into everything.

"A whore gets more respect than a woman forgotten! You come to me with your arms out because on this one night you feel passionate? Or daring? Is that it?"

"Emyn, you—"

"Why?" she shrieked as Rialos reached out as if he could calm her, but she held up her stick like a club. "Touch me again and I'll break your arm, I swear it!"

"Do what you want!" He turned and his shadow dissolved into a cluster of trees. "I am done with you, madwoman!"

She lowered the stick. He was gone, swallowed in darkness. Emyn looked around and caught a couple of faces turning away, pretending they hadn't heard.

Do what you want, he said. The man who'd killed all hope told her to do what she wanted as if she could want anything again. The irony was funny, but not even the ghosts were laughing.

Should she try to sleep in the same place? No one went home on Beltane, at least not until the sun broke over the eastern fields. She shook with weakness, as if her temper had burned all of her, leaving a shell of ash. She was arranging her large shawl around her when she—and everyone else—heard the scream.

It split the darkness and drove all other sound out of the night. When it ended, every animal stood alert, and every human searched another pair of eyes, wanting an answer. The cry was desperate and insane. Emyn knew in a heartbeat that it tore from Rialos' throat.

"Can your ghosts tell you anything, Gutumaros?"

The sleepless night weighted Satto's face, deepening the grooves around his eyes and mouth. He was Rialos' friend. She knew he had looked everywhere, even places he probably wouldn't want Emyn to know about.

"He doesn't want to be followed," a soft voice said.

Emyn repeated the words.

"No?" Satto grimaced. His bloodshot eyes glittered in the

morning light. "I don't trust the living when they say to do nothing. Why should I trust the dead?"

Emyn's laugh turned into a sob, and Satto patted her shoulder. She knew she looked as haggard as he did. "Who will care for the Honored Master Nanto while he's gone?" she asked.

"The queen attends to those things. They are your friends, aren't they? His student and the child?"

"Yes." A tremor passed through Emyn as she stifled a yawn. "I will visit his house."

"Good." Satto frowned and struggled for the right words. "He worries about you, alone in that hut. He asked that we all watch out for you. It's probably better that you're not alone." He ended with an uneasy shrug.

Emyn hesitated, not sure if she read Satto correctly. "You think I should stay in the Honored Master's house."

Satto nodded.

"Will he be angry? When he comes back?" He would come back, she told herself. Of course he would.

"No. He will be grateful." Satto turned and left.

THE QUEEN, the old healer, and even the warriors seemed relieved that Emyn was willing to stay in Nanto's house. The spirits didn't care; Emyn's surroundings mattered little to them. The dead king intruded no matter where Emyn slept.

"Chiefs bow before the Roman general." The dead king's voice swelled with spite. "They give him their daughters and even their sons, yes! 'Anything, mighty Caesar, if you leave our homes and fields intact.'"

"Who?" Emyn asked. "Who bows to him?"

The ghost named tribes. "But none exceed the Aedui in

flattery. Aeduan men chop their hair short and raze their moustaches to be more like Rome."

When King Vlidorix visited his silent elder druid the next day, Emyn passed on the dead king's words. The king rested his hand on Nanto's arm as she spoke.

"Caesar summons Diviciacos. The Roman dispenses orders like a master to a servant. He tells Diviciacos to drive his Aeduan warriors north to raid and provoke fights among those who might unite against Rome. Always north."

After her words settled, Vlidorix asked, "Is there anything else, Gutumaros?"

"No, sir," Emyn murmured.

"Nothing about our Master Rialos?"

Emyn waited but heard only the hisses and complaints of the dead king. She shook her head sadly.

HER MIND DRIFTED OFTEN. Why did Rialos want to lie with her and leave? Emyn had heard enough of Venetona's gossip to know he had no other woman—not even a favorite whore, though he visited them on occasion.

"Do you want some crabs to cook?" The question came from one of the queen's servants. Emyn tried to pay attention while the woman described how to boil and eat the creatures.

The woman left; the wind stilled and the sunlight dimmed. Emyn stood outside the druid's house, the wooden bucket with crabs in her hand. The scent of pine and sea gave way to the odor of bodies in a cramped space.

Emyn groaned. She did not want to see visions or think of Romans now! She wanted to bring these crabs inside, that was all. Was she still even holding the bucket upright?

But here she stood—in a corner, surrounded by clean-shaven men. Beyond the bodies, a lamp cast its feeble glow against the planked walls that enclosed them. The doorway revealed a larger room beyond this boxy space. She looked down. Her feet rested on mats, not the muddy paths of Venetona.

A centurion passed through the doorway, holding a woman by the arm and pulling her roughly with him. He wore pants. A Roman in pants. "What is this, dead king?" she called, not expecting an answer.

Shoulders blocked the woman's face until one fellow shifted his weight. Emyn recognized the Helvetian princess who had married Dumnorix, though she'd changed. Gone was the spoiled wife who played with mirrors. She watched these men, her eyes shadowed with suspicion and cunning.

The centurion who held her arm said, "Tell us again about Dumnorix."

"You tell them."

He gave her arm a shake. "You must say it."

"Why?" She looked at the walls. "They won't understand me anyway."

"Do not argue with me, woman! Say it."

The woman fixed her gaze on the centurion's feet. "Dumnorix is forbidden—"

Emyn sucked in her breath; she wouldn't dare!

"By whom?" the man demanded.

"By his ancestors. By the druids."

"Go on."

"Dumnorix is forbidden to cross the sea."

"And this is a sacred ban, correct? You called it a geis?" Without waiting for a response, the man chittered in his own language to the others. After answering their questions, he turned back to her. "I told them this geis is a secret. No one else knows of it."

The princess looked at nothing while the men talked. Did she understand them, Emyn wondered; had she learned their Latin? Was she alert and listening behind that vacant stare? She lifted her head suddenly. "You cannot trick him, not really. He will die rather than defy that geis."

The crowded room faded. Emyn blinked at the misty daylight and looked down. The bucket was on its side, the crabs escaped. They would die in green grasses, too far from the beach to find their way back to the sea. Freedom would do them no good at all.

DAYS LATER, Emyn tied string to branches, and then held a ladder for Gorio as he climbed up and hung the plants from the beams of Nanto's house. After that, she began chopping vegetables for the stew pot. If she kept her hands busy, she hoped, her mind would follow. There was little to clean here: no woven hangings and few shelves. Had it always been so sparse? Had Nanto no taste for ornaments? But Emyn found work; today she arranged chives and savory in one jug and rose petals in another.

"Are those love potions?" Moradag called from the doorway. He had been practicing with Satto and the warriors as he did each morning.

"No, just vinegar." Emyn finished pouring water into the jugs. "Eventually."

"Ah. If a girl named Pama asks you for a love potion, would you give her some of that?"

Emyn tied a piece of linen over each of the jugs. "I know Pama. She is too young for love potions. Did you flirt with her?"

"I swear I did nothing," Moradag wiped sweat from his face and arms with a wet cloth, then ran the rag over his hair as he talked. "She comes with her father to watch us train. I don't even talk to her."

"Ah." Emyn ladled warm broth with onions and cabbage into a bowl. Gorio and Nanto had nearly finished the portion they shared; the child would tear bread into small pieces to soak up the last of the broth and feed it to the old man. "Your voice is her music. She doesn't notice your words."

"That is a chilling thought for one who would be a druid, Chiomara." Moradag set a bucket of oysters between him and Emyn and pulled out his knife. "We are taught to believe our words can solve all problems."

He opened an oyster and slurped out the contents, then pried more apart, passing half-shells to Emyn as she sat beside him on the mat. Gorio crept up and Emyn handed some to him as well. The pile of discarded shells grew.

Finally Moradag sighed and said, "The men sent north have returned."

Emyn waited. If the news was good, Moradag would have burst out with it before now.

"No word, no sign. They followed the Visona River for two days, as far as the forest. They cut east and came back along the Visambu. No one has seen him."

Emyn nodded. When she badgered them about Rialos, the ghosts had pointed west, not north. Now spirits whispered that he was out of their ken, which could mean many things. Had he died, or boarded a ship, or crossed to an island like Gundori's? No path made sense.

Yesterday–her birthday—Emyn had dropped a silver coin into the Morrigu's spring, asking that Rialos return whole and sane.

"He will come back," Emyn said to Moradag. "His duty to you is sacred."

"Madmen can forget their duty—"

"In stories, maybe. But your master is not a madman. He will return."

Moradag took a breath as if he might argue with her, then nodded. "Yes. He will."

EMYN'S MIND SKITTERED AROUND day and night, though she tried to contain it. He would return. She slammed a door against any other possibility. He would return . . . but what would she do then?

Could she go back to her hut and live with the sight of him each day—at the well or the stable or sitting by the king? She could not stop wanting the man, that was clear. Should she leave?

Common sense rose up. She could not travel alone nor did she want to. Leaving Venetona would be foolish, a child's solution. Emyn was welcome and protected here.

Rialos would find his way home, she repeated to herself, and she would find a way to work through each day, stifling the ache when she saw him and the disappointment when she did not.

THE MOON DWINDLED TO NOTHING. The time of losing and mourning ended, according to Iomat's practical wisdom. Emyn remembered how the wise woman wove all duties into cycles of light and dark. "Gather food, build up your stores while the moon grows," she would say. "Forget your lack for awhile."

Emyn repeated the words to Nanto just so she could hear them spoken again. One part of his mouth turned up as he grunted and nodded. Shouts from outside intruded; the warriors cheered each other on as they sparred and wrestled. The dead king thrilled at such noises. "An audience assembles."

"Not for you, dead king." Emyn smiled at Nanto. "The sun is shining. We waste it inside, don't we, Master?" She turned to Gorio. "Go watch for Moradag. Tell him to bring strong men to carry the Honored Master outside."

The boy ran off. Emyn sat down and took Nanto's hand. "I'll put a pretty girl by your side in the sunshine. How is that?"

"You spout nonsense for the weak."

"Hush, ghost!" Emyn patted Nanto's hand. "A pretty girl to sing you songs . . . ." She kept talking, chanting as she would to a child. Nanto might understand; she could not tell. Maybe he found her silly and amusing. His eyes flickered from her face to the door and grew large.

Emyn turned, expecting to see Moradag and Gorio. They might have been there, but she saw only one form. He stood just inside the open door, daylight casting his face into black silhouette: Rialos.

Other men, full of questions, followed him into the house. She picked out Satto among the tall warriors. They blocked the light as her eyes followed the shadow of Rialos. Emyn wanted to cry out in delight as some of the men did, but she trembled and fought back unwanted tears instead.

Joy mixed with hurt. Time hadn't dulled the sting as it should; instead the aches piled up each time she saw him.

The king was coming, someone shouted.

"Now announce my words!" screamed the ghost.

Emyn put Nanto's hand back at his side and tried to explain, but choked. She could not speak, not before kings or druids. Her voice would crack if she tried. She shook her head in apology to the old man and picked up her stick. No one noticed her as she edged toward the door.

 34

"We have earned this house! Why do you leave when my words elevate you?" The dead king screamed at Emyn, stinging her like an insect as she hobbled behind buildings where the smell from latrine ditches wafted close. "You slink away like vermin seeking the darkness."

She ignored him. She could not weep without reason before all those men.

Emyn pushed open the door to her hut. For half a month, no breeze had touched this space and the stuffy air strangled her.

"The house of a druid holds comforts and the tokens of wealth!" The dead king softened his tone in an attempt to coax. "Let *him* search for new shelter!"

Emyn's soul knotted inside. Rialos had come back; that was good. He seemed whole and uninjured. Why could she not be happy?

"Look, look!" The old man ghost appeared and waved away the dead king. "You are a funny shadow. You don't even see what's in front of you!"

She peered through the gloom. The hut seemed a stranger's.

Even the little goddess over the door had been carried to Nanto's house; nothing blessed this place.

A long object—a stick or sword—lay on the ground, wrapped in leather. Emyn knelt, curious and thankful for anything that took her mind off Rialos. She untied a strip of cloth and lifted one edge of the leather. The object tumbled out and settled on the dirt. Three faces winked at her—the faces that Nonicos carved in the summer evenings as Bodocnos talked and Moradag recited his lessons.

"It has lain in blood," said the old man. "How did that happen?"

Emyn stretched her fingers to touch it. She had dropped this stick; her hands had lost feeling when the crazed king called her his Morrigu. Could this be real? The day had not changed; no vision moved her . . . yet here lay her stick, like an old friend that walked in to visit.

The old man and all other ghosts vanished. Rialos' voice rose out of the deep silence. "I came here first."

Had he brought her stick back to her? Her blood raced when he spoke.

"You came here?"

"I hoped—" He looked at her, then away. "Please don't cry."

"I'm not." But tears rolled off her cheeks and soaked into her shawl. Her fingers curled around the stick in her hands. Too many questions crowded her mind; she couldn't pick one to ask.

"I'll make a fire." Rialos bent before the hearth, and then stood, looking around for tinder, flint, and wood.

Emyn wiped at her eyes and took deep breaths as pine cones and branches began to crack. She looked out the door, wondering if anyone had followed Rialos here. "The king was coming to your house."

"I am a druid. The king cannot keep me if I wish to be elsewhere." He looked at Emyn again and the bluster went out of him. "I will explain my actions to him later. Don't worry."

Emyn shook her head slowly. Don't worry? He'd been gone from the full moon to the new—

"And it's not my house, but Nanto's. You didn't have to leave. You can go back. You can live there."

Emyn gripped the stick tighter. She felt as Micco must, searching for sense in the sounds that flew overhead.

"I hoped that if I brought that to you, we could talk." Rialos pointed to the stick. "Can we?"

"We are talking." Did he think she would throw him out? The last thing he'd said to her, weeks ago, was 'madwoman.' She lifted the stick; perhaps to him it was an offering of peace between them. "You have brought me something that means more than all the gold of this tribe. I am grateful."

A small fire warmed her hands as she lowered the stick.

"Gratitude is not enough, Emyn," Rialos whispered. "I thought it would suffice, but no. Gratitude blows like the north wind on my face. It gives no comfort."

"I don't understand."

Rialos sat close to her and rested his arms on his raised knees. "I will explain. I can say it simply: I lost my soul to you when you were fifteen. The lack of it finally drove me mad."

The words described no memory that Emyn held. Resentment burst out of her without warning. "I don't have your soul! You came to Samarnum and left without a backward glance."

His face jerked as if he'd been slapped. "That is what you remember?"

"I remember the night and the day." Emyn shut her eyes; she

did not want to be angry. "I will listen, but I am no druid. Say things I can understand."

Rialos stared at his hands. "I have been silent so long that my mind reshaped the past. I left, that is true. I did not dare look back.

"I was an outlaw, Emyn. Did you know that? I had no tribe or clan. My mother was a slave, and I'd run away from my father's family. I had none of the rights of a free man. No house was obligated to shelter me. Truly, I had no chance for a life of honor apart from Bodocnos' teaching. Even something as simple as courtship was beyond my status. Leaving your village was not a choice that I made. I had to follow my master. Is that clear to you?"

There was no mockery in his tone. Emyn nodded and—since his eyes remained on his hands—whispered, "Yes."

"In the years since, I won my serpent's egg and became a druid. Just as important, I am no longer an outlaw. Vinnia gave me back my tribe and family. Whatever grudges I bear, I must acknowledge that. She didn't have to act so."

In the long pause that followed, Emyn imagined those grudges. The offer of a child slave for pleasure—from a woman who would never stop reminding Rialos that he might still be a slave, but for her—must rank high.

He lifted his eyes. "I saw you again, on the same day that she accepted me as her brother. I could barely speak."

"I remember."

"Do you?" He scooted closer to her and took one hand from the stick she held. "Here is what I should have said that day: In all the years since I left your village, I doubted my memory of you. I thought I decorated it with extra charms. But you were . . are . . . always more beautiful than I could imagine."

He let the words rest on her for a moment before continuing.

"Druids do not often apologize but I must. I regret the mistakes I've made. I'm sorry I believed my sister's gossip and betrayed your friendship. Will you accept that?"

"Moradag delivered those words months ago and I accepted them. He made a fine speech for you." Emyn tried to meet his eyes. She had learned much since she was fifteen, but not how to arm herself against such flattery, not from him. Nor was she any wiser about how to hold on to a man. "That is not what hurts me. You must know that."

"No man can know a woman's mind." He gripped her hand tighter as she tried to pull away. "I am not done with my apologies. Listen, Emyn, a little longer. That night, after the trial . . . I ached for you. I sent Moradag off with the coins and words, then walked along the beach alone.

"Please hear me." He bent close; she had never seen this earnest side of him. "I'd been a slave and become a druid! I'd earned a tribe, a position—and all that crumbled to dust. You hated me. That filled my mind and drove out everything else: you hated me.

"Then, from outside an ale house I heard the word 'Gutumaros.' It burned my ears and I followed it . . . and saved your life. I and Moradag. What god should I thank? I've made offerings to all of them since that night. Emyn, would you ever have talked to me again or clung to me as you did, were it not for that?"

The room dipped and spun; Emyn grabbed Rialos' arm and pulled herself up to her knees. "You think I would lie with any man just because he saved me? Don't think that!" His face was close. The living and the dead waited outside the door but Emyn had his attention now for a moment—a moment that she could not waste. "For seven years, I dreamed of you. Only you—"

The fire cast little light; Emyn could not read his expression. He kissed her more gently than he ever had. "Is that true?"

"Yes!"

"But as a husband?" He took a deep breath. "I am—"

"Do you fear my ghosts? Could you live with them in your house?"

"Fear your ghosts?" He pulled away to frown. "Woman, no spirit unmans me! What are you thinking?"

"That you are brave." She laughed and fell against him. "That you are the bravest man I know. And there is nothing else that I want."

Her life ran out of order, not like a story at all—yet here was Rialos: holding her as the hero of a great story should. His kisses fell like summer rain, washing the hurts away.

The closed hut and its fire grew oppressive. She giggled when Rialos whispered a suggestion in her ear.

Low scattered clouds, their edges bright, drifted overhead when Emyn and Rialos emerged. She carried her carved stick, but her other hand held the druid's arm.

Satto and Moradag leaned against the stable, talking casually as if they had not been waiting. "The king invites you to share a fine catch of trout this day, Honored Master." Moradag bowed, but his grin was broad. "Although he realizes that your own catch far exceeds any fare he could offer."

Rialos raised an eyebrow. "The Gutumaros and I have plans to discuss. You will attend to Honored Master Nanto this afternoon until we return."

He led Emyn along the path and into the trees. Surely they would not be the only couple to seek out their own patch of sunshine and soft grass but just as surely, no one would dare follow.

* * *

THERE WERE FEW PROPRIETIES to be observed; neither Emyn nor Rialos held property or animals to negotiate over. She simply returned to Nanto's house with him. A marriage existed because they said so.

The warriors, nobles, traders, artisans, and servants who lived nearby watched and waited. Could the young master be tamed, they probably wondered; could he live with ghosts? Would his strange little wife blurt out nonsense to annoy him? Would his aloof manner spark her temper? It had before, after all.

Emyn knew they watched but didn't care. Living or dead, someone always watched. She tended her hearth, glad not to be alone. When the sun set and a new day began she wrapped herself in darkness, sharing secrets and caresses with her husband. Life finally moved forward as it should.

BOOK FOUR

The End of Time

 **35**

Emyn woke from a dream of Iomat. They sat in Volio's empty house . . . Rialos flexed the arm that lay over Emyn and pressed closer against her back. Dawn was near, and the dream escaped. She dozed again.

She stood outside Volio's house, breathing air heavy with the smell of summer fruit. Heaps of strawberries and buckets of apples and pears sat on carts around her. Emyn saw more carts and wagons than had ever been gathered in Samarnum, holding not just fruit but sacks of grain, boxes, pans, stools, and the crossbeams and weights of looms. Dawn broke, and Emyn looked up. The skulls that sat over Volio's doorway were gone.

Rialos squeezed her shoulder and stood. Sunlight streamed in as he propped opened the door with a rock. Emyn was not in Samarnum; she had been dreaming. She stared at the cold fire pit, remembering all that she could.

Every summer visitor to Venetona brought rumors, and Emyn was as eager for news as anyone else. Caesar marched as far as tribal lands bordering the Bellovaci, she heard. Would he go further? Would Caesar challenge the Nervian chiefs?

"More news!" the old healer called at midmorning as she passed Emyn's home. "You won't like it, though."

"Tell me," Emyn urged.

"The chiefs of Belgic tribes bow before Caesar. They feed his armies, men say. Though how any tribe can feed so many—"

"Who spouts such nonsense?" Emyn demanded.

"Don't blame me!" the healer cackled. "Wool traders from the east, there." She pointed to the descending path that led to several inns.

Emyn hurried away, anxious to hear this news from its source. A wagon hitched to two old and thin horses had to belong to the wool traders.

"What tribes feed Rome?" she demanded of a stranger who packed a bag of grain and some fruit behind the wagon's seat.

"Whoever is next on the march, I suppose," he shrugged. "They all bow to Caesar, from what we hear."

"Why would they do that?"

"If Roman armies camped outside your door, wouldn't you treat them as friends?"

"Friends?" Emyn bristled. "The Belgae are not cowards! They will fight Caesar!"

The traders exchanged glances. "We only know what men say on the other side of the gulf."

Emyn snorted and returned home, indignant. The druid and student were gone, but she spilled out the news before Nanto and Gorio. "The northern tribes should stand together!" she fussed. "Those men were wrong. It's gossip. I shouldn't have listened."

"Men plot to steal each other's fields even as they swear to fight side by side," the dead king said. "Why are you surprised after all that I've shown you?"

Emyn waved a hand at the ghost and stomped outside. The

ghost was not done with her, though. Blinded by the dazzling sunlight, Emyn blinked. The sun sparkled off a ribbon of the Samar on the other side of a familiar path—a path leading east from Samarnum. Cesua walked beside her, struggling to push a cart along the road.

In a heartbeat, Cesua and the Samar vanished. Emyn backed into her house and reached for Gorio. She didn't trust herself to speak. Her dream of carts and wagons packed with all Samarnum held dear and all its people would need—from food to skulls— had been as real as the crucified corpses along the Roman road, years ago. The people of Emyn's homeland fled their village.

MORADAG ENTERED THE HOUSE ALONE. Rialos, the student told her, drank ale with Satto. Emyn grimaced. She had hoped Rialos would make sense of the dream, her vision, and the news, but he did not even come home.

"Your husband tires of you already!" the dead king taunted. Like a bullying child, he grew meaner when the druid wasn't around to silence him.

"Shut up, ghost!"

Moradag's hand stopped in midair as he ladled stew from the pot.

"It's the dead king," Emyn dropped to the bench. "He maddens me sometimes. Eat."

The ghost would not be quieted. "Why does he drink with a man instead—"

"You are Belgic like me." The words burst out of Emyn. "Why would northern tribes ally with Caesar?"

"Do they?" Moradag looked surprised, but Emyn knew how easily he could pretend.

"That is the news. I know you've heard!"

The student drained the bowl, tipping it to get all the broth. As he wiped his face he nodded. "That was discussed today."

"And what do men say? What does your master say?"

Moradag chose his words carefully. "He reminded me that tribes large and small have borders to protect. They have raided other tribes for generations, and those tribes return the favor, stealing livestock, burning farms, back and forth. So when a strong army offers an alliance, a chief may view that as a good way to scare off his neighbors."

Emyn considered this as Moradag refilled his bowl. She knew Rialos would make sense of the news—but why was he not telling her this himself?

She thought of Samarnum and the tales of raids in her grandparents' day. "My village bordered Ambiani lands. The Ambiani king sent visitors each year with questions for me."

"Your village was luckier than most border lands. The presence of an oracle probably stopped the Ambiani from attacking."

"Maybe." The idea of Samarnum in flames, its people killed for their sheep and pigs, sent shivers through her. Emyn glanced around. Nanto and Gorio were already asleep far from the fire; she got up and shook out a blanket to cover them.

Moradag knelt before her when she returned to the fire. "May a lowly student offer advice to a friend?"

"Of course." Emyn's thoughts had been on Samarnum and the rich feast that Volio offered each year to visitors. What troubled Moradag?

"My master—your husband—is a good and wise man. But his passion for you sparks jealousy even without reason. He saw you talking with strange men today. You stood before a public inn—" he stopped when Emyn gasped. "Do I presume too much?"

"Is that why he is not here?"

"I believe so." The student glanced to the door. "He did not ask me to speak but I noticed a change in his mood after he saw you there."

Emyn nodded and moved her mouth into a smile. The gesture was empty. She did not feel like smiling.

"Fool," the dead king hissed. "You listen to a boy, but shut out my words."

"I will go sleep with the warriors tonight," Moradag said.

While some of Vlidorix' men had wives and homes, the unmarried warriors lived together in a large house, and Moradag stayed with them often. Rialos encouraged that. "He may command such men one day. He should know their jokes and complaints."

Moradag would not tempt his master's suspicions by sleeping near his lonely wife; that was the real reason the student left. Rialos indulged in jealousy the way some men drank or gambled. Emyn sat before the fire for a long time—until the smell of stew burning in the cauldron roused her.

Aruca had warned her last winter. "Would you be happy with a man who might love, but never trust you?"

"Yes," Emyn said aloud. She limped to the door, holding the cauldron in rag-wrapped hands. Night had come and she was weary. With every movement she wished that stronger arms would lift the cauldron from hers. He didn't have to explain, just return.

FERDIATH PASSED THROUGH VENETONA on another of his many trips, this time arranging prices for shipments that included Roman sauces and oils. He brought news from the north: the Ambiani surrendered to Rome.

Rage and shock took Emyn's breath away at this announcement. She had been sitting in the shade, sorting lentils with three other women, and stood so abruptly that her wide basket fell, spilling its contents into the dirt.

Ferdiath glanced toward her and bowed. "Gutumaros, I beg forgiveness. How thoughtless of me to shout out such news! You are Ambiani, aren't you?"

"Viromandui," she said with pride. "The people of the White Horse. But Ambiani towns lay only a day west."

The dream of ten days past made sense. Samarnum would not host Rome; its people left to join other Viromandui clans and honor their ancient alliance with the Nervians. Had they burned the houses and poisoned the well as they left? Or did they hope to return?

"Ask this man who he left behind," the dead king said, but at that moment the living king strode from his doorway.

"If you're still advising treaties with Rome, you'll find no sympathetic ear with our Gutumaros, Honored Master," Vlidorix called out cheerily. "She's gone and married the young druid. They stand united."

"Indeed? But . . . ," Ferdiath looked around. "Surely not Rialos?"

"Yes, Rialos!" The king slapped Ferdiath on the back. "The man she sued in that trial you decided. Love is a strange fish. Isn't that what they say? Slippery, but easily hooked with the right bait?"

"My congratulations, dear lady," the druid of Eire bowed toward her once more. "I should have known that such a jewel would not long remain unclaimed."

Emyn bowed back and nearly stumbled over a girl at her feet: a slave who had scurried forward to pick the lentils she'd spilled on the dirt. Ferdiath turned to follow the king into his house. Without looking up from her basket of lentils, one of the women hissed, "Watch out for him now! It's married women he likes best."

"Because they don't fuss when he leaves," added another.

"There are plenty of married women in Venetona for him." Emyn sat, and the slave handed her a basket with fresh handfuls of lentils. "He doesn't need to come sniffing around me."

"He might."

The last time Rialos had seen her talk to strangers, it had taken a night of drinking to purge him of his suspicions. "I'll blacken his eye if he does."

"Get your fist ready, then. He'll be sleeping in your home."

Emyn's stomach jumped. Ferdiath was a druid; of course he would stay in Nanto's house.

"Oh, to be a newlywed!" the oldest woman snorted. "When you've had the same man in you for a handful of years, Ferdiath might not look so silly."

"Even when I lacked a man, I had no taste for him," Emyn reminded them. "Who wants the last drop of ale when a cup's been around the room . . . twice?"

They all laughed at that.

She kept her gaze from Ferdiath throughout the day. "I know you are trustworthy," Rialos had told her when he'd finally returned after drinking with Satto—the closest he'd come to apologizing. "But when you smile at any man, the fire in my mind consumes what I know."

VLIDORIX ORDERED HIS BENCHES and tables moved into the sunshine and set his cooks to work out of doors as well. Lively breezes carried the smell of roasting fish beyond sight, drawing everyone near. All were invited to share; bowls of lentils and vegetables and baskets of bread made the rounds along with the platters of fish.

Warriors carried Nanto to a place in the shade where he could hear Ferdiath's news with everyone else. The old man was still treated as chief druid of the Veneti: he rested at the king's right hand, ate before all others, and was included in every counsel.

Emyn sat beside the old druid, waving away the bees that circled a bowl of strawberries passed to her. A cup came next; she held it to the old master's lips, and then passed it to Rialos.

With Samarnum abandoned, Emyn's past had been ripped away. Truly, her home in Venetona contained her entire world now. To protect it, she prayed and offered sacrifices, even drops of her own blood. Tears pressed her eyes when she thought of Samarnum—the village that gave birth to her—now dead.

Ferdiath kept talking. Moradag, standing just behind his master, clenched his fists as Ferdiath announced that the Bellovaci as well as the Ambiani had laid down their arms before Rome.

"Ask him who he left behind!" The dead king repeated his earlier question.

Ferdiath spread his arms. "The kings of these ancient tribes thus ensure the safety of their people and land—"

Nanto let out a high-pitched sound.

Rialos put his hand on the old man's shoulder. "He is distressed. Since when did ensuring safety become preferable to living free of a Roman yoke?"

"Better a light yoke than to watch your fields burn," said Ferdiath.

"Brave men and women would disagree—"

"Brave men and women have left this world, and their children were carted to Rome as slaves," replied Ferdiath.

"Helvetians never lacked bravery, but what good did it do them?"

"Much, I say." Rialos rose. "We do not judge solely by what happens in this world, but on honor earned for the next."

The two druids glared at each other. They disagreed on most points, but both were smart enough to draw back before giving serious insult. Now Ferdiath smiled, took up a cup and raised it toward Emyn. "My congratulations to you, Rialos. I should have offered them earlier."

Those with cups joined Ferdiath as he drank. "The Greeks say that a man without a woman is imperfect and homeless. You have a fine woman now, so you must be improved." He winked. "But why are you no wiser?"

Giggles erupted from the females, young and old, who clustered on the other side of the cookfire.

"I might ask you the same," Rialos grinned. "You should be the wisest of all men since you have had so many!"

When the laughs died away, Ferdiath spoke of the druids' gathering in Carnute, now more than two months past. Other travelers had described the bickering among the wise over how the Romans should be met. Ferdiath's admiration of Rome was obvious, but no one interrupted him as he talked. News was news.

Emyn shifted her seat to lean against Rialos and whispered, "The ghost has a question for Ferdiath."

"Ask, then."

"No, you ask," Emyn said. "Ask who he has left behind."

"Across the wide river," the dead king prompted.

"Across the wide river," Emyn sighed. "The dead king wants this asked."

"Most likely a wife or a murderous husband," Rialos groaned.

Emyn shrugged; the same idea had occurred to her. The dead king repeated his question.

Ferdiath finished his stories and sat. Rialos motioned to his student. "Who did he leave behind, across the river?" he whispered to Emyn. "Maybe the question will offend him, and he'll want to sleep in some other house."

Emyn lost sight of her husband as he joined the crowd around Vlidorix. Soon, though, whispers spread like the eddies from rock dropped in a pond, and a name hissed round the cookfire.

Ferdiath addressed the king as the name reached Emyn. "Rome sends a noble emissary to the west. The Namnetes, beyond the Liger River, host him with all due respect, and will reap the benefits of Rome's goodwill. He wishes to visit and convey Rome's respect to the master of the seas, the king of the Veneti. I have enjoyed many hours with Crassus as we traveled. The Romans do not lack culture—"

"Crassus!" Emyn shrieked when she heard the name. "Crassus, the murderer?" She grabbed Nanto's hand; the druid caught her eye helplessly. "Crassus, who crucified thousands? You remember, Master? I saw those men when I was a child!"

Emyn's heart pounded as she pushed herself up. "Six thousand men! That is Crassus' boast. Six thousand men were crucified to satisfy his vengeance! The ghosts showed that to me when I was a child, King Vlidorix, so that I could warn you today. Have nothing to do with Crassus!"

"Not the same man!" Ferdiath cried. "The crucifixions—what a gruesome sight for a child! Lady, no wonder you are upset. But it is not the same man, I assure you."

"No, it is not." Rialos smiled grimly as he placed himself between Emyn and Ferdiath. "It is his son. No son would behave as his father did, would he? If the father slaughters men by the thousands, why should we suspect that the son would do likewise?"

"King Vlidorix," Ferdiath spread his arms, taking the floor. Even on this hot day, his overly long sleeves fell to his fingertips. "If you judge the son by the father, then I must argue against misconceptions of the father. The men crucified by the elder Crassus were slaves that had carried on a two-year rebellion, terrorizing the entire Latin peninsula. Crassus succeeded where other men failed. He ended the slave rebellion.

"He crucified the men he captured. I point out again that they were slaves captured in war. It is a different death than what we mete out to prisoners and certainly disgusting to the eye! But remember how much of industry, commerce, and trade depend on controlling slaves. This rebellion, in which slaves killed free men, inspired more escapes and lasted for years. These outrages disrupted shipping and caused food shortages and panic in Rome itself. Punishment had to be public and cruel. Crassus ended the threat to his people and re-established the rule of law."

Ferdiath had circled around as he spoke, and at the end he faced the king. "Should he be ashamed of such a feat? Should his son? Publius Crassus is proud of his father's unwavering courage and with good reason!"

Rialos waited a polite moment before speaking. "You praise courage in Romans and disparage it in Celtic tribes. Why is that? Crassus is brave and his son proud, but Helvetians are simply dead and their children enslaved for showing that same virtue."

"The Helvetians," Ferdiath began, but the clamor of horns in Emyn's ears rose to bury his words. The druids, king, warriors, and women of Venetona disappeared.

Emyn cried out, but could not hear her own voice—only the long scream of other-worldly beasts. She had never seen war horns before; they rose from the bushes, their slender trunks like saplings, taller than men. She had time to notice that their mouths were shaped like beaks before the polished bronze caught the westering sun and blinded her.

The horns screamed for battle, and from all sides, men responded.

36

Horses reared, throwing centurions off their backs. The few Romans who managed to hold onto their mounts crouched and raced away like scared dogs, their red cloaks flailing behind them.

Shrieking to match the horns, tribal warriors burst from the bushes to give chase. The gentle slope in front of the bushes changed from green to speckled brown, alive with men leaping down as if it were a disrupted anthill. Emyn tucked in her arms and turned away, overwhelmed.

The war horns blared again. She stood in a river that seemed shallow and still as death for a moment. Then the warriors ran past her, holding their swords and axes high. One man tripped over tree roots and fell. Before she could jump out of his way, others ran straight at her, screaming in triumph. Emyn threw her hands over her face as river water splashed up and soaked her.

The screams and horns stopped; a crowded murmur filled the silence. She shuddered against Rialos and felt solid ground beneath her feet. "Tell me what you saw," he said.

"A battle begins." Emyn shook. Though her dress was dry and the sun warmed her shoulders, she still felt the cold water and the terror of the attack. "A river separates Romans and tribal warriors. War trumpets cried out, and the men crossed."

"Now?" Ferdiath asked. "Or do you foresee what will happen soon?"

Emyn pictured the men and their shadows as they ran down the bank to the river. "Now, this afternoon."

"It's a good surprise, isn't it?" The old ghost from the Morrigu's pool grinned at her. "To attack while the Romans are just setting up camp, tired after their long march?"

Emyn repeated his remark.

"It *is* a smart tactic." Rialos smiled toward the king's warriors who stood nearby.

"It might be my own people," Emyn moaned.

"Who are your people?" another ghost asked. The voice seemed to come from Nanto.

"The Viromandui," she said. The old druid pawed at her hand and gave a clumsy squeeze.

"Only them?" the voice tittered.

Satto and the other warriors parted, making way for the king. "Gutumaros, what battle did you see?"

"Warriors attack the Romans."

"The Nervians and their allies?" asked the king.

Emyn shivered; Rialos wrapped a shawl around her shoulders and rubbed her arms. She'd seen no white horse. "Men wore helmets with antlers. Their shields held lizards, fierce boars—"

"A mouth opened to scream," said a ghost.

"Those represent Nervian clans," Rialos said.

Vlidorix nodded. "What else, Gutumaros?"

"The horns rang out and the battle began." Where would her people be but there? "I saw warriors rush out of bushes and chase the Romans across a shallow river. There were not many Romans, though. Maybe those they chased were guards. Maybe the legions and their camps were on the other side of the river."

After a momentary silence, Ferdiath asked the question they were all thinking. "Will the ghosts tell you more of this battle?"

She waited for the ghosts to respond, but none spoke. Lights and shadows played around the living.

The dead king laughed, and the grating sound of his voice grew into a confused jumble of faraway cries. Beyond that, the rhythm of her grandfather's songs rang out: the Nervian warriors approached from the east, running uphill.

Emyn sat far from the battle now, at the rear of the Roman camp. Frightened legionaries scattered, cresting the hill to disappear into hedges and trees, like rabbits into their warrens.

One Roman raced from the opposite direction, up toward the fighting. The sunlight reflected off his scalp through short, sparse hair. He stopped a fleeing soldier and grabbed his shield. As the accosted legionary stammered in terror, the first man lifted his foot and kicked him away.

The balding man ran on, shouting names and strange words as he neared other Romans. Men turned at his voice; they called back to him and raised their swords. They stopped cowering and began to fight.

"Caesar!" Emyn screamed. Who else could drive men forward into danger, bolstering their courage like strong drink? If she were truly there . . .

She grabbed at knives as men paused, then at rocks on the ground. The metal and stone felt firm in her hand, weighting her arm as she pulled back to throw—but her weapons dissolved into air as they left her grip.

The hill shifted; Emyn's stomach seemed to be flipping as

well. Rialos held her arms down from behind. Some of the warriors were chuckling.

"The woman's fierce!" cried one.

"You'll be breeding heroes with her!"

"If Nervian men fight like that," called Vlidorix, "Caesar's legions have seen their last sunrise!"

Emyn shut her eyes against the spinning faces as Rialos laughed into her hair. "You can't fight them," he muttered. "But you poked Moradag in the eye."

Someone handed her a cup as she repeated what she had seen. The king asked questions until Emyn ran out of answers.

Time passed; Emyn shrugged off the glances and stares of those who hoped for more words on this sunny day. It seemed the ghosts were done with her for awhile.

"The Honored Master Ferdiath is never without a song or a story," Rialos called out. "A tale of brave actions would fit our mood, wouldn't it?"

Pleas from men and women filled the air. Ferdiath began a lively story of a cattle sale gone awry, starting a feud that led to war. Emyn listened for a bit, but lost interest. Ferdiath's tale made bravery look foolish. His voice grew distant; the sun warmed her. As her head dropped and then jerked up, Rialos pulled one of the pillows cushioning Nanto toward her.

As she fell asleep, Emyn saw a sacred warrior, one consecrated to the war god. Such warriors fought nude. The man was tall and broad-shouldered; his hair caught the sun and set his whole body sparkling. A heartbeat later blood spurted wildly and his fine form collapsed. She started; was this more of the battle that raged far away or the beginnings of a dream?

* * *

SHE WOKE AT A touch and shot up.

"What is it?" Rialos asked. "Did you dream?"

"No." Emyn hadn't—not a single image entered her mind. What did that mean? She looked around; shadows were long and the light golden. Hours had passed. "Have you been keeping the ghosts away?"

"When a battle decides the fate of so many? I would not dare."

Satto and others were carrying Nanto home. Men and women stood near, shuffling their feet and pretending to talk while keeping Emyn in their sight.

Armies could not fight in the dark. The battle to the east must be ending. An empty, sick feeling gnawed at her. When she left Samarnum, she had realized that she might never see Esmios, Cesua, or Iomat again—but not knowing whether they lived to see this sunset twisted her soul.

She wanted the truth. She asked for it out loud.

Instead of the shade, she found herself standing in light cast by the setting sun. Piles of bodies were everywhere.

"The battle ends!" she cried out. "There—before me—warriors stand on top of the dead. There are more dead than living. So many that the bodies form hills!"

She didn't dare take a step, but her eyes swept up and around. "The Nervian warriors stand on top of the corpses to fight. They have only their swords. The Romans surround them, waiting and laughing. The warriors are weary, all cut and splattered with blood. They know it is over, but they will not surrender.

"The sun passes beyond a hill. The Nervians swing their swords, but they have nothing left to throw. It is all a joke to the Romans. They stand out of reach, their shields before them. They are brave, now that they outnumber the warriors! Romans surround five warriors, only five, facing outward. They—one falls, a knife in his chest."

Emyn choked on the smell of death and waste; the ground blurred. Trimmed robes and leather shoes circled her. "Nothing more," she sighed. "It is over."

"The ghost showed you Rome, victorious?" Ferdiath's voice was somber, but his eyes were wide and pleased.

Emyn looked to her husband. "I saw only four warriors standing at the end. All the rest were Romans."

Rialos called to his student, but the other druid held up his hand. "No need. I will tell the king. I have your words exactly, Gutumaros."

"I'll go too," Satto said, exchanging a glance with Rialos.

EMYN'S DREAMS WERE FILLED with horrid sights that night: her brother, Esmios, lying on the ground, his side slashed open; women she had known since her earliest days throwing rocks at Roman soldiers until, one by one, they were killed or forced to the ground and raped. A few were tied up for the slave merchants. Cesua went down with a spear through her chest, a fierce and frightening scowl on her face.

Woe to the vanquished.

Emyn thought she woke between images, but maybe the waking was part of the dream.

She opened her eyes once to see Rialos sitting by the fire, talking with Moradag in a low voice. "The Romans were a tribal people once," he said. Then the thatch roof dissolved.

Emyn stood under the moon again. She saw Volio lying among the corpses that clogged the river, his dead eyes staring straight up.

* * *

TWO DAYS PASSED. She knelt before the fire, stirring broth: her stewpot, her home. Her only home. Samarnum was gone. The gods led those she had known to new homes, sorting through the villagers as if they were lentils in a basket. Some went to the land of promise, others to Rome in chains.

Emyn shook her hair back. What had she been thinking? Nights with little sleep broke her thoughts apart like weak thread. Rialos had fussed over the circles under her eyes. Now he stood with his student outside the door listening to Moradag recite, prodding him for one line after another. Their voices drifted in with the breeze.

Gorio held a bowl steady as Emyn ladled stew, then he carried it to Nanto. "Awa," he crooned to the old man. "Awa, time to eat."

Emyn knew that messengers would come eventually with news from the east. They would speak of the Nervians and their battle with Caesar. But who would tell her of Samarnum? Of one little village among so many—

A child whimpered behind her. Emyn turned and saw many children, some sleeping, while adults stood watch. Iomat hunched over, no longer able to straighten her bones. And no wonder! Emyn could feel the dampness; the air was thick with it. Where were they? This was not the moisture of a sea; more like a swamp, unhealthy and suffocating.

They'd been here too long, someone whispered. "The men won't return."

When shouts sounded from far away, a child wailed, then all the little ones began to cry. Coos and stern words did not calm them. The children made so much noise that Emyn did not hear the Romans until they splashed through the marsh, shouting and swinging their swords. They were drunk. They always got drunk for this kind of work, a ghost whispered.

"Better this than to be left to starve, isn't it? Better blades than wild beasts or slave traders." The dead king formed in the dense air, as real as her vision. "Slaves flow like gold to Rome, but these are weak and worthless!"

"Emyn!" Her body jerked. The vision wouldn't release her; she drowned in it, gasping as Rialos shouted her name again.

The scream lowered and turned to wind in her throat. Her scream. Hers only; the children died thirty times thirty leagues away—far from home, separated from their mothers, terrified. "Dead," was all she could say, but the word didn't come out whole. "Dead."

"Here." A cup pressed against her mouth. Soon emptiness cushioned her, and her body lay heavily against Nanto's pillows.

"What did you see?" Rialos prodded her.

"Children—"

"Whose children?"

"Samarnum . . . more. Village children." Her mouth moved clumsily. Rialos' voice rumbled as he pulled answers from her.

"Where were they?"

"Swamp."

"Who was with the children?"

"Iomat, old uncles . . . Romans came."

Her son's death had been quick, though brutal; he hadn't feared the shadow that caught and smashed him. These little ones—so little! —knew the creatures that tore at them with knives and swords. The short-haired monsters, the demons that killed their A'ers—

She couldn't get out all she wanted to say, but Rialos understood. He told her to sleep, and the attack sank to a dark place in her memory like a scary story she'd heard as a child. When she woke again Rialos sat close to Ferdiath as the druids murmured near the fire.

"There are more ways to call spirits than dismiss them." The druid of Eire faced the fire and she caught only bits of his sentences. "In sacred caves . . . they hide in mists."

Ferdiath knew the ways of divination, he'd told her once.

"Please," Rialos' voice was sweet. "Search your memory for stories known on your island. Any hint, no matter how small." He could charm when he wished; he wanted Ferdiath's help.

Both men rose. Rialos leaned near and put his hand over hers. His palm was hot: Emyn turned her hand to hold onto his.

"I swear you will have peace in your own home," he whispered.

He kept his word.

Rialos banished the spirits from the house of the chief druid. Most masters of learning could make them leave for moments. But Rialos circled, chanted, and drew lines in the dirt, purging the house of ghosts as if they were stains scrubbed away. The dead king, the warriors, ancestors, tricksters, shadows, lights, whirlwinds, and smoke, all answered to him and departed. Even the sounds, the cackling, hisses, hums, scratching, taps, and flutters were swept out.

For as long as he lived, Rialos swore, they would never again intrude. "Not over this threshold. Not under this roof."

It was a marvel; Ferdiath swore that no other man exerted such skill. "I confess it freely: I am astounded. This will make a fine tale, and for once I won't have to exaggerate!"

Emyn nodded and wrapped her arms around Rialos' waist. Now that the ghosts were absent, she hoped their guest would leave soon as well. She knew Ferdiath watched her when her husband's back was turned, and did not like it.

 37

Days later, Emyn walked along a favorite path thick with moss, searching for the black mushrooms that sprouted in damp, overlooked places. Spirits wavered behind leaves and trunks. Banned from her house, they now vied for her attention outside of it.

Without warning, Ferdiath stepped out of the shadows and reached toward her. She jumped back. His hands groped and she swatted them away. He babbled about unspoken words between them, insisting "You told me where you walk. You wanted me to find you here."

"Presumptuous goat!" cried the dead king.

"Foolishness!" Emyn huffed. She followed known paths. Were habits now an invitation, like smiles and whispered promises?

"Is it? Try a bed here in the soft ferns and tell me—"

Emyn pushed hard and he fell back; the dead king laughed.

"You lack judgment, honored Ferdiath." She glared at him. For two days he had helped her husband cast out spirits, working beside him like a friend. Now he would betray him for the sake of one last hump in Venetona? "I will never be your lover. I'll tell you one thing more: the Romans are not your friends. They use your honor and your reputation—"

"Bitter lies!" He jerked away and his hands dropped to his sides. Embroidered sleeves fell and again hid the malformed finger. "It is not I who lacks judgment, woman." The whine of a hurt child crept into his words.

"Go," she hissed. "You shame our hospitality! Go now!"

The wind carried other voices near; the healer scolded her granddaughter for lagging behind as they explored the path. Ferdiath's face turned murderous for a heartbeat, and then he was gone.

SUMMER FADED AND FERDIATH LEFT. Did he return to the Namnete king and his guest, the younger Crassus? Or did he worm his way through other tribes in the west, spewing more of his bad advice? Emyn didn't ask, nor did she tell Rialos about her last meeting with the Irish druid.

As autumn brought more wind and rain, Emyn grew used to thinking of her friends and relatives as dead—all but Nonicos. Occasionally a memory of Iomat's voice seemed so real that she halted and looked around, but it was never more than a memory.

"Are you unhappy?" Rialos asked her. She knew his tones by now. He didn't want to ask, but felt he must.

Emyn took his hand. "I grieve for my brother and my friends who died. But I am very happy in this house with you."

That was true. Without ghosts, her home swelled with quiet. No spirits roused her from sleep; during the day, her own humming echoed back from the walls. Fire crackled, wind whistled, rain splattered, and mice rustled through the thatch. Birds added their own songs, night and day. Each sound vibrated like bells in the stillness.

* * *

Nonicos arrived to honor Bodocnos on the anniversary of the druid's death. Emyn didn't have to tell her brother of her visions; the story had been repeated up the river, and messengers from the east had carried it past Nonicos' home as well. As they talked by the fire, she found he knew almost as much of the battle as she did.

The sight of Emyn's stick astounded him even more than her marriage, and he was mightily impressed by the story of its return. Emyn had a husband to be proud of: a hero who dared any challenge.

As the sun rose on the fourth day of Dumann, Emyn, Rialos, Nonicos, and Moradag hiked deep into the trees to a hidden pool banked by carved stones. "The oldest gods of the Veneti, as well as those of the forgotten, visit these waters," Rialos said.

Those of the forgotten: his mother's people—and Gorio's. Rialos once told her, "The Veneti call them the forgotten because their gods—for whom they raised stone monuments—have forsaken them."

But this day belonged to Bodocnos. She and the men circled the pool holding their offerings. Emyn brought coins. Except for her stick, she owned nothing from the time she'd spent traveling with Bodocnos. But coins made her think of the summer evenings when, with the aging druid at her side, she spoke about Caesar and Dumnorix at inns and under the stars.

The memories pulled tears from her eyes more than once. They would all sleep better when the sun set, Emyn knew; that was the purpose. Bodocnos built his life anew in the next world; those left behind now released their sorrow.

Or had they? She woke that night while rattling snores filled the house. Nanto, Nonicos, Moradag, and Gorio slept, but Rialos sat at the fire. Emyn pulled the heavy blanket with her as she crawled to him and lifted the wool over both their shoulders.

"What troubles you?"

She had to ask twice before he whispered an answer. "I never told him."

"Bodocnos?"

"I meant to." Rialos shuddered. "When I saw him again."

"Told him what?" He said nothing. "What? Tell me and ease your soul."

"When I first crossed Bodocnos' path." Rialos rubbed his hands together. "It was in the forest of the giants where pebbles are the size of a man. You've heard of the place."

"Yes."

Rialos sighed and leaned his head close to hers. The words were a burden that he seemed reluctant to shed. "Moradag must never know this. It was at night. Bodocnos slept . . . I thought he slept. I crept up to steal from him."

Once that admission was made, the words came faster. "I didn't know he was a druid, but I would not have cared. I was always hungry. The smell of his dinner drew me. By the time I found him, he was sated and sleeping. I saw a bag beside his head —too small to hold food, I thought, but maybe there would be something to trade. All my attention was on moving quietly, but now, looking back, I wonder if he slept at all.

"I touched the bag, pushed it open a little, then suddenly I was thrown back. I felt cold sharp iron at my throat." Rialos took a deep breath. "'Will you die for a flint and a bronze coin, boy?' he said. I remember those words clearly. I believed them. I could see his eyes in the moonlight; he looked like a killer."

Emyn waited as long as she could, but Rialos said no more. "What happened?"

"The gods intervened, I think." He let out a harsh laugh, then lowered his voice again. "I waited for the cut, terrified. He asked questions, this lunatic: *was I alone, where were my friends?* I said nothing; I was too scared to think of a way out. Then he pushed the knife—the blunt edge—hard against my neck and demanded to know why I wouldn't speak. He said, 'Answer me! Or do you want to die?'

"I thought that was a stupid question. No one wants to die! I must have smirked and that made him even angrier . . . so angry that he reared back, and I twisted and kicked and nearly got away.

"He caught me again and pinned me down. He laughed like a banshee. I was amazed. He said he'd never met a boy smart enough to keep his mouth shut. Then he asked when I was born."

Rialos had kept his voice low but clear; now it hissed like distant waves. "He still had that knife. He looked insane. He dug his knee into my stomach and said, 'Tell me, you lawless weasel!' I didn't know the answer, but I called out a date. He never forgot it."

"What date?"

"Don't ask," he shook his head. "It was a lie I grabbed it out of the air, but it pleased him. The more he thought about it, the happier he was. He made me his student because of that date. It was the luckiest guess a man ever made. For years I believed it saved my life."

Rialos sighed, not seeming to notice Emyn's arm around his waist. She pulled it back and linked it through his arm, squeezing his hand.

"When Coath came back—because even then he snuck away as soon as the master slept—Bodocnos told him my birth date and demanded that he work out our paths, so Coath could see why I would be as close to him as a brother. And we became so, but not because of the stars. I lied about the stars." Rialos cleared his throat. "My master died believing that lie."

They sat together for a long time as the wind threw handfuls of rain against the thatch. The last time Emyn delivered a baby, the dead king had told her, "Rome steals your destinies and mocks your stars." Maybe Rialos had found a way to thwart them.

She broke the silence between them. "You created a future." Was such a thought disrespectful? Rialos lifted an eyebrow, and Emyn explained. "You named a date as if you arranged your own stars. And now you are a druid."

"Because of a lie—"

"No." Emyn shook her head. "You claimed the future you wanted. I think the gods rewarded your daring."

That raised a smile from him.

WINTER CAME, but did not feel like winter. Though homes were damp, the air did not grow as cold as it should. Still, the salty winds of this land unsettled Emyn's bones. Through quiet days and evenings she listened as Rialos drilled Moradag on property laws, rituals, and the oldest stories and riddles. She collected rhymes to distract herself.

When Moradag was absent, Rialos spoke his odd language with Gorio. Drizzling rain and the fire whispered around them as Emyn asked questions. Gorio remembered living by a river. His people hid from the boats that traveled on it—with good reason. "When the market for slaves is good," Rialos said, "merchants go hunting for young men and women, even children. They are considered trainable."

Gorio was not the boy's real name, she learned, but simply what a slave trader decided to call him. He did not offer his real name. "What are the forgotten people like?" Emyn asked.

"They are very different from us," Rialos answered. "They do not spin thread, or strike coins to trade, or even keep animals. They dress in fur. No place shelters them for long. They are ancient, yet their lore is despised."

On another day he watched the clouds move and said, "My mother's brother taught me to read the sky when I was very young. Not the stars but the clouds."

"He could tell the future from the clouds?"

"The future, no." Rialos smiled at a memory. "He did not care about the future, only about the day before him. The clouds told us where the winds came from and how much rain they brought."

Rialos would not be coaxed into saying more than he wanted. The dark evenings were long and quiet, though, especially when Moradag stayed with the warriors. Word by word, Emyn assembled a story and an understanding of her husband.

Almer had excited her into marriage and then filled her life with disappointment. She'd been even less thoughtful and more passionate when she married Rialos, but this time she had no reason for regret. Her husband's moods flustered her, but his deeds and the secrets he shared made her proud, not sorry.

Weeds sprouted into tiny flowers, and the ground quivered with the beginnings of spring. Emyn made another trip to the hidden pool where they'd remembered Bodocnos. She pricked her finger and dropped blood into the water. "A baby," she whispered, her breath rippling the surface. "Dirona, be kind. Let us have a child."

She visited other shrines as well with the same prayer. "You are a selfish fool," the dead king grumbled one day. "Would you bear a slave for Rome?"

Emyn waved him away. The future was as unknown to him as it was to her. If women stopped having babies each time an enemy threatened, no one would walk the land today.

As she returned home, Gorio ran toward her. "Your honored husband looks for you, lady. Men came from Moradag's king." He wrinkled his brow. "Is Moradag's father a king?"

"He is. Our Moradag is a prince." Emyn grinned. "What did the visitors say?"

"They bring news, some for the master alone, but some for everyone. Our king said, 'Come to my house so all can hear!' The warriors carried Awa, and I came to tell you."

38

"This is the oracle whose life you saved, Moradag?" A warrior's torque flashed orange in the firelight as Iotros bowed. His face was round and pock-marked and sat on a body that looked as solid as an oak tree. "The song does not exaggerate her beauty. I am honored to meet you, Gutumaros."

Song? Emyn bowed back. The man's accent was like Moradag's.

"The Bellovaci have a new song honoring their prince," the queen announced. She clapped her hands, signaling the slaves to refill cups of ale. "But if we ask for it again, I think Moradag will catch fire, he blushes so fiercely!"

Iotros slapped his thigh and laughed as two warriors behind him began to sing badly. They were Iotros' companions, but Emyn hadn't heard their names. "This song pleases King Mortirix so greatly that he has it sung at all feasts! It tells how the young prince and his teacher saved the beautiful oracle from brigands. I'll tell the bards it requires a new verse, lady. We did not know that you'd claimed the hero as your husband."

"My wife is Belgic," Rialos stepped forward. Emyn knew from

the set of his jaw that he'd heard the song too many times already. "I told you that we knew of the great battle between the Nervian Confederacy and Rome. The Gutumaros saw it on the very day it was fought. Her own people were there."

"Then I am doubly honored to be in your presence." Iotros bowed again toward Emyn; his face grave and his mouth suddenly set, losing all merriment. "The courage of the Nervians will live forever."

"Forever?" The dead king snarled. "What do you fools know of forever?"

"Courage is easy to sing about, but difficult to sustain." Other ghosts joined in as Emyn nodded.

"Courage makes men drunk."

"It blinds them."

"They crave glory more than gold."

Emyn wished she could ask blunt questions of Iotros: his people should have fought with hers.

"You were about to tell us," Vlidorix called out, "About new alliances, cast after Rome's victory."

"Indeed, sir." Iotros turned back to the king. The other two men had stopped singing when Iotros grew somber; they sat quietly now. "Alliances prompted by fear and greed. My king does not expect those bonds to last. They are like scabs covering wounds; they'll fall away when they're no longer needed."

Emyn sat beside Nanto to listen. Food and drink passed by, but her mind wandered. Iotros' stories sounded more like gossip than news; he might as well have been spinning tales of unfaithful lovers. Belgic chiefs made promises in the heat of a moment, he reported. They lied and wriggled out of their vows, betrayed old friends and sought forgiveness, abandoning what they had for the sake of something new and enticing.

Was there truly, as Rialos once said, nothing new under the sun?

Her chin dropped, and her eyes shut for a moment. She started as Gorio pressed her spindle back into her hand. "Who will weave your fine thread into cloth?" the dead king grunted. "Better to sleep." She looked around; several men were nodding off. The afternoon had passed quickly. In the fading light, Emyn sent the spindle twirling once more.

"Surely they know they are not welcome here," the queen said sharply. Emyn made another attempt to follow the conversation.

"They go where they please—"

Iotros held up his hand, silencing his friend. "Lady, the Romans travel in small groups: a pair, a trio. Who can refuse them hospitality when they pose no threat?"

"I hate the sight of them," said another of his companions. "Strutting like roosters."

"Romans foul your roads," hissed the dead king.

"What is the purpose of these travels?" Rialos asked.

"They ask for pledges of grain so that they do not exhaust the stores of their hosts," Iotros began.

"Hosts!" snorted the first warrior. "They set up camp without a hello, cleared a forest for their legion—"

"Threatened to burn the chief's home to the ground," the other put in.

"Yes, and then they call him *their host!*"

"A whole legion. As if it were their own land!" The visitors were indignant and the Veneti warriors hollered insults toward the absent Romans.

"We saw them at the home of King Sotirix, just north of here."

"They boast of their strength—"

"Asking the king if he wanted a friend or an enemy—"

"The way they treat women is shameful!"

"That's true," Iotros shook his head balefully. "All females are whores to them, even if they wear a serpent's egg."

Emyn shuddered and took old Nanto's hand. "I'm glad the king told Master Ferdiath that his Roman friends weren't welcome here," she murmured close to his ear.

"You are blind, woman," the dead king scolded.

The Aeduan warrior took shape beside her. "Rome shakes its fist. You cannot ignore these men."

HIS COMPANIONS AND THEIR servants rested with the Veneti warriors, but Iotros accepted the invitation from Rialos to stay at his house. Emyn was glad; she wanted to know why these men had traveled so far from their home. Was it just to visit Moradag and learn that he was well?

As she made sure Nanto was comfortable and warm atop his cushions, she kept one ear toward the fire where Iotros spoke to her husband and Moradag.

"King Mortirix has much to thank you for," the warrior said. "Let me first express his appreciation for how you have sheltered our prince and continued his training this last year. The king's gratitude toward you is as unlimited as the stars in the summer sky. I have gifts to show his good will and thanks."

Coins jingled as they changed hands. "Gold enough for two cows," Iotros continued, "and a personal token as well, from the hand of his own smith." Emyn stretched her neck to watch him unfold a small piece of leather and tip it to spill silver into Rialos' palm.

The druid raised an eyebrow as he held up a large brooch: the strong, curved back of a boar ended in bristles—the sign of a people at war.

"I was honored to take up the work of Bodocnos." Rialos' voice was full of charm; only Emyn and perhaps his student guessed that his soul remained unmoved. They knew that Rialos must be as curious as they were. "Moradag warms our home with his wit. You know that he saved our lives. Your king's generosity is appreciated, but Moradag's presence itself has been a gift. I hope it may continue."

For a heartbeat, their guest looked pained. Emyn felt suddenly sick again. He'd come to take Moradag away; she was sure of it. She stepped forward to hand Iotros a cup of ale. The small fire lit Moradag's face; his jaw was tense and his eyes alert.

"I brought something else: an offer," Iotros said after he drank. "I see now that it's inappropriate. We did not know of your marriage."

"So you said earlier." Rialos accepted the cup from him.

"I was to propose a home for you near King Mortirix' own if you could be persuaded to leave the Veneti."

"A gracious offer, but as you've guessed, one I cannot accept." Rialos stole another glance at Emyn. "This implies that the king wishes his son to be near him."

"It does." Iotros sighed heavily. "My king had an agreement with the Honored Master Bodocnos—but you are not bound by their oaths. This year, he was to bring the prince back to Bellovaci lands to the long house of his father and continue teaching him there. The king's warriors would see young Moradag trained to lead them, and he would learn their habits and strengths. The prince would . . . will sit beside the king's druid as he judges civil cases and sets fines, studying the subtleties of our laws."

"He has been chosen to take his father's place," Rialos stated.

"From birth," Iotros nodded.

Emyn refilled the cup; she carried it to Moradag and rested

her hand on his shoulder. Had he known of the agreement? Had he expected this? The eyes he lifted toward her were troubled. He'd learned patience though, or at least restraint, and made no sound as Iotros and Rialos talked of King Mortirix and the Bellovaci chieftains, and then rehashed the news of Roman treaties and demands.

"Have you come to take him back to his father?" Rialos asked when the question could no longer be avoided.

"Ah, Honored Master, you are more forthright than most druids. I like that. Had you been willing to travel north, my men and I would be proud to serve as your escort. My king foresaw that other courses might be followed, though. That is why he sent us now on the eve of the light season, so that the months of summer would lie before you as you made plans."

Iotros lifted the cup again, but Emyn noticed it was still half full. The man stayed deliberately sober. "These are difficult times. My king wishes to have his son at his side, but he trusts in your wisdom to find the best way to bring the prince home. My men and I are yours to direct."

YOURS TO DIRECT.

It was an odd choice of words since Rialos had no particular power over the Bellovaci warriors. They knew he would not refuse to send Moradag home; nor would he simply wave farewell as the youth walked off without a teacher. The druid's sense of duty ran too deep.

"I wish," Emyn began to say to her husband more than once, and then choked back her words. Her thoughts were foolish; she did not need the dead king to tell her so. She wished Iotros and his companions had not come. She wished Rialos would discover a path that she herself was too dull to see; a way to stay and keep their home as it had been.

Days passed, and the question of leaving was chewed to mush. From their seats around the fire or under the pines, the men described the landmarks and perils of every direction and listened as Rialos weighed the stars and signs. At the end of each conversation, the same flavorless course remained their sole option.

Rialos would go with Moradag and the Bellovaci warriors to the annual gathering of druids in Carnute territory. He would arrive before the longest day to find a new teacher for Moradag, one who would respect his father's wishes and live among the Belgae for the next few years—exactly as he had whispered to Emyn on that first evening after Iotros had fallen asleep.

"I think I must," he had said. All their discussions came back to that. They would go to Carnute.

Wasn't there another way? "I wish . . . . "

"Tell me," Rialos insisted one night. "What do you wish?"

Emyn sighed; the sound scratched in the darkness. "I wish that nothing had to change."

"All things change," he whispered.

"Everyone says so, but I don't see that."

"No?"

"In my village, nothing changed, not for years and years." She felt his breath over her. "I was born in the house my great-grandfather built. Little things changed, but not the place. Not the homes, not for three generations. I want our home to stay the same."

She knew she spouted nonsense. Tears slid sideways from her eyes into her hair.

"It is an illusion." Rialos wiped the wetness away. "Your great-grandfather died. Your mother died. Your home did not stay the same."

"I wish ours would."

"Do you?"

"Yes, until your hair turns gray. Homes should grow, not shrink."

Such wishes were childish and he laughed quietly. She felt the low rumble, the shake of his shoulders. Beneath the wool blanket, the heat between them thickened. "Then ours will. If not in this world, then the next. Or the next. Eventually you'll have your wish."

"Eventually?" She frowned. "How many lives do we get?"

"Many, over and over, in this world or the other one. Our lives continue in a circle; they don't end. Rebirth, over and over—"

"Over and over," she chanted as he settled on top of her, his breath hot in her ear, making her smile as he teased.

"We're in this world or the next." His kisses were soft; their bodies merged like paths converging. "Together. We are never nowhere."

They were like rocks rolling downhill. Maybe a god chose the hill and gave them a push to start their descent. What good did it do to worry about how far they might tumble? They couldn't stop. But at least they could hold on to each other.

39

Rialos and Moradag left with the Bellovaci warriors.

They allowed only a month for their trip to Carnute lands.
Emyn and her group had taken much longer to travel that distance
in the opposite direction, but these strong men had servants to
carry and cook for them. They would move quickly along the
rivers.

The days alone in Venetona dragged by. Emyn stayed outside
as much as she could, where the chattering ghosts surrounded her.
By day she felt like the fishing boats left high on the beach by the
receding tide, their paint dried and cracking in the sun. At night
she lay like the wheat stored in pits beneath houses, buried in
darkness, far from warmth.

Rialos had been gone six days when a messenger arrived from
the west: a servant sent from a wealthy family on Gundori's island
brought news to their son.

The son realized the importance of the message and carried it
to the king himself. Emyn sat with Nanto in Vlidorix' longhouse
and listened.

"Two Roman soldiers arrived on the island, demanding a

ration of food for troops quartered with the Namnete. They were offensive and rude, my mother says, even to the chieftain. Gundori holds them under guard. He says they are his hostages."

Silence followed the announcement. Did King Vlidorix remember, as Emyn did, Rialos' warning? "It is the Roman way to make examples of those who defy them."

He'd said that last summer, not even a year ago. Merchants had visited, telling the tale of a certain tribe in the north. That tribe had hidden from battle and surrendered to Rome. Later, the warriors found their courage, overthrew their chieftain, and tried to fight. They died in great numbers, greater than Emyn could count. Caesar sold the survivors, the women, and the children to slave traders and wiped the tribe's name from the earth. No one would say it again.

Now Gundori defied Rome. Would Caesar think that the Veneti would make a fine example in the west?

SOON, folks from the west arrived daily, many with all their belongings. Some stayed; others boarded ships. Emyn intercepted Haebro one morning as he pushed his wheelbarrow toward Nerrus' house. After greeting him, she asked if he would stay or return home.

"Return to what?" he shrugged. "Suttia stays. And your rich friend, Lorsus. They've got too much to leave behind, I guess." He winked at Emyn. "Or maybe they're too fat to run!"

They sat in the shade and Haebro shared the village gossip—which girls had married, which men strayed or drank too much—as though nothing more momentous were going on. Haebro told Emyn he had relatives on the southern side of the bay and would find a boat and pilot to ferry him across in the morning. "That's where I came from. But they didn't need another ale house there and I wanted to make my own way . . . well, not anymore." Haebro sighed. "We all get old."

"THE GODS PUZZLE ME, Honored Master," Emyn murmured to Nanto. They sat outside where cool breezes from the sea swept over them, relieving the heat from the sun. Nanto grunted, so Emyn went on. "My people fought and died. I am proud of them. Other tribes did not fight, but they prosper. It seems that some are punished for their weakness, others for their strength."

Nanto could not respond, but the Aeduan warrior and his crouching allies appeared around their ghostly campfire.

"Your story is not complete," the familiar spirit said.

Another looked up. "How can you judge?"

"Only the dead can look back on a life."

"The living still have tales to play out."

As quickly as they had appeared, the warriors dispersed like smoke.

Emyn turned to look at Gorio, who knelt on a mat. The healer's youngest grandson squatted beside him. She'd put the boys to work crushing oats.

"This one's Caesar." Gorio pushed the oats into a pile and grinned at his friend.

"That's his head!"

"Bam! Smash it to mush!"

The rock rolled over the pile, and the other boy giggled. "Now get his arm!"

Were males born to create mayhem? Emyn couldn't remember playing such games when she worked before Iomat's hearth.

She took Nanto's hand. "Rialos once told me that it is easy for a happy man to convince himself that death could be faced another day." She could almost hear his voice. "So they choose to preserve their hearths, and their flocks, and their gold. They pretend they will stand and fight when they must—when the time is right, and the signs are more favorable. But they won't. He said, 'There is no other time but now, and no man should waste it.'"

She could not tell if Nanto agreed or even understood.

EMYN STIRRED THE POT of millet over her fire. Each morning brought Rialos closer but also increased her impatience; in the afternoon she watched the paths for any sign of excitement. How long could the journey take when he likely traveled alone?

Today she would see him at last, she was sure. The stars promised surprises just as they had on the day he'd brought back her stick.

"Today," she whispered into the heat that rose from the bubbling pot. A servant, one of many sent by the queen to help care for Nanto, glanced from side to side as she always did when Emyn spoke to no one.

A crone entered the house and walked over to the fire. Emyn remembered her rotting teeth that smelled so badly—where had they met? Before she could recall, the Aeduan warrior, his shield raised, stood by her side. How could they be here?

"Heroes live faster than farmers," her grandfather grunted.

Emyn whipped around; the house was full. Ghosts crowded into every corner right up to the thatch. Rialos would be furious; he had banished them.

"Get out, all of you!" This would be a terrible homecoming, the spirits trespassing when he'd forbidden them. He *had* forbidden them.

He had. The truth pounded at her head but she wouldn't open the door to let it in, not even a crack. "Get out, get out, get out!"

SHE THREW THE SPOON, and it flew right through the ghosts. She pulled at her hair; why wouldn't they listen? Rude ghosts, all where they couldn't be! Living men walked right through them, asking her what was wrong while women held her arms down.

What was wrong? "The ghosts are here!"

"But you always see ghosts—"

"Not here! Not in our home!"

"They can't." Satto's familiar voice brought logic back. "They can't be here."

He was right. But they were. Emyn couldn't block out the awful, whispering spirits. Her knees buckled beneath her. Truth rang in her bones, vibrating till her body threatened to shatter from the inside. She tried to say his name and couldn't, as if she'd been socked in the chest. All air emptied out of her.

If the ghosts were in her home, Rialos was dead.

Time raced and slowed with Emyn's mood. No part of Venetona seemed real to her now, especially her own home. This was a shadow world, a trap, and death was her only possible escape.

But death would have to wait for duty. Gorio's eyes reminded her of that; panic and tears pressed just behind his gaze. He retreated to Nanto's side when women filled the house. They were kind, but perhaps they reminded him of Vinnia and her friends. They wailed and held Emyn while she cried, and they offered wine and whatever numbing brew they could think of.

Vlidorix sent men to search for the druid. The ghosts might be wrong, Satto said; who could interpret the plan of the gods? Emyn knew better than to hope.

For a few days, she drank whatever was brought her. Sleep offered her only comfort, with the chance she'd wake feeling that Rialos had just been there, sitting beside her on the mattress or holding her arm while they walked through grass damp with morning dew.

The healer held up the pot of herbs one night. "Can you sleep without it?"

Emyn shrugged. Did it matter if she slept or not?

With Gorio at her side, Emyn left her home and walked past the stable the following morning. Men and women stopped talking when they saw her and bowed.

She found Satto. "Has anyone returned with news?"

Strangers surrounded the well; news and gossip must be everywhere. But Satto knew what she meant and shook his head. "Not yet, Gutumaros."

Who were all these people? Entire families, some with tents, filled the spaces between houses. Makeshift shelters stood in clearings, and carts and belongings rested under the shade of pine and linden.

"People come from King Gundori's island every day," Gorio whispered, clutching her skirt as he looked around. "Every day more." Did he fear that Vinnia would jump from the crowd and lay claim to him once more?

In the end, it was Nonicos, not Satto or strangers, who brought the answers Emyn dreaded. The approach of another road-weary traveler was no longer news, so Emyn heard nothing of a one-eyed man's arrival until her brother simply emerged from the bunches of people who constantly filled the paths.

Nonicos carried more years than she remembered. He barely spoke as she embraced him and led him to her home. There, before she could pull away his cloak or offer him water, he untied a leather bag from his belt and held it out to her. "You must have this."

She knew what the bag protected when he laid it in her hand. Rialos' serpent's egg: what he had spent half his life earning. How her brother gained possession of this was as blurry a question as asking where the wind came from.

The stone rolled onto her palm. Flecks of blood clung to the metal wires that held the serpent's egg on its chain. It seemed too vivid to look at, too heavy and full of pain to hold. How had Nonicos carried it so far?

"He was returning home," Nonicos whispered.

Emyn insisted that he wash and eat before telling the tale—a tale that she did not want to hear. Once fed and clean, he repeated the words. "He was returning home. Over a month ago, he came with Moradag and the warriors so that we could see the boy a last time. He promised to stop back and he did.

"He had news, Emyn. No one else knows this. He carried news for the king, and he told me what it was. I think he died for the sake of that news."

Nonicos shook his head with sorrow and confusion. "I took Laurina and the children to a safe place before I left to come here. I thought that once I saw you the words would come, but I don't know what to tell you first."

Emyn opened the leather bag and eased the serpent's egg back into it. Rialos was dead; did the rest matter that much? "Children? You said the children are safe."

His one eye lit up. "I have a son, three months old. A strong boy; we named him Isminos."

Emyn reached over to squeeze his arm. "So there is some good news in the middle of all this. I'm glad." She pushed herself up from the ground. "You know what news he carried?"

"I do."

"If it cost his life, we must deliver it."

DOORS WERE LEFT WIDE open in the summer, and all were welcome in the king's long house. "Pretend it's Volio," Emyn whispered as they crossed his threshold. Nonicos nodded; she could not see his good eye or tell if he were nervous. The rumble and laughter inside stopped as eyes picked Emyn's figure out of the shadows.

Men and women touched their hands to their foreheads as she passed, signaling their shared sorrow. This gesture followed her everywhere these days and brought a simple comfort: she was not alone. All grieved for the young druid and shared her loss.

Satto greeted Nonicos as an old friend while men carried Nanto to his customary seat. Gorio curled himself beside the old druid, ready to lift a cup or tear bread into small pieces. Nanto had grown frail; should they trouble him today? Maybe Emyn should follow him back home while the men talked. She looked around for help, but ghosts clouded her sight, pressing her back and urging her to sit.

"We are grateful for your news," Satto whispered to Nonicos. "You don't have to speak like a druid; I never could."

Her brother was not the only visitor here. At Vlidorix' side sat two tall men, one with a serpent's egg. It surprised her that Nonicos was already speaking and that the attention of these powerful men fixed on his every word.

Moments had been slipping away from Emyn lately, a few heartbeats at a time. Conversations and simple movements jumped past. It was like being caught in a windstorm, holding her ground as leaves and dust flew by. She put her hand over the pouch that held the serpent's egg and tried to pay attention. She did not want to ask Nonicos to repeat the words.

"The Honored Master Rialos had run for leagues. He was tired to the bone when he arrived at our home. He said, 'You deserve a more gracious guest, but I have urgent news for the king of the Veneti.'"

Nonicos looked up for the first time. "He was my sister's husband; I knew he did not exaggerate. Once he'd eaten some stew, he told me what he'd seen: a legion, a Roman legion on the Liger River."

"An entire Roman legion?" the king barked.

Nonicos jerked and then lowered his gaze again. "Yes, sir. He said he'd seen them building ships. He counted five handfuls of ships already completed, sitting in the water. He talked about the felled trees, the planks stacked up, the Romans walking to and fro —I could see it all in my mind when he talked. I wish I could remember the exact words. He spoke of pots of tar and . . . ."

Nonicos shook his head to clear it. "The numbers are important, sir, even if my words are poor. I remember those, clear as the sunlight. Five handfuls of ships completed, the Honored Master said, and more than that number under construction. And a whole legion there doing the work. That is what he was in a hurry to tell you."

"When did he leave your home?"

"Sir, he didn't leave." Nonicos turned a twisted face to Emyn. "My sister brought me here to give you his news. I haven't even told her what happened."

"Ah?" Vlidorix looked to the queen, then Satto. "Come closer, then, both of you." Another bench and pillows appeared. The king whispered to Satto, who called a command to the warriors and vanished.

Crowds drifted away. With a start Emyn recognized the druid beside Vlidorix. He inclined his head to her when their eyes met: Dumnorix.

The queen sat beside Emyn on the bench and took her hand; a row of ghosts backed Dumnorix. The living prince stood shoulder to shoulder with his Aeduan ancestor. Emyn sensed the dead king above, watching as he had since her mourning began. Whatever his reasons, she was glad for his silence.

"Satto was Rialos' good friend; we will wait for him to return," the king announced. "He will want to hear the tale, sad as it must be." Satto was no doubt selecting men who would hurry to the Liger. How many? Emyn wondered. Vlidorix would also send out spies, traveling as traders or farmers. Rialos excelled at such games—

Sorrow washed over Emyn like waves on a sandy beach, carrying bits of her away.

She could not endure sitting here. Who would stop her if she jumped up and left? Why should she listen? She found comfort in her dreams now; what if Nonicos' story turned those dreams to nightmares?

He was already speaking again, facing her as if they sat before her hearth, not the king's. This was her brother; she couldn't run away. She clenched the leather bag and felt the egg inside.

"We have a horse. I told Rialos to ride her and get to Venetona faster. He could send her back, maybe even bring you to visit. So at first light, he went out to the stable. Micco followed him. You know how he was about horses." Nonicos' mouth stretched as if he meant to smile but couldn't quite manage it. "He followed your husband everywhere. I think he didn't want him to leave.

"Neither came back from the stable, so I went to check on Micco." Nonicos swallowed hard; Emyn squeezed the egg. "I saw right away . . . he lay there, your husband. His throat was cut. Laurina kept saying the horse must have kicked him, but she didn't see. Someone murdered him."

Emyn moaned; his blood spilled onto the stable floor and no sacred vessel caught it. She'd seen that years ago in Samarnum's grove, when bluebells covered the ground. She'd demanded the truth then and gotten it.

"Who could do this, and where were they hiding?" Nonicos

went on. "I looked everywhere. There was no sign of Micco, no sound. Finally, I led out the horse and put my wife on it, with the baby in her arms and the child holding on behind. I led them to her cousins, a half league away. I ran beside the horse. I couldn't send them alone. What . . . what lunatic would kill a druid?"

No one answered him. The murder of a druid could not be repaid, not with all the riches of a tribe. Only death remitted such a crime.

"We left without Micco. I couldn't find him. The trip didn't take long. The men were in the fields, but her old uncle and his daughters were home. I didn't want to wait for the men to return. I knew my family was safe, and Micco was missing—but mostly, I could not leave your husband where he fell." Nonicos placed a hand over both of Emyn's, folded around the bag that sat in her lap: the bag that held the last piece of Rialos' soul left in this world.

"So I ran back to my house, and the stable. We have our places there for bodies. I arranged him properly. He faces the sky and the summer sun . . . but not alone. Another lies beside him."

"Who?" Did she say that out loud?

"Before I could pull your husband from the stable, I heard Micco squealing. A man held him by his shirt. Micco was terrified.

"The man was a druid. He pointed to the body and shouted, 'What crime is this?' I tried to explain, but the master interrupted. He shouted questions at me and kept shaking Micco. He wouldn't let him go. With one shake, the serpent's egg bounced from inside Micco's shirt."

Nonicos looked at Emyn. "Micco wore your husband's serpent's egg around his neck. I don't know why. Micco did not lay a hand on your husband. You know he could not, no more than a rabbit could attack a wolf."

"I know."

Nonicos caught Satto's eye. "You remember him? He wasn't strong enough to cut a man like that. Not Micco."

Satto nodded, and Nonicos gathered his thoughts and went on with his tale.

"The druid asked—loudly—why did the halfwit have the egg? Did I think such a rare object was a toy for a fool?

"I told him, no, of course not. I didn't know who killed the master—I never even had a chance to tell him that this was no passing visitor, but my sister's husband. The words were there, but he wouldn't let me speak. He accused me of killing him myself and asked me how I would pay for the life of a druid.

"I said, 'I would never kill—not a guest, not a druid! I have a family,' I told him. 'Why would I shame them and break our laws?'"

Nonicos shuddered. "The druid said, 'Do you think you can lie to me? Your only hope is the truth, man. Tell me why he was here and who has done this!'"

Emyn wanted the story to end. The queen's arm was around her shoulder, a gesture that comforted Emyn. She tried to rise but the arm, like iron, held her down. Nonicos continued.

"'He spent the night,' I said. 'He was anxious to get to Venetona by horse.'"

"'Why?' The druid screamed at me. 'Why? What was his reason?'"

Nonicos ran out of words. He stared at Emyn for several heartbeats. "I—I did not tell him. My mind distrusted this man. I held the truth back. I said that this poor visitor was a druid like him and I did not dare ask his reasons."

With his one eye, he looked at the others. "Micco had a child's mind and never spoke, at least not clearly. All the time the druid questioned me, he held Micco by the shirt. Micco squealed and wailed, so much that I could not think."

Emyn bent over the egg and sobbed. No one could escape the blighted stars that rose over them nightly. Not Micco, not Nonicos —an honorable man who never wronged a living being.

She put her hands over her ears as Nonicos told how the druid declared Micco a killer and executed him for the murder of an honored master. "He looped the rope around Micco's neck, tightened it, set a stick in it to twist tighter and strangled him while I begged . . . . Then the druid fell on me again with more questions. 'What did the murdered man say? Where did he come from?'"

"Shh." The queen pulled Emyn's hands from her hair with a firm grip.

Nonicos breathed hard; Emyn saw a tear on one side of his face. Only the one.

"'How did you lose your eye?' he asked me. The master looked at me, like . . . like everything was clear to him. 'How did you lose your eye?' He said it a second time, very softly.

"Laurina's cousins arrived then—several of them. They gathered around poor Micco, but since the man before me was a druid, they could do nothing. They stared at the two bodies.

"The druid looked around then shouted at me, 'The gods protect you this day! Do not think you can meddle in their affairs again without punishment!'

"When he left, Emyn, we laid them out together, Micco and your honored husband."

"Two victims of the same hand." These were the first words Emyn had heard from the ghosts since Nonicos began his tale. The living would not make such an accusation against a druid, not without proof. But Emyn was sure that everyone in the king's house thought it.

"This second druid." Vlidorix barely moved; his voice was low like a cauldron just beginning to boil. "Did he ever pronounce his name?"

"No," Nonicos answered. "I asked, but he threw questions back at me and never answered. He had an island accent, though."

"Eire, do you think?"

"Yes, sir, I do."

ONE THING REMAINED TO BE DONE.

"Where?" Several voices asked the question—over the sea, among the trees, by the well, outside his house, the paths he liked best?

"Tell us where, dear." Emyn looked up at the queen. She meant well but Emyn had no answer. Did it matter to a soul where it was released?

"By the Morrigu's spring." The words seemed to find her rather than the other way around.

"A worthy choice." Servants scurried away to tell the king.

The afternoon passed, and gray twilight raced toward her like an arrow. One day would be ending soon, another beginning. Emyn sat, heedless of the living and dead who tried to comfort her.

She was led to the Morrigu's pool where men had piled stones and built up a little altar. It stood before her, waist-high. Someone pried the leather pouch from her hands. The serpent's egg rolled onto a gray stone and cast an oblong shadow across its mottled surface. A rock as big as her hand rested next to it. She shuddered in rebellion; she didn't want to do this.

The king spoke. "Gutumaros, it is time."

Emyn stepped forward, leaned her stick against bluish rocks, and saw that the air vibrated with a golden glow.

She stared at the serpent's egg in its wire cage. Except for their first meeting in Samarnum, it always hung round his neck, even when he lay naked beside her. How could it have been parted from him?

"Emyn." Nonicos stepped close to whisper. "You cannot hold him in this world."

She knew he spoke truly, but her arm wouldn't lift. How strange to see her own body as if from far away, with her arm refusing to move. Like a door that stayed bolted while the walls crumbled around it.

"He has left you," the dead king hissed. "I remain. What is there to dread? He is already gone."

Duty loomed before Emyn. She forced herself to think, to push against the lethargy that was drowning her. She could do one thing at a time. Today's task was hard, but it brought her closer to the time when they would be together again. Every step brought her closer to that.

She picked up the rock. It was heavy; she nearly dropped it. Twice she tried to lift it high, twice she failed. Her arm was strong, it was her spirit that weakened.

"Gutumaros, lift again." Long fingers curled over hers and hefted the weight of the rock. The strange hand rose with hers above her shoulder, then dropped faster than she could see.

The serpent's egg shattered between the stones. Dumnorix released her hand and studied the shards that settled on the altar, the ground, the bushes, and even the fine pieces that fell and floated in the sacred pool. He was druid as well as prince and warrior; he would read the signs.

"Your enemy comes to this land," he announced finally. "You choose the battleground, but the gods choose the victor."

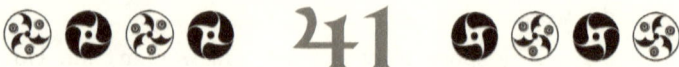 41

Dumnorix stayed three days, conferring with the king and his warriors, rousing them to action. Gundori's rash abduction of two legionnaires insulted Rome and drew Caesar's attention to the west, Dumnorix pointed out; they must prepare to confront him.

The prince walked near the shore, drawn by the sounds of hammering and the smell of bubbling pitch. All of Venetona's men worked on ships and weapons now; all were eager to hear from Dumnorix, the hero who defied Caesar and kept his freedom.

"You have the advantage," Emyn heard him shout. "Your ancestors mastered these seas! Their Latin gods are ignorant of its currents and moods."

Emyn could not imagine sea warfare. How did the fervor of battle spread on the water? Did ships charge, as men did on land? It seemed to her that only archers would be useful there; no warrior's sword could reach an enemy on another vessel.

"Hold nothing back!" Dumnorix cried as the men cheered. In the harsh summer glare, she saw that the Aeduan prince had aged.

* * *

A FEW STRANDS OF hair sparkled white, and his eyes were circled and grooved.

Dumnorix visited her home to offer his respect to the druid Nanto before turning to Emyn. "I recall a child who stood resolute before warriors twice her size." He smiled grimly. "Your village was Viromanduan, was it not?"

"It was, sir. My people—my village—fought and died with the Nervians last year."

"They live triumphant over their enemies in the land of summer, then." The prince touched his hand to his forehead. "You have lost much, Gutumaros. Men call me brave. I lead warriors in battle and fight beside them, but it is the courage of women that never wavers. You brandish no weapons and carry no shield that can soften the blows of life. I can lay down my sword, but a woman's battle never ends, does it?"

"You are a wise master," Emyn whispered and bit her lip to hold it from trembling. He read her soul.

"I knew your husband as a worthy friend who did me great service once." Dumnorix' gaze was steady, but not intrusive; he looked past her eyes. "I had hoped to see you united, not torn in this way."

She would like to learn more about that service; Rialos had told her only a little. He had gathered outlaws to carry Dumnorix' messages, messages that his brother must not hear. Emyn was sure, though, that the prince had not come here to share such memories as old friends might in times of peace.

"Tell him," the dead king rumbled.

"Sir," Emyn said, "my ghosts have shown me things you must know."

"Indeed?" Dumnorix smiled. "You gave me a sure warning about my brother years ago. I should have acted sooner on it."

"What could you have done differently?" Emyn said, aware that she sounded presumptuous. "It is your ancestor who asks you this; he stands beside you often. Now he says that we cannot change events; we can only meet them."

She glanced at Nanto and lowered her voice. "You have a geis on you. You should know that the daughter of Orgetorix has told the Romans of it."

He set his jaw. "She lives, then."

The Aeduan ancestor allowed Dumnorix no time to dwell on this before giving Emyn more words to repeat. "Your ancestors guide you. They want you to know that you were born with the gifts of a great king, but that the time for kings has passed. No songs will be written for you. There are no victories to be won. The choice before you is to live and die a free man or to submit to conquest."

Her hands were shaking. These were not words to say to a prince or to anyone else. Could the future of the Aedui really be so bleak—and did that of the Veneti hold any more hope?

"Your spirits tell you this?" he asked.

"Your spirits, sir."

Dumnorix considered her words. "This sounds as if the choice is personal; as if my decision was for no one but myself. That is not the choice of a leader."

"Choices do not have to be spoken to be made," whispered a gentle spirit.

Emyn nodded. "Though all men look to you, Honored Master, it is a choice you must make for yourself. We live at the end of time. This is what the ghosts say."

* * *

THE DAY AFTER DUMNORIX left Venetona, Nonicos departed. He returned to his wife and children after pleading with Emyn to seek safety there as well. "Upriver, away from the sea. We farm; the Romans have no reason to bother us."

"My duty is here," she told him. She held back the hopeless words that she heard so often from the ghosts: no place promised safety. No one could hide.

Within days, Romans attacked Gundori's island by land, crossing at low tide. The legion arced north of the Liger, avoiding the great bay of the Veneti to sneak into Gundori's realm. The king and wealthy families collected their slaves and livestock and gold and escaped on ships from the island's west shore. What happened to those left in the village where Suttia's long house stood—or used to stand—Emyn never heard.

In the midst of the wild tales and uproar, the warrior Satto disappeared. Emyn suspected that he went to the Liger to see the Roman camp for himself.

Caesar's makeshift fleet had not dared the open sea yet, but rumors spread daily about his intentions. Venetona swelled even more, with folks arriving from villages all around the gulf by land and sea. Grain, fruit, ale, and even pigs and sheep were ferried by Veneti ships to different islands, some outside of the gulf. The large ships then returned to the port to wait.

The people of Venetona made bundles of their cloaks and treasures, easy to grab when the time came. The refugees who filled the inns and empty spaces were ready as well; most of them never unpacked. With so many people, tempers were quick to ignite over small insults. Fights broke out each afternoon when men began to drink.

Satto returned after the full moon. He looked at no one as he passed, but went straight to his king where—so the gossip flew—they spoke alone. Not even a slave overheard.

"It must be bad news—terrible news that can't be shared," the healer told Emyn, shaking her head. "Satto looks like he swallowed poison."

The gossip was thick at the well. "The Namnete threw in their lot with Rome."

"That's what my husband says too."

"They've cast a dark eye on us for years, everyone knows it."

"Rome promised them the salt trade, I'll bet."

"Can't trust them—"

"He practices his story as he practices with his sword," the Aeduan ancestor's voice cut across the women's nervous chatter.

"Who?" Emyn hissed softly, turning from the well. A ghostly campfire glowed and the warrior spirits sat round it. Trees showed through their forms.

"The lone warrior," said one.

"Satto?"

"He knows more than he tells, that one!" A living woman spoke; Emyn tried to block her out and listen to the ghosts.

"His tongue is not used to lies. He must practice them," said one.

"The same words, over and over," added the Aeduan spirit.

"Until they are perfected."

"He polishes his tale." The spirit who said this smiled in appreciation of the irony. These ghosts, as usual, tended to their weapons. One wiped an oiled cloth along the rim and boss of his shield while others polished axes and swords.

Did Satto lie to the king—was that what the ghosts meant? Or did he practice his lies for others? With clusters of people surrounding her, Emyn did not dare ask this question aloud.

"The Romans have launched their fleet." So many voices

repeated the words that Emyn wasn't sure if she'd heard them first from the dead or the living.

THE DARK DAYS OF ELEMBIU BEGAN. Several druids, refugees themselves, crowded into Emyn's house each night. They conferred with Nanto, letting his expression direct their words. Most kept their own servants and slaves to serve them and help Emyn cook; one even brought a nervous student with him.

On the third day of the month, the druids brought Nanto into the pine trees, nearly a league away from buildings. The trek took most of the morning. None of the druids were very strong, but they insisted on touching the bars of Nanto's litter even though slaves bore most of its weight. Emyn followed with Gorio.

King Vlidorix waited at a spring that bubbled from the ground between two ancient oaks. He bowed before Nanto and whispered into his ear, embraced the old man, and left. All heard a sob choke the king's breath as he waved his servants away.

Gorio held Emyn's hand tightly. She had explained to him that Awa was too old and frail to begin a new journey in this world. Instead, he would leave it now with honor. The boy said that he understood; he wanted to stay with Awa till the end.

A druid with hair half-gray, half-yellow, faced Nanto. "Are you prepared, Master?"

Nanto looked at Gorio, his eyes dancing.

The other druid smiled at the boy. "You are a great comfort to the master. When you are as old as he is, remember that a wise and dear friend waits for you in the next world."

They might have gathered to share ale and stories, so light was the mood. One druid shook the contents of a bag into a cup, careful not to touch the pulpy stuff. Aconitum? The masters had whispered of this for days, but Emyn didn't ask for details. She sat at Nanto's side and watched as the poison was poured into his mouth. One by one, the druids took Nanto's hand, offering words of respect and admiration and bidding him farewell—at least for awhile.

When her turn came, Emyn stood and leaned over Nanto. Her thoughts felt tangled like wool that needed combing. Nanto went to his place in the land of summer. She supposed he would see Rialos there; what should she say?

"Tell my husband I miss him," Emyn whispered. The words sounded foolish. Of course she missed Rialos; could she think of no better message to send into the next world? She lowered her voice even more. "I do what I must."

Nanto pushed a sound from his throat. Emyn remembered how Gundori's poison had paralyzed her body and her voice. Nanto might want to speak badly; had she upset him? She squeezed his hand. "I will see him soon, and you too."

Suddenly it was over. Nanto had slipped away, and Gorio buried his head in Emyn's lap to silence his sobs, his head and shoulders jerking.

Looking more like a beehive than a harbor, Venetona spread out before them as Emyn and Gorio returned from the hidden place. Along the shore, beached boats tilted and their rigging snapped in the wind. Figures scrambled around them. Men, women, and children formed lines; the biggest and strongest tossed their baggage onto the decks where slaves caught and arranged the parcels. Some folks handed up cages of noisy geese. Yapping dogs got in the way as waves began to lick at feet and ships.

These ships would carry the wives and children of Venetona to a well-stocked fortress, on a peninsula outside the bay. No ship could sail with ghosts in attendance, though, so the king assigned three men and a woman—warriors all—to escort his Gutumaros to the same shelter by land. Emyn would ride in a chariot again, circling the entire bay.

Her clothes, blankets, bowls, cauldron, pots, and everything else she owned were stacked on a cart outside the house, ready for slaves to lift and push to the shore. The effort seemed wasteful; would she use them again, ever? Her home had been stripped; it felt dank and lifeless like a cave. Satto stood in its darkness staring up at the one item the slaves had missed: the little goddess carved by Nonicos.

Satto cleared his throat. "Should I take it down for you?"

Emyn managed a smile. Once Satto handed it to her, she hugged the little statue to her chest. Wind blew along the thatch; its sound echoed through the empty room.

"Go find the queen's servants," Satto said to Gorio. "Ask them for a bowl of food and some bread for the lady." He turned back to Emyn as the child ran off. "We leave the town tonight, everyone, when the tide rises."

She nodded; it was rising already. "Before dark, then," she said.

"Your warriors have only to harness their teams to chariots; everything else is ready. I'll let them know you're here." Satto's eyes darted around the bare walls as if he expected to find hidden enemies there. How many times had he sat under this roof sharing a cup and a joke with Rialos? Venetona was more his home than Emyn's; to see it abandoned must stab the warrior's soul.

A hand rested on Satto's shoulder, then disappeared. Lights, soft and pale like fires seen behind a screen, surrounded him. He straightened his back and looked Emyn in the eye. "Before you leave, there is something I must tell you."

She waited.

"I found him." His voice cracked in the silence. Suddenly, Satto could not meet her gaze but spun and addressed the walls, the cold hearth, the posts. His words spilled out like water overrunning its banks. "I found him: the Honored Master Ferdiath. Honored! He had no right to that title.

"He didn't deny what he'd done. He laughed at me and called me a fool! He called Rialos a fool too, a dreamer. 'Look around you!' he said. 'Where are the towers and spearmen who could defeat Rome?'"

"He admitted that he killed my husband?" Nausea weakened her knees, and Emyn put both hands on her stick for balance.

"I accused him of murder and he smiled. 'The one-eyed man was her brother, wasn't he?' he said. 'I realized that too late.'"

"He has no shame," Emyn moaned. Ghosts rested all around her, but they were strangers. Rialos waited in the land of promise; she would not find him in this world. What use were all these ghosts, and what use was she to them?

"He mocked us all," Satto's face twisted. "He told me that the Romans are coming and will not be stopped. 'Profit from this, if you have any wits,' he said. Profit!"

"No shame," Emyn repeated weakly.

"He turned from me, Ferdiath did. What has a druid to fear? But he took the life of a druid in a stable, when *his* back was turned. That's how it happened, I am sure. He could not match Rialos in a fair fight." Satto stopped pacing and faced her. "I took his life as he took my friend's. Do you understand?"

"Yes." How could she not?

"This consumes his soul," a ghost murmured.

Satto fell to his knees, covering his face.

"The king has pardoned you, hasn't he?" Emyn finally asked.

The man moaned and pulled at his hair. The murder of a druid was an unforgiveable act.

Over the crown of Satto's head, Emyn's hands wove an ancient pattern that Iomat had taught her years before. She pushed Satto's arms from his face, then spat into her hands, touched her palms to his forehead, and blew on his brow. "With sacred air I bless and thank you. May Camulos strengthen your arm and the Morrigu clear your path in the battles to come, and may all your ancestors stand by you."

"I am theirs to use," Satto groaned, "but my soul is cursed to the next world."

EMYN AND HER SMALL group rode only two leagues before stopping for the night. Arrangements had been made: a young man welcomed them to a large house and passed around bowls of hot soup. Their host would join other warriors on a ship once his visitors left in the morning.

Gorio curled next to Emyn, but she lay awake for a long time, too overwhelmed for sleep. Nanto's passing, Venetona abandoned, Satto's confession—was that not enough for one day? Her soul felt pummeled and weak.

A ghost stroked her hair; another sang a lullaby. Emyn shut her eyes.

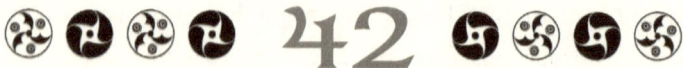

42

Small fires dotted the fortress, heating cauldrons filled with cereal. Women cooked to feed their children, maybe for the last time. They paused to touch their hands to their foreheads and bow as Emyn passed.

"Gutumaros, what do the spirits say?"

"Our ancestors stand with us," she repeated over and over, and those who listened assumed that meant victory.

Men and women believed the dead simply because they were dead. Spirits held secrets that inspired hope or brought power, they thought. Emyn's ears heard different omens, but she would not repeat the words.

By mid-morning, hundreds of Veneti women, children, and grandparents lined the wide walls of the fortress. Emyn planted her feet and leaned on her stick.

"There! I see them!"

Ships sailed by, their leather sails afire with the sun. The hulls and masts were built of oak, the favorite wood of gods and men. The ships rose to crest waves and splash down on the water, like giant warriors with souls of their own. Soon, distant vessels dotted a blurry horizon, so many that Emyn could not count them.

"Look!"

"Where?"

"South, coming up. Do you see?"

The Roman fleet approached and the crowd shifted to get a better view. A man laughed out loud, then a woman, and soon all were calling out insults as if the Romans could hear them.

"Fishing boats would look scarier!"

"Those ships are stunted—"

"Like their men!"

What could the Romans hope to achieve with these puny boats? Emyn wondered if Caesar stood on one of them. The ghosts could tell her nothing of what went on across the water.

"They sit too low," an old man shouted. See that?"

"Couldn't sail into the gulf without ripping the bottom out."

"Not even in high tide—"

"By Camulos, I wouldn't bet a lost tooth on them. Toy boats!"

"Arrogance!" snarled the dead king.

"The sails are cloth!"

"Cloth?"

"Look at them! Cloth!"

Men and women shrieked in scorn. "That won't last—"

"One storm will shred them!"

"Fools!" shouted the dead king, and dread rose in Emyn like bile. She'd seen Roman tricks before; she'd seen them gloat over fallen enemies. Their ships might be built all wrong, but they didn't have to survive a storm or sail into the gulf. They had only to fight today's battle.

The insults grew stale, and silence fell on the waiting crowd. Everyone scanned the sea until a youth with sharp eyes yelled and pointed. Emyn could not see what alarmed him; the ship he pointed toward bobbed and shrank behind the waves.

As the sun rose higher and the heat and smell of many bodies filled the air, fingers pointed in a different direction and then a third. This time the Veneti ship was close enough for Emyn to see clearly; she could even name one man who gripped the ropes like a spider on a web.

A Roman vessel closed on the Veneti; for the first time Emyn saw long-handled oars swinging from holes in the side of the hull. Were these Roman ships nothing but large rowboats? The Veneti ship towered over the smaller boat, and men threw rocks and spears down on the Romans. Below, shields were lifted and flashed in the sun.

A pole rose over the Romans.

"What's that?"

No one answered.

"What are they lifting?"

"Is it a spear?"

All held their breath as the long pole pointed toward the rigging of the Veneti ship, then another pole arced upward.

"They're going to slash the sails," said a woman.

"By poking them?" asked another.

"Maybe there's a knife tied to the poles," the first offered.

Archers shot at the Romans, but the poles remained upright. An arrow found its mark and sent a man into the sea, and shields flashed once more. The poles thrust, retreated, and thrust again.

At a Latin command the smaller ship moved away from the larger, leaving a pole bent in the air as if caught on something. Once the distance between the enemies widened, the pole jerked and sprang back.

On the Veneti ship, the sails collapsed. The crowd in the fortress gasped.

"They've brought down the yard!"

The yard, Emyn remembered, was the horizontal beam that held up the sail. No—it held up the ropes that in turn held up the sail. Now she understood the Romans' pole and how it reared back and snapped: like a line pulled taut by a fish until the fish got away.

Even as she reasoned this out, two more Roman ships rowed close to the disabled vessel. Hooks and ropes swung up and onto the Veneti deck, and Romans scurried like bugs onto the ship. Fire sparked and spread. Men jumped from the rails to the deck with blades drawn and hacking.

"Scavengers!" Like everyone else who watched from shore, Emyn screamed without hearing herself.

By then another two ships had come together, closer to the mouth of the bay. The Romans' pole rose again to catch and pull on the ropes of the larger ship until the rope broke, and when it broke, the yard, the sail, and all the marvelous, intricate equipment that propelled the Veneti ship before the wind fell useless to the deck.

Throughout the morning and afternoon they watched. All the Roman ships carried long poles. The Veneti captains kept their distance, staying just close enough to rain arrows down on the Romans. This was no way to fight!

The worst happened in mid afternoon.

Emyn knew the bristling tinge of the air that signaled an oncoming storm; now she sensed the opposite. A void approached. A stillness that defied sunlight and wind settled over the bay. The breezes died; the air grew stagnant and heavy. Even the birds ceased to fly.

She looked around. A crowd of ghosts stood on the wall of the fortress. Though indistinct, she could see that some wore furs and others armor; they seemed of all ages. *Our ancestors stand with us.*

If she'd ever doubted the words of the gods or the power of their will in the living world, those doubts vanished. This weird calm that dissolved winds and melted waves came from beyond the boundaries of this world. It brought death to the Veneti.

Without wind, the large oaken ships were easy prey for the Romans, who used oars to propel their boats close. The poles rose over fierce fighting, hooking the ropes and yanking down the sails on one Veneti ship after the other. With no wind to fill the sails anyway, the tactic seemed hardly worth the effort—but the Romans were methodical creatures.

The enemy had fewer ships, but those they had could move without wind. Rome butchered the Veneti piece by piece, ship by ship, surrounding them one at a time, maiming the crews and leaving the hulls to burn so that eerie, floating fires sprouted in the bay.

Satto fought on one of those ships; so did the warriors who'd brought her to this fortress. Vlidorix insisted on sailing on the largest ship. All were gone.

Now the faces near Emyn were streaked with tears, mouths open: people unaware of the mournful cries that came from their own aching throats. They began to look around; they tried to shake off the gloom that fell over them. Mothers called to their children. Women grabbed bags that held coins and jewels, maybe food.

The druids standing on the highest wall of the fortress did not weep, but their faces were as gray as the standing stones. For a moment, Emyn imagined that ash had covered them, but that was impossible; no wind had risen to carry the ashes of the burning ships.

The druids had sworn that the Veneti would drown Rome. The stars promised it, and their charms and incantations ensured victory, they said. For men of logic and sense, the outcome was certain. Gods, however, weren't bound by the logic of this world.

Gorio appeared beside her, carrying a bag. He shoved her carved stick into her hand and cried, "Come, come!"

How many times had he tried to get her attention? Finally, she roused as if breaking from a nightmare and followed.

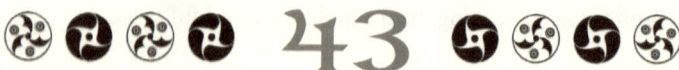

43

They fled the fortress and stumbled along the shore, two among a multitude.

Some refugees sobbed. Most seemed as dazed and sick as Emyn felt. She heard women say they must stay away from the roads, that Roman butchers would be watching those.

Strangers approached to ask where they should go for safety. Emyn glared at them. No place was safe, and her mouth was tired from screaming.

One man was insistent. He hugged a canvas bag to his chest and gripped the strap of another, slung over his shoulder. Coins jingled inside both bags.

"What should I do?" He expected her to guide him. She was an oracle and must know; he was rich and could pay.

Her throat hurt as she growled out an answer: "Die bravely."

Gorio pulled at her skirt, urging her to move. She and the boy were slower than most; the wealthy and desperate soon left them behind. She thought they put leagues between them and the fortress, picking up one foot and setting it down, then the other . . . but she had no way of measuring. Did it matter?

Slowly, the sun rolled to the west and its golden light sparkled off the waves. A summer sunset—yet nothing could mask the ugliness. Each breeze carried the stench of decay along with the tang of salt water.

As the tide fell back, body parts washed ashore along with charred timbers, scraps of leather, and other wreckage. The highest waves left a line of dark, wet ash that snaked through the sand as far as Emyn could see. Gulls and carrion birds cawed and landed to pick at the leavings.

Gorio tugged again. She kept up with the boy—or maybe he slowed—but she could not stop looking. Shreds of striped wool and a rope belt caught her eye. These scraps of fabric belonged to someone, a man hot and alive in the morning. So did this twisted piece of iron with a chip of coral still attached.

A few steps more . . . Emyn wedged her stick between rocks and leaned on it to stare at a severed hand. It posed as if it just that moment dropped the knife or sword that failed in its defense.

None of the flotsam strewn here wore armor—that would have sunk. What washed up belonged to fishermen, peasants, and slaves pressed into service to sail the ships: men who could not afford the mail shirts or helmets that dragged their owners to the ocean floor. Men whose children would cry for them as darkness fell, just as the children of the warriors would.

They walked while the sun lowered and turned red, stepping around bits of clothes and shoes, leather sails, cups, empty sheaths, apples, small carved gods, lengths of rope singed at both ends, and light chains of tin. Wood was everywhere: beams and planks splintered into small segments, carved and polished or rough and weathered, and ashes. Charred wooden handles twined in seaweed had burned free of their metal blades. The wood of ten times twenty ships.

The pair veered inland before sunset. The dark days of Elembiu left them no moonlight; Emyn and Gorio slept side by side on a soft slope. They spent the next day walking, and the next. The smell of burning was everywhere.

If Emyn sought refuge, she would not know where to look. The land was strange to her, its paths a mystery. Refuge was not what she expected, though. She knew her stars and could read many signs.

Spirits swarmed in every shadow. Some were curious and some whispered but Emyn had no reason to pay attention. Her fight was over, and there was no one besides Gorio to receive their obscure messages.

Thoughts fell away as if her mind lacked room for them. Why did she walk? For Gorio. His life lay ahead; hers fell into the past. Venentona and Samarnum were gone. The idea grew in her that Gorio's forgotten tribe still lived in the forest; the Romans knew nothing of them. Their stars told different stories than those of the Veneti. She would find the forgotten people for Gorio's sake. It was not much of a plan, but it led her footsteps forward.

"Men are near," the dead king announced as they neared the thick trees. The last of some plums they'd found had been eaten, and both Emyn's and Gorio's stomach gurgled with hunger.

"Who?"

"Men known to Caesar, men with food and wine. Stay on this path. Call out! Promise them gold; I will guide you to treasures." Emyn suppressed the urge to hum loudly, blocking his words as she motioned Gorio from the path and into the trees. The ghost scolded, but she ignored him. Did he think she would let him lead her to Rome?

"Will you starve?" The dead king rattled in her ear. "You

accomplish nothing this way. Rome values oracles. With my words, safety and honor are yours!"

She waved him away. What did he know of honor or anything else?

Perhaps the dead king tasted fear at last. He had forsaken Samarnum to follow her. Could his voice be heard by anyone else? He faced death too, in a way.

Before dark, they stumbled across a hunter's hidden cache of dried fish and grain. The bounty surprised her: two handfuls of millet in a pot large and strong enough to heat over a fire.

Emyn and Gorio ate the dried fish and some berries they'd found, but neither was sated. Silently, they watched the sliver of moon outpace the sun to the western horizon. The third day since the defeat of the Veneti began.

They slept. The sun rose; the moon stayed behind. Emyn and Gorio lit a small fire, shared the millet and set out walking. A few clouds drifted and Emyn raised her head to look at them.

Would Caesar bring his bright southern sky with him to shine over the lands he'd conquered? She's seen it once as a child, that ugly Roman sky behind the stark outlines of hammered trees and dead men. Under Rome's rule such sights might become common. Years from now, would a child of this land look up to see slaves crucified along the roads laid out by the ancestors? Would that child speak Latin and worship Roman gods? Emyn was glad such a life would never be hers.

They pushed through shadows and early morning dew until her stick dropped into a hole hidden by mulch. Emyn jerked, thrown off balance, and her feet slid over the wet, dead leaves. Her shoulder twisted as she tried to stop herself, but there was no ground—she just kept falling.

* * *

WATER DRIBBLED OVER HER FACE. It didn't stop the blinding pain in her skull, but it felt good anyway. Sunlight touched her skin as well. Gorio whispered, begging her to wake.

She opened her eyes, shut them quickly, and pushed away from Gorio as she vomited. The stench was awful, but worse—the confusion. Where was she? Pain reverberated in her head and down her spine. Who had hit her? If enemies were close, they kept silent. She opened her eyes again, just a little.

"Here is water." The boy reached around her shoulder with a pot and a rag. She stared at it. Gorio scooted closer and wiped her face. "You fell," he said, and his voice shook. "You slept."

"Slept? Here?" Dirt banks rose on either side of them. Why this place? Where was her house? "Who else is here?"

"No one else." The water touched her face again. "Maybe your ghosts talk." The boy was frightened. Emyn protected him; that was part of why they were here, wasn't it? "Are you broken, Lady Emyn?"

Her stomach heaved again, but nothing came up. At Gorio's suggestion, she moved her legs and her arms. Nothing hurt more than her head.

"I help you up," Gorio said. He knelt beside her and put her arm around his shoulder—thankfully, he touched the arm that was not sore. "You try."

It took more than one attempt. Her head screamed. The ghosts whispered, but too many voices muddled their words. Once he had her up, Gorio propped her against a tree. The roots sprawled around her feet like veins in the earth.

"Your stick." He pressed it into her hand.

Emyn's eyes fixed on the carved knob, then on the hands and skinny arms that steadied her. Gorio. She was with Gorio and they were . . . "Where?"

"Up," he said. "We were up there. It's easy this way."

He led her up a gentle rise. She had more questions, but he would be scared if he knew she'd forgotten what this place was.

Maybe the ghosts knew. Ancient spirits darted in and out of tree shadows. She didn't need them, a sprite laughed. The Morrigu had her hand on Emyn.

"Will you trust me?" Whose voice was that?

The lights were strong around Gorio, whispering that they would take care of their own.

EMYN FELL MORE THAN ONCE, blinked, and lost her way. They didn't walk far, and when they stopped, she could not stay awake. Dread filled her. Her head was injured badly enough to keep her from walking. Who would help the child? She knew him only by his slave's name; it did not seem enough.

He knelt beside her anxiously as she dozed and woke once more. The day slipped away from them. No food remained, and he would not leave her. What now?

"What is your name?" Gorio's eyes grew wide; he must imagine she was losing her mind. "What—" Emyn's voice cracked. She swallowed and tried again. "What did your mother call you? When I pray I would like to know."

His lips barely moved; she had to ask him to repeat his name.

"Vael." He bent his head close, sharing a secret. "That is what mothers call their sons, Vael. We get names when we grow tall."

Emyn lifted her arm. She was awkward, but managed to grab his smaller hand. "You are Vael to me."

SMALL NOISES WOKE HER; the sun still lit the world. Gorio slept beside her, but beyond him leaves shifted. Emyn's head would not move. She waited for the animal to come into view, wondering if she should try to shake Gorio awake.

An oversized crab scurried forward: a creature with a dark, bent head. Shaggy fur covered its shoulders and back. It crossed a shadow and disappeared briefly, and then the head lifted.

Their eyes locked. The other was a woman, neither young nor old. Matted hair fell over her eyes.

Ghosts murmured, but it was noise to Emyn, like a running stream. She was done with ghosts and their messages. She tried to move her arm and failed, but she did push a word out of her mouth: "Vael."

Did she dream? She saw the woman between gaps as the sun peeked through branches overhead. First came a flash too bright to look upon, then darkness blew in with the breeze. Emyn shut her eyes, opening them when she heard a grunt very close.

Lean arms slid under Gorio's knees and neck. The woman set her muscles and lifted. The boy stretched and the woman froze. He slept so lightly; slavery had taught him that. Emyn wanted to touch and reassure the boy, but could not.

The woman's soft furs cushioned his head. Gorio settled back into sleep, and the stranger threw a last glance at Emyn. She got to her feet, and then hurried away.

Emyn stared at the empty space where Gorio had lain. It was too much to hope that this was the family he'd lost, but he would have a home. He would grow and be given a name.

If this was real. If it wasn't, what could she do?

Blood pounded in her head. When the wind blew the clouds away, the sky was as beautiful as a jewel, but she couldn't keep her eyes open long.

How would the summer sky look in the next world? Emyn would not lack for company there. All the heroes who had died filled the land of promise. One soul, though, she ached to see more than all the others.

Emyn let her eyes fall shut as if it were night. She imagined resting against Rialos, his body arranged around hers like a cloak, heat passing back and forth between them. She could feel his breath dancing over her hair.

It was real, more real than the pain. Just that: his breath ruffling her hair.

Epilogue

A year after the Veneti's destruction, Julius Caesar crossed the English Channel briefly. The next year he returned to Britain with a larger fleet, intent on conquest. Because he wanted no trouble in Gaul during his absence, Caesar summoned many tribal leaders to a northern port on the continent. Those he could not trust, he decided, would accompany him to Britain as hostages. Dumnorix, the rebellious Aeduan prince, was judged too dangerous a man to leave behind.

Caesar writes, "Dumnorix pleaded all kinds of reasons why he should be left behind in Gaul. For one thing, he claimed, he knew nothing of sailing and was afraid of the sea; for another—or so he alleged—religious obligations prevented him from going."

Caesar would accept no excuses and accused Dumnorix of plotting mischief and rabble-rousing. As the Romans made ready to sail, Dumnorix escaped with his cavalry. Caesar sent his own cavalry after him with orders to kill the man if necessary.

Not surprisingly, it proved necessary. "He continually cried that he was a free man and a citizen of a free state. Caesar's men surrounded and killed him, as ordered."

Julius Caesar, *The Gallic War*
Book V:6-7
Translation by Carolyn Hammond

Acknowledgments

I would like to thank my extraordinarily patient friends and fellow writers who proofed, read, and reread this work. One writing buddy in particular has painstakingly gone over the manuscript no less than four times now: Debra Ann Pawlak, author of *Bringing Up Oscar: The Story of the Men and Women Who Founded the Academy*. Deb, you deserve much more than a shout-out, but I don't have the authority to issue Medals of Valor.

I'd also like to thank the wonderful members of a critique group that met every Tuesday in a now-defunct Borders, who walked me through so many chapters. Libby, Doc, Brenda, Laura, Jim, Armon, et al: I appreciated every comment and word, even when I argued with you! This group was an offshoot of the California Writers' Club, Inland Empire branch. For those of us who need to see a friendly face and get a reassuring "Well done!" every now and then, a critique group of fellow writers can be invaluable.

To readers Mary Watkins, Linda Lichtman, and of course my daughter Katie Kaopua, muchas gracias as well.

To Mary Klifman, scourge of unnecessary commas everywhere, a huge and sincere thank you.

To Stacey Aaronson of The Book Doctor Is In, who designed this book. I owe a huge debt of gratitude for your help, advice, and kindness.

Finally, I'd like to thank a man whose name I never knew, who sat at the counter of LAX's Terminal 4 in the mid-1970s, asked me to bring him a burger, then turned to his grown son and said, "Why is it that waitresses have no ambition?"

Sweetie, you'll never know how determined I was to prove you wrong.

About the Author

VICKEY KALL lives on the fringes of Los Angeles where she blogs on local history and mosaics at:

HistoryLosAngeles.blogspot.com

She holds a master's degree in history and enjoys burying herself in research, but her real passion is writing. Under the name Vickey Kalambakal, she's contributed many articles to magazines and books about such diverse topics as Caesar's Battle with the Belgae, Pet Rocks, Abraham Lincoln, the Modoc War, and Aluminum Christmas Trees. All of this makes her a frightening competitor at trivia games.

Death Speaker is her first novel. *The Boomer Book of Christmas Memories* was released in 2013, and a novel of greed and destruction set in California's Gold Rush is set to follow.